THROAT

Throat

R. A. NELSON

Alfred A. Knopf
New York

THIS IS A BORZOI BOOK PUBLISHED BY ALFRED A. KNOPF

Visit us on the Web! www.randomhouse.com/teens

Educators and librarians, for a variety of teaching tools, visit us at www.randomhouse.com/teachers

Library of Congress Cataloging-in-Publication Data
Nelson, R. A. (Russell A.)
Throat / R. A. Nelson. — 1st ed.
p.   cm.
Summary: Seventeen-year-old Emma, having always felt cursed by her epilepsy, comes to realize that it is this very condition that saves her when she is mysteriously attacked and left with all the powers but none of the limitations of a vampire.
ISBN 978-0-375-86700-2 (trade) — ISBN 978-0-375-96700-9 (lib. bdg.) —
ISBN 978-0-375-89731-3 (ebook)
[1. Vampires—Fiction. 2. Epilepsy—Fiction. 3. Supernatural—Fiction.] I. Title.
PZ7.N43586Th 2011
[Fic]—dc22
2010027969

The text of this book is set in 9.5-point Versailles Light.

Printed in the United States of America
January 2011
10 9 8 7 6 5 4 3 2 1

First Edition

For Charles Brian Nelson,
who took us to the moon

CONTENTS

1. THE CURSE

When I was thirteen, I ran away from home because of a curse.

Mom caught up with me miles out in the country, standing in front of an abandoned grain silo. The sky was full of what looked like baby tornadoes. I had just been examined pretty thoroughly by a three-legged dog. I was sweaty, thirsty, filthy with road dust, and my heart was completely fractured.

Mom turned the car around and headed back to the apartment, yelling the whole way how badly I had frightened her. I turned my head to the window to shut her out. I just wasn't up for it. For the first time in my life, I didn't feel like fighting back. I was broken in too many places.

Instead I thought about the curse, how crazy it had been to try to outrun it. How do you run away from something that's inside you?

But I had learned something from walking all that way. I had learned the world was an amazingly big and strange and unknown place. There could be anything out there. Anything at all.

Four years later I was sitting in that same junky old car and we were headed east toward the north Georgia mountains. This time the sky was dotted with innocent-looking spring clouds. Mom was driving and my sister, Manda, was shrieking Disney Channel tunes in the backseat, helping me to get my game face on.

After we crossed the state line, the landscape began to change. We passed through sagging towns that could have been renamed Foreclosureville, then nothing but red clay fields, mossy farms, and small, lonely houses clinging to rocky hillsides.

In the last clear place before the mountains I saw a slash in the forest where brown and white horses were cropping grass. The horses made me ache. I'd always wanted to ride, but my neurologist, Dr. Peters, had convinced my mom it would be too dangerous. Because of the curse.

When we got to the Appalachian foothills, the forest took over and the road began to rise. Mom's old Kia labored and whined. A blue Mustang shot past us, honking, its emergency lights flashing. Three girls were hanging out the windows, laughing and screaming, hair blowing across their faces.

I knew before I looked that Gretchen Roberts was driving. Gretchen had been my best friend in the eighth grade before the curse had changed my life forever. Now she was beautiful and had her own car and all the guys called her G-Girl. We didn't talk a whole lot anymore unless we had to on the soccer field.

Every time we traveled to a tournament, Gretchen played cat and mouse with us, knowing I was the only junior in our entire high school that didn't have a license.

I swore quietly and glanced at my mother. She was hunched over the steering wheel, long brown hair covering what I knew was a look of worried annoyance.

In two more days it would be my hands on that wheel, my foot on the gas. Nothing in front of me but the open road. Forty-eight measly little hours and I would be officially seizure free for six consecutive months. Long enough to satisfy the Alabama Department of Motor Vehicles. For once, I would beat the curse.

Now we were climbing long switchbacks into a shaggy forest.

Tall trees hung over the road, and thick clumps of kudzu and poison ivy made the day seem darker.

"I heard they filmed *Deliverance* around here," Mom said, eyes cutting back and forth nervously. "That old movie where the redneck makes the city guy squeal like a pig?"

I could believe it. I could only see a few yards into the gloom. But the feeling of mystery and danger made me hungry to go exploring. *To escape.*

"How do you make somebody squeal like a pig?" Manda said. She was five and the main reason I remembered how to smile most days.

"Like this," I said, and reached back, going "Oink! Oink! Oink!" and tickling her stomach until she screamed.

Now it was Mom's turn to swear. "Stop it, Emma! You're going to cause an accident! And put your seat belt back on!"

We passed a historical marker that said SOUTH EDGE OF DAHLONEGA. That's all I was able to catch. I knew Dahlonega was some kind of mine. Coal? Silver? Gold? I couldn't remember.

It would be useless asking her to stop. Mom didn't even care about her own history, let alone anybody else's. The last time I asked her about my dad, she told me to Google him. I did, and all I could find was a service that wanted $39.95 for a peek at his latest utility bill.

I had already made up my mind: the first thing I was going to do after getting my license was take my mother on a long road trip and pull over at every marker. Read each word lovingly. I knew what she would say.

"You have no sense of time, Emma."

Sure, Mom. As long as you don't count the kind that's measured in centuries. *Or driver's licenses.* Two more days.

* * *

We made a wrong turn looking for the soccer fields, and eventually the pavement dead-ended in a shadowy clearing. In front of us sat an old gray building perched on stacks of flat river stones. Its windows were specked with mud, and an algae-coated stream crept along beside it.

"Nice place for a murder," I said.

"Let's get out!" Manda said, straining against her seat. "I want to see!"

Mom cursed and jerked the wheel around crazily, throwing up gravel and road smoke. After we found the main road again, the forest magically opened up, revealing ten soccer fields smothered in sunshine and dozens of girls romping around in the most bizarre color combinations you ever saw.

"Thank God," Mom said.

We got out and Manda hauled her to the concession stand for a shave ice while I joined my teammates under the main tent. I hated the sign-in stuff at tournaments. By the time the ref in the short yellow shorts quit tapping our shin guards, I was ready to knock down anything wearing cleats.

I kicked streaks of shadow in the dewy grass as Gretchen waited for the ref to blow his whistle. She tapped the ball my way. Not because she wanted to, but Coach Kline would have killed her otherwise.

I floated toward the ball casually, then exploded through it. The power of the kick caught the other team completely off guard. Two of their mids had already started forward to defend, and now they had to retreat, stumbling, the ball sailing over their heads.

I blasted down the middle of the field after it, sideswiping two of their defenders along the way. A confession: I love hitting people. Maybe because the rest of my life has always been so safe. The only reason Dr. Peters let me play soccer at all was that my feet stayed on the ground. *Well, most of the time.*

The ball bounced thirty yards in front of me, bounding so high, the keeper was backpedaling, only now realizing it was going over her head. That's what I was counting on. I barreled past her and caught the ball coming out of its hop, pounded it straight into the net: 1–0 good guys.

The rest of the half wasn't much different. The Georgia girls were shell-shocked, 3–0. I had one yellow card pulled for trucking a forward who completely deserved it. The Georgia kids were finding out what my own league already knew: Emma Cooper will push it right up to the edge . . . and sometimes beyond. I could see them over there at halftime, muttering through their orange slices, talking and pointing. They hated me already. *Good.*

We played three games that day, dominating our way through the tournament. So far none of the other teams had come within four points of us. By late in the evening, our last game, the Georgia players were so focused on me, the rest of my team was able to keep the ball on offense most of the time.

This seemed to be okay with the Georgia kids. They crowded me, rushed me even when I didn't have the ball, making me furious, and that's what I wanted too. The angrier I got, the more aggressively I played. And then it happened.

Gretchen nutmegged one of their defenders, kicking the ball between the other girl's legs, and looped a shot at the goal. I rushed the keeper, saw the ball ricochet off the post, and sprang in the air leading with my skull. At the last possible moment, Gretchen cut across me. My head collided with her shoulder. *Whack.*

It was already dark, but I saw the sun. Then nothing.

*   *   *

5

The first time it happened, I was in the eighth grade. His name was Lane Garner. He was standing across a volleyball net from me in his parents' backyard. The afternoon sun blazed behind his head, framing his face with fire. I fell in love without even knowing the color of his eyes.

Lane Garner slammed the ball off the top of my head. I blocked a couple of his spikes. By the end of the day we were sitting on the back porch chopping ice with an ice pick and trading turns cranking an old-fashioned wooden ice cream maker between our knees.

After that he came over to my house every day. Shot basketball with me in my driveway. I couldn't sleep for thinking about him . . . his long, muscular legs, lanky arms, the way the collar of his T-shirt always shifted toward his left shoulder. Lane Garner was the most beautiful human being I had ever seen.

I have never taken drugs, other than prescription stuff, but those months must've been what an addict feels like. I wanted to be with Lane every second. Hold his hand for the rest of my life. More than that, I wanted to absorb him. Be absorbed.

I covered my notebooks with his name. He gave me a fake gold necklace that said LANE. One night I rolled over and nearly choked to death in my sleep, but still I wore it.

I was wearing the necklace in the Explorer Middle School gym one morning when a sick odor of overripe oranges came up into my nose and the world flashed off. When I woke up, everything was strangely round, as if I were looking at a reflection in a Christmas ornament. My nose was snuffling in a puddle of warm urine. A hundred of my not-so-closest friends were watching, including my soon-to-be-former BFF Gretchen Roberts . . . and Lane Garner.

I never held his hand again. Never kissed him. Never got to watch him grow from a tiny dot at the end of my street into a boy who was the whole wide world to me. Game over. The curse was upon me.

What they don't tell you about epilepsy: there's much more to it than the flopping and flailing stuff. The curse messes you up in all sorts of secret ways too. Especially girls. My metabolism was off the charts, but I still had to watch my weight. The only reason Mom let me play sports was so people would call me voluptuous rather than voluminous.

Epilepsy can also wreck your period and give you a tendency to hirsutism. Wikipedia explains: "From Latin *hirsutus* = increased hair growth in women in locations where the occurrence of hair normally is minimal or absent."

Sweet.

But yes, the worst is the tonic-clonic. A tonic-clonic is not a mixed drink you order at the Star Wars bar; it's a kind of seizure my old-school neurologist, Dr. Peters, called a *grand mal.* An electrical storm in the brain.

Sometimes you get a warning a big TC is coming on, called an *aura.* White spots. Numbness. A sense of dread. Unexpected smells. Tonic-clonics can be brought on by lots of things: chemical imbalances, malnutrition, lack of sleep, flashing lights, patterns, anxiety, antihistamines, etc. Or, as in my case that day on the Georgia soccer field, a violent blow to the skull.

After the sun exploded inside my head, I disappeared inside myself for a little while. How long? I could never tell. Experiencing a tonic-clonic is not like dreaming. I never saw any images at all. There was no sense of the passage of time. I was just there and then I wasn't. Then I was back again. I had to rely on what others said about what I did.

Waking up from a big seizure is awful. They tell you a lot of mumbo jumbo about neurotransmitter depletion, postictal states, general amnesia. None of that describes just how disorienting it is to wake up from a storm inside your brain.

When I came to that evening in Georgia, the ground curved upward to meet the bluish black of the twilight sky. Everything else in my field of view was curved too: lights, goalposts, legs, cleats, the clipped grass, trees against the darkening horizon. I didn't know where I was or what had happened.

The first thing I saw was a curved face with a mustache that hooked around both sides of a gourdlike nose. It was the ref in the yellow shorts. His mouth opened wide, becoming a gaping hole followed by a sound I can only describe as coffee-shaped, slow and sludgy. I couldn't recognize the words.

More faces and legs appeared. It took some time before all the parts of my body felt connected again. Then my mother was there, and when I saw Manda, saw her eyes, I finally understood and began to cry.

At least twenty players from both teams were grouped around me by then. I finally was able to get to a sitting position. Several people were speaking at once. Someone brought water. They forced me to sip it while I tried to get hold of myself.

Manda threw her arms around my neck and tried to coax me to my feet. Her hands were still sticky with blue shave ice.

"Emma, Emma, Emma."

I mumbled a bunch of slurry words, head spinning. I dropped the water and went down on all fours. This seemed to help as I slowly padded back and forth on the grass on my hands and knees. I came to a soccer cleat and looked up.

Everything began to flood back in as soon as I saw her face. Gretchen Roberts.

My license. The license I had been cheated out of for nearly two years. There it went. Floating away on little electroencephalographic wings. *Because of her.*

A hot stream of volcanic bile pulsed through me. I got to my knees wobbling, looking into Gretchen's face. She had done it. It was all her fault. Somehow I was sure of that.

"Oo," I said, trying to jab my finger into her chest. "Oo. Oo."

The volcano gushed up to my head, filling my eyeballs with molten magma. She grinned at me. *Grinned.* I hit her. Hit Gretchen as hard as I could in the face. Felt something crack. She tumbled at my feet. I stood there swaying over her, a drunken, enraged monkey.

Hands grabbed me from all sides and they led me away, stumbling, to a little bench behind the sign-in tent. I cried explosively. The only time I ever cried was right after a bad tonic-clonic. It was as if my head were full of pipes and some powerful force had blown the gunk out.

Manda was clinging to my leg, crying too. My mother wouldn't touch me but instead settled in front of me, legs crossed, like a model for a painting titled *The Last Straw*.

"You. Broke. Her. Nose," she said. "Her nose, Emma. The league . . . I don't know what they're going to do. This is the last time. You're out of second chances, you know that."

The world was fuzzy through my tears. I didn't know what to say.

"Emma . . . ," Manda said.

"Be quiet," I said. "Please be quiet."

"Please don't cry, Emma. It's all right."

That made me cry harder. I couldn't look at her. I pulled up my jersey to wipe my eyes, exposing my sports bra.

The first thing I saw as my vision cleared was two tournament officials sitting with Gretchen at the first aid table, blood spurting from her nose down the front of her shirt, her dark eyes smoldering. Ms. Roberts stalked up to me. She was one of those people who were polite on the surface, but anything nice about her was just that, surface, and the cracks were constantly showing.

"That's the last time—so help me—the last time—you, you—!" She jabbed a fat finger in my face and dragged one of the officials over.

"I want her off this team, I want her out of this league, and if you don't do it immediately, I will press charges for assault. And I will hold you personally responsible. I'll sue you! Do you hear me? I'll sue you for all you're worth. What has to happen to get you people to wake up? Maybe the next time, she'll kill someone. Did you think of that? She's a danger to the other players on the field."

"Now wait a minute," my mom said. "Let's calm down here. You're getting a little out of control. My daughter—"

"Your daughter," Ms. Roberts said, sputtering now, "has gotten away with murder all year, because of her, because of her . . ."

Say it, I thought. *Because of my seizure disorder. Say it and I'll break your nose too.*

She turned to the official, face pale with frustration, unable to complete her thought.

"This is serious," the official said. "There will have to be . . . a board hearing . . . to see . . . what they decide from there. We will see—"

"Did you see my daughter? She will never look the same again, do you hear me! That's it. If you won't do anything, I'm filing charges for assault." Ms. Roberts turned to her son. "Give me your cell, Trevor. I'm calling 911."

My mother was screaming at her now. Manda was screaming in general. I saw Mom's car keys dangling from the side pocket of her big floppy purse. I don't know why I did it. I reached and grabbed the keys while they were all still screaming and ran for the parking lot. I got the door opened before anyone noticed it, shoved the keys in the ignition. Put my foot on the gas and roared out of the parking lot, no idea where I was going.

Night had fallen. I turned out onto the country highway and floored it, feeling the Kia complain but noticing it only with my bones. No streetlights and I didn't even have the headlights on. I fumbled, looking for the switch, tears streaming down my face, my hands slick on the wheel.

So far nothing in my rearview mirror. Guess they didn't care what happened to me. Soon the brightness of the soccer field lights was only a glow above the trees swallowed up by the hungry dark of the woods. I sped on, chasing the cone of my headlights.

I turned at the first side road I saw, gunning the engine and making the car fishtail. I was ready to point the wheel in any direction, let it carry me.

The level ground fell away; almost before I knew it, I was plunging down the plateau. The tires squealed as I slid into the curves like a motorcycle racer, foot barely letting up on the gas. I jounced over a series of rough bumps that made the beam of the headlights jitter and leap. At times I was bouncing so hard, the headlights weren't even shining on the road but instead up into the endless mass of trees and vines.

I didn't care. I pushed harder on the gas, and when I didn't see the curve, I felt the car go suddenly airborne, sailing off the shoulder and down into the woods. I screamed and came to earth hard with a big banging crash that threw me toward the dash, then back against the seat.

Dirt fell on the hood like rain. I sat there breathing a moment.

Held my hands up stupidly, feeling my fingers shake. I tried to swallow, but my mouth was too dry. Somehow the air bag hadn't gone off. I sat there listening to the engine tick and feeling my heart gallop.

The forest was bone white in the headlights. The engine was still running, but I was stuck. Mom's car was resting on a downslope that was covered with skinny saplings. I had rammed into a muddy bank above a small spring.

When I could find my voice again, I swore. My cell phone was in my athletic bag back at the field.

I pounded my fists on the steering wheel, cursing again and then jerking at the wheel as if I could tear it out by the roots. I couldn't get the driver's-side door open; it was lodged against something. So I climbed over and tried the latch on the passenger side, then kicked the door open with my cleats.

I tore off my shin guards and threw them in the backseat. Rolled my sweaty socks down and loosened my cleats; Coach Kline always made us lace them really tight to get more toe into the ball. Mom kept a flashlight in the glove box for emergencies. I got it and slid out into the stream. The water was shockingly cold on my legs. The ground was tilted and I had trouble standing, but I didn't seem to be hurt. I had to put my back against the car and move along the bank like a crab, then used saplings to haul myself uphill to look around.

I couldn't even see the road, which was still farther above me, but by swinging the flashlight beam around, I could make out the black-gray shape of some kind of structure in the woods.

I pointed the light in front of me, beating back the vines with the handle. Maybe someone would be there and I could use their phone. *Stupid. You are so stupid.* I had stopped crying and the terrible anger was starting to fall away, leaving me feeling flat and empty and embarrassed. *What is wrong with me? Why do I do things like this?*

It was harder to get to the little house in the woods than I thought. The ground was so unlevel, I kept slipping and sliding. The flashlight beam glinted off some windows, but there were no lights on in the house. I wondered how it even got there. I couldn't see any road or driveway or even a path. It was as if it had grown up out of the ground.

The siding was rough, wide planks the color of old barns. I went around to the front and came to a door with a design shaped like a Z. I knocked several times, but no one came. My feet hurt. I sat on the little porch and took off my cleats and rubbed my toes, the flashlight beam pointing up to infinity.

I could see the lights from the car still burning over by the stream bank, reflecting into the woods at a crazy angle. I should have cut them off, was probably burning up the battery or whatever it is that happens when you leave them on.

I wondered if I should try to walk back to the soccer fields. Mom was going to be so furious, I'd be under house arrest for a year. I beat my fists on the tops of my legs, fresh tears springing up. *The license*. It was mine. I had earned it.

Manda must have been so scared, seeing me take the car like that. I put her in the room in my head where I put stuff that I didn't want to think about right now. I needed to get out of this situation somehow, then I could start trying to fix all the things I had broken. Maybe—

"Hello," a voice behind me said.

I have never been the skittish type, but I jumped about three feet and even let out a tiny bit of a shriek. It was a deep, deep man's voice that somehow made me instantly conscious of the bones inside my arms and legs, as if they had separated from the tissue and I couldn't use them anymore.

I spun around, fists raised; there was no one there. But the door, the big wooden door with the pattern like a Z, was gone. There was nothing there but a tall black rectangle in front of me. *It's open.*

"What were you expecting?" the deep voice went on. "For me to say, 'Enter freely and of your own will'?"

I never heard the door open, not a creak. No one was standing there that I could see. The flashlight was at my feet, still aimed up at the stars. I reached for it and the voice spoke again.

"My God, you are young, aren't you? A girl. What are you doing here by yourself?"

The voice was coming from the black rectangle inside the house. I pointed the flashlight. I could see at least twelve feet of empty space beyond the open door, the flashlight beam tacking a spot on the far wall with a nail of light.

The floor was rough-sawn and littered with dust bunnies and little bits of trash and leaves. There were no footprints in the dust. I was just about to say something about the car being stuck, and now I was glad that I hadn't.

"Where are you?" I said, feeling a pulse start up in my neck.

"Ah, I like that," the voice said.

The voice was outside now, somewhere to my right. I swung the flashlight beam over. Still no one there. I turned in a frantic circle. Every direction was empty.

"Your throat is . . . *vollkommen*. Perfect," the voice said. "I can smell just the slightest hint of . . . *Salz*. And your feet are bare. More than perfect. And is that some kind of u-ni-form?"

The word *uniform* was pronounced in three slow syllables as if he wasn't used to it. Not a hint of redneck; the voice almost sounded cultured. I felt my skin freezing in horror.

I stepped backward, keeping my eyes on the house. The car was about forty yards away, up a slope and then over the top of the stream bank. I was fast, but could I make it before he could catch me? All those branches, vines, the incline. But if I did make it to the car and hit the door locks, then what? He could pick up a tree branch, bash the windshield in, and drag me out. A sound was coming out of my mouth now, an animal kind of mewling.

"What are you thinking?" the voice said. "I cannot read thoughts, but I would dearly love to know yours." Now the voice was behind me. I whirled around in a panic, saw nothing but the bones of more trees.

"I can't see you," I said. "Come . . . come out where I can see you."

"But I'm right here."

I turned a complete circle, seeing nothing.

My heart was pounding. The car was my only chance. Find some kind of weapon in there. Something—maybe something on the floorboards or hidden in the glove box. *This isn't happening. This isn't—*

I tensed the muscles in my thighs, preparing to spring up the slope.

"Here," the deep voice said, "I am."

I looked straight up. A towering black figure stood on narrow branches directly above me. His eyes were black. He dropped, and I felt the world come down on top of me.

2. CHANGES

Something was fluttering around in my head. I grabbed at it, but I was always too slow. I tried to catch it for a while, then got tired and fell asleep again. The next time I woke up, I heard a voice.

"I think two days at the most, maybe three," a man said.

But it wasn't a deep voice. More like my art teacher last year, Mr. Mancuso, whose passion for painting sometimes got away from him. Some of the kids called him Mr. Manicure behind his back. Why was I expecting the voice to be deep?

Why was it so light in here? Something told me it should be dark, but I could see the brightness through my closed eyelids. I tried to open my eyes, but they were gummed shut. Tried harder and a crack of visibility became a slice of bright room with a tiled floor and green walls framed by the prison bars of my eyelashes.

I raised my arm to brush at my eyes and something tugged painfully: a plastic tube with a needle was stuck to the back of my hand. The tube led away from the needle beyond where I could see. I let my hand slump back down, felt sheets and a thin blanket. I was in some kind of bed.

"But two transfusions? Two?"

My mother's voice, but I couldn't see her. Someone passed in the hall, a small heavyset woman in rumpled blue hospital togs. I watched her, not totally comprehending.

"She's lost a lot of blood. It's a miracle she was still on her feet."

The man's voice again, somewhere to my left. I tried turning that way and it felt as if my head were going to twist off my shoulders. My neck was killing me.

"Mmmph," I said. Then said it again louder when nobody noticed. I never felt so tired in my life. Everlastingly tired. I pushed away from the bed, trying to sit, gave up, and collapsed back into the bunchy pillows, ears muffled.

"Emma!"

Mom swam into view and took my hand, accidentally jerking the plastic tube.

"Ouch." I was too tired to be alarmed.

Mom's eyes were baggy and ringed with dark circles. Her hair was limp, her thin face creased with concern.

"She's awake!" she said, and wrapped her arms around me. Well, as much as the sheets would allow.

A man appeared at her shoulder. He was a head taller than Mom, young, though already balding, with small eyes and arms too long for his white coat. Behind him I could see a gold cross hanging on washed-out yellow walls.

"I'm Dr. Williams, Emma. You're in Saint Joseph's Hospital of Atlanta. You've been in an accident. What do you remember? Do you know what happened to you?"

I pushed up to a sitting position and nearly howled in pain. Yanked the sheets back and saw a blood-soaked bandage on my upper thigh.

"What's this?" I said, touching the bandage.

"Lie still, please! You—your leg was apparently injured in the crash. The wound was deep, cut into the subcutaneous tissue. Another inch and it would have severed a tendon. Thirty-six sutures to patch it up. You're a lucky girl."

For the first time since waking, I remembered about my license. *Lucky. Yeah, that's what you'd call me.* But I hadn't remembered being hurt in the— *Oh. Oh no.* The crash . . .

"I'm . . . I'm sorry, Mom," I managed to croak. "Sorry about the car."

She shushed me, shaking her head. "You rest. The doctor says you have lost a lot of blood, Emma. We have no idea what you cut your leg on. The state police said there wasn't any blood in the car."

I ran my tongue over my lips. They were cracked and raw.

"Are you thirsty?" Dr. Williams said.

They sponged my eyes with a warm rag and I sucked on a cup of ice chips awhile and felt a little better.

"How did I get here?" I said.

"What do you remember?" Dr. Williams said again.

"I don't know. Is it . . . is it night?"

I searched the room with my eyes. An overstuffed chair sat in the corner along with a white plastic bag, my bloody soccer uniform peeking over the top. A TV on a metal bracket, a set of double windows with the plastic shades closed. Dr. Williams stepped over and drew the shades, and a grainy light spread across the end of the bed. The glass was dotted with raindrops.

"Morning," he said.

"You've been in and out all night," Mom said. "We've been so worried."

"I remember it was dark," I said. "The last game . . . the one where . . . Gretchen cut me off and we collided . . ."

"But after that?" Mom said.

"I don't know. I can't remember. Just taking the car. Something happened after that . . . after I drove off in the ditch."

"We believe you had a second tonic-clonic, Emma," Dr. Williams said. "It's not all that uncommon—"

"I know," I said.

"She's had two in one day before," Mom said. "You remember, Emma, that time with the swing?"

"Yeah, yeah."

"Anyhow, that's most likely what's causing your lack of memory," Dr. Williams said. "In a high percentage of incidents, patients recovering from a strong tonic-clonic experience what is called transient epileptic amnesia, which is a temporal lobe—"

"Yeah, I know. I've heard it a million times. Okay, so what did happen to me?"

"We had the state police out, everyone searching," Mom said. "A farmer found you. You were walking up the middle of a deserted road nearly three miles from where they found the car."

"Three miles?"

"You collapsed into his arms. He drove you out of the mountains in his pickup."

My head was churning as if something was trying to surface from the subconscious part of my brain. I closed my eyes and tried to remember.

"What did he look like?" I said.

"Who?"

"The farmer."

"I don't know. We never saw him. I wanted to thank him, but we don't even know his name."

"You've had a couple of transfusions," Dr. Williams said. "We want to keep you another night or two until you are strong again."

I lifted my hand. A tiny blue ribbon was tied around the needle.

"We call that a butterfly," Dr. Williams said. "The ribbon, I mean. Usually we reserve those for children, to keep from frightening them. . . ." He probably saw my eyes flash. "Not you, of course. You were pretty shaky when they brought you in. Not many people could have still been on their feet, let alone walking up a mountain road, having lost that much blood. You have wonderful endurance. How do you feel?"

"Hungry."

"Great. That's a great sign. They'll be bringing you something soon."

"You should see how pale you are!" Mom said.

"How's the car?" I said, looking at the sheets.

Mom touched my hand. "Thank God for Triple A. It's going to be all right. But if you ever, I mean ever, do something like that again . . ."

"And I'm off the team," I said.

"Let's not worry about that right now. That's not important."

"It's important to me."

"You just get better."

I ate a big lunch and talked on the phone to Manda, who cried and told me she was sorry I had a "conclusion."

"Convulsion, Manda," I said. "I had a convulsion."

"I wish Gretchen had one. She's a real—"

"Don't say that word," I said. "Say 'witch' instead. No. Gretchen didn't have a convulsion. She doesn't have epilepsy."

"Then I hope she catches it," Manda said. "It's not fair, Emma. Emma, are you going to come sleep with me? In the hotel?"

"Not tonight, girl."

"You'd better."

"Why?"

"I'm tired of staying in the Tuckers' room," she whispered. "I can't work their clicker. Besides, you might have another conclusion, and I would be right there to help. And then we could go in the pool. They have an inside pool. With a big red slide that has three curls and . . ."

Mom buzzed in and out and finally slumped in the corner chair, snoring. The rest of the day moved achingly slow and the night was worse. Everything was so bright, for one.

"Don't they believe in letting you sleep in the dark?"

Mom stirred sleepily. "Huh?"

"I'm fine. Go back to the hotel, check on Manda, and get some rest."

She shuffled out, still half asleep. Nurses came in at least four times to give me pills or change the dressing on my leg. I couldn't sleep anyhow—couldn't shut my brain off, trying to remember what had happened after the wreck. I had seen something, hadn't I? *Something in the woods.*

My leg throbbed. That was the strangest part of what I could remember. I had gotten shaken up pretty good when I drove off into the stream, but nothing that would have cost me nearly three pints of blood.

Finally I must have fallen asleep without realizing it. I woke sometime later certain someone was standing beside my bed staring at me. No one was there.

The next day I felt stronger. So much stronger, it surprised Dr. Williams.

"Well." He kept tapping my chart.

"They teach you how to do that in school?" I said, trying not to smile, which hurt my cracked lips. "Bedside Manner 101?"

"What?"

"Nothing."

"Well." He was doing it again, the tapping. "You've really gotten your color back. It's almost unbelievable."

"I'm a quick healer. So when can I go home?"

"Today, I think. As long as there is no secondary infection." He tickled the bottom of my foot.

"Hey!"

"Can you feel that?"

"What do you think?"

Mom came in rubbing her neck.

"Well, I'm glad somebody is feeling better," she said. "Your sister is driving me crazy."

"When can I see her?" I said.

"Would you like to look at it?" Dr. Williams interrupted, pointing to my wound as they changed the dressing.

I sighed. "I saw it last night. Going to be a fun scar."

The wound was all purplish and knotted, the skin bunched around the stitching. The clipped ends of the sutures felt like wires. Something had ripped a pretty terrible gash into my upper thigh.

"You were in surgery for over two hours," Mom said.

"Why is it all knotted up like that?"

"The damage was fairly extensive," Dr. Williams said. "We had to stretch the skin in places to make it reach. If it had been any worse, you would have required cosmetic reconstruction. But I think it will heal fine. Your regular doctor will remove the sutures in fourteen days."

"Oh." I couldn't hide my disappointment. I basically hate going to the doctor. "I thought you had stitches that just melted away or something. Can't I just do it myself?"

The doctor grinned. "Right. We had to repair the femoral artery as well. That was the touchiest part. No worries. A good strong flow was immediately reestablished. You're my best patient this week, Emma. If all of them were like you—"

"Thanks." I was tired of talking about it. I clutched at the hospital gown and looked at Mom. "Where can I get some real clothes?"

No walking allowed for at least a week without crutches, the doctor told me. Mom threw them in the trunk after some nurses helped me into the backseat from the wheelchair. I was pretty clumsy with them. All the sports I had played, and I'd never been on crutches in my life.

I couldn't wait for the fun I'd have back at school. *Oh boy.* I'd seen what the boys had done with Molly Walton's crutches when she'd torn up her ankle: taken turns pulling the rubber cushion off the top and putting it down their pants.

I sat in the backseat of the rented car and kept my seat belt unbuckled so I could sit sideways and stretch out my hurt leg. They had me on painkillers so strong, they were making me nauseous, and still my leg was killing me.

Manda was banging her head against the back of her car seat, singing a song she had made up on the spot for the occasion.

"Emma's got a hurt leg, funny hurt leg, funny old, funny old, funny hurt leg."

"Stop bouncing, please," I said.

When we pulled out from the overhang, the rain had stopped and sunlight poked my eyes with burning fingers. I threw my arm across my face. "Oh my God. When did it get so bright?"

"Bright?" my mom said. "It's been overcast all morning."

"It's really hurting my eyes."

"It must be the antibiotics. Funny they didn't say anything about it—"

"Do you have your sunglasses?" Without waiting for her to answer, I felt around in her purse and opened the little glasses holder and put them on. "Ah, that's better. Some."

"This looks bright to you?"

"Please just drive. I'm sick of this place."

"Listen who's back to normal. Touchy, touchy." She reached and gave my shoulder a squeeze.

"Hey, watch the road. This is a city, you know," I said. Mom scared me to death in places like Atlanta.

We got back home in one piece. I had to wear the sunglasses the whole way.

The next day Dr. Peters upped my seizure medicine and put me through a full EEG schedule and blood work. An EEG is an electroencephalogram, which tests your brain waves. They marked my scalp with a styptic pencil and attached sensors to my head and flashed strobe lights in my eyes and did other tests to see if there was anything abnormal.

I couldn't fall asleep for the sleep test, even after staying up all night watching old movies with Manda snoozing on my lap. Dr. Peters did the next-best thing, taped my eyes shut, which always made me completely uncomfortable. I wasn't claustrophobic, but for some reason having my eyelids taped shut made me feel that way.

Everything checked out normal. Well, normal for someone with a seizure disorder. Though my eyes were still "extraordinarily sensitive to sunlight." Dr. Peters's words, not mine. They sent me to an optometrist for special sunglasses until they could find out what was wrong.

The sunglasses were a big hit at school. The first person I ran into was a little dope named Robbie Putnam.

"Nice," he said. "They give you a stick and a tin cup to go with those?"

I told him no . . . or they would already be lodged in a particular part of his anatomy.

Crutches were a miserable way to travel, robbing me of my one point of high school superiority: my physical grace. For the first time in my life, I experienced what it felt like to be clumsy, a dork. I banged the crutches into doors, spread them too wide or too narrowly, whacked kids in the shins.

I'm not into dreading, but I genuinely dreaded first-block English. Gretchen sat three desks away. We had gotten a letter from her mother's lawyer that scared my mom nearly catatonic. Insurance. Lost time away from work. Etc. Whatever credits I had built up in my motherly bank account by nearly bleeding to death in the forest had rapidly been depleted.

I hobbled into Ms. Rose's room, trailed by the little sophomore office aide flunky who was toting my books. Luckily, I was early. Gretchen came in, her nose buried in a mass of white bandages, raccoon circles under her eyes. Her tawny lion's mane hair was restrained in a strangled ponytail.

Bite the bullet. I struggled over to her desk before the classroom could fill up. She wouldn't look at me.

"Gretchen. I'm sorry. There is nothing I can say . . . but I'm sorry. What I did was . . . it was really . . . stupid." I waited for her to say something to ease my fledgling conscience, but she never looked up from her notebook. "I just wanted you to know—"

"Get away from me," Gretchen said.

"What?"

"I said get. Away. From. Me."

I went to my seat, dragging my tail between my legs. When Ms. Rose came in, she tripped over my crutches.

*　　*　　*

The bus was a complete nightmare. When I finally got home, the apartment had never looked better. The minute I struggled through the door, I threw down the crutches, dropped my backpack, and hopped over to the couch.

"We're having cheese sandwiches," Manda said, bouncing up from *Hannah Montana* and throwing her arms around my leg. "And lentil soup."

"Nice. Is Mom home yet?"

"It's Wednesday, Emma."

Wednesday. I was losing track of time. Mom worked days for an accountant, but three nights a week she filled in as a waitress at a restaurant called the Blue Onion.

"Can I wear your glasses?" Manda said.

"Sure. Are you really watching this?" I changed the channel and dropped my shades in her hand. "Don't lose them. I'm blind if I go outside without them."

We watched TV together until I couldn't put it off any longer, then I made supper. Manda sat on the counter next to the griddle, peeling the American cheese slices out of the plastic and putting them on the bread. That was her job.

After we ate, we watched several more hours of sucky TV. Then I carried Manda piggyback to her bedroom and read to her like I always did. Manda's all-time favorite was Dr. Seuss. We read about Sneetches who were the best on the beaches until she fell asleep in my arms. I tucked her in bed and watched her while she was sleeping. Her golden hair was spread over the pillow. I wondered how old she would be before she learned about real disappointment. She still had my sunglasses in her hand. I turned her light out and went back up the hall.

I tried not to notice the calendar where I had been crossing off my seizure-free days with big red *X*s. It was too early to even start counting again.

I loaded the dishwasher—had to start building up that motherly bank account again. I replaced the bandage on my leg, slathering the wound with goopy antiseptic while watching a rotten movie on Lifetime, Television for Battered Women. Ate some stale ice cream I found in the back of the freezer. When Mom came in at eleven, I had turned the TV off and was sitting at the kitchen table making a halfhearted swipe at my homework. She dropped her purse and fell over my backpack.

"Emma!"

"What?"

"Where are you! What's going on?"

I came hopping up the hallway. "I'm right here. What are you talking about?"

"Why are all the lights out?"

"Huh?"

I didn't believe her until she flicked the switch and the sudden light drilled my eyes back into my skull. It was true. I'd been able to see everything. Even colors. In complete darkness.

3. POWERS

"It's called photophobia," the eye specialist said a few days later.

"Fear of photography?"

He ignored me. "It could be from a corneal abrasion. Or uveitis. Sometimes a retinal detachment. Even a nervous system disorder like meningitis."

My mother drew in her breath. "Oh my God."

"Do I look sick to you?" I said, glaring at her. "I feel fine. Besides, there's nothing wrong with my eyes. I mean, it's not that I'm having trouble seeing. It's like . . . I'm seeing too good."

"That's not possible," the specialist said. I never caught his name. He was an old guy with hair going from gray to white. For some reason his jacket smelled faintly of wet dog when he leaned in close with his little penlight. "Any of the things I mentioned— they would all bring about a decrease in vision. The decrease might be temporary, but—"

"But she could see," my mother said. "I turned the lights off and tested her. She could see things across the room that I couldn't see in my hand. She could tell me details about objects in the pitch dark."

"Maybe there was more light than you realized?"

"Test me, then," I said.

He did. The specialist made sure no external light was coming in and held objects before me. I could see them easily. It wasn't like looking at them in the daylight, no. It wasn't that they were reflecting light either. It was . . .

"They're giving off their own light," I said.

"Emma likes to tease," Mom said, as if she were talking about somebody Manda's age.

"No, I don't," I said. I hated people who tease. I liked to tell the blunt truth.

The specialist's pen gave off a spectral kind of glow. Everything did.

"Good guess," he said, holding the pen up in front of me. He was smirking. In the dark.

"Okay, want to know what is written on it?" I said. "'Mid-South Medical Supply, Memphis, Tennessee.' Did you swipe it in Memphis?"

The specialist frowned. "They give them to us. Sales reps. Wait." The lights flicked back on, making me wince. "There is no possible way you could be seeing all that in the dark. You must have seen it before. Maybe you don't remember?"

I was shading my eyes with my arm, looking down at the floor. "Nope. I didn't see it before."

"Fluorescents hurt too?"

"Not like sunlight. And only when they first come on."

He went to his desk and sat down. "Let's try this again." He flicked the lights off, and after a moment I could see him there, frosty hair almost glowing as he slid open the top drawer of the desk and took out a stapler.

"Now what is—"

"A stapler," I said. "Swingline. Beige." He brought out other things. "A Phillips head screwdriver with a square orange handle. Gray cell phone. A CD, some group called the Carpenters. A book of Liberty Bell stamps."

The specialist swore softly. "Excuse me. . . . It's just that . . . Give me a second. Okay, I'm going to turn the lights back on now, Emma. Close your eyes."

When my eyes adjusted again, we just sat there looking at each other.

"And you're sure it's not meningitis?" my mother said.

"Absent any other symptoms, I would say no." The specialist took off his glasses and massaged the bridge of his nose. "I have never seen anything like this. Never read about it in any of the journals, either. If I even told anyone about this, they wouldn't believe me."

Mom's voice was shaky. "But what are we supposed to do? We told you about the accident. She's been this way ever since then."

"What is it like?" the specialist said, looking at me. "How bright is it? It must be pretty bright for you to see colors and read things. Colors wash out pretty quickly in dim light."

I thought about it. "It's . . . hard to describe. When I've been in the dark awhile, I almost can't tell the difference. I forget the lights are off. But when the lights come on, it's . . . like a lightning flash in my head until I get used to it. But after I've been in the light and go back to the dark, I can tell the difference. It's dimmer, but . . . somehow I can still see the details. I told you. It's like things are giving off their own light."

The specialist smiled, but his brow was furrowed at the same time, giving him a pained expression. I didn't like this. I was starting to get pictures in my head of me stuck in front of hundreds of eye freaks in white coats shining things in my eyes, lecturing. Stretching my eyelids back while I sat on a cold steel table in nothing but one of those backwards hospital gowns.

"Let's go," I said to Mom. "I want to go."

Mom looked embarrassed. "But the doctor—he's not finished, Emma. He wants to run more tests. . . ."

The specialist started to speak, but I was already up and moving to the door. I left without ever looking at his face again.

"Why do you always have to be so much trouble about things like this? I get so tired of it," Mom said.

I tore into another slice of pepperoni. God, I was so hungry these days. We were sitting at one end of the food court surrounded by moms who were hustling their kids around the play equipment. The tables were about half full. I liked the feeling of anonymity my sunglasses gave me. I could stare at people without them knowing.

"You think this is my fault, don't you," I said, tearing off another bite.

"Well, I wonder why? It was you who lost your temper. It was you who stole the car. Crashed it in a ditch." Her voice started to break. "What do you want me to say? And now this." She waved her arms around. "You're going blind."

"I'm not going blind, Mom. How good can a specialist be who has an office at the mall? It'll be okay. I bet it's already starting to go away."

"You're lying. You know I can always tell when you're lying."

"Not possible. I don't lie."

"So why did you just say that?"

I sighed. "Because I know this is scaring you. I don't want you to be scared. I'm not scared. I just want my shorts back." I was tired of wearing jeans. I would wear shorts year-round if I could get away with it. But nobody was seeing that bandage on my leg until the stitches were out. I turned my head away, indicating the conversation was over.

I never held things back. But I was holding something back now. Something I had seen when the lights were off and I was watching my mother's face. *Blue.* She had been giving off a faint bluish glow in the dark. So had the specialist.

31

"You're doing it again," Manda said, yanking on my arm. "Hey. Emma. Stop, wake up!" She snapped her fingers.

I was looking at something outside the window, a tree framed by the light. Only I didn't see it as a tree anymore. It had gone out of focus. Now I saw it as a shape. Saw a light inside it. My mouth was hanging open. My eyes had this comfortable feeling. It felt as if they were getting rounder and rounder, wider and wider, expanding. And the longer I stared, the more comfortable my eyes felt, until that feeling of complete and total comfort spread through my whole body. As if what I was seeing was going so deep inside me, made me feel so good, I could look at that tree that was no longer a tree the rest of my life.

"Emma!" Manda screamed.

"Huh?" I blinked. Shook my head. The comfortableness of the tree and the light was gone.

"You were doing it again."

She meant I had had a seizure. If I lost consciousness for a brief little moment of time, say thirty seconds, it was an absence seizure. What doctors used to call a *petit mal*. Otherwise, it was a simple partial, which is similar, but you're aware the whole time. Sometimes it was a little hard to tell them apart.

What I thought of as my "small" seizures were generally pretty mild. When I came out of one, it was like my life had jumped over a minute of time, completely skipped it, before settling back into its groove. Those little blips of time were lost forever.

Sometimes I had several small seizures a day. Other times I didn't have any for a week or more. Most of the time I wasn't aware I was going through it, unless Mom or Manda or somebody else brought it to my attention.

I took Dilantin, which was supposed to cover the "big" seizures, the tonic-clonics, which it did for the most part, with obvious breakdowns like the soccer tournament. We tried Depakote and then Zarontin for the small ones, but nothing seemed to make them go away completely. And the sleepiness from the extra drugs was wiping me out in school, so we stopped them. Besides, I was lucky that the small ones were generally pretty harmless. Only something about this one didn't feel quite so benign.

"Do I look crazy to you?" I said to Manda.

"Only one million percent," she said. She dipped her finger in the peanut butter jar for another lick.

"Don't do that. You really shouldn't do that."

"I don't care, Emma, it's so good."

I didn't say anything. For some reason my seizure had gotten me thinking about what I had seen in the eye specialist's office. The way my mom had been glowing blue in the dark. Was this some weird new offshoot of my epilepsy? What was happening to me?

"Emma? Are you listening?" Manda yelled. "I said, did you know I can count to a billion? Emma!"

"What? Um, oh, you can?"

"One, two, three, four, five, a billion," Manda said, and collapsed into giggles on the living room floor.

I was thinking that I could try it again right now. Take my little sister in the back bedroom, close the curtains, cut out the lights, and see. See if it happened with Manda too. But I didn't. I don't think I wanted to see.

The next change came all at once. I told Mom I was trashing my crutches, no matter what the doctor said. I had been walking around the apartment just fine and was sick of dragging the things to school. She knew it was useless to try to force me, so instead she turned the situation on its head.

"Okay, if you're all healed up, tomorrow is garbage day, right?"

"But my poor leg," I said.

Mom smiled sweetly. "Besides, you can take Manda to the playground. She's been cooped up all afternoon."

I grumbled and grabbed my sister and we headed across the Autumn Creste complex to the Dumpsters. She held my hand the whole way, skipping and practically jerking my arm out of its socket. Manda spent eighty-eight percent of her waking life either dancing or singing or both.

I got her started on the swings, then headed over to the Dumpster to jettison the bag of kitchen crap only to notice that some doofus or, more likely, team of doofi had blocked the Dumpster door with a huge yellow refrigerator.

I knew the Dumpsters had tops that opened so they could be raised and emptied into a truck, but the Dumpsters at the Creste were old. Iron Age old, complete with lids so rusty they looked like they were welded shut. I thought I would give it a try anyway. Maybe I could get it open a crack, enough to slip the bag in. I found the cleanest-looking grungy spot along the rim of the lid and heaved with my left hand . . . only, it didn't just open a crack, it kept going. Flipped all the way over and slammed against the back of the Dumpster like a bomb.

"Holy . . ."

One of the kids over at the swings finished the thought for me. All of them were watching. I looked suspiciously at my hand. *Huh?*

I took my shades off, kept my eyes closed against the light, and mopped my brow. Put them back on and opened and closed my fingers. Something . . . *something moved inside me.*

I didn't know any other way to put it. It was as if there was a new kind of energy there—an energy that was suddenly loosened to where it flowed freely down my arms and legs and back. I had the sense that if I flexed my calf muscles and jumped, I could fly to the top of one of the apartment buildings.

I looked at the refrigerator. *No way.* But why not? I stooped next to it, stuck the fingers of one hand underneath, and gripped the bottom edge. Stood very rapidly . . .

The yellow refrigerator came completely off the ground. I watched in shock as the metal trim at the bottom came level with my eyes, then the whole thing kept going higher and higher as it left my hand. It all felt so effortless. The refrigerator tumbled in midair a moment, then gravity caught up and it came crashing down on its side.

The sound boomed off the nearest buildings. The kids at the swings came running over, shrieking and laughing, all wanting to touch me, calling me superhero names like Spider-Man and the Hulk. Manda was right in the middle of them.

"Emma! Emma! You're Superman!"

"No, shhh, no, I'm not!" I said. "It was just really light. I didn't do anything."

"Emma! You're a superhero!"

They begged me to do it again. I shook my head over and over. Thankfully, none of them was older than five or six. Nobody would believe them if they told anybody what I'd done. I thought it again.

What's happening to me?

I was stunned and more than a little afraid. It was almost as if . . . as if I were turning into something new. *Some new kind of human.*

But what kind? I didn't know.

One thing that hadn't changed: my impulsive nature. Why couldn't I have waited until after dark to have tested my strength?

But it had been impossible to ignore once I had felt it—that power—inside me. The moment it had surged through me, I didn't give a rip who was watching. *Who cares?* I would have thought if someone had tried to warn me not to do it. *What? You think you can stop me?*

I took Manda's hand and hustled her back to the apartment with her complaining the whole way. I stopped when we got to our steps. "You can't tell Mom about this," I said. "You just can't."

"Why?" Manda said. "She has to know. She has to know you're Superman, Emma."

"I'm not Superman, Manda. I'm not."

"Supergirl, then."

"No."

"Superwoman."

"No, I'm nothing. I mean, I'm just strong, really, really strong. This has to be a secret, do you understand? A secret just between me and you. If you tell anyone, even if it's just Mom, she'll get really scared and other people will find out. And then . . ." I wasn't sure what I could say to convince her. Then I had an idea. "The bad guys will get me, Manda. Do you see what I'm saying? You don't want that to happen, okay? The bad guys would get you too. And Mom."

"Oh! Like Peter Parker."

"Yeah, just like Peter Parker. Nobody else can know or—"

"Or the bad guys, they will come and hurt us."

"Right. Okay. Talk about something else when we see Mom. Anything else."

"Okay."

My head was bursting with thoughts, so many I couldn't keep up with them all. The most disturbing was this: while it was happening, what I was doing didn't feel disturbing at all. Lifting that refrigerator didn't feel strange. It felt natural. *The most natural thing in the world.*

The next morning I begged out of school and nagged my mother until she drove me to one of those doc-in-the-box places to get the stitches removed.

"But it's more than a week early!" Mom kept saying all the way there.

"I know, but it feels fine," I said. I didn't want to tell her what I already suspected.

I looked at the doctor's name tag: OLOKOWANDI.

"And may I have your name, miss? Call me Dr. Olo," he said when I climbed up on the paper. He was a dazzlingly handsome black guy with the most striking smile I had ever seen. Though right now he was looking kind of perplexed.

Dr. Olo had just taken the bandage off my leg and run his finger along the top of my thigh. Where the sick-looking wound had been, there was a slight ridge of flesh about three or four inches long—and nothing else. The skin was perfect, otherwise.

"I don't mean to . . . say this," Dr. Olo said. It sounded like an accusation. "There are no sutures. You took them out, didn't you? You are a strong girl to take them out yourself. Or did your father or mother do it for you?"

My face must have told him that wasn't the case. His expression changed. "Take your finger, there."

Dr. Olo guided my hand over the same ridge of flesh he had just touched. It was smooth, but . . .

"See how hard it feels? That is the scar tissue. If someone did not remove the stitches, I would say it is almost as if they have been . . . reabsorbed." He shook his head wonderingly. "The only thing I would know to do, Miss Emma, is to take a scalpel, so . . ." He pointed the tip of his fingernail against the raised place, drew it along like a knife. ". . . And see what we will see is beneath." Dr. Olo laughed heartily. "Of course, I am making a joke. There is really nothing to be done. You are healed! It is a miracle! Please have a glorious day."

When my mom saw me back in the waiting room, she asked, "How did it go?"

"Butter," I said. And we left.

The next impossibly weird thing came later that day. It had rained all day, so I knew the soccer fields would be closed, which was good because I wanted to test my leg with nobody watching.

Besides, I just needed to get away, do something physical. Running had always been my therapy, ever since the curse had come on the scene. Running helped me to think, settled me out when I was feeling over-amped and crazy.

I would have loved to run on the grass, but the fields were damp and spongy from the storm. So the asphalt jogging trail it was. A fresh mass of black clouds was threatening in the west and the light of the day was already failing. Well, failing for everyone else.

It had been more than a week since I had really put the hammer down, so I went through a light stretching routine. Then I was off.

Supreme.

The word popped into my head as I rounded the first long curve in the running trail. I was moving uphill and already gaining speed. My injured leg didn't hurt at all. But that wasn't really accurate. It was more than just a lack of pain. I had never felt anything like this, anything this good.

I felt fantastic every time I ran. In spite of my size, I was built for speed. But this . . . I glanced around me. The glowering clouds were starting to spit rain. Nobody in sight.

Push it.

I lengthened my stride, intending to kick like I would for a sprint, the kind of flat-out running a person can only hold for a few seconds.

Something inside me kicked back.

Oh my God . . . I was moving. Really moving. Faster than I had ever run before. It was so easy. But I could instinctively feel it wasn't a full sprint. I was still in a lower gear.

I pushed harder and could feel wind whistling past me now just as if I were sticking my head out the window of a moving car. Only unlike in the movies when someone is going terrifically fast, nothing was a blur. Everything was as rock steady as if I were standing still.

I felt my heart as I ran. It should have been racing like a high-performance engine, but I couldn't even feel the beat at first. There it was, about like the pulse you would feel lying down, maybe sixty, seventy beats a minute. Up to then I had thought I was blazing. But now I realized I could go faster. Much faster. *Try it.*

I opened the throttle all the way, running as if I'd heard a baby crying in a burning building. It was like flying. It *was* flying, while still touching the earth. The black cloud above me burst and lightning shivered across the horizon like the glowing ends of a witch's broom. Rain ricocheted against me—I was racing into the big fat drops so fast, they were bouncing off of me sideways like liquid bullets. It felt amazing, transcendent.

I would have lapped the fastest Olympic runner on the planet three, four, five times already. I was something beyond human, more than human. *I'm a god.*

I began screaming. I screamed over and over. At last I slowed, finally stopping next to a giant spreading oak. I sat beneath it and watched the rain thunder down. Checked the time on my cell. I had been sprinting like that for more than thirty minutes.

The next morning I floated through school in a dreamlike state. In homeroom, kids moved around me sleepily, slinging their books down, talking about their weekends. The box on the wall blared the usual scratchy salute: "It's a great day to be a Red Raider!" Followed by announcements I ignored. My body was in the room, but my spirit was still on that track, flying.

The truth is, I didn't know if I even belonged there anymore.

What was I becoming? Would it end or just keep on going? I turned my hands up and looked at my palms. Not one crease out of place, everything just as I remembered. But I was something different and new. Maybe some kind of genetic anomaly? A new kind of human being, anyhow. I refused to consider any possibility beyond that.

After lunch we rehearsed a school lockdown, cutting the lights off and locking the classroom doors, pretending a shooter was on the loose in the halls.

We huddled in the dark. Only—*oh my God*—I could still see everyone by the ghostly bluish light their bodies were giving off.

I turned my head right and left in complete disbelief.

James Wharton was kissing D'Shika House and feeling her up. I could see D'Shika's wet eyes blinking, their bodies moving. I could see kids waving their arms blindly, trying to poke other kids.

I felt uncomfortable watching what people do in the dark when they are certain no one can see them. Kids scratching in embarrassing places. Picking their noses. But the hardest thing to watch was the faces. Once I got used to the blue, I got to see each kid's secret face. What their public faces relaxed into in the safety of the dark. Some of the kids looked happy, well adjusted, sure. But the faces that haunted me were the others. Sad. Depressed. Frightened. Overwhelmingly tired.

My math teacher, Ms. Timms, who was new and young and hot, fresh out of college, and Ben Wheland were right next to each other, leaning against a table at the front of the room. Not touching. Not moving at all. But so very close, their hips were less than an inch apart.

One of the most interesting things about the lockdown was this: knowing that if someone really did attack the school, I could very easily walk out there and stop him.

No matter what weapons an intruder had, from pipe bombs to an M16—unless he had a gang of shooters with him, he would be completely helpless against me. I was just too fast. I could dodge around behind him, make it seem as if he were moving in slow motion. To the killer it would seem almost as if I had the ability to disappear in one place and reappear in another.

I could basically do anything I wanted to do.

"Emma. Emma!"

"Huh?"

The last class of the day, creative writing, and Ms. Walker was looking at me as if she was expecting something. She'd already accused me of trying to sleep behind my sunglasses.

"We're selecting partners for the Argumentative Essay project. Like to join us?"

I sat up straighter in my chair. "Anybody is fine with me. Could I go see the nurse?"

"Is there something wrong?"

"I don't know, I just need to see the nurse."

Given my medical history, Ms. Walker was afraid to say no. She made out the pass and I left. I strolled past the nurse's office and then right past the checkout office too. Out the front door. *A clean getaway.*

I spent the rest of the day walking aimlessly all over town, finally sitting on a bench outside the library. For a while I tried not to think about anything at all. Just absorbed my surroundings. The brick dentist office in the little house across the street. Broom sage blowing in the empty lot next door. The smell of french fry grease from the McDonald's up the road. A ladybug crawling along my finger. The world seemed so incredibly alive. Alive in a way I had never imagined before. Beautiful. Interconnected.

Then I heard something . . . a kind of whirring, fluttering sound. I looked around trying to find the source. Then I saw it, a bird with blue-tipped wings, fifty yards away, landing in the top of a locust tree.

I can hear its wings flapping.

4. SICKNESS

Of course I thought about it. How there must be some connection between my accident in the Georgia mountains and what was happening to me now. If only I could remember . . .

That night Mom was working at the Blue Onion again and I had read to Manda and gotten her in bed. She wasn't sleepy, though. Five minutes after I had her down, she charged up the hall to where I was sitting in the living room with my trig book, trying to care about homework. A nature show about vampire bats was on, but I wasn't paying much attention to it.

"Can't sleep," Manda said.

"How come?"

She jumped into her favorite place, my lap. The trig book fell to the floor, closing itself. "I keep thinking about those pale green pants with nobody inside them," Manda said. "What's inside them, Emma? There has to be something inside them. Or they couldn't move, could they?"

I let out a deep breath. "It's just a story, Manda. You know what Dr. Seuss is like. Everything he writes is all made up and crazy."

"But Horton is not made up. Horton is an elephant. Elephants are not made up. I've seen one at the zoo."

"But a talking elephant? Who sits on an egg and hatches it?"

Manda looked at me as if I were slow. "That's just for the story, silly. But the pants . . ."

"There's nobody inside the pants."

"Not a ghost?"

"It's just drawn that way. The pants are supposed to be alive. They are alive, but that's all they are. Pants. It's supposed to be . . . a mystery. You're not supposed to know how the pants work. That's why the story is so good."

"Like the secret you showed me?"

"What secret?"

"About your superpowers?"

I swore to myself. "Well, yeah, I guess so. That's a mystery too, isn't it? That's why it has to be kept secret." I put a finger to my lips.

She threw her arms around me and clung to my neck. When she spoke again, she was speaking very softly, just under my ear. "Fly me away, Emma. Fly me away from the pale green pants."

I squeezed her hard. "I can't fly. That's silly." Was it? I didn't know. I had never tried. *Stop it.*

"But . . ."

I pulled her away and got up to take her back down the hall. But she wouldn't let me go. "Let me watch something, Emma."

"You need to be in bed."

"Just a little bit, so I won't think about the pants."

So we settled down again and watched the nature show. Five vampire bats were hopping around a pig's legs in the middle of the night. I never imagined they would move that way. There was something unsettling about the way they bounded around and around the pig. At last they climbed aboard, settling onto the pig's back.

"Vampire bats have heat-seeking sensors in their noses," the announcer said. "Let's look at that in infrared so you can see exactly what the bats are searching for."

The screen suddenly changed from normal nighttime hues to brilliant yellows, oranges, and reds with little dots of white in between, each about the size of a quarter.

"Those white spots are just what the bats are looking for, and their special noses lead them right to it: the most promising locations for easy blood," the announcer explained.

The bats each found a white spot and dug in, lapping pig's blood into their wedge-shaped mouths along a groove in their long tongues. Three bats were suddenly fighting over a particularly promising spot. "Like miners who have struck the mother lode," the voice-over said. "Why doesn't the pig wake up? Because the vampire bat's teeth are razor sharp. So sharp, the pig doesn't even feel it. Vampire bats will feast for as long as thirty minutes on one victim. By the time these bats are done, they each will have lapped up about half their weight in hot juicy pig blood."

I began to feel sick. I didn't know why. I'd never had a weak stomach before.

"Okay, that's it," I said to Manda.

"But it isn't over!"

"You know what's worse than pale green pants?" I said.

"What?"

"Momma if she comes home and catches you out of bed. Get."

She scooted down the hall and I tucked her in. I put the Sneetches book back on the shelf so maybe she wouldn't think about the pants so much. When I came back to the living room, I changed the channel. Five minutes later, I felt so sick, I climbed into bed.

I threw up three times before Mom got home. It had been years since I had had any kind of stomach bug. She blamed it on the

Italian dressing chicken breasts I had baked for supper, but Manda had eaten them too, and she was fine.

I was afraid it was something else. The worse the pain got, the more cursed I felt, connecting my sickness to the changes in me, as if my new gifts had somehow come with a terrible price.

I felt completely empty inside. I started shivering violently and Mom covered me with blankets. I drifted in and out of a feverish sleep. At one point I felt something on my leg, so I pulled the covers back and the old wound on my thigh was open and raw again, oozing pus and blood.

Then vampire bats were crawling all over me, hopping from my knees to my chest to the top of my head. I feebly tried to shake them off, but they didn't seem to notice. Now six of them were feasting on the wound in my leg, like cows around a tiny pond. On TV they had said the pig couldn't feel the bats feeding, but I could. I could feel every tearing little bite.

One of them sank its teeth into my scalp. I must have screamed, because Mom came running in after that.

"Emma! Are you okay?"

She swabbed my head with a damp cloth and said she was calling the doctor's exchange. The doctor called back and told her to give me twice the recommended dosage of Tylenol. All we had was the liquid variety. I threw it up. It looked like fresh blood on the carpet.

Somewhere in the middle of the night my fever broke and Mom left me alone to sleep. When I woke again, the sheets were drenched and the room was strangely cool. I could see every inch of the space so clearly: my glass-topped bedside table, the oak dresser, stacks of clean clothes on a chair, my closet with the poster of David

Beckham in his white and yellow LA Galaxy uniform, the square panes of the window. Beyond that a light in the parking lot shone red through the thin white curtains. And I remembered.

A man is standing in the trees.

A tall black figure. He was about thirty feet off the ground, his long legs spread from one slender branch to another. Branches seemingly too small to support his weight. His eyes were open and his arms were crossed in front of his chest like a corpse in a casket.

I stood there looking at him, feeling my blood turn to powder. I wanted to run. Ached to run. I even started moving my legs. Until the man appeared—just appeared—on the ground right in front of me.

I recoiled, dropping the flashlight, and reflexively threw up my hands for protection. The man towered over me. The light was between us, spraying up the tall man's chest. He was wearing a dirty white linen shirt that looked old-fashioned and buttoned up the middle with what looked like little pieces of cork. Long creased pants and a wide buckled belt. A coat that came to his knees, something like a cowboy might wear in wintertime. He was dirty, but the coat made him look somehow elegant. *His face . . .*

"Welcome," he said.

I started running for the car, scrambling up the slope. The man in the coat just stayed where he was. I got to the top of the low hill, where I was close enough to temporarily blind myself in the headlights. I lunged toward the little stream—

The man was already there, standing between me and the car. I don't know how. I never saw him move. He was suddenly just there.

I swung my fist with all my strength at his terrible face; his big hand locked onto my wrist. I never saw him move. I struggled, using both my hands, trying to pry myself free. His arm stayed locked. His fingernails were unnaturally long and cut into the skin of my wrist as I fought. I drew back my bare foot and kicked him hard enough to break his shinbone. He laughed and threw me on the ground.

The man knelt, placing one knee on my side and bringing his awful mouth close to mine. His black eyes were blazing in the glare of the headlights. His skin looked translucent and tight. Something was gruesomely wrong about his scalp; part of it was peeled away, hanging like a long flap of skin, making me think of autopsy photos I had once seen of John F. Kennedy's head after he had been shot. The flap moved a little as the man moved. He couldn't be alive. Not with a wound like that. But he was.

He got both hands on my arms and pushed them easily to the moist ground. Lowered his face. He was smiling. He opened his mouth and spoke a phrase I couldn't understand. It sounded like German.

"Geben Sie mir Ihr Leben."

His breath stank of rotting leaf mold. For one horrifying second I thought he was going to kiss me.

The man's ragged lips trailed across my cheek and dropped to my neck instead. I could feel them brush me there. *Rape. I'm going to be raped,* I thought.

The man lost concentration for a moment, because I was able to slip one arm free. I smashed him in the face as hard as I could, trying to drive his nose into his brain. The man's head snapped back and he howled in rage and surprise.

He raised his arm and backhanded me so hard that lights flashed inside my head. I heard a crunching sound in my neck and felt an electric pulse shoot up behind my ear and thought my neck might be broken. I fought hard to stay conscious, blinking at the tears in my eyes.

"*Was erlauben Sie sich,*" the man said, voice spitting with fury. "How dare you."

He slammed one long arm across my chest, knocking the breath out of me and pinning me to the forest floor. He turned his body so that he was no longer facing me. Began to tear at my soccer shorts.

I felt something in my chest, felt it like my body was filling up with something. Then I realized what I was feeling: my own death. A premonition of it. I was crossing a line into a new place, a place I could never return from. I started kicking and flailing with an insane fury, bucking up in the air, scratching, hitting, clawing, even though I knew none of this was doing any good. In fact, it only seemed to make things worse.

"I would have honored you, *Mädchen,*" the man said, growling deep in his throat as he easily held me down. His face was turned away as if he would no longer look me in the eye. "And this is how you show me respect. If that is what you want, then this is my answer."

He drove his teeth into the fleshy top of my thigh and began to tear the skin away. I screamed. I screamed again and again, thrashing my body. The man kept ripping at my leg with his teeth. The pain was indescribable. But the pain was nothing compared to what he did next.

Once my leg was torn open, my ruptured artery spurting blood into the leaves, the man fastened his mouth there and began to drink.

I don't know how long he drank. I was too horrified to think, too horrified to do anything but act on animal impulse. The man held my head so that I had to watch as he slobbered and gulped. I was sick to my stomach watching his mouth dipping and raising, his ash-colored teeth stained with my blood, his jaw and cheeks splashed red. The wet sucking and gobbling sounds . . .

I don't know why I didn't close my eyes, but I couldn't. After a time I started to have the sensation of falling. But not falling on the outside, falling on the inside. As if some part of my life or mind or spirit had broken loose and was dropping inside of me, dropping with no bottom in sight. This man, this creature, was going to drink from me until I was dead.

I remember seeing my bare foot, my muddy toes. That was somehow the hardest moment. It felt like . . . like I was failing myself. That I had let this happen. That somehow I could have stopped it. *All my fault* . . .

My world filled up with light.

Was this it? Was this my death? This nuclear blast inside my skull? Whatever it was, it lifted me away from that place; I could look down now. I was somehow free. I could see my body down there beneath me next to the stream, the headlights cutting a beam across my blood-spattered leg. The man still bent over me, drinking. And then nothing. An explosion of nothing.

The nothing began to go away. I was barefoot on a country road, dragging my hurt leg, one hand clapped over the pulsing wound. The moon had risen, giving just enough light for me to stay on the road. The sharp stones should have been hurting my feet, but all of me, my sensation, my pain, had retreated into my head. The rest was just walking.

Finally I saw headlights and was terrified. Knowing I had a chance to live. That's when he would step in and take me. Finish the job.

*　　*　　*

Mom let me stay out of school the rest of the week. It wasn't too hard to convince her. Even after my physical symptoms went away, I was still sick. Sick in a way I had never been before. Sick in a way I couldn't understand. The sickness of trying to process the unprocessable.

I had been attacked by a vampire.

As the hours crawled by, my mind dizzy from too much thinking and lack of food, I tried every other possibility to explain what had happened to me. Someone had put some kind of drug in my lunch at the soccer field. The first seizure had rendered me temporarily crazy. The man in the dark coat was nothing but a psychopath. A flesh-and-blood human being, just one with major issues.

But what psychopath could have done what he did? Who in the real world had the strength that he had? The quickness? The supernatural ability to stand in a tree on the slenderest of branches without falling?

Anything to spare me from staring long and hard at the two most likely scenarios: either vampires existed or I was insane.

When Mom came home each day, I would roll myself up in my blankets and pretend to be gone to the world. It wasn't so easy to turn Manda away, but at least she understood that I was temporarily out of order.

By the end of the third day, I was finally ready to accept the truth.

No matter how badly I wanted to disbelieve it, vampires existed. I was sure of something else as well: the attack had caused a massive seizure while the vampire was still feeding. The doctors in

Atlanta had told me I had had two seizures that day. Now I was convinced the curse had somehow saved me. But I had also been changed.

Transformed.

I felt crazy even considering the idea. *Vampire.* I didn't even like saying the word.

But something had happened that night. All the changes had occurred after the attack: strange colors in the dark, superhuman vision, strength, speed, hearing. Only something important was missing: the part where I ran around in a cape after dark, hungrily slurping up blood. The thought of drinking another person's bodily fluids made me nauseated all over again. Until I had gotten sick, I had been eating stuff like tuna fish and cheeseburgers for days. Also, vampires supposedly couldn't go out in the daylight without dying or otherwise dissolving into a pile of dust.

So what did that make me?

I also knew I wasn't dead. In fact, I had never felt more alive. The man in the dark coat wasn't dead either. At least he didn't seem that way. Flappy head wound aside, that was not a walking corpse who forced me to the ground and drank from my leg. It was a living, breathing human being of some sort. Maybe a genetic offshoot, runaway science project, you name it, but I was sure he was a living man.

I tried to remember the German-sounding phrase he had said to me just before I had smashed my fist into his face. *Gaybin zee meer ear laybin.* I spelled it out phonetically and plugged it into Babel Fish. No luck. I would have to try it on my grandfather, Papi, the next time I saw him.

As I started getting better, I spent more and more of my time researching vampires on the Web but almost instantly got tired of the subject. I found a million and one sites on vampires and vampire lore. Depending on the site, they were gross, silly, ridiculous, shocking, stupid, you name it. But most of all they were contradictory. There were the purists who deferred to Bram Stoker on all things bat. Historians who preferred Vlad Tepes, the Impaler, the infamous Romanian prince who loved to invite guests to "stake" dinners. Then every imaginable variation when it came to powers, from flight to shape-shifting.

Honestly, and I knew this was sacrilege in some corners, I had never found vampires all that interesting. Finally I just told myself that whatever I was, whatever I was becoming, I would have to figure things out for myself.

But what if I started manically craving blood? Was I doomed to spend the rest of my life . . . feeding off other human beings?

Oh no. I spent so much time alone with Manda.

I cried off and on for hours, consumed with horror at the possibility. If I noticed even a hint of a bad change, I had to leave, I decided at last.

But where would I go? What would I do?

That week felt like a whole year. I started having nightmares where I had grown fangs. The scariest was a dream about Manda. My little sister sprouted wings from her back that looked like knobby bits of bone splitting their way through the skin. Once they got large enough, she opened them like a huge bat and flew away. I jerked up in the middle of the night, a scream catching in my throat.

After I finally hit bottom, it took forever to climb back out of the poisonous hole of fear and confusion I had found myself in.

But climb out I did. By the end of the week I was sleeping better and keeping my food down, and as far as I could tell, there were no new changes. The nightmares stopped.

But my whole world had been wrenched violently out of joint.

I could never look at the "real world" the same way again. I had to question everything I had ever known to be true. If vampires were true, then maybe a tree could suddenly start talking. Maybe the ground under my feet would open and swallow me up.

And if vampires really existed, that meant they were still out there.

5. THE VISITOR

I got my chance to talk to Papi sooner than I expected. The following weekend Mom decided I was well enough to drag me out of the house. She drove us to my grandfather's place in the country so she could "spend a little time with myself."

It was always interesting to me that Mom never "spent a little time" with her own father, but she always told us she had gotten enough of that growing up. "Fondness skips generations," she liked to say. Which I took to mean that she and Papi didn't get along.

But today I was much more interested in other things. Like on the trip there I couldn't help thinking how long it would have taken me to run it. *Bet I could have beaten this Kia.*

My grandfather lived in a tiny one-story stone house in the nowhere town of Pineville, Alabama, population 302, give or take a stray dog or two. The only landmark was a BBQ joint called the Pig Stand that served Papi's favorite white sauce. "The reason I came to live in Alabama," he liked to say.

"I'm not sick, Papi!" Manda said, skipping up his wide stone steps.

Papi swept her up in a bone-smashing hug. *"Sehr gut,"* he said in his thick German. "But I did not expect my *Liebling* would be."

Papi was wearing what looked like a mechanic's blue uniform, but without a single smudge of grease. His wispy comb-over was perfectly in place, as always.

He put Manda down and turned to me, touching his left temple with his index finger the way he always did when he was "puzzling a little problem out."

"You . . . you are different," Papi said to me, leading us into the kitchen. "Don't tell me. Let me discover it on my own, *Enkelin*."

Enkelin is German for "granddaughter," which is what he called me, not because it was cute—Papi was not into cute—but to remind me who my elders were. Papi was German to his toes and bumpy and prickly and precise and loving all at the same time. It worked for him. I loved him more than any human being on earth. Other than Manda, of course. My grandmother died so long ago, I didn't have many memories of her. But Papi was my sun and moon.

The kitchen smelled of apples. "I have heard it has been you who have been the sick one," Papi said as we sat down to a snack of cheese and crackers and *Apfelwein,* a kind of German cider he made from trees in his backyard. He had his own cider press in the garage.

"I'm fine now, Papi," I said. *The lie of the century.* Like Papi, I hated liars.

"But that is not the difference, this sickness," he said. "I will have located it by the time we finish supper." He smiled so broadly, his thick eyebrows came together.

We went in the backyard. Manda was glued to Papi's side the whole afternoon and he threaded his way around her the way you walk around a cat. I wondered if I was ever going to get any time alone with him, hoping I wouldn't chicken out when I finally did.

We ate BBQ on Papi's rolling front lawn. Not one inch of his small lot was level, but the grass was cropped like a golf course. His garage was just as neat. I could see his old-fashioned rowboat and fishing tackle hanging above his Buick.

The T-shaped bars where my grandmother used to hang clothes out to dry were still there—my only clear memory of her was standing by her side between billowing sun-blown sheets as she snapped wooden clothespins to her line. Papi had been bellowing a bouncy song from the kitchen window called "Ein Prosit." "Stop singing that beer-drinking fighting killing song!" my grandmother had yelled. Papi swatted her on the butt as she came inside.

Papi was a stonemason from the old school and had built the little house himself with native rocks. You wouldn't think he was an educated guy. Mom said he never got beyond the eighth grade because he had to quit school to work for his family when his father died. But looks were definitely deceiving.

The house had only five rooms and a bath, but it was stuffed with books, all history. I knew just exactly what he would say if I asked him if he believed in vampires. Papi believed in combustion engines, Jitterbug lures, and his hero, the German NASA engineer Wernher von Braun, "who put Mr. Armstrong on the moon." Bloodsucking monsters? Forget it.

"Now," Papi said, putting aside his plate of BBQ and fixing me with one squinty eye. "Something is wrong, I can tell this, *Enkelin*. You want to talk about it? You ask your mother, I promise you, I am not a good listener. But for you, I listen."

I didn't know how to begin. I talked about everything but the real thing. He could tell I wasn't revealing anything and said nothing about it. That was one of the best things about him. Unlike my mom, Papi wasn't a control freak about other people.

Finally I couldn't stand it anymore. We had settled down in the living room to talk about history, books, that kind of thing, just like we always did before going to bed. It was now or never.

"Papi, do you believe . . . What do you think . . . about . . . supernatural things?" I said at last.

His eyebrows jumped. "Religion? I am surprised you ask this

question. You would have been better to have known your grandmother."

"Not religion, Papi. You know, just things."

"Things?"

"Things like you can't . . . understand. Things that are beyond understanding. Beyond explanation."

"Could you give me just a little bit example, *Enkelin*?" There he went with the elders thing again.

"What about . . . what about vampires?"

I cringed as I said it. Papi could be pretty brutal when he wanted you to know just how dumb you were. But I was built for brutal. *Here it comes.*

Instead Papi put a finger to his lips, then walked me up the hall to the little room that used to be Grandmother's bedroom. Where Manda was sleeping now. We both peeked at her. She had kicked off her covers but was completely out of it. I wondered how Papi would react if I told him she was glowing softly blue in the dark? I followed him back to the living room. He poured us fresh mugs of cider and sank back in his recliner. I could tell he was settling in for one of his stories.

"Something I never told you. It was a story my own grandfather told me. There was a man in his village who was his good friend when he was a young man. And this good friend had an elder brother named Dieter. Dieter was a stonemason and he was also a suicide. Something to do with a love that was not returned. My grandfather was told this man Dieter, three days after his death, because of the suicide had become a *Nachtzehrer*.

"A vampire. He ate his death shroud and began to eat the corpses of his neighbors. The people noticed this defilement and began to place clumps of dirt under the chins of the dead or coins on their tongues to prevent any others from doing this."

My skin went cold all over. Papi went on.

"Once this Dieter, the *Nachtzehrer*, had devoured the limbs of those buried around him, he began to walk abroad in the village at night drinking blood. He practiced on the blood of pigs to begin with *und* then graduated to human beings. There was a panic in the village and all the doors were smeared with *Knoblauch*."

"*Knoblauch?*"

"Garlic. At last it was determined who was the identity of the *Nachtzehrer*, and a crowd came from the village to the cemetery to cut off its head *und* drive a spike through its mouth, to pin its head to the ground. When they opened the crypt of this Dieter, he was found to be lying in a pool of blood, so gorged was the *Nachtzehrer* that it could not retain all the blood it had consumed."

I sat there blinking, not knowing what to say. "Jeez, Papi. That's really messed up."

"*Ja.* And so why do you ask about such things?"

"It's just . . . I have been wondering. About something like that. Did you believe his story? Your grandfather's?"

"I believe that he believed his friend."

"But you, what did you . . ."

Papi snorted and thumped his hand on the arm of his recliner. "Complete nonsense. People are . . . what is the word . . . *leicht-gläubig*. Gullible. They want to believe what they want to believe. It has been so down throughout history. That is one reason it is so interesting to study. The history changes, but the people? Never." He smiled again. "You did not answer my question, *Enkelin*. It is your choice. I just want you to know I noticed."

We waited, looking at each other. No one, I mean no one, could beat my papi in a staring contest. I blinked.

"Papi, another thing . . . Could you please translate something for me?"

I took a small piece of paper from my pocket where I had spelled the words out phonetically and did my best to repeat what the man in the dark coat had said to me.

Papi frowned. "I don't think maybe you are pronouncing it a little bit right. Is it this: *Geben Sie mir Ihr Leben?*"

"Yeah! That's it. That's what it is."

Papi's frown deepened. He dropped the footrest on his chair and sat forward, eyes shining intently. "Where did you hear this? Did someone say this to you, *Enkelin*? Tell me."

"Never mind, Papi. Just what does it mean?"

"It means this," he said. "'Give me your life.'"

It took me a very long time to get to sleep on the rollaway cot in Manda's room. Papi snored so loudly, it sounded as if the house would break apart from the sheer decibels. That was the reason my grandmother had demanded a separate bedroom. But the sound had never bothered me before. In fact, it had comforted me.

But tonight I couldn't stop thinking about the *Nachtzehrer*. The story, the way he told it, had the feel of truth to it. No matter what he said about it being nonsense. Maybe that was Papi's way of dealing with something he couldn't, didn't want to, understand.

What if . . . what if the lust for blood . . . what if it was a change that I hadn't gone through yet? What would I do if it came? How could I live? *Can a vampire commit suicide?*

Most of all, I couldn't stop thinking about the man in the dark coat. The vampire, I reminded myself. Back on the mountain, he had wanted to kill me. I was helpless. But something had stopped him. *My seizure?* That had to be it. Maybe when a person dies in a vampire attack, they are just plain dead. But because I survived, I was turning into one. . . .

I didn't want to think about it. I looked over at Manda, her tiny hand dangling over the edge of the mattress, one leg pointing at the floor. *So small.*

What chance would she have if . . .

Could I stop myself? Would I even be able to think like a human being anymore if the change came? Or would I be a ravenous beast, hell-bent on nothing but feasting to drive off my terrible hunger? The vampire . . . his face . . . I refused to ever let that be my face.

In the end, I didn't tell Papi. I couldn't. As we were leaving the next morning, he suddenly grabbed my arm.

"You have lost weight, *Enkelin*. That is the difference, *ja*?"

Actually, I had. Who wouldn't have, going through a sickness like that? But I still liked hearing somebody say it.

"Is that it? I believe it is, isn't it?" he said.

"Yes, that's it, Papi." I looked at him, trying to figure if this was just his way of letting me off the hook.

"You can't fool these eyes," Papi said. "I never will remember a name well, but I remember faces forever. Appearances. Personalities. These are the things that do not change for me."

He held me to him and hugged Manda as Mom pulled into the gravel drive. "You can tell me anything," he said into my ear, making it look like a goodbye kiss. "You are never afraid. You are my *Kämpferin*."

He had said this before. I felt tears in my eyes. I knew a little German from hanging around Papi over the years. *Kämpferin* meant "fighter." I took Manda's hand and we ran to the car.

After coming back from Papi's, I began to feel better again. There were no new changes. I was still going outside in the sun with no ill effects, and the bloodiest thing I craved was the prime rib Mom always got for us on birthdays and at Christmas.

It's interesting how quickly a strange situation can melt into the background and become the new "normal." At school everybody was used to my shades by now, even me. My grades even picked up. I was hanging around the apartment so much, I spent more time with my books out of sheer boredom.

I hadn't even had an argument with my mother lately. Not a bad one, anyhow.

"You worry me," she said one night.

"Why?"

"I'm starting to think you might almost like me."

"Mom."

She was sitting on the floor in the living room. An old movie was on that wasn't very good—Cuba and dancing and a butt-ugly singer with a receding hairline who we were supposed to believe was making all those beautiful girls swoon.

"Emma, do you ever miss your father?" she said, looking down at the laundry basket in front of her.

That one caught me off guard. "I don't really think about him all that much." I wondered if I was telling the truth, thought about it, and decided I was. He hadn't entered my mind much since the attack.

"Do you ever wish you could see him?"

"I used to."

"Why? Do you miss him?"

"I wanted to ask him things."

"Like what? Why he left?"

"I know why he left."

Mom scooped out more clothes to fold. It was late; Manda was in bed. The laundry tended to back up, so the living room was crowded with little piles. I sat down in the middle of them and started sorting socks.

"What, you're actually going to help?"

"Hey, come on, I help."

"Okay. You do. Sometimes. Do you really know why he left?"

"I don't think I want to talk about it."

"It's okay."

"For you, maybe."

"He met someone, Emma. You know that, don't you?"

I reached for more socks. "I really don't want to talk about this."

"It wasn't anything you did, honey. It wasn't your epilepsy. That was just . . . timing."

"I'm not stupid, Mom." My seizure condition was usually off-limits when it came to talking about Dad. She knew that. She was supposed to know. We worked together for a while not speaking.

"I think he's embarrassed," Mom said.

"Who?"

"Your dad. He's embarrassed. It was supposed to be one of those happily-ever-after things, you know."

"So do you hate him?"

She watched her hands working on a shirt. Picked up another one and folded it. "There's no future in hating someone, Emma."

"Even if he deserves it?"

I looked at her face. She was swiping one of Manda's socks across her eyes.

"Are you okay?" I said.

"Why don't you go to bed or something?" she whispered.

"Not sleepy," I said. I would have patted her on the back or given her a hug, but I was not big into the comforting thing. I figured it made you weak. But I touched her arm. "Mom?"

"What."

"Sometimes you believe in something, you think you know what it is, and it changes. Your world is suddenly completely different and you have to figure it out all over again. I know what that's like."

"Because of your epilepsy?"

I let her believe that's what I was talking about.

Later I lay there looking up at the ceiling in my room. My window was cracked open and somewhere across the complex I heard somebody say, "I really can't stand living like this anymore." I listened to them going back and forth, a man and a woman somewhere out there in the night. Nothing earth-shattering, but still something no one else should have been allowed to hear.

I didn't want to believe it, but I knew my old life was coming to an end. It had to. I was different. I wasn't my mother's daughter anymore. Not the daughter she knew.

I looked at the clock: 12:03 a.m. I stared at it. Kept staring. The numbers were red. Someone once told me the best clocks had red numbers because the light was softer than blue in the dark. I couldn't see how that was true. Blue was robin eggs, soft spring skies, water that was not stormy. Red was war and sunburn and ambulance lights and warning beacons. *And blood.*

I was still staring, but I didn't really see the number on the clock anymore. Actually, I saw it, but it wasn't a number. It wasn't even a light. It had become a colored thing with edges and a shape. Something about the shape pleased me. I kept staring.

Pretty soon I was experiencing another "small" seizure. I didn't know it at the time, of course. You usually don't, not till afterward. Sometimes not at all. I just kept staring and staring at the number on the clock, feeling more and more comfortable.

Then the clock went away, and the comfortable feeling was all there was, and I was basically staring at a place in the center of the dark. I could see perfectly that there was nothing there but the wall and my bedroom closet. But then something different happened: instead of becoming a blip of lost time in my life, I was completely aware of what was going on.

It started like this: the feeling of something physical pushing itself into my head . . . a solid, invisible finger digging straight into the comfortable feeling of my absence seizure. I kept staring at the wall; I suddenly became aware that someone was standing there. A tall man with long legs and a coat that came to his knees . . .

"Good evening, *Mädchen*," he said.

If the bottom of the sea could make a sound, that's what his voice sounded like.

He was with me, right there in my bedroom. The vampire. I should have screamed, should have jumped up, run for the door, anything. But I was somehow still locked inside the seizure, experiencing that feeling of endless, openmouthed comfort. So I only stared. That's all I could do.

The vampire was not seven feet away. I could see his black, creased pants. His dirty white shirt with the cork buttons. Eyes with no color. There was a lavender glow about his entire body. Not blue, like with everyone else. Lavender with an edge, as though the blue of his original color had been mixed with blood.

I couldn't speak. Couldn't move. I was paralyzed. As if there wasn't room for anything else inside my mind. *Only room for him.* I wasn't even sure I was breathing.

"So this is your . . . room," the vampire said. He spoke the words slowly, the hint of a bottoming-out snarl in his throat. "How nice to have found you home in bed."

He watched me and I watched him and we waited.

Wirtz.

I heard the word like a sound inside my head, not a voice, but more like the ping of a small bell. The vampire's lips hadn't moved. He hadn't spoken it, but somehow I knew that was his name. *Wirtz.*

The vampire stared at me without any particular expression. My mouth was wet at the corners and my face felt as if it were immersed in cotton.

The vampire, Wirtz, turned his face away slightly. I could see the pinkish flap of torn scalp on top of his head. He was looking at something else. So I looked there too.

A pair of tiny sneakers was on the floor next to my dresser. The sneakers had yellow and blue flowers and pink laces.

Manda.

Wirtz looked at her shoes and licked his lips. His tongue was unnaturally long and slightly squared at the tip rather than pointed.

"Delikatesse," the vampire said, nostrils flaring as he inhaled deeply. As though he was tasting something on the air. *Tasting her.* "A delicacy, you know," the dark man went on, looking at me again. "Very new blood. So warm as it slides down your throat, it almost burns. But that is not the best part. New blood is also very energetic. As I drink from someone so young, I can taste the lack of age. The lightness of the years. But drinking young blood is also something like eating new fruit. So . . . *scharf* . . . tart." He extended a long finger, pointing at Manda's shoes. "You will watch as I drink from her, *Mädchen.* You will see it in my face, the tartness of her sweet young blood."

I was still trapped in the middle of the seizure, but now I started to feel a trembling sensation in the cottony thickness wrapped around my face. A rippling from deep inside, trying to bring me up to the surface.

"Come to me," Wirtz said. "You must answer my Call. It would be so much better for her if you would come on your own, as you should. It is unnatural that you have resisted, stayed away from me for so long."

I couldn't remember resisting anything. This sure didn't feel like resisting. It felt like . . . *surrender*.

I started to push back on the inside. Wirtz turned his head the other way now, looking around the room as if trying to remember everything there. My soccer posters. Bookshelves. Nightstand, laptop, the quilt on my bed.

He looked at me again. "I will find you, you know. I will never stop looking. Come to me now and I will let her live."

I was still locked inside my mind but could feel the tumblers beginning to fall. I was coming up from someplace that was very heavy and deep and far away. But I was surfacing. The more he stared at Manda's shoes, the faster I rose to the surface.

"I am your father," the vampire rumbled. "I created you. You are one of my children. How did this happen? How did you make your escape? Help me to remember. The last thing I know, I saw . . . *Lichter* . . . lights. After, nothingness. You did this? *Unbegreiflich*. Inconceivable. You have hidden secrets from your father. Come to me so I may learn them too. These secrets will not buy your life." He glanced at the shoes. "But they will buy hers."

Snap out of it, Emma, a voice said. It was my own voice, coming up from far below. *Now. Now. Now.*

"If you do not come to me," Wirtz said, "let me tell you what I will do. I will find you, and through you I will find your family." He smiled. "I will have her. I will hold her in the air and break her spine across my leg. With luck, she will still be alive. Alive enough to know she has been paralyzed. But do not worry. Her condition will not last long. I will rip her throat open and suck her dry until she is shriveled and gone almost completely, but not quite. I will save some spark of life, some *Funke,* until the very end. And then I will tear her head from her shoulders."

The voice in my head was screaming now. *Come up, Emma, come up!*

"Very well," the vampire said. "Your silence is your answer." He gestured at the sneakers. "This is your decision. I will find you. Her blood will be on your hands."

He stooped beside Manda's shoes, reaching as if to stroke them with his dirty fingernails.

"All I need is something that will tell me . . . where . . . you . . . are. . . . *Ah.*"

The fingers stopped just short of caressing the shoes. . . . The vampire had spotted something else. A scrap of paper. *My school lunch menu.* The menu was upside down. If Wirtz turned it over, he would see the name of my school in bold print across the top.

He reached for the paper, then his face twisted with something that almost looked like pain. The vampire drew back his hand and stood, looking at me. Mouth like a wound. He sighed.

"No matter. It is only a question of time. And I have so very much of it. Run if you prefer, *Mädchen.* I will still come. I will never stop coming until I find you. Never. *Das schwöre ich.* This I vow."

Hurry hurry hurry!

I was close now, so close; the part of me that the seizure had buried was moving fast, about to break through the top.

The vampire smiled. *"Sie werden wie ein Schwein sterben."*

You will die like a pig.

6. RUNNING

The clock read 12:04.

An animal sound gushed from my throat. The seizure was over; I was free of the paralysis. I flung myself off my bed and leapt across the room at Wirtz. *Kill him. Kill him.*

I flew straight through the vampire and smashed into my closet door instead. The door groaned as it was knocked off its track; I lashed out furiously, splitting the wood in half and throwing shards of it up in the air. Sheetrock rubble from the ceiling fell on my head. I looked wildly around the room. Wirtz had disappeared.

I shouted Manda's name at least five times before my mother came in and grabbed my arm from behind. I flung her away, not realizing she wasn't the vampire. She slammed against the bedroom door, shutting it with her back, looking at me with crazy eyes. Manda's voice came crying through the crack.

"Emma, Emma, Emma!"

My mother put her arms out toward me, eyes wide as she took in the destruction of my room. "Emma, what's wrong! What's happening?" She was almost screaming the words.

I felt all the air leave my body. *Oh my God. What am I doing?* "I have to . . . I have to go, Mom," I said. "I have to go now. . . ."

She put her hands out again. "What . . . what are you talking about? What's wrong?"

Manda banged on the door, but my mother was still leaning against it.

"Emma! Emma!"

My sister's voice sounded alarm bells in my head. I took a step backward and looked around in a panic. I could still feel the vampire in the room. His cold, heavy emptiness filling the space.

Manda was still screaming. Mom was struggling to keep the door shut so my sister wouldn't see this. *See what I've become.*

I had to do something. Seconds counted. *It's me he wants,* I thought. Wirtz was looking for me; I was leading him straight to them. If I stayed any longer . . . the vampire would be back . . . holding Manda in his hands. His mouth on her throat. As her life ebbed, when he was drunk on her blood, when he had gorged on my sister's blood, he would throw her away like a broken doll. *And it would all be my fault.*

I'm the monster.

I had to draw him away. *Now.* I turned and grabbed the first thing I saw—my sunglasses off the nightstand. I shoved them in my pocket, rushed across the room, and threw my shoulder at the window, hitting it full force. I could feel it as I blasted through the glass and wood, and the window exploded outward with the force of my body.

I was nearly twenty feet off the ground. I fell in a shower of shards and debris and landed in the grass. I shook the glass out of my hair. I didn't have a plan but to run, just run. Run as far and as fast as I could, before Wirtz could close in on them. *Draw the vampire away.*

I ran down our little side road, then streaked across four lanes of traffic without waiting for the cars to pass.

I was barefoot and wearing pajamas. I kept going until I broke through a band of trees. I was in a field, then another band of trees and then another field and a farm road. I put on more speed. *Power* station. *Gravel. Pavement, leaves, woods.* I was flying past hills, rocks, fences, walls. I chewed up miles of countryside until I had no idea where I was or how far I had gone.

I burst through a wood and came to a wide river. I could see a barge moving through the water that looked as if it wasn't really moving at all. I took a tremendous leap and hit the water hard and then was stroking for the barge, kicking up a wake behind me.

I grasped the edge of the barge's nasty saturated wood and threw myself over, sailing past the heads of two men smoking on deck. The smell of their cigarettes filled my nostrils and I could hear a tiny piece of their conversation as I zoomed over—"That's how you pick up girls"—then I fell into the water on the other side and was swimming again.

I came up the far bank, battling through river trash and vegetation, streaking through the woods and leaving a trail of drops in the air behind me. I crossed another field and came to a fence. The fence was twice as high as my head and strung with razor wire at the top. It had a large white sign that said:

US ARMY INSTALLATION
NO TRESPASSING
TEST RANGES

I took two steps and bounded over, hit the ground running on the far side. I ran through one big field after another, then nothing but thick woods. I came to a hillside with a farm road running along its edge and a broad drainage wash that emptied into a big concrete pipe.

I ran into the wash and threw my body into the pipe. Lay there listening to the sounds of the nighttime around me. They were loud. Insects chirruping and creaking and buzzing. Wind in the trees. Twigs crackling as something moved over them.

I curled up and made myself smaller, holding my head in my hands and drawing my knees up to my chest.

Had I gone far enough? I could imagine the vampire out there in the dark. Tracking me. Licking his lips, biting them. If he found me here . . .

I waited, certain any moment I was going to see Wirtz's terrible face peer over the edge of the pipe.

Finally my heart began to slow. I couldn't believe what I had just done. I lay on the rough cement listening and watching. My pajamas were still wet from swimming the river. My hair dripped into my eyes and down my back. I was used to a bed, a home, pro-tection, warmth. . . .

I shivered miserably and wept.

As the hours crawled by, my vampire ears had me jumping at everything that moved. I had never felt so far away from the things I knew. Everything was alien. The sounds, distant lights across the fields, the smell of wildness . . .

I think I slept.

Where was I?

I blinked and opened my eyes, starting violently. Directly over my face was the grodiest-looking spider I had ever seen. I raked my fingernails on the inside walls of the pipe, scrambling to get out. Flopped on the moist ground, then almost started bawling all over again.

Sunshine.

The unimaginably bright ball of the sun was rising over the hill.

So intense, it nearly made my eyes bleed. I dug my sunglasses out of the pocket of my pj's and put them on, then lay there a long time letting the orange glow wash the night out of my skin.

I sat up. Nobody else was around. I was sitting at the base of a low woody slope surrounded by fields and woods as far as I could see. *Mom . . .*

A fresh wave of tears rolled down my face. She had to be scared out of her mind. I put my hand back in my pocket. *Stupid.* My cell was lying on my nightstand at home, plugged into its charger.

I got up and scaled the hill behind the pipe and found a clear place to get a look around. I could see a fence to the north and beyond that a line of traffic crawling up a highway that ran alongside a town. The skyline—or lack thereof—looked familiar. *That's Huntsville,* I thought. The highway was I-565. So I was about thirty miles from home, give or take.

The vampire could be anywhere.

I sat on a limestone outcropping, forcing myself to slow down and think. I could still feel that invisible finger entering my head—the burning connection between us. It was insane, but I was certain of it: somehow my seizure had let Wirtz through to me. But the real, physical vampire had never been in my room. That was an image of Wirtz I had seen. A projection. I had gone right through him when I had lunged against the closet door. But he had spoken to me and could see everything around him— *Can all vampires do this stuff?* I wondered.

And what was stopping him from visiting again? Without warning, given the nature of seizures. It terrified me to think of what could have happened if that lunch menu had been right-side up. . . . *If I hadn't run away . . .*

Manda . . .

For once my instincts had been good. The only way I could help her now was by keeping alive and staying away from home until I could figure out what Wirtz was up to. *How to stop him.*

I looked at the horizon. The sun was supposed to make everything better, wasn't it? For the first time in my life, it didn't. I had never felt so miserably alone and frightened. But it did remind me of one thing.

I have a power you don't, I thought.

If the legends were true, right now Wirtz was dug in somewhere like a rat in a hole. And he would be there for at least the next thirteen or fourteen hours. The daylight belonged to me.

The first thing I had to do was find something to drink. I knew all about giardia, the little germs that get in streams when an animal like a deer dies in the water. I didn't care. I was about to fall over from thirst. I found a stream at the base of a hill, a brook that was clear and cool and rushed over small stones. I lay on my belly and drank until I could hear my stomach slosh. I felt dirty, so I splashed my streaky face and washed my arms and legs.

Feeling a little better, I scaled the hill again and scouted the surrounding territory.

I faced west and saw three long roads, one of them wide like a highway with at least four lanes of slowly creeping traffic. The other two roads were narrower and swung toward one another and eventually joined. A lot of the cars were headed to a cluster of tall buildings straight in front of me.

Scattered all over were breaks in the woods. I could see other groups of buildings, most of them long and low to the ground. There were lots of fields as well, some of them dotted with cows. What was this place? It looked weird seeing livestock so close to office buildings.

To the east I could see nothing but thick woods and more low hills. To the south the Tennessee River, which I had crossed the night before, sparkling in the morning light. Near the river was a tall brown structure that appeared to be made of iron surrounded by small square buildings with low concrete walls.

First things first. Right now I was hungry. I crept down from the hill and followed the long curve of the old farm road, staying just in the edge of the trees, heading in the general direction of the cluster of tall buildings.

There was a broad pasture between me and the office complex. I would have to be less cautious if I wanted to find something to eat there. The parking lot was full—most of the people seemed to be inside now. Hopefully they weren't staring out their windows.

I came out from the trees and scrambled over a low fence. The buildings were so big, they were farther away than they seemed. It would take a little while to get there. I could unleash my feet, but it couldn't be good if anybody saw a barefoot girl in filthy pajamas and shades setting a new land speed record.

I circled the complex from a good distance away. It felt a little safer when I got to the back of the parking lot. At least I wasn't so exposed. I trotted around to the front and saw a sweeping semicir-cular entryway. In the middle of the entryway was a grassy oval on which sat something that looked like a funky piece of abstract art. Dark golden in color, roughly cone-shaped, wide at the base and narrow at the top. As I studied it more closely, I realized it was a huge piece of machinery of some kind.

The golden machine was covered with twisted metallic pipes and thick, painted wiring. It reminded me of something I had seen before. Suddenly it hit me: *An engine.* An enormous, otherworldly engine, but yeah, an engine. It was perched in front of a large sign that read:

GEORGE C. MARSHALL SPACE FLIGHT CENTER
NATIONAL AERONAUTICS AND SPACE
ADMINISTRATION

Holy crap.
I had stumbled onto a NASA base.

7. MY CASTLE

I had heard of this place, sure. I had never been inside the fence, but back in middle school I had visited the world-famous Space and Rocket Center just outside the base. It was NASA's scaled-down version of Disney World, complete with zero-g rides, antique space junk, and rockets you could climb through. That's where I remembered seeing an engine like this one before.

I remembered they had told our class that the actual Space Center was surrounded by a huge army base called Redstone Arsenal. Which made sense, considering they would have to protect the secrets of the space program from foreign governments. So some of those cars I saw coming through the gate probably belonged to soldiers.

As I watched from about a hundred yards away, people from the parking lot mounted the steps and entered, sweeping some kind of badge in front of a bar code reader to get inside. There was no way I could find any breakfast in there without being spotted. I turned and trotted back to the woods.

I crouched next to a sassafras tree, stomach growling. *Guess I could eat the leaves.* Looking back at the sea of cars, I thought of Manda and smiled, thinking how she would drive me crazy if she knew I was here. Wondering if the astronauts ever came to visit and where they kept the moon dust hidden.

Hidden.

An idea popped into my head. I was tucked away from the rest of the world, surrounded by thousands of acres of woods, fields, and hopefully about a million army tanks. Finding food and shelter couldn't be all that tough, either. Not on a place this size with this many buildings.

I started to feel a little better about my situation. Then I remembered Wirtz's face as he spoke the words: *I will never stop coming until I find you. Never. . . . This I vow.*

No matter how careful I was, sooner or later he would find me. He had superpowers, was driven by some kind of murderous vampire vendetta, and had all the time in the world. My skin prickled with the realization.

Wirtz would never stop coming until . . . *until one of us is dead.*

Okay, as hungry as I was, my most pressing need was a safe place to sleep. I refused to spend even one more second in a concrete pipe. But my home base couldn't be just anywhere. I shuddered at the thought of facing Wirtz out in the open. But as long as I stayed here at the Space Center I had certain advantages, and I was determined to exploit them. Through instinct or sheer luck, I had found the perfect place for a siege. And, thanks to my grandfather, I knew a thing or two about sieges.

The first thing to do, Papi always said, was find the most defensible position. This usually meant high ground with a full view of the surrounding terrain in 360 degrees.

But just camping on top of a hill and trying to keep watch felt like suicide when facing a creature as powerful and deadly as Wirtz. I had powers of my own, sure, but I would feel a lot better at night in some kind of defensive structure where I had ways of slowing the vampire down.

In the Middle Ages a noble family would build what was called a motte and bailey: an enclosed area, usually on a hill, surrounding a group of small wooden or stone structures. Later they would start on the actual castle itself.

No matter how strong and fast I was, I didn't have the time or the serfs for that. What I needed was something already built. I immediately thought about the tall brownish structure I had seen and took off for the river.

With no other eyes to see, I turned on the jets and raced through the forest. Soon I broke into a pasture full of cows. I rushed through the herd at supersonic speeds, and they fled in a panic, mooing crazily.

I pushed harder, using the run to experiment with my vampire abilities. I leapt into the air, twenty feet off the ground, and soared through the notch of a tree without touching a leaf. Came to earth again on the far side, soft as kissing a baby.

I burst into a meadow, empty except for tall wildflowers that blew over in my wake. I threw my arms wide, bounding through clouds of yellow pollen.

On the far side of the secret meadow, something caught my attention: a large white board near the edge of the woods. I walked around to the other side to look.

DANGER!

BURIED MUNITIONS

NO TRESPASSING

DO NOT DIG WITHOUT GPR PERMIT

I stopped breathing. I had just been running and bouncing through a minefield. I could have blown myself up. I sat down shakily, looking back at the innocent yellow flowers.

Can a vampire die?

If Wirtz was to be believed, they sure could. *Keep going.*

I could smell water and knew I was close to the river. Moving much more carefully this time, I walked a little ways into the woods and a new place opened up before me, a wide circle of grassy gravel and weeds.

No signs around, so it seemed safe enough. I moved into the clearing. In the center was a towering structure that rose up like a big squarish grain elevator emblazoned at the top with a huge peeling NASA logo. Metal stairs zigzagged up the tower's sides to doors placed at different levels. The tower itself was made of thick metal plates studded with giant bolts, and the whole thing was laced with ladders and catwalks. From the top protruded a monstrous arm that had to be nearly a hundred feet long running perpendicular to the tower, making the whole structure look like an upside-down letter L.

Directly beneath the arm was a gigantic iron chute that disappeared into the ground, then bent and reappeared at an angle pointed at the woods on the other side.

I walked around to the front of the chute. It looked like a fireplace big enough to drop a house in.

I glanced around, tingling all over. I had the sense the tower hadn't been used in decades. It looked as if everything had been left to the elements. So quiet, undisturbed.

Perfect.

I had found my castle.

Before climbing the tower, I did a little exploring in the immediate area. There were a couple of abandoned one-story cinder block buildings nearby with peeling paint and doors that had never seen a bar code reader. I pushed inside and immediately caught the rank smell of a structure returning to a wild state.

A couple hundred feet from the base of the tower, a huge concrete bunker had been built into the side of a low hill. The bunker had square observation windows, but the glass was long gone. The walls of the bunker looked to be about two feet thick, something not even Wirtz would be able to get through, only the opening leading inside was much too wide for me to block.

I stepped inside the bunker and slipped my shades off. A little ways in I found a water faucet sticking out of the wall beneath one of the observation ports. I turned it on and was surprised to see it still worked. *Ewww*. I was thirsty, but the water came out brown and ropy. I left the faucet running, hoping it would clear sooner or later.

The interior was cooler than the outdoors because it was partially underground. There wasn't much inside. In the back I came to a steel mesh curtain with only darkness beyond. I could see into the darkness, of course, but there really was nothing there. Only more concrete floors and walls running deep into the hillside. I could smell dirt and hear water dripping somewhere far off. The underground exhaled, ruffling my hair. *Save it for later.*

I put my sunglasses back on and sprinted to the tower and began climbing, launching my body up the side rather than taking the stairs. The strength of my legs was incredible—I flew upward at least fifteen or twenty feet with every kick, propelling myself higher and higher from one handhold to the next using my newly discovered vampire senses to judge distances. I felt so confident I wouldn't fall, it was almost as if I could fly.

It didn't take long to reach the flat metal roof at the top. The only things higher than what I was standing on were the supports at the end of the big iron arm that jutted out over the clearing. I dusted rust from my hands and looked around. The view from up there was perfect. I could see everything for miles around: NASA buildings, the river, the interstate, acres and acres of swamp, forest, and fields. With my eyesight, it would be next to impossible for anybody to approach without me noticing.

Assuming I'm awake to see it.

I dropped to a catwalk one floor below and found a steel door leading to the inside of the tower. The door was old but still locked. I put my shoulder against it and used my strength to smash it open.

"Oops."

The door came completely off its hinges. I was holding it by the steel knob. I held the door over the drop below and let go, just to get it out of the way, aiming for the next catwalk. It missed and fell to the ground seventy or eighty feet below with a reverberating crash. *Oh well.*

Behind the gaping hole where the door had been was a dingy little room. It smelled as if it had been closed for decades. I stepped inside and found a gray desk, a couple of folding chairs, and a green filing cabinet, all covered with patches of rust.

The desk was empty and the filing cabinet drawers were rusted shut, so I ripped them open with my bare hands. Inside were masses of moldering yellow and pink paper. If I needed a fire, here was plenty of starter fuel.

The carpet was the color of dead grass, and the lumpy steel walls reminded me of oatmeal. A mildew-spotted fire extinguisher hung next to a shelf that was bare except for a single stained coffee cup half filled with pieces of bugs.

I went back to the doorway and sat down. I wondered where Wirtz was at exactly that moment. What did vampires do to avoid the sun? It was ridiculous to think of them dragging coffin-loads of dirt around, plunking them down in some sweaty basement whenever they needed a rest. As for me, I could bed down in this room as soon as I found something decent to sleep on. No way was I going to stretch out on that nasty carpet.

There's something in the trees, I thought.

No, not a monster, but something monstrously large, and only a few hundred yards away. A shiny aluminum structure with a long drive leading up to it.

I scrambled down the tower and went uphill through the forest to a little high point of land. I lay on my stomach and hands, creeping forward cautiously because I could hear a car coming. Over the crest of the little hill a Mini Cooper was swinging around the curve. I ducked my head, then leapt across the road as soon as the car was out of sight again.

The woods thinned on the other side of the drive, and there was a long building nestled in an even longer clearing. At the end of the building was a tall metallic dome glinting like aluminum foil in the sun. A sign at one end of the drive read:

MSFC SOLAR OBSERVATORY
CONTRACTOR'S ENTRANCE

The building had windows so narrow they looked like medieval arrow ports—what Papi called balistraria. I picked a spot between two of them, took several long hopping steps, then sprang right up the side. It felt just as natural as walking. I grabbed the rim of the flat roof and hoisted myself up.

Something immediately clutched at my stomach: *Oh my God.* Hot dogs.

I dashed to the far side of the roof and flipped myself over to where I was hanging upside down. I lowered myself slowly, and sure enough, there it was, a cafeteria. I looked both ways; nobody was around. I dropped to my feet and found a door that led to a kind of air lock. I got through the outer door, but the inner one was sealed.

The sight of those steamy-wet hot dogs turning under the heat lamp almost had me battering down the glass door. I saw two cooks in white aprons moving around in the back, but no one else. *Must be preparing for lunch.*

I looked at the cafeteria door again: it had the same kind of bar code reader I had seen at the first complex. My anger flared. I would need a special key card or badge to get through it. *Hey, this is an emergency here—* I briefly considered tearing the reader off the wall and smashing my way in. I would get my hot dogs, sure, but I was also pretty certain I would scare the cooks to death and set off an alarm somewhere. Not the best way to treat one's neighbors.

I stepped out of the air lock and slipped back into the woods, frustrated. Making it worse, the breeze was still bringing me a fresh scent of those tantalizing . . . A noise behind me made me flinch. I dropped down, feeling ridiculously exposed. Two men were walking up the sidewalk without looking my way.

"Hey, you still watch *American Idol*?" one of the men said.

"Yeah, but it's crap," the other said. "The singers this season are crap. The songs are really terrible. I miss the old days."

One of them was tall and fat, the other short and thin. They both had badges with their pictures on them swinging from cords around their necks. They headed straight for the air lock door I had just left and stuck their badges up to the reader and they were inside.

I was right behind them, moving so quickly and silently, I

caught the door in mid-swing; neither of the men even turned around.

The inside of the building was shaded in lights and darks. I slipped behind a large pillar in the cafeteria that was decorated with posters of outer space and let the men walk away from me. Now the only people I could see were the cooks in the back, one of them stirring something in a large stainless steel pot while the other rapidly chopped onions.

I sprinted to the hot dog case without making a sound and fell to the floor in front of a steel counter directly below the revolving wieners. Saliva was practically dripping down my pajama top. I raised my head slowly, reached around, and snagged two hot dogs before the guy chopping onions could even bring down his blade. They tasted so wonderful, my eyes started to water. I stole two more hot dogs and gobbled them.

Now I was thirsty again. But it was nothing at all to grab a cup of orange drink from the dispenser. It was kind of funny, actually. The cook doing the stirring kept looking up every time I thumbed the dispenser, but by then my hand was already gone. It took several tries to get a full cup. Finally he put down his spoon and came over to investigate. By then I was gone.

Okay, food and shelter situation solved, at least temporarily. Now I needed to get busy. I still had several hours before I had to start worrying about the dark again. I skirted the minefield, wishing I had shoes, and made a beeline for the nearest highway. *Time to do a little shopping.*

8. DESPERATE

"Fear makes the wolf bigger than he is."

That's something Papi liked to say.

Still, I had never stolen anything in my life. Not a stick of gum or even a grape from the produce department. *Okay, hot dogs.* Just like my grandfather, I had always thought thieves were complete creeps. Now I was standing in the power tool aisle at Home Depot about to commit a felony.

Papi had been in the army in East Berlin and had plenty of guns, but he never taught me anything about them. "You are *ein Fräulein*," was all he would say, shrugging. He'd let me watch him plink cans with his .22 in the gully behind his apple trees and that was about it. "Little girls shouldn't know such things."

Maybe he was right: I was probably more of a hand-to-hand kind of chick.

I knew nothing about weapons or defending myself, other than plain raw fury. It had been all I ever needed. *Until now.*

I had one of those long flatbed orange carts loaded to the rims with a thirty-inch Poulan chain saw, a battery-operated nail gun, a roll of wire, a five-gallon bucket of swimming pool chlorine, a hundred feet of nylon rope, a shovel, a pick, an air mattress, a hand pump, liquid soap, a battery charger, bungee cords, a small generator, a five-gallon gas can, a double-bladed ax, the biggest garden hoe they sold, and a large assortment of smaller items, from duct tape to nails to whetstones.

I was scared to death. But that was good. When I got scared, I got angry. And when I got angry, I could do scary things.

"Where do you keep your ankle grinders?" I said to a Home Depot man in the orange suspenders.

He was about sixty, rumpled, with thick glasses and a bulbous nose. He gave me a look. "You mean angle grinders?"

"Oh yeah. Angle. That's right." I guess that's what my mom likes to call a "Freudian slip."

The man looked at my nasty pajamas and stolen rubber Home Depot gum boots with raised eyebrows. Hey, you haven't been to high school lately, I wanted to say. After a night in a concrete pipe, I was pretty rumpled myself, which is one reason I thought of Home Depot in the first place. You can look like anything in there and nobody bats an eyelash.

The man took me to the proper shelf. The angle grinder was a small handheld tool with a diamond wheel like a miniature circular saw used for cutting anything from concrete to tile. I liked the heft of it in my hand.

"This thing is brutal," the old guy said. "You have to be really careful, or it can cut your hand off. Literally. Whatcha planning on building?"

"A belfry," I said, and hustled away before he could ask me anything else.

I had briefly thought about breaking into a gun store or a place that sold samurai swords, but those kinds of weapons would be more conspicuous to haul around. Plain old tools would be less likely to arouse suspicion.

I already had the sense that Wirtz was not only dangerous but cocky. One of those guys who was so confident in his physicality, he didn't figure he needed anything else. *Especially against a half-vampire girl.* Let him keep thinking that way.

Like I say, I didn't know weapons, but I knew tools. Papi and I had spent many an hour trolling through Home Depot over the summers, building everything from bird feeders to rabbit hutches. I had selected the hoe in his honor. The hoe was Papi's favorite tool.

"You don't have to bend so much to use it," he liked to say. "*Und* you can lean on it when you are tired." He would turn the hoe and show me how the sharp corner of the blade could make a razor-thin line in the soil. "You see? It can be *ein Skalpell*." Then he would turn it back flat and crush a row of weeds. "Or a road grader."

Or, in the right hands, it could split open a man's skull.

I strapped my load down with bungees, then rolled it to the back and parked in a quiet aisle that was aimed directly at the big contractor's entrance. I waited. At last when the clerk moved away, leaving the doors temporarily unguarded, I blasted off toward the wide automatic doors.

By the time the shoplifting alarm started whooping, I was already burning rubber halfway across the parking lot and gaining velocity.

I finally stopped running half a mile from the store and looked behind me. Not surprisingly, nobody was there. Who could have kept up with me? I pointed the cart toward the Space Center and bounced across a field. I felt rotten about taking the stuff and promised myself to someday come back and pay for it all, whether that was really true or not. But now I had one more errand.

I parked my load behind a Dairy Queen that was part Texaco gas station. Nothing else around but fields and a greenhouse nursery. My "purchases" would be safe. I went to the front with my five-gallon can and waited until I saw a guy leave the hose on while he went inside to pick out some junk food. I took the hose out of his tank and squeezed the can nearly full before he even got back to the counter.

I hid the gas in the back with the other stuff and went inside, hoping the clerk hadn't noticed me. She was busy with several customers. *Great.* I would never get a better chance. I peeked into the little office in the rear. *Empty.* Snuck in and uncradled the phone, dialing my home number. After the fourth ring, the answering machine at home picked up and I blurted out a message. It cut me off at thirty seconds, just as I was saying something to Manda. I swore and dialed the number again.

"Hello?"

Mom's voice startled me. I could hear everything at once—terror, sadness, frustration, hope, all in a single word.

"Emma!"

She must've just gotten in from work and snatched up the receiver as my message was running out.

"Darling! Darling, that *is* you, isn't it! Oh God, where are you? Are you okay? You must be hurt, oh God, darling! Oh please say something, anything . . . !"

"Mom," I started.

She screamed and I tried to talk, but her relief and joy were so loud and messy, I'm sure she couldn't understand a word I was saying.

"Mom, I'm okay! Please . . . don't worry! I'm fine, I just had to leave . . . really fast. It was so stupid, what I did, going through the window that way, but I didn't—I didn't know what to do. I had to go, Mom."

"Tell me. Are you in a hospital? Oh my God, Emma, what happened to you? Has somebody done this to you, made you this crazy? Tell me where you are! I'm coming right now. But please,

please, God, be okay, please, oh please . . . !" She was practically sobbing and screaming at the same time.

"Mom, Mom!" Now I was bawling too. I had to speak louder to even be heard. "I'm not in a hospital, I'm fine. I'm not hurt."

"But . . . how could you be okay? I saw you. You jumped through a window! I don't understand . . . ! Whatever . . . whatever it is, we can fix it, honey. I'm so sorry! I know I haven't been the best mother, I haven't."

"Come on, you've been fine! It's not you, it's me. It's all me! But I don't mean I did anything. I didn't do anything bad! I mean—the window, yeah, but—it . . . it wasn't my fault, I had to. I had no choice. I was afraid if I had stayed a second longer . . ."

I didn't know how to finish the sentence. I knew I wasn't making sense, was only making things worse. But I couldn't tell her the truth, I just couldn't. She begged me to explain and I had to deal with a fresh bout of shouting and weeping. Finally I just held the phone against my leg, afraid the clerk would hear us from the other room.

"Mom, would you listen. Please! Just listen . . . just . . . for a second, could you?"

"I called the police, Emma. You are making me crazy," she went on. "Oh please, dear God, please come home. Please just let me come pick you up."

She was practically shrieking now. I took my shades off and swiped my sleeve across my face. I had to get under control here. "Please . . . please, Mom. Calm down. I can't tell you where I am, Mom. I can't explain why I left. You will just have to accept that. There was nothing else I could do. You'll understand—"

"Drugs! It has to be drugs. I have told you time and again—"

"It's not drugs, Mom. You know me better than that! I would never put that crap in my body."

"Someone gave them to you! I know it. A boy. Someone . . . someone slipped them in your food, something you drank."

"Nothing like that, Mom. I'm okay, I swear."

"But where are you?" Her voice was choked; she was running out of steam at last. "What am I supposed to do, Emma? Knowing you are out there—somewhere dangerous . . . and I can't even help? Oh dear, sweet God . . ."

I saw the clerk moving around the counter out in the store.

"Look, I've got to go now, Mom. I've got to go. I'll be okay, I swear. You don't have to worry. I'll call again. Okay? Soon as I can. Tell Manda I love her—"

I had to hang up. The store clerk was coming through the door.

"Hey, you can't be back here," she said, sweeping her dark bangs out of her eyes. "You could get me in trouble. What are you . . ."

But I had already brushed past her and soon was roaring up the highway with my stolen Home Depot cart practically sparking the road. My face burned from crying.

It was an adventure getting all my stolen junk back to the base. I had to cross a couple of major thoroughfares, jouncing over the uneven pavement and drawing looks you wouldn't believe. The last trouble spot involved heaving everything over the NASA fence. But I managed it without breaking anything and stashed the orange cart near the bunker after unloading everything back at my tower.

I scaled my new home, lugging the tools up, and furiously threw myself into action. Anything to keep from thinking about Manda, Mom, all the stupid things I had done. *The trouble I'm in.*

I started by stringing what felt like miles of wire around the tower and catwalks, complete with noisy jangly things like metal outlet covers to provide some early warning. The generator I left up on top, and the tools I dispersed at important locations all over the structure, mostly hidden behind posts and beams where they would not be easily seen, but I could get at them in a hurry.

The rest of the day slipped by faster than I thought it would. I couldn't help but wonder what all my classmates were doing and if they even wondered why I wasn't there. Probably not. It felt ridiculously strange and guiltily shameful being outside on a school day. You do things a certain way year after year, it just doesn't feel right when everything changes.

The sun marched across my little enclosure, the tower's ginormous shadow gradually leaning this way and that, almost like a sundial. I wondered if I could figure out how to use it as a way to tell time.

After hours of hard work, I felt pretty satisfied with my preliminary defenses. I could tweak them some more tomorrow. At least I would sleep a little better tonight. I filled the generator with gas and cranked it. It was kinda noisy, but my ears were so sensitive, it was hard to tell what the noise sounded like to someone with normal hearing. I plugged in the battery charger and the battery pack.

I was feeling hot and sticky, so I climbed down with soap and headed inside the bunker to clean off.

The concrete floor of the bunker was submerged two inches deep in cool running water. *The faucet.*

I had left it going all this time! I splashed inside and followed the gurgling rush of water to the spigot. All of the brown was gone; I collected a mouthful in my palm, sniffed it, then finally tasted it. It was slightly metallic, but other than that it was okay. I drank my fill, then cut the tap off, praying there wasn't a sensor going off somewhere that would bring a NASA repair crew.

I made sure nobody was around, then stripped and hung my clothes over the windowsill. Turned the water back on and bathed.

So cold! But so good too. While I drip-dried, I shook my hair out, using my fingers for a brush. It felt so wonderful to be clean again, I hated the thought of putting my filthy pajamas back on.

Laundry, Emma.

I swallowed a lump in my throat, hearing my mom's voice in my head. I retrieved my pj's, gave them a squirt of soap, and started rubbing fistfuls of material together under the cold water. It was harder than I would have ever imagined. After ten minutes of this caveman stuff, I told myself I would never again complain the next time she asked me to throw something in the washer. . . .

The next time.

What was wrong with me? I never used to cry at all, and now I always seemed to be teetering right on the verge. To distract myself, I watched out the little bunker window. A hawk was circling a distant field and the sun was still a ways above the horizon. As soon as I finished, I would go foraging again—

Something fell out of the pocket of my pajama bottoms. It was floating on the standing water next to my bare feet. I reached to scoop it up. *What in the world?* Macaroni noodles painted gold and sprinkled with glitter, glued together to form a small oval . . . and in the center of the oval, a picture . . .

Manda.

She was grinning at the camera, golden curls on either side of her head. One of her front teeth was missing. I turned the macaroni frame over; on the back was a little heart drawn in now-blurry red marker.

She must've slipped it into my pocket that last time we were reading the Sneetches. . . .

I dropped to my knees and stared at the picture as if I could somehow pull my sister through it. Absorbing every line and feature and the points of light in the corners of her eyes.

Now I couldn't keep from blubbering. It was as if this frail little thing in my hand, charged with all my sister's trust and love, was standing alone against the horror of Wirtz. My logical mind knew that if the vampire had found us in that apartment, my family would now be dead. But I couldn't help feeling I had abandoned them when they needed me most. *I will tear her head from her shoulders. . . .*

I put a wet knuckle to my mouth and bit down. Hard.

Get it together, I thought. *You just need something to eat.*

When I arrived back at the Solar Observatory, it was starting to get dark and there weren't many lights on in the building. *Perfect.* Nobody around to bother me. Except now I wouldn't be able to get in by piggybacking behind some employee with a badge.

The roof turned out to be the easiest access. I found a metal door that came loose when I put my strength into it, and from there I climbed down a ladder to a closet that locked from the inside.

The building was harder to navigate than I expected—lots of long hallways with side junctions. I saw acres of cubicles. Most of the offices were completely dark, but one cube was strung with chili pepper lights that gave the whole room an eerie red glow.

By the time I found the cafeteria, I was ready to eat toilet paper. But the serving lines and warming pans were empty and stainless steel shiny. I hurried back into the kitchen . . . everything spotless in there too. Not one crumb of food. There were bags of potato chips and cookies behind a plastic shield, but I was looking for something a little more substantial. *Like a bucket of chicken.*

I noticed my appetite had been increasing lately. Did half-human non-bloodsucking vampires have to eat every two hours or something? Maybe I was not only the first vampire with epilepsy, but the first with hypoglycemia as well. I laughed out loud at the thought. It felt good to laugh for the first time since . . . *Since the last time I tickled Manda. Stop it.*

I told my stomach to be quiet and rifled through the steel cabinets and overhead bins. There was a walk-in freezer, but it had been turned off and was stacked high with boxes of napkins, paper cups, and plastic utensils. What kind of cafeteria was this?

I went back out front, ready to rip into the plastic bin full of chips. I raised my hand to smash the plastic shield. . . .

"Hey."

The voice was not loud, but it made me turn around so hard, I cracked my head on a metal shelf. I cursed and grabbed at my forehead to see if it was bleeding.

"Oh, man, I'm sorry."

A young guy was standing there. Tall and thin with straight blond hair that was parted at the side and came just over his ears. He looked a few years older than me.

"My bad," he said. "Are you okay?"

"No," I said.

My second night on the run and I'd already managed to get caught. What was he doing here after everything was shut down, anyhow?

I slowly straightened up and looked at my hand. No blood. Looked back at the guy. His mouth was wide, nose a little long, eyes large and icily blue. The kind of blue where it seemed like there might not be anybody inside. But so striking. He was wearing khaki shorts, leather slip-ons, no socks, and a T-shirt that said HUBBLE TROUBLE.

"They bring the food in," the guy said, coming closer. "Every day. In this big truck with warming pans. Some contractor. It must be a cost-saving deal. My dad says in the old days they had full cafeteria staffs. Now they just bring it in, sell it for a couple of hours, shoot the leftovers back on the truck, and zoom, they're gone."

"Oh." I put a hand to my head again.

"Let me look at that," the guy said.

"What?"

"Your head. You banged it pretty good."

"Oh. It's okay. No blood, no foul."

He frowned in a surprised way. "You sure? You want to sit down? Most girls would be wailing after a lick like that."

"Most girls?"

He put his hands up in the air. His fingers were long and thin. "Okay, okay. People. You with the crew?"

"What crew?"

"You know. Custodial. Cleanup. You sure you're all right?" He came even closer, staring at me intently.

"No, I'm not with the crew. . . ." I didn't know what to say I was. I felt completely embarrassed standing there in my damp pj's and gum boots. At least I was clean.

"What's with the Ray-Bans?" the guy said.

"Huh?"

"Sunglasses."

"Oh. I have . . . an allergy to sunlight."

He smiled. "After dark?"

I took my shades off. I had forgotten I was wearing them. Now he was so close I could smell the remnants of shaving cream on his cheeks. He had a dark mole along his jawline that was unbearably cute.

"Oh. I have a cousin with that," he said. "Breaks out in the worst rashes ever. Sun poisoning . . ."

"It's not like that," I said, feeling slightly dizzy. "Maybe I will sit down." I pulled out one of the plastic chairs and plopped into it. "It's just my eyes. They're really sensitive. I forget when I have my sunglasses on."

"Oh." He sat down beside me. His eyes were amazing. I felt like I was staring, so I dropped my gaze to his arms. The hair on his arms was golden.

"You Swedish or something?" I said.

"Norwegian. Most of my relatives are from Minnesota. Lutefisk every holiday and smother everything else in cheese. I'm Sagan. Sagan Bishop." He held out his hand and I shook it. His fingers were cool.

"Sagan?"

"My parents came up with that. One is an astrophysicist, the other a solar astronomer. They work out here."

"Okay?"

"Carl Sagan? The astronomer?"

"Never heard of him."

"One of the co-founders of the Planetary Society? Heavily involved with SETI?"

"SETI?"

"Search for Extra-Terrestrial Intelligence. They use the big radio telescope down in Puerto Rico. Haven't you seen *Contact,* with Jodie Foster? Any of this getting through?"

He moved his eyebrows in a way that made me think he would like to rap me on top of my head with his knuckles. In a sweet sort of way.

"Oh. One of those guys," I said. As if I knew what he was talking about.

"No, not one of those guys. *The* guy. Carl Sagan was brilliant.

He helped design the plaques they sent into space on the Pioneer and Voyager probes for aliens to find. Always went around saying, 'Billions and billions.'"

"So he was rich?"

Sagan Bishop laughed. I liked the sound of it and started to feel a little less self-conscious. "He was talking about how there are so many stars out there," Sagan said. "His theory was that it's a mathematical certainty there are other inhabited planets with intelligent life-forms."

I smiled. "Gotcha. So, didja ever meet him?"

"Who?"

"Your hero, Cal."

"Carl. Nope, he died in 1996."

"Well, good God, that was ages ago. How was I supposed to know—"

"Struck on the skull by a meteorite."

"Really?"

Sagan leaned in closer, grinning. "You're pretty gullible, aren't you?"

I liked how quickly he was able to tilt things back in his favor. But I wasn't letting him get away with it.

"Nope, just honest. When I feel like talking at all. Mom calls it blunt."

"Ah! So you have a family."

"Who you will never, ever know anything about."

Sagan mimed being struck in the chest by an arrow and slumped over on the table. "You're blunt, all right. Anyhow, that's where my name comes from." His face was still down on the table. "And you're . . . ?"

"Hungry."

He sat back up. "I noticed. When I came in, you were about to fracture your arm on that case over there, weren't you? No, seriously, who are you? Could you at least tell me your name?"

"No."

"Then I'll have to report you." He pointed at my chest and I thought for a second he was looking at my boobs. Guys were always doing that.

I leaned back in my chair, looking into his eyes again. Ready to run. Part of me would enjoy knocking him down on the way out. Although I had to admit . . . compared to what I had been through the last couple of days, this was a blast.

"What are you doing out here so late?" I said.

Sagan grinned. His bottom teeth were a little bit crooked. "Hey, I'm the one who should be asking the questions." He pointed at my chest again.

"What? Is something hanging out?"

"No badge," he said. "A big no-no out here. They give us security briefings about it all the time. I'm supposed to 'challenge' you, then wrestle you to the floor and wait for security to come."

"Good luck," I said.

"What?"

"Nothing."

"So how'd you get in the building, anyhow?" Sagan said. "How'd you get on the base?"

"'Bishop' doesn't sound very Norwegian."

"It's not," he agreed. "Does anybody ever tell you you are great at avoiding questions?"

"Does anybody ever tell you you're nosy?"

"You got me. Okay, so you don't want to tell me your name or how you got out here. I can live with that. I like mysteries. That's the reason I do what I do."

"What?" I said.

"I'm going to be an astronomer. You know, mysteries of the universe and all that?"

"Not for the billions and billions?"

Sagan reached over and tugged the hem of my pajama top. "Those are pj's you're wearing, aren't they?"

"Sleepwear. That's what they call it these days. The latest thing in high school fashion. Are you an albino?"

"Only on my father's side." Sagan looked down. "And you're wearing . . . rubber boots. And . . . is that gasoline I smell?"

I couldn't help it, I giggled a little. I never giggle. "Do you really work here?" I said.

"I'm a NASA co-op," Sagan said. "I go to classes at UA–Huntsville by day, then work here after hours. Right now it's volunteer stuff. But starting in June, I'm going to be a summer intern." He rubbed his hands together. "The big bucks!"

"How old do you have to be to do that?"

"Nineteen."

"So how old are you?"

"Thirty-seven."

I laughed. "Divided by two?"

Could this really be happening? I had spent the day preparing to fight a vampire to the death. Now I was joking around with some strange guy as if knowing him was even possible. But it felt so good to think about something else.

"So you still live at home?" I said.

"Sure. All of us do."

"All who?"

"I've got three sisters."

"Wow. Big family. And where are you?"

"I'm the oldest."

"So come on, how old are you?"

"Nineteen."

Please don't ask, I thought.

"What about you?" Sagan said.

"I'm . . . um . . . I'm eighteen."

"I thought you were always honest?"

"Okay. Seventeen. But that's my final offer." *And if you call me a kid, I just might break your face.*

I got up from the table and walked back over to the chip case.

"Stand back," I said.

Sagan got up too. "Hey, hold on. You don't have to get violent. We'll figure out something."

I dropped my arm. "No joke, I'm starving. You got anything on you?"

"Food? Maybe a candy bar back in my desk."

"Maybe?"

"Okay, so I was saving it for later. I have to eat chocolate every 11.3 hours to survive. I'll split it with you. Just tell me your name."

"You'll give it all to me or I'll beat you to death with a stapler."

"I sense issues with anger," Sagan said, grinning. "I'm kind of gifted that way. Glimpsing the inner person."

I started to grin too. "Let's go."

9. SECRETS

"So you're basically homeless," Sagan said.

"I didn't say that," I mumbled.

My mouth was full of Snickers. God, it was so good. He was lucky he kept his arm when he offered it to me. We were sitting at a tiny wicker table in Sagan's cubicle, the kind of wicker they use for outdoor furniture. The cube was micro-sized, just big enough for the table, a desk, and two chairs. We were surrounded by the walls of other cubes. If I stood on my tiptoes, I could see them going on and on into the distance. Most seemed to be empty. And not just because it was after hours, either.

"Devoid of human habitation," Sagan said. "They used to use this building for something else, before they built the Solar Observatory. All these long buildings out here are pretty old, most dating back to before the moon landing."

"Don't you ever get creeped out at night?" I said.

"I'm not the type."

"Me neither." Well, I wasn't until yesterday, but I wasn't going to tell him that.

"Well, actually I might be the type, but . . . I'm too focused, I guess?" Sagan said. He leaned back in his government-issue chair and kicked his feet up on the table. It started to fall over, so he took them off. His legs were long. "When I'm thinking about something I'm interested in, everything else just goes away," he said.

Kind of like a seizure, I wanted to say, but didn't. I studied

Sagan's desk—none of the usual stuff you would expect to see. No pictures, nothing personal, not even a calendar. Maybe he just hadn't been there long enough? I stuffed the last of the Snickers in my mouth. I was still ravenous.

"Do you ever get tempted, you know . . ."

"What?" he said.

"To look around?"

"At other people's stuff? Sure. All the time. Well, not all the time. Most of the time what I'm working on is so interesting, I don't think about anything else."

"Ever found anything weird?" I said.

Sagan looked disappointed. I could tell he was itching to explain all about the work he did, but astronomy just wasn't my thing.

"Weird like how?" he said. "Mostly I'm just grazing for food. I look for places where somebody put out a bowl of something. I don't go through their drawers and stuff. I wouldn't do that."

I smirked. "Sure you wouldn't. I really believe you. I would."

He looked at me. "I bet you would."

I couldn't get over the washed-out blue of his eyes. Nice complement to the blue he gave off in the dark, I bet. "I've always been the curious type," I said.

"What about privacy? Somebody's personal space?"

"I never respect that."

Sagan laughed. No doubt about it, I really liked his laugh. "Actually, I bet nobody does," he said.

"Yeah. I bet when someone is alone, they do whatever they want, just as long as nobody finds out."

He swung his head left and right, as if he could see through the cube walls. "Some of these people—I wouldn't want to know. If you're so curious, how come you haven't asked me what I do out here?"

"Astronomy is boring."

"What!"

"Deadly."

"Have you ever looked through a telescope?"

This time I put my feet up. The table didn't move. I had taken the gum boots off to give my toes a rest. In spite of all my scrubbing, they were green. *That's what running through miles of grass barefoot will do to you.* I wiggled them.

"A couple of times," I said. "Back in the eighth grade we went up to the Von Braun Astronomical Society on Monte Sano."

"Hey, I'm a member!"

"You would be."

"So? Whatcha think?"

I glanced at him. I could tell by his face he really cared about my answer. "The telescope was pretty impressive, if size is a big deal with you. I was all ready for blazing fireballs, dust storms on Mars. Rainbow stripes on Jupiter—"

"Hubble stuff," Sagan said, nodding. "That's what everybody expects their first time—"

"I guess so. But everything was so small. Just tiny little white dots. Even Jupiter. I could barely see the red spot, and it wasn't red. And the stars weren't even dots, just pinpoints of light. . . ."

"Stars can't be resolved down to disks. . . . They're too far away—"

"There was this funny old guy there. . . ."

"Dr. Hermann."

"Yeah. He had hair growing out of his ears and showed us a binary star and practically had a stroke, he was so excited. And it was just two tiny pinpricks of light."

"What about galaxies?"

"They showed us one. . . ."

"I bet it was M31. Andromeda. That's the one he always—"

"Who cares." I made my voice deep, imitating Sagan imitating his hero. "Billions and billions of stars. And nothing but a smudge. See? Boring. Okay, put me out of my misery. What do you do here?"

"I hunt for comets," he said, the disappointment unmistakable. "The observatory is booked solid doing solar stuff during the day. Comet hunting they save for late at night for the cheap help."

I took my feet off the table and let myself slump over, making snoring sounds.

"No, it's really cool if you find one," Sagan said, perking up again. "They name it after you. Well, unless some guy in Japan has snagged it already. So every time it comes around again . . ."

"People all over the world pass out from sheer excitement."

Sagan grinned.

"You have a really big mouth," I said before I could think to stop myself. *Good God, Emma.*

"I get that from my grandfather, I guess," Sagan said, smile fading a little. "Everybody says I look like him. Works for me."

"Hey, I'm sorry. I like it. Your mouth, I mean. A lot of the time I just blurt out the first thing that jumps into my head."

"Yeah, well, it still jumped in there, didn't it?"

We didn't say anything for a while.

"So . . . what do your parents do out here?" I said finally to break the silence.

"My mom works here doing solar stuff," Sagan said. "My dad is in another building dreaming up deep sky projects."

"Why don't they work together?"

"They figure it works better this way. You know, so they aren't on top of each other 24/7."

"Oops," I said.

"That didn't come out right, did it?" he said, blushing like mad.

"You ever find one?" I said.

"What?"

"A comet."

"Not yet."

"And you've been out here how long?" There I went again. *Shut up.*

Sagan's eyes widened. I actually think he was excited. "Believe it or not, some guys do this stuff for years before ever finding a single one," he said.

I thought about saying something positive, like, "You'll get yours soon, I bet." But I kept my mouth shut. No sense going against type this late in the game. Besides, what was I doing? It's not like I was crushing on this guy or anything. Okay, I liked him. But I had business to get to. A vampire was looking for me.

"So. Food," I said.

Sagan picked up the Snickers wrapper from where I had thrown it on the wicker table. "What, that didn't do it?"

I just looked at him.

"Okay. Let's say I order a pizza," he said. My insides practically convulsed in delight at the thought. "What do I get in return?"

"Nothing," I said.

But I tried to make my eyes bigger, give him the kind of face Gretchen Roberts was so good at. I'm pretty sure I looked more like a wolf.

"Deal," Sagan said.

We had pepperoni, of course. Sagan got us drinks from a machine and we moved back into the cafeteria. I ate all of a large except two slices and didn't feel quite so anxious. Maybe there was something to that hypoglycemic vampire notion. Afterward I felt a little more generous.

"I have a home," I said, gnawing on a piece of crust.

Sagan blotted pizza sauce with a napkin at the corner of his mouth. "And it's . . . where?"

"Not here."

"Are you going back there tonight?"

"No. I can't."

"Why not?"

I glared at him to let him know that one was off-limits. "Okay," he said, holding up his hands for mercy. "Your family. Do they know where you are?"

"No. I called my mom to let her know I'm all right. She was pretty crazy."

"Are you? All right, I mean?"

"Don't I look all right?"

Sagan studied me a long time until I started to feel uncomfortable. *Those eyes.*

"Well, you don't look homeless," he said. "Except for your clothes."

"Profiler."

"And you're not emaciated."

"Watch it."

"And you're clean." He glanced at my boots, no doubt remembering my green toes. "Well, mostly."

"I told you. I'm not technically homeless," I said. "I'm just temporarily . . . hiding out."

"And you won't tell me what you're hiding from? Okay, let me guess. Violence at home. A weird father. The cops?"

I shook my head in a way that didn't say no. It said, "None of your business."

"I'd still like to know how you got on the base," Sagan said. "It's not the most secure place in the world, but no way could you get through any of the gates. Not without a badge and a vehicle. So you had to climb the fence somewhere. Or you walked in through the alligator swamp. But you're not all—"

"Alligators?" I said.

"Hundreds of them. Big as Escalades. You ever see *Primeval*?"

"Bull . . . ," I swore.

"Okay, not so big. Probably just pets somebody threw out their car doors or flushed down the toilet. But they found a guy's head out here a few years ago. I'm not lying. Just a head."

"Yeah, yeah."

"They didn't know if the gators got him before or after."

"Before or after what?"

"The drug deal. But like I was saying, maybe you came in by the river—that's a possibility. But I think they have fences down there too. I haven't been in a while."

"You act like you know this place."

"You'd be amazed," Sagan said. "I practically grew up here. My parents have taken me all over. I've seen stuff most people never get to see. It was much easier back before 9/11."

"Nine-eleven?"

"Yeah. You could just zip through the gate barely waving at the guard. No barriers or anything. When I was a little kid, they brought me out here just about every Sunday to watch kid flicks in the auditorium at Building 4200."

"I didn't know the buildings were numbered."

"4200 is the most famous. That's where they planned the moon landings. . . ."

I made the nodding-off sound again.

"Okay, okay. No more space stuff."

"Thank you."

"At least for tonight."

I didn't say anything, and he kept waiting for me to. "Is that . . . okay?" Sagan said, touching my arm. "I mean, that I want to see you again?"

"Well, I don't know. My schedule is pretty jammed."

He started laughing.

"No, it's true. I'm really, really busy," I said.

I suddenly remembered the little generator chugging merrily away on top of the tower. How long had I been gone? Night had closed in, and I hadn't even blown up my bed. The vampire would be up and about now.

"Doing, um, what?" Sagan said.

I stood up. "Huh?" I couldn't remember what we had been talking about. The huge empty cafeteria suddenly felt too close.

"I need to go," I said.

Sagan stood up too. "Okay, no joke. Let me shut up the observatory for the night and I'll give you a ride home. That way you don't have to . . . um, walk."

"Sagan. I am home."

"Here?"

"Well, no. Of course not. Not here. I mean—it's here. On the base."

"The Space Center?"

"Yeah."

"No, really."

"Really."

He ran his fingers through his hair. I would have liked watching it fall back into place, but . . .

"I thought you were joking," Sagan said. "That this whole time you were just having some fun."

"I told you, I'm honest to the bone," I said. *At least I used to be.* "And I have been having fun. The most fun I've had in a while." *A good long while.* "But I need to be ready. . . . I mean, I need to get some stuff set up so I can get to bed."

"But you can't . . . It's impossible. Where will you sleep? This place is huge, but it's just not fixed up for camping out—come on, are you being serious?"

"Deadly."

Sagan stared. "But it's dangerous! There are so many ways to get killed out here. Industrial chemicals. Buried army stuff. Scary machinery. All kinds of electrical hazards. Radiation, lasers. Take your pick."

"I'll be careful."

"You know, all it would take would be a phone call. They would come get you. Escort you off the base. That's what I should do . . . to keep you safe."

I almost said, "I'd like to see them try." For once I caught myself. Instead I did something that wasn't easy for me because I didn't like giving people the wrong idea. I took his hand and said, "But you won't, will you?"

"How do you know I won't?"

"I just do." *Because if you do, you'll never see me again,* I wanted to say.

"How will I know you're okay?" Sagan said.

"You don't know me. Why would you care?"

He sighed. "You're right. I don't know you. I don't even know your name. Do you have any food? Real clothes?"

"I'll manage."

"Like you managed tonight?"

I felt my face flush. "Hey, when do most people get out here? What's the regular schedule?"

"My parents get here at seven. But they're the exception. Most people, it's probably around eight or eight-thirty. The base is mostly empty after five-thirty."

"Good."

"Why, so you can do more breaking and entering?" Sagan was smiling, but it was a serious smile with concerned eyes. "The next person who catches you might not be so cool with things. Most of these people are engineers. Not even green toes will save you."

"I'll take my chances," I said.

Now he looked anxious. "Look, really, let me go close down. Then I can at least take you somewhere so you won't have to walk."

"You're not getting me in a car."

I left the room and started walking up the hall with Sagan following.

"Okay, so let me just walk with you," he said. "But I have some applications running that I need to shut down. Come on, I can show you things."

We stopped close to the air lock that led outside. "No thanks, I'll just wait for you here."

"You will? Great! It'll just take me a few minutes. . . . Some routines I left running . . ."

I leaned against one of the columns and patted my mouth, showing how sleepy I was. All of a sudden I did feel sleepy. I yawned.

"Okay. Be right back." Sagan started to go, then stopped again. "Look, sometimes guards come around the buildings late at night, checking the exits and stuff. If you see headlights coming up the drive . . ."

"I'll duck into the bathroom." I genuinely needed to.

"Great." He pointed. "The closest one is about halfway down that hall on the left."

He headed outside and kept looking back over his shoulder all the way up the sidewalk to the observatory. As if he was afraid I was going to run out on him.

He was right.

Even with the thought of Wirtz being awake somewhere out there, I walked back. I just didn't feel like running. Something was bothering me, and the vibe only got worse once I climbed up to my hideaway in the rocket tower. The feeling of decay matched my mood. The sense that the room had gone feral and my asking it to be a room again was somehow wrong.

I did my best to make things more comfortable. I didn't really need a light, but I lit a small battery-powered lantern just for the gleam. I took a can of Lysol and sprayed it all over, then shoved my remaining Home Depot loot into a corner. I spread out a tarp that covered most of the floor—the thickest Home Depot sold. The electric air pump didn't work so well—it seemed to be missing a part—so I blew up the air mattress the good old-fashioned way. Something that would have once taken me hours, if I could've done it at all, now was over in minutes. Turns out vampires have extra-powerful lungs as well.

I lay down and pulled the excess tarp over me. *Crap, no pillow.* I would have to fix that tomorrow. It's funny all the little things you miss.

Speaking of—I still needed to go to the bathroom.

In the end I decided I couldn't stand sleeping in the little room at the top of the tower. Aside from the creepy factor, I didn't like feeling cornered. If Wirtz showed up unexpectedly, he could trap me in there.

I moved the air mattress to the roof and laid my head on my

arm. It was breezier and much more comfortable. I had the ax next to me, my hand on the handle.

What if I fell off? There were no guardrails and it was a long ways down. A really long ways. Maybe vampires bounced? *Go to sleep, Emma.*

The dark does weird things to you, even when you can see in it. I lay on my back looking up at the stars trying to think about anything but Manda. A knot of guilt lodged itself in my stomach—I wondered if she was missing me right now? I thought of her lying in her little bed, the Sneetches book beside her, worrying about the pale green pants.

I squeezed the handle of the ax and forced myself to think about Sagan Bishop instead. *Cool name.* Now I wished I had told him mine. I wondered if I would ever see him again. I guess that was really up to me. Who knows, he might be calling security right now to run me off the base. Still . . . he didn't seem like someone who would do that. Then I couldn't stop thinking about him. His image ran round and round in my mind. I kept coming back to the same place: wondering what it would be like to kiss that mole on his jaw.

I exploded awake sometime in the middle of the night—one of the trip wires was jangling.

I was instantly up on my knees on the air mattress, heart slamming the inside of my chest, both hands gripping the ax. I looked around crazily. A half-moon was riding on a raft of clouds, moonlight filtering through the trees below. Wind lifted my hair. I was someplace very high. *Outdoors.*

The strange noise shattered the quiet again and I remembered. Wirtz, the tower, my alarm system. It sounded as if someone was caught in the wire and trying to get untangled.

I threw myself across the top of the tower on my stomach,

landing on toes and fingertips as silently as I could. Peeked over the edge.

Nothing there. The sound came again, and I realized the intruder was on the north face. I slipped over the edge of the east face and dropped to a catwalk. I shifted the ax to my right hand and padded barefoot toward the corner of the tower where the east face met the north. The catwalk ran out about two feet shy of the corner. I stepped to the end and put my belly against the railing, leaning over as far as I could. Just as I was about to poke my head around the corner, the jangly noise stopped.

I drew my head back and flattened myself against the side of the tower, my cheek pressing the cold, rusty iron.

I gulped. This was it. *It's really happening.* All my nerve endings came alive, giving me the sensation of fingers being dragged over every square inch of my body. *I could die,* I thought. *I could die right now.*

I fought to keep my brain from locking up. Looked stupidly at the ax. Should I climb back up and crank the chain saw?

No time. The vampire hit the trip wire again. I glanced at the shiny forest below and wanted to jump. Anything would be better than this. But I had to do it, had to take a look.

I lay against the railing a second time and let my body hang out into space. Stretching my neck, putting my head closer and closer to the corner. Exposing my throat to whatever was on the other side.

Please . . .

All of the air rushed out of my lungs. I could see it now: a long piece of old black pipe was hanging down the north face of the tower. The wind was causing it to sway back and forth, banging against the wire.

I slumped against the catwalk, swearing. Slid down until I was sitting on the cool steel mesh. Finally I got to my feet again and slowly climbed back to the top. I went to the north side of the tower and used the ax to chop the old pipe loose, watching it fall over the side. I lay down on the mattress again and pulled the tarp over myself. As if I could actually sleep.

But I did. I woke up several more times during the night, but not because of the trip wires. I don't know what woke me until the last time, when I was awakened by a dream. I could see the vampire, Wirtz. He had his long arm outstretched toward me. He was holding my sister's head.

115

10. FIGHTING

Crap. It was raining!

I blinked and jumped up and hauled my things back inside the little room one floor below. The room smelled even mustier in the rain, as if the humidity and the rot were mating.

I put my sunglasses on and poked my head out—*overcast, duh*—trying to gauge what time it was. It didn't feel like I had been asleep long. The slanting gray light over the hills to the east told me it must be barely sunup.

Now that I was completely awake, no way could I go back to sleep. Not in here. Besides, I didn't really want to—that was enough scares for one night.

I wrung out my pajamas as best I could, shivering. This was getting ridiculous. I had to find something better to wear.

The rain kept falling. Perfect. But then I realized that the dim light would make it harder to see me and fewer people would be out in the weather at this time of day. Time for another "shopping" expedition.

Fifteen minutes later I was standing behind Madison Square Mall, the closest one I could find. There was one car in the parking lot, a clunker so far away, it might as well have been in the next county.

I was looking for a particular kind of store. I walked along outside the building, checking the names stenciled on the gray back

doors. The Gap? *No.* Dillard's? *Nah.* Parisian? *Double nah.* Aéro-
postale? *Nope.*

United Outfitters sounded promising, but after I ripped open
the door and battled my way through cardboard boxes, empty
racks full of clattering hangers, etc., it turned out to be more froofy
than the name suggested. I didn't hear an alarm, but that didn't
mean that one wasn't going off down at the police station.

I found a stack of fluffy towels and—*thank God*—an overstuffed
throw pillow. I mopped my dripping hair and jammed everything
into a bag. On the way out I also snagged a fancy toiletry kit with
hand soap and shampoo.

I went back outside and raced on to the next store. American
Barn. Suncoast Video. Spencer Gifts. Pac Sun. I didn't strike pay
dirt until I came to a place called North Creek.

This time an alarm definitely sounded, nearly rupturing my
eardrums as I moved through the back of the store. Try finding your
size with that racket in your ears. No time to try anything on, either.
I would just have to do the best I could.

It felt weird loading up on clothes—Mom had never had the
money to be able to take us shopping very often. At the most, it was
one top or pair of shorts at a time. But now, thanks to my flourish-
ing criminal enterprise, I was going to be better dressed than I had
ever been in my life.

The clothes were a little too prep for my taste—*eat dirt,
Gretchen*—but I had no right to complain. Nike gym shorts. A silver North Face rain jacket. A couple of Izod pullovers. Puma
straight-fit jeans. And for my feet, Adidas socks and a pair of Zugo
trail shoes with Velcro flaps.

I threw aside the rubber gum boots and stuffed my bare

feet into the Zugos. Crammed everything else in bags and headed out.

The back door was still hanging open, with feeble morning light peeking in. I heard the police car before I saw it. Unlucky for them, their radio squawked just as I was about to jump down to the loading dock.

"Hey, you! Stop where you are!"

I thought those guys were all supposed to yell "Freeze!" My heart sure did. This wasn't Mom's rusty old ride I would be up against if I took off running. Was a vampire bulletproof? I jumped back inside the shop, pulling the door shut. I heard a couple of car doors slam. Then I was off, flying to the front of the store so fast, some of the hanger ensembles were temporarily horizontal. Sweating and cursing, I got both hands on the cold steel fence between me and the rest of the mall and forced the mechanism up two feet. Kicked my bags under, crawled through, and let it shut behind me.

I could see the two cops now, a male and a female, entering the back of the store, pistols drawn. Which freaked me out more than a little. But they were being way too cautious, ducking behind boxes, dodging around pillars and clothing racks. I was fifty yards away and gathering speed before they even reached the front of the shop.

All I had to do now was find another way out. A mall is a weird place when it's empty. Every sound was so magnified. I could hear the cops' footsteps and the hissing of voices on their walkie-talkies as if they were right on my tail. But I got so far ahead, I felt safe enough to stop and steal food from a vendor. I crammed one of the bags with soft pretzels, cookies, and cheesecake. *Oh my God.* At this rate I was going to be the world's first obese vampire. I turned back to look, but the cops had only made it as far as the central fountain. I was surprised to see there were at least five of them now. They slowly fanned out, checking stores in both directions.

I heard other footsteps as well, farther back. Probably mall security guys. For the first time, I started to feel a little nervous. I knew I could blaze right past one or two, but seven? Nine? I hopped the food vendor counter and raced down a side alley.

That turned out to be a dead end. I rushed back to the main artery again and went left, hearing the cops getting closer all the time. From the chatter on their walkie-talkies, I knew they were systematically closing off every avenue of escape and pushing their way in my direction.

At last I came to the end of the line: JCPenney. I tried jerking the double doors open, but the cool metal handles came off in my hands. I threw them down and turned to look for a planter to throw through the glass if I had to. That's when I saw about eight or ten cops moving methodically in my direction, calling back and forth to each other. They had me trapped and they knew it.

No guns—I guess they didn't want to shoot at a perp inside an empty mall—might accidentally damage a storefront, huh? Instead they were each brandishing what I figured had to be Tasers. I had never seen one up close, but they looked like little plastic ray guns with yellow stickers on the side and rectangular barrels.

"Halt!" one of the male cops yelled. Now that was more like it. "We've got all the exits covered! Put the bags down and put your hands above your head."

Oh boy, I sure would like to. My loot was slowing me down. Not the weight, just the general awkwardness. I briefly considered dropping the bags and bull-rushing the cops, figuring they would barely see me as I passed by at supersonic speed. But I didn't want to chance it.

"Stop!" the same cop said, speaking more angrily now. "I said, put. The. Bags. Down."

No, I thought. I had already gone to too much trouble to get this stuff, and I wasn't giving it up now. The lead cops were less than a hundred feet away now, moving faster, sensing they had their prey cornered. I had to admit, I was feeling a little frantic, my back to the JCPenney store. It looked as if I was going to have to test my permeability against that glass. . . .

Wait.

I looked up—there was a giant oval of empty space cut into the ceiling about twenty feet over my head. It was surrounded by a railing, adding another four or five feet. So maybe twenty-five feet in all if I wanted to make a clean getaway to the second floor. I took a deep breath—I had never tried a leap like this before, not without a long running start. Bounding through forests and the boughs of trees was one thing. . . . If I missed . . . I didn't want to think about the consequences. Would they Tase an unarmed vampire who was crumpled on the tiled floor?

Go.

I gathered my shopping bags in either hand, then took off running straight at the cops, bellowing like a crazy midfielder about to waffle-stomp a keeper. I saw the cops all raise their Tasers in slo-mo—*this had better work*—and took a long step up to the rim of a low planter wall, pushed off mightily just as they fired, and there I went, soaring right over the ficus.

I heard at least five separate pops as the Tasers went off, saw four of the little square metal thingies jerk out their length of wire and clatter harmlessly to the floor, while the fifth embedded itself in the toe of my left shoe.

I was still gaining altitude when I felt the electric charge leap through my leg—it wasn't really so bad, not as bad as the time I stuck a fork in an outlet when I was Manda's age. But I could still feel it, that horrible, pulsing sensation of voltage roaming through my insides. *Humane* is not the word that comes to mind.

The Taser that had shot me was yanked out of the guy's hands as I sailed higher and higher, body quaking with the stun force. I could already tell I wasn't going to make it over. My stomach slammed into the second-floor railing with a tremendous *oomph*, knocking all the air out of me. My shopping bags tore loose from my hands and hurtled over, riding the inertia of my leap. As I doubled up with the force of the blow, I could see the bags skittering and tumbling ahead of me, clothes and goodies flying everywhere.

The cops were shouting below, mostly swearing in pure astonishment. I was doing a little cursing of my own as I hoisted myself over the bent railing and flopped onto the floor. I broke out in a cold sweat and could still feel the paralyzing effects of the Taser, but I was quickly coming around. I didn't have much choice if I wanted to retrieve my stuff and get out of there in one piece.

I rolled over onto my hands and knees, stomach lurching. I yanked the Taser wire loose and threw it away, scrambling forward like a crab, and started furiously collecting my things. I say *furiously* because there was beautiful New York cheesecake splattered across the tiles.

I managed to salvage most of my stuff, moving sluggishly, then staggered away on unsteady legs. At least I wasn't lying on the floor wiggling in a spasmodic electricity dance.

In seconds I was really motoring again, though I still didn't have much of an escape plan. If the place had been jammed with people, I could've possibly blended in—sure I would, wearing shades, pajamas, and trail shoes—but the mall wouldn't be officially open for at least a couple of hours.

A second group of cops and security types were already

scouring this floor as well; I could hear their walkie-talkies and the clicking of their shoes running toward me. Jeez, how many guys did they need for one seventeen-year-old girl? I felt cornered and let out a snarl.

Listen to yourself, Emma, I thought. *You're the bad guy, not them.* They were just doing their jobs.

I didn't want to hurt these guys, but I just might if they Tased me again. I looked around desperately for an exit, someplace to hide. Then I saw it: an enormous domed skylight above my head. The kind with the candy-colored glass. *There.*

I shoved my sunglasses into my pocket, looped the bags over my arms, and sprinted for it. Just when I was beneath the skylight, I coiled my legs and sprang, closing my eyes and hunching my back against the impact. I blasted through the glass—the frame was made of tougher stuff than I had expected—and flew like a mini-missile out into the open air.

I landed hard on the wet, pebbly roof. I was breathing raggedly—the Taser had taken more out of me than I had realized. Even in the rainy light I was blinded. I stood, stretching my back, whipped out my shades, and put them back on. I glanced around. The skylight now had a jagged hole the size of a merry-go-round. I could hear more curses rising through the opening.

Time to scoot. I gathered my bags and sprinted to the nearest wall at a dead run. I peeked over and saw a handful of police cars and two little trucks that said MALL SECURITY, but they were pulled up closer to the far end and appeared to be empty.

No time for ladders—I leapt over the edge and fell the whole three stories, landing on my backside with a big *whoomp*ing thump in an open Dumpster, pieces of shirt boxes and colored tissue paper *shoomp*ing up around me. Thank goodness it wasn't the one close to the food court. I kicked the door open and aimed myself for the Space Center as fast as I could go.

By the time I got back to the base, the rain had stopped and the sun blazed through, making everything steamy. I carried my load up and rested awhile in the little tower room, munching on mall fare and gleefully checking out my haul.

Then I thought of what Papi would think of me and felt an acrid twang of guilt. Burglary. Property damage. Resisting arrest. *What next? Assault?* I was rapidly becoming the kind of person he would want to see put under the jail. I vowed to do a better job of curbing my impulses, something I hadn't had too much success with in the past. I remembered how I had felt when I lifted that refrigerator in broad daylight. Untouchable, arrogant. Maybe that was all part of the vampire transformation, but it only magnified my worst flaws.

Life without rules was more complicated than I thought.

I spent the rest of the day working around the tower, streamlining things and improving my defenses, while waiting for the NASA employees to leave. After the adrenaline rush of the chase, I felt jangly and overstimulated. No wonder; I was stuffing my face with nothing but Fudgey Nut, soft pretzels, and chocolate chip cookies the size of Frisbees.

I was aching to try on my new things, but I was completely filthy. When I saw the last of the government workers pouring off the base, I picked out clothes, cleaning supplies, and a sinfully thick burgundy towel and hurried down to the bunker. After days in pajamas, I was almost goofy with anticipation. Twenty minutes later, spanking clean and dressed in jeans and a frothy orange top, I couldn't believe how much better I felt. But somehow it still wasn't enough. Something was missing,

"Go away," Sagan said.

I felt hurt. Here I was all freshly scrubbed in my brand-new North Creek preppy togs, and he was refusing to let me in.

"Oh, come on," I said, looking at him through the glass, making my eyes as sorrowful as possible. "Or I'll huff, and I'll puff, and I'll . . ." I couldn't believe it. I was actually flirting.

"I mean it," Sagan said for at least the third time. He was standing on the other side of the air lock doors—just beyond my reach, because of the bar code reader—and speaking to me through a little wall-mounted intercom. He gestured at the white phone hanging next to the door. "I'll call security. They'll be here in ten minutes."

"What's your problem?" I said into the speaker box.

"You."

"What'd I do?"

"Just please go away."

Okay, I was going to have to do it. . . . I'd never been very good at pointing the finger of blame at myself when somebody else was handy. But—in spite of the empty calories I had inhaled—I was half starved. And besides . . . I just wanted to see him again.

I rapped on the glass pleadingly. "Come on, Sagan. I'm sorry I ducked out on you. I had a great time last night. The best night in practically—forever."

"No."

"It's me, okay? Sometimes I do things without thinking. That's part of the package. I know I should have hung around and said goodbye. Come on. Give me another chance."

He seemed to sag a little. He was wearing shorts again and a faded blue polo shirt with none of the buttons buttoned. And this time he had glasses. Thin little wire-rimmed specs. I loved the way he looked in them . . . like a sexy lab guy. He was leaning with his forearm pressed against the glass, making the long muscle below his elbow spread out into a powerful oval. He looked strong, like he could pick me up and run. . . .

He thumbed the speaker button. "Whatever."

Ouch. *Guess I deserved that.*

He took his finger off the intercom and turned on his heels and walked into the cafeteria.

I looked behind me into the forest. The sun would be going down soon, and I wasn't too cool with the idea of going back to the creepy spider nest I called home. Besides, I had never been the type to give up easy.

Five minutes later I was descending the little ladder that led down from the roof and negotiating the maze of hallways back to the cafeteria.

Sagan was sitting at one of the tables. He had a thick paperback book held open with one hand while he stirred a spoon around in a little bowl of microwave chili with the other. I could see steam rising from the bowl, and it made my mouth water. He must've heard me, because he looked up.

"Okay," he said. He almost didn't seem surprised. He took his glasses off and leaned around a pillar to look at the locked door. "So how'd you get in here?"

"The same way I did last time," I said, sitting down next to him.

"Which was?"

"Through the roof."

Sagan looked up as if he expected to find a hole in the ceiling. "I can still call security, you know."

Not after I beat you to that phone and rip it out by the roots, I thought. I resisted the impulse.

"But you won't," I said.

"You don't think so?"

"Well . . . I hope you won't."

He put his glasses back on, looked down at his book.

"Please go away. I'm busy."

I looked at the title of the book: *Brisingr.* "Dragons, huh?" I said. "I read the first one. It was pretty solid. I don't read a whole lot of sword and sorcery stuff."

"I'd like to get back to it," Sagan said. "You know the way out."

I made a face he didn't see. "Papi—my grandfather—he turns me on to history books he likes. He's got unbelievable taste. For an old guy, I mean." *Oops, watch the family references.*

Sagan turned a page, and his washed-out blue eyes shifted. I loved the way his straight hair fell over his glasses.

"You're pretty mad at me, aren't you?" I said.

He read at least half a page before answering . . . and then he didn't really answer. Just sort of grunted.

I leaned toward him, wanting to touch him on the arm. "What's wrong?"

"You're welcome for the pizza."

"Thank you. Got any left?"

"Um. And you are still here because . . . ?"

I touched his arm. He didn't exactly jerk it away, but I felt his muscles tighten.

"How was school today?" I said.

"College. It's called college." What he was saying underneath it was this: I'm not a kid anymore like you.

Whoop dee frickin' doo, I started to say, then decided I better soften it. "Must be nice."

Sagan closed his book with a thump and finally looked at me. "Please go away."

"Nope, sorry. Not until your mood stabilizer kicks in."

"Why should I even be talking to you?"

"Because I'm cool to talk to. Because you like me."

Okay, I had the bait out. Now let's see how he was going to respond. Sagan took a bite of chili, blowing on the spoon before putting it in his mouth. All that junk food in my system—watching him eat was a killer.

He put the spoon down and looked out at the setting sun, slowly exhaling. I waited, hopeful.

"It's happened all my life, you know?" he said, looking at me. "I've been the guy other people could get to do things for them. I've always had skills. Or was willing. That's what people always wanted me for. What I could do for them."

"A tool," I said.

Sagan swore. "You really were just after something to eat last night, weren't you?"

I rolled my eyes. "When you catch somebody rifling through a kitchen, that's a pretty safe guess."

"So you decided to charm me into buying you something. You used me."

Wow, nobody had ever accused me of having charm before. "I didn't use you," I said. "Okay, well, maybe I used you a little. But that's not why I came back. . . ."

"It was all a joke, wasn't it?" Sagan wasn't smiling.

"What?"

"You spent practically the whole night convincing me you were some kind of poor homeless person who had been abused or were in some kind of terrible trouble—"

"Hey—" I couldn't help myself; I was starting to bristle now.

"That's not fair. Everything I told you is true. I never said anything about being abused. And I said I was only technically homeless, remember? I have a home—but I have to live out here for right now. Because I *am* in trouble. And yes, it's pretty terrible."

"How do I know it's not just another trick?" Sagan said. "You probably don't even need those sunglasses either."

I took off my shades and put them in my pocket. He was moving another bite of chili to his mouth. His hand stopped and his eyes widened. He was staring at me.

"Look, how many times do I have to say I'm sorry?" I said. "You're right. Running out on you wasn't . . . it wasn't very nice." I had never liked that word. *Nice* was people who got the short end of the stick because they were too afraid to stand up for themselves.

"I still don't know your name," he said.

"Emma," I said. "My name is Emma."

Sagan looked at me questioningly. "Last name?"

"Sorry, that's all you're going to get."

"So how do I believe you?"

"I don't lie. Well, I didn't until recently. But I swear that's my name. They named me after my aunt."

"Okay. Emma. Keep going. Who is 'they'?"

"My parents are divorced. I live with my mom and little sister in a ratty apartment. I haven't seen my dad in . . . well, a really long time. I don't even know that much about him anymore."

"So why did you have to leave?"

"You wouldn't believe me if I told you."

Sagan gave me a genuine smile for the first time all night. "Hey, I believe in stuff like neutron stars and black holes. This is where I'm supposed to say 'try me.'"

I took a deep breath. "That's the movies. This is real. Only in the movies would somebody believe anything like this. I still don't believe it myself sometimes."

"So you really are living out here? Where?"

I looked away. "I have to keep that a secret. To protect you."

"Why? What could happen to me?"

"Like I said, you wouldn't believe me."

"You owe me," he said. "I took a chance on you. I could've gotten into big trouble letting you stay. The last time I saw you, you were wearing gum boots and pajamas. Your toes were green. Now you come here looking all gorgeous like you just stepped out of a catalog. You could be . . . anybody. You could be . . ." He didn't say it, but I knew from his face what he was thinking. *You could be crazy.*

"I'm not crazy," I said. "Wait a minute. Back up. Did you . . . did you just call me . . . gorgeous?"

"What if I did?"

"Where'd you say the restroom is?"

Oh my God.

I was looking at the proof in the mirror and couldn't come close to believing it. *I'm beautiful,* I thought. For the very first time in my life. *Beautiful.*

It wasn't the clothes; it was me. It. Was. Me. I had always been okay with my looks before but sometimes felt a little invisible to guys. Especially when girls like Gretchen Roberts were around. Now I still looked like myself: the same high cheekbones, thick brown hair, slightly wide nose, and big intense wolfish eyes . . . but something, some miraculous transformation had taken place. All of the parts of me that had never seemed to quite work together before—they all blended now.

It was a miracle. My skin shone. My curling bangs that had always driven me crazy—after camping out in rat holes, bathing with tap water—they fell just exactly across my forehead. My mouth was even poutier. And when I smiled . . . *Oh. My. God.*

Of all the surprising things that had happened to me today, this was the most shocking of all.

11. BURNING

I walked unsteadily back to the cafeteria. I say *walked*. But really it was more like floating. *Maybe vampires can fly.*

"I can't stand it anymore. Here," Sagan said when I sat down. He slid his bowl of chili over.

I stared at him blankly.

"You look like you're about ready to fall over."

"Oh! Thanks, but I'm not hungry." I pushed the bowl back. I didn't care if I ever ate another bite of food in my whole life. *I'm beautiful.*

"The girl who ate practically a whole pizza is not hungry," Sagan said. "Okay. So what have you eaten today?"

"Huh? Oh. Nothing. Well, nothing but a ton of mall junk."

"You went to the mall today?"

My luminous mood plummeted. I could have bitten off my tongue. "Well. Um. I did some . . . uh . . . shopping."

"That's where you got the clothes?"

I waited, figuring out what to say. "You have to understand. I'm not a bad person. I'm not. But lately . . . I've had to do some bad things. I've never stolen anything in my life, I swear. Well, except . . . lately."

"You stole those clothes?"

I could only nod.

Sagan sighed. "So why didn't you just go to a thrift store or something?"

"What? You think I should have stolen from poor people?"

"Oh. So you don't have any money?"

"No. Not even a debit card. I've lost everything. My cell phone. All the stuff in my room."

"It's not lost if it's right there," he said.

"I can't go back there. I don't know when I'll ever be able to go back. I barely made it out as it was."

"Sounds like you had to leave really fast."

I thought about how I had smashed through my bedroom window two nights ago. It already felt like another world, another life.

"You have no idea," I said. "Besides, even if I had my debit card, my cell, if I used them, they could trace it. They could find me."

"They?"

"Anybody who wants to find me."

"So it's somebody in your family you're hiding from?"

"I didn't say that. But they sure would like to know where I am. My mom is scared half to death."

"Why not just tell them? So they can help?"

All the questions were starting to make me feel uncomfortable. I got up and turned toward the window and watched a truck rumbling by in the distance.

"It would be too dangerous for them," I said. "I can't be seen around them. There is no way I could go back home right now, Sagan."

"Why?"

"Somebody is . . . after me. If they find out where my family lives, they would hurt them to get to me. That's why I left."

"Who?"

I started to say something, and he held up his hand.

"I know, I know, I won't believe you."

"Right."

Sagan cursed. "Come on, Emma. If somebody is trying to hurt you, you have to call the police! If you don't call them, I will."

I felt my jaw tighten and took a couple of steps toward him. "Look . . . if you say a word about this to anybody . . . you're going to get me killed. My mom and my sister too. Seriously."

Sagan's eyes widened. "Drugs. It's got to be drugs."

Now I cursed. "No! You're just like my mom. I hate drugs."

"I don't mean you . . . but you saw something, some big drug deal—"

"Not even close."

"But it has to be something . . . crazy. Really bad."

I felt like pulling my hair out. "What do you think I've been try-ing to tell you? It just happened to me. It could have happened to anybody. I was in the wrong place at the wrong time. I nearly—I nearly died."

"And you're telling me the police—they can't do anything about it."

"They would make it ten times worse! If I did that, they—the bad people—they would know for sure where my family lived." *They can't stop this,* I wanted to say. *Not what is coming.* "It wouldn't do any good," I said. "The police couldn't protect us. They'd be as helpless as anybody else. Swear that you won't call them."

"Okay, okay, I swear," Sagan said. "Emma . . . you make it sound like . . . it's the Mafia or something."

"It's worse than that. Much worse."

I started to cry. Which I hated. I had seen so many girls do this . . . use tears to turn things in their favor. But I couldn't stop.

Sagan got up and came toward me. "Hey, look. It's going to be okay. Come on. It'll be all right."

His concern made everything worse. Now I was really sobbing. All the stuff I had stored up inside me was about to come flooding out. I bit my lip. Bit it hard and shook my head. I turned my back to him.

"I'm stupid. Really stupid."

He came up behind me and I could feel his big hands on my shoulders. I wiped my eyes, willing myself to stop. Nothing made me madder than somebody feeling sorry for me.

"Hey. Hey, it's all right," Sagan said. "You don't have to tell me. You're okay. You're safe, all right? Nothing is going to happen to you now. . . ."

"Nothing . . . right. You don't know. . . . You don't. They're looking for me right now. I can't talk about it. I won't. . . ."

"Okay . . . look. Let's do it this way. I can handle not knowing. Just don't tell me, okay? Until you're ready."

I couldn't speak for a while. I wanted to fall into his arms. He had said exactly the right thing.

We walked up the sidewalk to the aluminum dome of the observatory. There was a grassy smell on the breeze, and the sky still had a little blue. The only stars out, Sagan said, were really the planets Venus and Jupiter. How could anything be wrong on a night like this?

Where is he? I wondered. Wirtz? Out there waiting for the blackness to fall. What kind of place was he in? How far away? How did a vampire know when it was safe to awaken? Was I the first thing he thought of when he shrugged off sleep, some new way to get at me? Or did he think of something else . . . his hunger . . . *No. I won't think about that right now. I won't. You don't control me.*

I stopped in front of a door.

"Okay. You'll never have a better shot," I said. "Show me everything."

But Sagan kept going, taking my hand and pulling me with

him. "No, come on. That's the Vector Magnetograph Facility. There's a telescope, but it's not all that huge."

"Magneto-flidgy what?"

"It gives you views of chromospheric structures. Weblike patterns on the sun caused by bundles of magnetic field lines . . ."

"Bleh. Enough."

Sagan winced. But only a little.

"But the observatory—" I said.

"The dome? That's not really the observatory. The observatory my mom works with is . . . in a different place. Come on."

He took me past the dome and let us through a door with his badge and we walked down a long, dark hall to a long, dark room. Sagan began to glow, a nice robin's egg shade.

"Okay. Let me find the lights."

I could already see a couple dozen desk chairs perched in front of computer monitors. Most of the monitors were blank, but a few were scrolling some kind of data.

"You probably shouldn't touch anything," he said.

"Wasn't planning to," I said.

"A guard comes around just about every night. He's cool. Most of the time he comes in and walks around and we scare each other."

"And if he caught us?"

Sagan showed a wicked smile. "If he caught you, you mean. We would both be in it pretty deep."

I must have looked alarmed, because he added, "Don't worry, we're fine. It's usually in the middle of the night when he comes through. And even if he did, you would just have to keep on your toes. Go to the opposite end of the building, duck in and out of places."

"I'm good at ducking."

"I've noticed that."

Sagan turned and lifted his hand majestically, as if we were standing before the pyramids.

"This is STEREO."

I could see an enormous oval conference table flanked with cushy chairs. The table was crisscrossed with wires that went to telephones and a couple of computer keyboards.

"So, play me something," I said.

"It's not that kind of stereo."

He walked over to one of the keyboards and bumped the mouse. The giant screen popped alive, showing a Windows log-in page.

"STEREO is short for Solar TErrestrial RElations Observatory," Sagan said. "Actually two nearly identical observatories. One ahead of the earth in its orbit, the other trailing behind. Here's the cool thing about it—for the first time ever it gives us a view of the sun in 3-D."

He clicked his way deeper into the program. "This is a remote station. Mostly I get to look at what STEREO is looking at. I can't send it any real commands. With over a hundred million bucks on the line, I'm locked out. But it's cool just getting to work with the data it collects."

"Oh. So what do you get for a hundred million?" I said, dramatically stifling a yawn.

Sagan clicked the mouse. "This."

The screen burst with supercharged greenish light, making me flinch, even with my sunglasses on. I had to step back and turn my head away, shielding my eyes from the otherworldly radiance.

"Pretty amazing, huh?" he said.

When my eyes adjusted, I saw an image of the sun, actually about a quarter of the whole ball, slowly rotating, massive coils of fire shooting out from the edge of the sphere, then turning back in on themselves. As the coils moved across the surface, they swayed and danced, reminding me of videos I had seen of tornadoes ravaging a pasture. I had never seen anything like it.

"Yeah, now that's cool," I said, peeking through my fingers, genuinely enthralled as the flames whipped back and forth.

Sagan's eyes glittered with reflected green light. "That's one of the 'wow' images they throw at people the first time they come to the facility. You should see their heads rock back when they aren't ready for it."

"Except . . . why is it green?"

"Oh. I toned it down, put it into an easier spectrum for you to handle, knowing your eyes are sensitive. The full spectrum would've knocked you over. It's that intense."

"Thanks. Hey . . . what's that bright spot where so much of the fire seems to be bursting out?"

"A CME," Sagan said. "Coronal mass ejection. Basically an explosion on the sun. You ought to see a CME in yellow-orange! You'd be blinking white circles for a week."

"I bet," I said, but the sarcasm in my tone went right over his head. "So tell me again, what's it for?"

"STEREO traces the flow of energy and matter from the sun to the earth. The two observatories can show the 3-D structure of coronal mass ejections so we can study 'em. CMEs can seriously mess with satellites and power grids. It gives us more data we can look at, see how we might possibly survive a giant CME. At the very least, give us some advance warning."

"Survive? Advance warning of what?"

He nodded at the fireball on the screen. A loop of flame was wiggling like an electric charge.

"If you get one big enough, a CME or a flare, it could throw us back into the Dark Ages."

I looked at him. He was serious.

"You really think something like that is possible?" I said.

"Sure. It would knock out satellites. Could fry the utility grid. No power. No communications. No lights. Very little water if you can't pump it. The food distribution system would break down. People could start to riot. Did you see that story about the bread truck that stalled on the interstate during a bread shortage out west?"

"No." I seemed to remember something about it but couldn't recall the details.

"People hijacked the truck, stole everything. And not just poor people. People in Mercedes."

"Oh."

"So, the longer we go without essential services, the worse it would get. Think about when a disaster hits a big city. People come from all over to help. Okay, imagine a hundred cities in trouble at once. There'd be no way to keep up. People would be helpless. And if they started to die . . ."

I wasn't hearing him anymore. A picture of Manda had appeared in my head. All alone, moving through the darkened apartment, crying. *Starving. Looking for me, and I'm not there.*

I turned around. No windows in this place, but I could still sense it—the darkness. I swore inside. I'd let myself get sidetracked.

"Let's go," I said, the mood gone.

"But I haven't shown you how I hunt for comets," Sagan said.

"There's something I need to do."

"Was it something I said?" he asked when we came back outside. I was scanning the woods, the highway. Sagan touched my shoulder, and I pulled away.

"Huh? Oh." I tried to smile. "No. It's not you, Sagan. It's me. I have to . . . keep focused. I can't let myself get too caught up in other stuff right now."

"Other stuff? You mean like . . . me?"

"Well . . ."

"Don't say it. I hate it when girls say that."

"What?"

He took a long breath. "The *F* word, you know."

I said the *F* word.

"No!" Sagan said, starting to laugh a little. "Not *the F* word. The other one. *Friends,* you know."

"Oh, you're worried that I—"

"I said don't say it."

"Okay."

"I could drive you," he said, pointing at a battered Jeep Wrangler.

"Nice," I said.

"Hand-me-down from my dad. One slightly used graduation present. Get in."

"Nope. Then you would know where I'm staying."

"Yeah, I would. Is that a bad thing?"

"I don't know. I hope not."

Sagan reached as if to grab my hand, thought better of it, and let his arm fall again.

"Are you coming back tomorrow?"

I rubbed my chin. "That depends. . . . Whatcha going to be eating?"

Sagan frowned.

"Oh, come on, I'm kidding. Thank you for the offer. I will . . . if I can."

I walked with him to the main door and made him go back inside the cafeteria before I would leave.

"You know this is crazy, right?" he said, raising his arm again. *He wants to touch me,* I thought.

"Yeah," I said. "But sometimes crazy is the safest way to go."

Now was the time to try it.

I was back in my little tower room. I would have preferred to do this test outdoors, on the roof, but if Wirtz's projection showed up, there were too many things up there that might give away my location. Besides, I worried that I could accidentally induce a tonic-clonic. I could all too easily imagine thrashing around until I flopped right over the edge, then *zam,* doing a gruesome face-plant on the gravel below.

I was sitting at the crappy old desk. I opened a pack of playing cards I'd snagged from Sagan's desk and fanned them out in front of me. The desk chair shrieked each time I leaned forward, putting the cards down.

How big of a risk was I taking? At the worst, it would be frightening, but Wirtz wouldn't be able to touch me. And there was nothing in this little room that would give away my hiding place. If the test backfired, it might even do some good, showing the vampire I had moved and he had missed out on his chance to get at my family.

I only knew I was sick of being driven into corners, playing the mouse to the vampire's cat. *I'm the one who does the driving,* I thought. *Let's see how you like being the mouse.*

I tilted my lamp toward the cards to increase the glare and studied the pattern. My eyes flitted from card to card, never staying on one card for very long. I heard a siren wailing somewhere on the highway. . . . *Focus, Emma.*

It didn't seem to be working. I collected the cards again, began shuffling them and fanning the deck before my eyes. *Ah, that's better.* I began to feel something soft and warm directly behind my eyes, as if a fluffy rolled-up towel had been tucked there, cushioning them from my brain.

Wirtz, I thought, picturing the vampire that night in Georgia. His greedy black eyes, his despicable slobbering mouth. *Take me to Wirtz.*

I instinctively touched the raised line of flesh on my thigh where his teeth had torn open my leg. Ran my finger along it over and over, feeling the skin get warmer and warmer. *Take me to Wirtz. Take me to Wirtz.* I repeated the words over and over again, finally just hearing them inside my throat, as if knowing the universe would listen and respond.

Then, just like the clock numbers in my bedroom, it began to happen. The playing cards became something that was only a shape with color. And then even less than that. I was looking at a chunk of nothingness. I pushed my way into it.

I could feel something hard pushing back.

I pushed again. It was like shoving against a door someone else was holding shut. All at once they let the door go and I fell through.

Oh wow. It had worked.

The world around me passed into nothingness. When I came back into the light, everything was different. I was there. In a place I had never been before.

I couldn't see Wirtz, but I could sense him somewhere close by. I could almost smell his woody leaf-rot scent. It was all so real; I could feel myself standing on a porch in front of a small darkened house. I was looking in through the big picture window in front.

Staring at someone inside. A young woman in a kitchen. The light to her stove was on, and she was stirring a wooden spoon around and around in a pan.

I moved along the front of the house peering into other windows. Lights were on in some of the rooms, but most were dark.

I looked up and down the street. *A sign. Look for a street sign.* But there were no signs, only some parked cars and a row of similar one-story houses with old trees in their yards.

I glanced at the woman in the kitchen; she was still happily stirring. Probably waiting for her family to get home. That's why I was here, I realized. I had picked her. I had been up and down the street looking for someone alone.

I crept along the porch to the front door. Could feel my hand on the doorknob. Really feel it—this was no projected image. The knob was cold and hard in my fingers. I turned it—the door was open— and stepped inside. *So silent.* I stood there a moment looking toward the kitchen. Light slanted diagonally across the living room. I had a moment's indecision. I didn't want to cross the triangle of light. Instead I stepped straight down the front hall and turned right.

I could see the woman from another angle now. She was young and pretty with blond hair pulled back with a blue headband. Her feet were bare. My tongue curled over my bottom lip as I watched her move.

I smiled. It wasn't just her blood—though I was aware of every inch of the woman's circulatory system, almost as if her skin were crisscrossed with a pattern of tiny webs of flame—but I could sense what she was like beneath her clothes. The weight and shape of her breasts, the flesh of her hips, at what depth the blood was swimming in her thighs. Where it was closest to the surface. It felt as if I knew her body, really knew it, even better than she did.

I stepped closer, making no sound. Strangely, the sensation of movement seemed to stop when I was actually moving the quickest. One moment I was in the hall, then I was just there, in the kitchen, my arm draped across the woman's back.

The woman dropped the spoon, and spaghetti sauce splattered across the floor. Her mouth opened wide, but before she could make a sound, I had lifted her into my arms and carried her into one of the back bedrooms.

The bedroom was dark. I threw the woman down on the bed. She looked up at me and started to scream. I fell upon her, putting the back of my arm across her open mouth. I put my hand on the side of her face, bent her head unnaturally to the side—tore at her soft throat with my teeth. . . .

My stomach filled like a bag.

Back in my little room at the top of the tower, I swung my arm in front of me and slapped the cards away. I shoved back from the desk and got up from the cracked chair, still feeling the heaviness of the woman's warm blood in my belly.

I staggered back a few steps until I collapsed by the door. I crawled out onto the catwalk and clung to the railing. Because I was in danger not of slipping, but of throwing myself over. I wanted to go over the edge. I couldn't live with a dying woman's blood inside me. I vomited into the forest.

12. DARK KISS

I lay on my back on the air mattress on top of the tower, looking up but seeing nothing. I felt broken in some important way. The experiment had been a success, if you could call it that. I had connected with Wirtz's mind, but not in the way I had expected. I had thought I would be able to visit him the same way he had visited me. As a projection, an image that could interact with the vampire. But I had done something completely different . . . and infinitely more disturbing.

I killed her. Killed that poor woman.

Hot tears streamed down my face. Yeah, I knew that Wirtz had really done the killing, but it might as well have been me. Tonight there was a family with no mother. A husband with no wife. A lost daughter. Sister. Friend. And it had all started with a long chain that led back to the Georgia mountains and pointed straight at me. She was dead because of my anger.

No.

I couldn't let myself think like that. I hadn't invited Wirtz to attack me. But I had sure put myself in his path.

That's what he wants you to think, I told myself. *Screw him.*

I needed that anger if I was going to survive. Besides, I wasn't going to make it that easy for the vampire to break me down. I reminded myself that I had just learned something here, gained a little bit of an edge. *I traveled inside another person's mind.*

I had briefly experienced life as a full vampire. But more than just the sensation of moving inside Wirtz's body: I was moving inside his needs, his wants—*his perversions* too. I had felt the vampire's excitement at the nearness of his prey. Her beauty. The certainty that she had no chance of getting away. His awful hunger. The horror and yet also the gloating satisfaction of the attack.

I wanted her blood.

I had wanted every drop of it until the sickening feeling bloating my body had knocked me out of the vampire's world.

What I had done was far more powerful than what Wirtz was able to do. When he came through during one of my seizures, he could see me, yeah. Could guess at my reaction to things. Maybe even find out where I was hiding—if I did something unforgivably stupid, like hang around a sign that said WELCOME TO MARSHALL SPACE FLIGHT CENTER until I had a seizure.

But I can go inside his head.

The problem was, now that I knew what it was like, I couldn't bear to go there again. I couldn't. I felt like it might kill me if I tried. But I had to. Not tomorrow. Maybe not even next week. But no matter how awful it was, I had to try.

I promised myself I would be stronger next time. Strong enough to stay with him, see what the vampire did after feeding. Maybe even learn where Wirtz was hiding. Then I could go over there during the day, take out a mallet and a sharpened stake, and . . .

There were just a couple of problems. Even in the midst of his feeding frenzy, I could feel more than Wirtz's satisfaction. I could feel his confidence, his certainty, that he was on the right track, that he was closing in on me. Killing this woman was just one step closer.

I closed my eyes against the thought and drew the tarp up over me.

I woke as soon as the sun came up. The forest was glowing with soft morning light. I sat up and took in a deep lungful of the spring air; my heart expanded with it. The horrors of the night had mostly evaporated. I changed into fresh clothes and climbed down from my tower.

Today was Saturday. I figured I should start making marks on a stick or something. But did that really matter anymore, now that my weekends were like any other days? I wondered if vampires forgot about time altogether, except for the simplest of observations: day or night.

I walked up the hill in the breezy air, not really caring what direction I took. I realized where I was when I spotted the dome of the Solar Observatory rising through the trees—and Sagan's Jeep sitting in the parking lot. He was leaning against the passenger door.

"Hey," he said. He was holding a crimped white bag. "Brought you some breakfast."

We sat at a little picnic table in the edge of the woods and ate bagels.

"How did you know I would be here?" I said.

"Took a chance."

"How long have you been waiting?"

"Couple of hours."

"Wow."

"Astronomers are patient. Want some cream cheese?"

"Yuck. No thanks. Now a little melted butter . . ."

"Sorry."

I waved my hand at the observatory. "You work on the weekends too?"

Sagan took a bite. "Not really. Sometimes. If there's an event."

"Event."

"Potential comet stuff. The latest thing is 'dark asteroids.' Somebody figured out that most of the sky surveys are skewed toward objects with highly reflective surfaces. But there are thousands of dark ones out there too. They're harder to find, but they could be every bit as dangerous to the earth as the ones that are easy to see."

I bit into a bagel. "You're kinda like the angel of doom when it comes to this astronomy stuff," I said.

"Really?" he said. "I guess I've never thought about it that way, sorry."

"It's just hard to think about anything dark on a morning like this. But I wish I had your passion for something."

"Okay, so what do you like?"

"Staying alive."

Sagan didn't smile. "No, really. What about history? You said you and your granddad—"

"Yeah, but that's his thing, you know? We like history for different reasons. He loves it because it's old. I love it because nobody was constantly telling you what you couldn't do. People just did things."

He smiled. "Yeah, women, for sure."

I hit him with a wadded-up napkin. "You know what I mean. There was more adventure, excitement. Mystery. Now everything's supposed to be careful, safe, known. Millions of rules." I stopped, feeling a knot come up in my throat, thinking about vampires. How my perspective had changed. "Anyhow, I want something of my own," I said.

"So what's holding you back?"

I considered telling him about my epilepsy for about half a second. But that would only give him one more reason to turn me in. *For your own safety,* he'd say.

"I'm working on it," I said.

Sagan crumpled up the bag and took a shot at a nearby garbage can. Missed.

"Loser," I said.

"I've got some surprises for you," he said.

"I take it back, then."

He walked over to the Jeep and returned holding a large blue gym bag. Sat it on the table and unzipped it. I looked inside. A toothbrush, toothpaste, some baby wipes, a bunch of snacks like granola bars and rice cakes, and . . .

"The piece of resistance," Sagan said, digging into the bag. I giggled. He handed me a small black gizmo that was fitted to a headband so it could be positioned over the ear. "The latest thing for hunters and hikers. It operates on a radio signal that can't be traced the way a cell can. Keeps your hands free and has a radius of fifty miles, as long as there aren't too many obstructions. I can keep the other one in my car and bring it into the observatory each night. In case you need me."

"Sagan. It looks expensive."

"Only five hundred bucks."

I nearly dropped it. "Oh my God."

"Happy birthday, Emma."

For a moment I was speechless. "Wow. Nobody . . . nobody has ever given me anything like this. But it's not my birthday. You have to take it back." I reached it out to him, but he waved me off.

"Call it a loan, then. My dad never uses them anyway."

"No, really. Please."

"Keep it. You're in trouble, Emma. You won't tell me what it is, so you have to let me help some other way."

"So you're just going to trust some homeless chick you might never see again?"

"No. I'm going to trust you."

I felt my eyes go wet.

"Oh, and here's the charger," Sagan said, putting it in my other hand. "Assuming you've got some kind of power source?"

"Um, yeah. But—"

"You won't tell me where you are living. You won't tell me who's after you. It's driving me crazy. Let me do something. You have to let me do something."

I touched the base of my thumb to my eye and didn't speak.

"All done?" Sagan said, sweeping away the last of the bagel crumbs. "Come on, I want to show you something."

"But . . ."

"I won't take you off the base. I promise."

We stashed everything in Sagan's Jeep and took off. The windows in the back were plastic and the seats were rocks, but I was smiling the whole time. I couldn't believe how good it felt, how normal, to be riding in a car again.

First stop, a group of five rusting rockets that reminded me of Russian dolls—the smaller ones could fit inside the bigger ones. "Okay," I said.

"Hey, this is historical stuff," Sagan said. I hoped he was kidding. "Steps on the way to building the world's first—"

"I know," I said, giving him a fake scowl. "Don't push your luck."

We motored on. Next on the agenda was something Sagan called "high bays" where engineers once tinkered with *Saturn V* rocket boosters. I tried to feign interest. "So what's inside there now?"

"A bunch of basketball courts with a ceiling two hundred feet high."

Next, the "world-famous Neutral Buoyancy Simulator, where the astronauts practice underwater to simulate weightless conditions," Sagan explained. It was a giant white tank shaped like a sphere with little portals around the sides.

The swamp was more interesting. I asked him to park and we walked down to the water's edge. Black and brackish and still as a painted picture. Every once in a while a dragonfly buzzed by or bubbles rose from the bottom, making concentric circles.

"Swamp gas," Sagan said. We didn't see any alligators.

"Any snakes?" I said. I wondered if vampires were vulnerable to moccasins and rattlers but didn't want to test the theory.

"All you can eat," Sagan said. "Come on, I saved the best for last."

"The wastewater treatment plant?"

"Funny. Get in."

We drove back in a big circle. It almost looked as if he was taking me to . . .

"The Solar Observatory? Why are you bringing me back here? No dark asteroids, Sagan. I'm begging you."

"Relax, grasshopper."

Instead we continued along the river. At last we came to a beaten-down gravel road with two iron posts standing on either side of the entrance, a rusty chain stretched between them.

I looked at Sagan. "End of the line?"

"No way."

He backed the Jeep up a little, then left the paved road and drove right around the post on the far side.

"We're not supposed to go here, right?" I said, a feeling of worry tickling my stomach. "Won't we get in trouble?"

Sagan grinned. "Nope. Security never comes out here. Why would they? No secrets. Nothing to steal. I used to come out here with my dad all the time. I never once saw the road actually open."

"So . . . where does it go?"

"You'll see."

We wound along in silence, zipping around saplings that had sprung up through the gravel and easing over fallen timber. The trees began to thin, and suddenly I started to recognize the clearing. He was taking me to my tower.

The Jeep rolled to a stop not fifty feet from where I had vomited the night before. I climbed out, trembling slightly, wondering how good a job I had done at hiding my defenses.

"Why . . . why are we here?" I said, deliberately turning my back to the tower. "You don't expect me to climb that thing, do you?"

"Huh? Naw. There's really not much to see. I've been up there a million times. That's the old test stand they were going to use to test-fire liquid oxygen rocket engines back in the sixties—that big flue-looking thing at the bottom is where the exhaust and fire came out. That was before they realized they couldn't use it and had to build a new one farther away."

"How come?"

"Too dangerous. Because of what it was built on top of."

"What?"

"You'll see."

He unzipped the back of the Jeep and brought out a small knapsack and two flashlights, handed me the red one and kept the blue.

"Okay?" I said.

"Follow me."

We marched over to the bunker. *My bunker, the one where I bathe,* I thought. There was still a little water standing on the floor.

"Huh, looks like somebody's been messing with the faucet," Sagan said.

I followed him inside, feet sloshing almost as loudly as my heart. Had I left anything lying around? Shampoo? Soap?

We walked past the faucet and came to the metal net at the back that I had seen before. Sagan knelt at a corner and flipped up a little flap of metal that I never would have noticed. There was a sturdy padlock hidden beneath it holding the screen in place. He took out a key and undid the lock. Slowly pushed the heavy net over far enough for us to get through. I could feel that same subterranean breath blowing in my face, and now there was nothing between me and it.

"Let's go," he said.

We had to step carefully. Here and there were little chunks of concrete rubble and something that looked like pieces of brownish wasp nests but were hard like stone to the touch.

"Karst," Sagan said, without explanation.

I could see everything, so following Sagan was like following a man who was practically blind. Concrete slabs. Concrete walls. Forty-gallon drums that Sagan said were full of old gasoline for the generators.

"They stopped maintaining this place years ago," he said. "Even before the fall of the Berlin Wall."

"What is it?"

"A nuclear blast shelter. Let's keep going."

We went deeper. The concrete walls gave way to big clunky shapes and long slanting fault lines, then pieces of stone that seemed to flow down the walls like solidified lava. The room was still mostly flat, but now there were big pieces of slag everywhere. Real stalactites. Side tunnels and channels. Pits in the floor and holes in the ceiling. We were in a cave. A real live cave.

"I've . . . I've never been in anything like this before," I said, barely managing a whisper.

"This is why they abandoned the old test stand. It was built on top of a series of caves."

"How far does it go?"

"How far do you want to go?"

"Any chance of us getting lost?"

"Oh yeah. It's a big cave."

I was pulling him along now, impatient to see.

"Hey, slow down, Emma! We don't want to fall into anything."

"I won't let us fall," I said. I had taken my sunglasses off. "I can see."

To my vampire eyes, everything had a ghostly tint of color. Greens, browns, yellows. The walls of the caverns seemed alive with it. We came to a place where the room narrowed down and the ceiling appeared to have collapsed. We duck-walked past the rubble, all the time slanting downhill. There were other places where the rubble was so deep we had to scramble over it.

"Watch your clothes," Sagan said.

I surged with excitement and raced ahead, my flashlight dangling from a belt loop. We entered a gigantic room with a rounded dome of a ceiling at least fifty feet high.

"Grotto," Sagan said, beaming his light up to show me the dagger-like formations above us and layers of concentric stripes that made the roof look like a huge stone target. "This whole system is part of a karst aquifer where everything has slowly collapsed over the centuries. What's left is mostly limestone. There are pyrites and gypsum too. They've mapped twenty-six separate caves, and geologic surveys show it's even more complex than that. They think the caverns we're standing in were probably inhabited lots of times over the last ten thousand years. Maybe longer ago than that."

"You sound like a tour guide," I said, accidentally putting my light in his face.

"Is that bad?"

"It's perfect." I wanted to squeeze his hand but didn't. We kept going down.

Now as we descended, the rubble gradually went away and the ceilings and floors got more and more smooth, almost glistening like wet clay. Finally we came to a place that had humongous humps of slick stone that rolled right down to something unbelievable.

"Oh my God. An underground lake."

I walked closer, in total awe. I had thought the swamp had been still—here the water was so motionless, I wondered if the molecules even moved. I looked up, could feel the eons sitting on top of my head. It was thrilling and strangely scary.

"What?" Sagan said.

"It's this weird little fear of mine. I've always been kind of freaked by things that never change, never see the sun. I always wonder what all that time and darkness has done to it."

"To what?"

"The stones, the water. Everything. I always think everything is alive. "Let's turn off our lights," I said.

"You sure? Have you ever been in a cave before and turned out the lights?"

"No."

"It's a pretty bizarre experience."

"Okay, now we have to do it."

We did a little countdown . . . "Three, two, one," and clicked off our flashlights simultaneously. At first I thought there was nothing but blackness there, which was kind of a relief when all your eyes ever do is see. But then I began to make out shapes and more and more detail as my eyes adjusted. I don't know how. We were so deep underground, there had to be no light at all. But I could see . . . the vaguest hint of color, but mostly the structures of things, stones, my hand in front of my face, and especially Sagan's body, even in this no-light, glowing dimly blue.

He extended his arms out in front of himself, not saying a word, and then I realized he was trying to find me. He was going in the wrong direction. I edged toward him and got in his way; he stretched right past my shoulders, reaching too high. Just as we were about to bump, I kissed him. I heard the intake of his breath and saw him flinch backward in surprise.

"Hey!"

Then our arms were around each other.

Sagan kissed me, pulling me close to him. I had never really kissed anyone before. Not like that. *Not even Lane Garner.* I had to fight the urge to kiss him too hard. I wanted to take hold of his head, pull his face to mine, tug at his hair.

It was hard to remember to let him breathe. I had to take Sagan's cue when to break free, and then started up again. I was so hungry for his mouth, I could barely stand how gentle we were being. I wanted to be fierce. I could hear water dripping. If he hadn't returned my kiss, I just might have thrown myself in.

We ate our lunch in the cave. Baloney and cheese sandwiches that Sagan had brought in the knapsack. Time went away. Hunger.

155

Thirst. Pain. Even feelings, to a certain extent. The only things left were the stones around us and his lips on mine and the way he held me.

We propped our lights on a flat rock, letting them fan out across the silent lake.

"I . . ."

I started to say something after we had been chewing awhile without speaking. How much this meant to me, how unexpected . . . how perfect. Then I realized I had no idea what words I should use.

"I . . . wonder . . . any fish in there?" I said a little lamely.

"Blind ones," Sagan said.

"No way."

"Want to see?"

My vision was about a hundred times better than his, but I couldn't see a thing beneath the water.

"You're looking in the wrong place." Sagan took me closer to the edge where there were shallow pools between the humped stone. Sure enough, there were tiny white fish there.

"Their eyes are like bumps," I said, totally enthralled. We watched them dart around, making the barest ripple.

"Here's the coolest thing," Sagan said. "Scientists took some of these fish out of here one time, put them in a tank in the light."

"So what happened?"

"After a few weeks, they started to grow eyes."

"You're lying."

"It's true. You can look it up online. It took about six weeks in all, but all of them had grown eyes. Think about that. Whatever message is coded in their DNA that grows eyes . . . it had survived countless births and deaths of fish without the code ever being turned off completely. It was just lying dormant, waiting for the sun to flip the switch. Generation after generation, maybe going back thousands of years, no contact with the sun at all, but somehow the light brought them back."

I thought about that for a while, watching the fish move. "Why don't they go out in the deep water?"

"Nobody knows. I figure . . . living things, they are so used to a place, so used to being what they are, they just keep following everything that is old. Nobody ever tries anything new. That's why evolution takes millions of years to do very much. They've found spiders in amber fifty million years old that look almost exactly like spiders living today."

That started me wondering . . . *vampires*. Was I the first step in some new phase of evolution?

"What are you thinking about?" Sagan said.

"Nothing."

He grinned. "I thought you were supposed to be so honest."

"Okay, something. I just . . . don't know what to think about it."

"Me?"

"Yeah. I was thinking about you."

We picked up our flashlights and kissed some more. I hoped I didn't taste like baloney.

As we left the lake, Sagan took me back by another path. "There are blind crayfish too," he said. "But you have to crawl on your stomach to get to them. It's in this ridiculously low stretch of cave hardly anybody knows about."

"Take me there," I said.

And he did. He led me to a place where there was a crevice in the wall that was nearly invisible if you didn't know where to look. We slithered through, then got down on our bellies.

Sagan wasn't joking about the crawl—I practically ruined my clothes. But I had to see them. The crayfish were smaller than my pinky and lived in little pools not much bigger than a birdbath. The ceiling was so low, you had the feeling you were seeing the very last days of a once-mighty chamber. Sagan called it "the King's Chamber." He said it had been dropping for centuries. We were there just in time to see the finish.

When we came out, the sun was so dazzling it hurt, even after I put my shades back on. I couldn't believe how green everything was.

"That's what a cave does to you," Sagan said. "The world never looks more beautiful than it does coming up from underground."

I nodded. But to me nothing could have been as beautiful as that strange, silent, monochromatic lake.

As we made our way back to the Jeep, I noticed something odd about the position of the sun.

"What time is it?" I said.

Sagan looked at his cell. "Five forty-seven."

"It can't be that late!"

He laughed. "That's another thing spelunking does to you."

"Spelunking?"

"Caves. They distort time. You don't have any frame of reference, so you're not as aware of time passing. Nothing moves. Not enough sensations."

"I had plenty of them," I said, resisting the urge to touch his mouth with my index finger.

"A French guy, a scientist, did an experiment," Sagan said. "He went down in a cave with tents, lights, all kinds of recording devices. His friends stayed on the surface monitoring everything he did. He stayed down there for six months."

"Holy crap. Dedicated."

"He wanted to acclimate to the cave's environment completely. No clocks. He ate when he felt hungry. Slept when he was sleepy. It was 'morning' when he decided it was morning and turned on the lights. Same thing for bedtime. By the end of the six months his friends were amazed."

"He'd turned into a bat?"

"Listen," Sagan said.

"Sorrrrry. So his friends were amazed . . ."

"Yeah. Turns out the scientist had been living fifty-six-hour days."

"What! No."

"Yep. Without any clocks or other references, his artificial 'days' settled into a pattern of fifty-six hours instead of twenty-four. He had utterly no idea how long he had been down there. . . . He thought it was only about three weeks."

"I could do it," I said.

"What?" Sagan said.

No way was I going to say it. But I thought it. *Three weeks in a cave. With you.*

I let him drop me off at the observatory.

"Is your thing on?" he said.

I smiled. "My thing?"

"Shut up. Your headset—the radio thing I gave you."

"Oh no. You gotta go?" I whined, trying to make him feel bad for leaving.

"I told my dad I would help him take the pool cover off. We always open it about a month earlier than anybody else."

"A pool! You didn't tell me you were rich."

He snorted.

"Yeah, right. It's thirty-two by sixteen. Mom's going to skin me alive. I was supposed to be home hours ago."

I put my arms around his neck. . . . He felt warm. "I thought you were going to help your dad."

"Mom's the official skinner."

"So where do they think you are?"

He looked at me funny. "With you."

I pulled my arms away. "You didn't tell them about me, did you?"

"That's my new nickname for the observatory."

"What?" I said.

"Emma."

"Oh! I almost forgot," Sagan said as I walked him back to his Jeep. "You'll love it. Not as cool as a cave, but . . ."

He reached into his pocket and pulled something out. It looked like a large gold locket on a short chain. Too heavy for a necklace. He showed me how it flipped open. My breath caught.

"A pocket watch!" I said. "I've always wanted one of those! Papi carries one around with him. He always used to put it in bed with me when I was really little to help me go to sleep."

"It's an old one of my dad's he doesn't use anymore," Sagan said. "Wish I could claim it's a priceless family heirloom, but they've got hundreds at Walmart for $12.95."

I put the watch next to my ear and listened to the ticking. I had to swallow a couple of times, feeling tears behind my eyes. I was thinking about Papi. How afraid he must be for me.

"Thank you," I said. "Are you coming back tomorrow?"

Sagan made a face. "Nah. Figured I would hang out with my sisters around the house. Maybe do some laundry."

I punched him.

"You're crazy," he said, rubbing his shoulder.

I kissed him. Then I started to smile. I tried to stop, but I couldn't.

"What?" Sagan said.

"A bat." I finally managed to choke it out. "I didn't see a single bat."

13. STONE HOUSE

Back at the tower, I knew I wouldn't be able to sleep. Not tonight. Not with the taste of his mouth on my lips. His arms around me.

Sagan. Just saying his name had my nerve endings on fire and my breath coming faster.

The darkness ticked.

I felt trapped. I had to get away. I wanted to run. Run somewhere as hard as I could. Fly right off the face of the world.

I actually only ran about seven miles, about half of it uphill. I ran down the middle of the road because it was the only way I knew to get there. I sailed along with my head down, only looking up to see the curves in the road, then looking down again as the white stripes flew past my eyes. I saw two cars just in time to get out of the way.

At last I realized where I was going: I was running all the way up Monte Sano. I was going to Papi's favorite place.

It was called the Stone House Hotel. Or the *Steinhaus,* as Papi liked to say. Papi helped build the *Steinhaus* in the 1960s. It was once a sprawling hotel built in a state park on the edge of Monte Sano, complete with a ballroom and twin hearths large enough to walk into.

There had been a fire only ten years after the hotel had opened. It had burned to the ground. A man was arrested for trying to incinerate his lover. Only the stones remained.

I knew the road into the park well enough to find my way. I

could see the picnic pavilion at the end of the dead-end drive just as clear as if I were looking at it in the daylight. You had to walk over a long ridge to see the ruins. Papi had brought me here count-less times to play, but what I liked to do most was climb the *Stein-haus.*

The stones provided plenty of handholds and footholds. When I was a kid, I loved sitting on the edge of the high wall and looking out over the spreading valley. Papi showed me a stone he remem-bered laying with his own hands.

"This one we called the *Bär.* Which is 'Bear,' " he had said, pat-ting a massive rock that bulged out from the face of the wall. "Not one of the boys wanted to touch it, it was so huge. But I did."

I stopped running as I topped the ridge. I could see the *Stein-haus* laid out before me, not one stone changed. And I saw my goal: as a kid I had always dreamed of scaling the main chimney, which rose higher than some of the surrounding oaks. There was no one to stop me now.

The ballroom was full of trees.

I patted the Bear's smooth, cold surface, planted one foot on its rounded hump, and sprang—and flew halfway up the chimney stack. I sprang again, and I was there. At the top. I wanted to scream—for joy? I didn't know. Joy was part of it, but it was too fierce to be joy. Something darker was in my throat, more like a war cry.

This should have been the best night of my life. But so much had been taken from me. Now Sagan. While he grew older and died, I would move unchanged through the centuries. *Alone.*

I dipped my hands into the chimney flue and coated my palms with soot. Painted my face in stripes of black. I stood, straddling the mouth of the chimney, threw my arms above my head, and screamed at the darkness. I wanted the monster to come.

* * *

When I came down, I sat on the Bear, thinking. I checked the watch Sagan had given me. *Already past ten.* I didn't realize I had been there that long. At last I stood and brushed myself off, ready to go back "home" to my air mattress.

I hoisted myself over the low wall and started along the front of the ruined hotel back toward the park entrance. I wondered—

Someone stepped out of the trees and threw a blanket over me. *Wirtz.*

I smashed at the hands holding me, but every time I got free, two more hands came from another direction. The vampire seemed to be everywhere at once, trying to crush me to him, suffocate me. I was thrown on the ground, wound in the blanket, and could feel his weight settle on me. I bucked my legs up, cursing and clawing at the edges, trying to work myself loose.

I got a hand free and snatched a fistful of hair and heard the vampire scream but was shoved back into the blackness. I bit at his fingers when I found them, never quite getting hold of one, my arms bound and then unbound as I fought my way out of his hold time and again. But he was so fast, so much faster than I had even realized. He seemed to be able to counter anything I tried to do.

Suddenly I was shaken loose, tumbling out of the blanket onto the grass, rolling down a slope. I caught myself in mid-roll and kicked off the ground, throwing my body into the air, landing like a cat on my feet.

I could see the vampire now, standing right in front of me, legs spread, hands on his hips, and . . . *breasts.* The vampire had breasts. It wasn't Wirtz at all. It was a tall, thin girl about Sagan's age with thick auburn hair tied behind her slender neck and wearing a long old-fashioned dress.

There were two others . . . a boy and a girl about my age. They could pass for brother and sister. Both were dressed in black shirts and blue jeans. They both had black hair—the girl's hair a little shorter than the boy's—and the boy was a little taller. They were crouched on either side of the tall girl as if ready to spring if I moved an inch. One of them, the boy, was laughing. . . .

I hurled myself at him. Hit him in the gut full force, hearing a giant *oomph* fly from his throat as his thin body was slammed backward to the ground. I was astride him now, moving so fast he almost couldn't defend himself, pounding my fists into his face, his neck, chest, but mostly his hands as he tried to cover up.

The younger girl came to help. She plowed into my side, bowling me over. But I was stronger than she was and instantly jumped up and smashed the side of her head with my forearm. Now the two of them were down, and I drove my knees into their chests, knocking them flat, and started hitting them some more.

"Enough!" someone yelled, and I felt myself being yanked up in the air by my shirt collar. It was the tallest one, the girl I had mistaken for Wirtz.

I whirled around, aiming to backhand her in the face, but she dropped me at the last moment. I got to my feet, scowling menacingly.

"You want some too?" I said, and lunged.

The older girl sidestepped my charge and slammed me in the back of my neck with the edge of her hand. It felt like being hit by a two-by-four. I collapsed to my knees and she put her foot on me. I twisted beneath her, got my hands on her ankles, and yanked. The taller girl sat hard. Her dress blossomed in the air around her and started to float back down.

We stared at each other. I was breathing fast and had spit in the corner of my mouth. Other than when I was Tasered, it was the first time I had ever been truly tired as a vampire.

. The two younger ones I had been pummeling got up and walked over to us, the girl helping the boy, who had a hand covering one eye. I jumped up, face hot, and crouched, ready to fight. . . .

"I must apologize," the taller girl said, breathing heavily herself, "for frightening you. We . . . were a little frightened ourselves, hearing you shout the way you did. We didn't know what you were doing here. My name is Lena."

Her voice sounded older than she looked. She had long sleeves, though it was plenty warm. Her dress came well past her knees and hung in folds like old curtains. The fabric was ragged along the hem, with dirty dangling threads.

Lena had big green eyes shaped like almonds, a long, smooth neck, a small mouth, and full lips. She looked like someone out of a movie and might have been the most beautiful woman I had ever seen.

"She's strong, Lena, and a fighter," the slightly built guy said.

He was still holding his eye where I had belted him, but smiling. He had straight black hair and the darkest eyebrows I had ever seen. His features and hands and fingers were small, his shoulders narrow. He came forward, taking his hand away from his eye and offering to shake.

"Anton," he said, trying to clasp my hand. I just looked at it. He seemed to have the slightest trace of a foreign accent, but I couldn't place it. His dark eyes were wide and interested. He nodded at the younger girl. "And this is Donne."

The girl named Donne continued to glare at me. She stood protectively close to Anton, still holding his arm. She had dark hair with chopped bangs, a small, pointed nose, and was slightly built as well. Their jeans were ratty with holes and their T-shirts dusty and stained. They could have passed for high school kids except for the fact they had no blue glow.

Their color was lavender.

"Who are you?" I said through my teeth, covering my fear with anger.

"Shouldn't we be asking that question?" said Donne, the younger vampire girl, speaking for the first time. There was nothing unusual about her voice. "Don't you know any better than to trespass on someone else's *Strecke*?"

The word sounded German, but I couldn't place it. Papi was forever scolding me for not taking more of an interest in the language of my ancestors.

"What are you talking about?" I said. "You grabbed me. . . ."

"*Strecke*," the girl said again. "Range. You're trespassing on our range."

"Range? It's a freaking state park."

"The way things are divided by humans in the daylight has nothing to do with us," Donne said.

"What's on your face?" Anton said. He shook off Donne's arm and came a little closer.

"My . . . face?" I put my hand to my cheek and remembered the soot.

"You look as if you have marked yourself for battle, yes?" Anton said. "We saw you climb. When we heard you shouting up there, we thought maybe the war was back on."

"War? What war?" I said. "I was just . . . messing around. I felt like screaming, so I screamed."

"The war between the—"

"Anton," Lena said, lifting her hand. Anton immediately shut up. Lena was obviously the leader.

They were trying to be subtle about it, but I could see that they were separating now, slowly circling me.

"We only wish to know what you are doing here," Lena said.

"Nothing," I said. "I've been coming to this place for years. What are *you* doing here?"

"You are not *Verloren*?"

"Never heard of her." I stayed in my crouch, ready to pick out a target. "And you'd better stop circling me, or one of you is getting trucked." I figured I would smash Anton again and just keep on running.

"*Verloren* is not a person's name," Lena said. She straightened up and lifted her hand. The other two vampires stopped moving. "*Verloren* is a way of thinking. You might call it an absence. An absence of faith."

"Um . . . okay . . . whatever you say." I looked from face to face, stalling for time, trying to figure out what to do next.

"She doesn't understand, Lena," Donne said. "I think she's a Fresh. Look at her color."

"My what?" So I've got a color too?

"You're right," Anton said. He looked me over. "Kind of a wispy blue. Very likely a *neues Blut.*"

"A Freshblood," Lena translated. "Someone who was just recently turned."

"So you really are . . . vampires," I said.

Lena's jaw tightened. "Yes, but we do not use that word very often."

"Too many negative associations, right?" Anton said, smiling.

"You still haven't told us what you're doing in our range," Donne said.

Lena looked at the two younger vampires and again waved her

hand. They went over and sat down on a low stone wall. I began to relax my guard . . . but only a little.

"So . . . if there are three of you here . . . then I'm assuming that means . . . the world is full of vampires," I said.

"Yes. But we try to remain . . . unobtrusive. Most of us," Lena said. She glanced at Anton, who grinned.

"How many?" I said.

"Who would know? Not nearly as many as the daylight men. Only a fraction. Maybe a very small fraction. I don't know of anyone who keeps up with the numbers. If we were to . . . confederate . . . it would make us too visible."

"And it would be seen by the *Verloren* as provocative," Donne said, leaning forward. "I don't think we should be talking to her, Lena. We don't know who she is. What she is . . ."

"What do you mean?" I said. "I'm like you."

"You're not . . . like us." Donne got up and came close to me now, reaching out as if to touch my arm. Instead she held her hand up as if collecting something out of the air. *My color.* "We told you. You're blue. Almost a human blue."

I held my arm up. It wasn't glowing that I could see. *Weird.*

"You can't see your own color," Anton said, starting to laugh. "What did you think?" He got up too and looked at me closely. "Wait just a minute. . . . You're not an *Unschuldig,* are you?"

"What's *Unschuldig*?"

"Oh man," Donne said.

"One who has never hunted," Lena said.

"Never made a kill, you mean," Anton chimed in.

Lena glared in Anton's direction. "It's not a polite word to use. But it has been a very long time since we have spoken with . . . anyone else. Please sit." She indicated the wall again.

Okay, so now I was sitting down with three vampires just like we were friends at school. The thought made my skin crawl. I also noticed that no matter where I was, there was always at least one of them on either side of me.

"How have you done it?" Anton said. He reached over and grabbed my arm. I jerked it away.

"Hey!"

"How have you survived? You look so good, hey? How long has it been since you were turned? You must be completely *blutrünstig* with hunger by now."

I didn't know what to say. I rubbed my arm where he had touched it. . . . His hand had been so . . . smooth. . . .

"It . . . wasn't that long ago," I said.

"And your name is?" He gripped my arm again, scowling a little.

"Cut it out," I said. "I . . . I don't . . ."

"Can't you see she doesn't want to tell you, Anton?" Donne said. "My God. You'd tell your whole life story to a complete stranger."

"Oh no! That's Lena, believe me. Just give her the chance!" Anton said, brightening again.

"I really should leave," I said, standing up. "I'm sorry I stumbled onto your . . . your *Strecke*. I won't come up here after dark anymore." *After dark . . . careful. Don't let them know your secret.*

"Wait," Lena said. "Please, sit with us awhile longer. It would mean very much to us if you were to stay."

Was it some kind of trap? I wondered. Were they working with Wirtz? They didn't seem dangerous, but . . .

"Why? So you can throw another blanket over me?" I said.

"I told you. We were frightened," Lena said. "You never know who may be *Verloren*. Your color is blue, so it is plain you are a *neues Blut*, a Freshblood, perhaps even an *Unschuldig*, as Anton so rudely put it. It is just that it has been . . . so long . . . only the three of us. We will not hurt you, as long as you promise not to hurt us. We are . . . isolated. We can observe the world of . . . people . . . down below, but that only gets one so far. . . . Could you stay for a little while? Tell us something about yourself?"

"I don't really know if I should," I said. "To be honest, I feel like you guys are okay. But there is someone else . . . who can't find me."

"Who?" Anton said.

I wanted to bite my tongue. "I'd rather not talk about it. I've said too much already."

"Let her go, Lena," Donne said. She hadn't smiled once. "I don't care if we are isolated. I don't trust her. She's so fresh. . . . She could go down into the city and tell someone we are here."

"What could she tell?" Anton said. "Three . . . vampires . . . are living at the state park? I'm sure that would bring the policemen running."

"You know what I mean. Maybe she wants to claim this place for herself?" Donne said.

"I have my own place," I said, glaring back at Donne. "I told you, I came here because of my grandfather."

"Does he live here?" Anton said.

"No. But this—this was our favorite place to visit. He helped to build it." I pointed at the stones. "It's always meant a lot to us . . . and I was feeling . . . alone. So I just came up here to see it. Impulsively."

I couldn't quite believe I was sitting there in front of Papi's beloved *Steinhaus* talking to three vampires. But I was so curious, so desperate to have my questions answered.

"Okay . . . what if I do stay a little while," I said. "Do you promise to let me go when I'm ready?"

Lena smiled warmly. "Yes. You have my word on it. But I will leave it up to them. Anton?"

"Sure! I'd love to talk with her some more."

Donne shook her head. "I don't want to take the chance. But I can see you two have already decided to trust her. As usual, I'm out-voted. She can stay."

"Wow, thanks a lot," I said sarcastically.

Lena looked at the younger vampire without saying anything.

"I'm . . . I'm sorry," Donne said. "It's just that we have to be so careful. We don't want to lose this place."

I wanted to dislike her, but I could see some of myself in Donne.

"Hey, I like your name," I said, working hard to smile at her. "Where did you get it?"

"My mother," Donne said. "She was . . . how would you say it . . . you're so fresh—a fan. My mother was a big fan of the poet John Donne."

"*Paradise Lost*, huh?" I said.

"That's Milton," Donne said. "Donne is the guy who wrote 'No man is an island, entire of itself. . . .'"

"Right, right." I remembered, feeling a little embarrassed.

"You still haven't told us your name?" Anton said. Almost everything he said sounded like a question.

"I don't know . . . ," I said.

"We told you ours."

"Okay. It's Emma."

"How old are you, Emma?" Lena said.

"Seventeen," I said.

Lena pulled at her lip. "I was your age, Emma, in . . . let me think . . . 1859."

"Oh my God." Just thinking about it made me start feeling a little dizzy.

Lena's laugh was high and musical. "Wait just one minute! I'm not even two hundred years old yet."

Anton got going again. "At least Donne and I are from the same century, only about twenty years apart. I was my last human age in . . . 1918. Donne in 1938. She is the youngest. We try not to let her forget it, right?" He laughed and nudged Donne with an elbow. She glowered at him. I was struck with the feeling that they were a couple.

"Can I . . . ask you some questions?" I said, feeling a little bolder. "I've tried to read about it . . . a lot of things in books and on the Internet."

"What would you like to know?" Anton said.

"Most of what I have read doesn't seem real. It's just people guessing who don't know what they're talking about. Like, I know we don't disappear in mirrors, for instance. I've seen myself."

"We are physical," Anton said. "So that's purely logical, right? A physical thing reflects light, or you wouldn't be able to see us, correct?"

"And so many other things," I said. "So many inconsistencies. I'm so new to all this and there hasn't been anyone . . . anyone who could tell me anything about it."

They all looked at one another, but didn't say what they were thinking.

"What would you like to know?" Lena said. "We will do our best."

"Um. Do we really . . . live forever?"

"Ah, that would be first," Anton said. "Of course not. We are physical, like I said. We have to stop sometime, don't we?"

"So vampires die of old age?"

Lena turned to look at Anton. "Have you ever heard it?" she said. "A vampire dying of old age?"

"No," Anton said. "That's true. But logic . . ."

"We don't know," Donne said. "That's what they're trying to say. It's something we've all wondered about for generations. If we do age, it's very, very slow. That much is certain."

"We are hopeful," Lena said.

"Hopeful that you'll live forever?" I said.

She shook her head. "Hopeful that we will live long enough."

14. BLOOD HUNT

"Live long enough for what?" I said.

"To experience the *Sonneneruption,*" Lena said.

A feeling seemed to pass through the three of them at once, as if they were all in one body. Ripples moving across a pond.

"*Sonneneruption?*" I said.

"It is a very old word," Lena said. "It describes for us an experience that is the . . . most holy, I suppose you could say it that way. It has been a very long time . . . years, perhaps, since I have even spoken this word out loud. *Sonneneruption* is the holiest word we have."

"What does it mean?" I said. "My grandfather is German. It's another German word, isn't it? I know what *Sonnen* is. *Sonnen* means 'sun,' doesn't it?"

"That is correct," Lena said. "Therefore *Sonneneruption* is exactly what it says . . . an eruption of the sun."

"Like an . . . explosion?"

"You could call it that, though we would say *explosion* would be much too small a word and too . . ."

"Physical," Anton said.

"But . . . an eruption of the sun? How could that not be physical?" I said.

"It is," Lena said. "But it is so much more than that. It is . . . what is the best word?" she said, turning to Donne.

"Spiritual," Donne said. "I would call it spiritual."

"A spiritual event?" I said.

"Yeah," Donne said.

"So what's supposed to happen?" I said. "The sun blows up?"

They all looked at each other as if they were humoring a child.

"The *Sonneneruption* has nothing to do with destruction," Lena said. "It is all about . . . cleansing. That is what you could say about it. Healing, perhaps. It is a glorious time for vampires—as you would call us—all over the world . . . a time of rejoicing. A time we wait for. A time when . . . our agony is over."

"I'm not sure I'm catching all of this," I said. "So . . . this kind of spiritual eruption happens on the sun, and somehow this is a cause for rejoicing for . . . vampires?"

"Well, not all of them," Anton said. "There are some. Quite a few, actually, who are not spiritual, okay? Most of them don't believe in the *Sonneneruption*. Some of them believe in it but feel they are cursed for all eternity."

"There is a madness to many of their kind," Lena said. "We call them the *Verloren*."

"Lost," I said, my sketchy memory of Papi's German kicking in. "*Verloren* means 'lost,' doesn't it?"

"Yes," Lena said. "It is not so much a physical losing as . . . a loss that is . . ." She couldn't seem to find the word, so she touched her heart.

"Spirit? Are you talking about a loss of the spirit?" I said, trying to help.

Lena nodded. "An absence. Loss. Most of the *Verloren* no longer have faith in the *Sonneneruption*. If they ever did. They are the ones we think of as the vampires. The monsters. Many have a malevolence that is bordering on pure evil."

Wirtz, I thought instantly. *They're talking about Wirtz. He's one of the Verloren.*

I wondered if I should tell them about Wirtz. *No. Not yet.*

Lena seemed to go all somber. "Emma, I have not seen the sun in . . . over a century and a half. You can still recall its warmth, the way it felt on your bare shoulders, the way it filled your eyes. The way it made water sparkle. Do you feel it yet, Emma? The eternal loss of the sun? Do you know what that is like? You will."

"So you miss it?" I said. "Miss the sun . . . even though it can kill you?"

"*Sonnen* is the healer," Lena said. "That is what is so misunderstood. We could step out into the sunlight tomorrow, and the healing would begin."

I gulped a little, thinking of Wirtz. "So, that's just a myth? About the sun killing us?"

"Oh, it's true," Donne said. "It'll kill you, all right. Surely you're smart enough to know that. Just try it sometime."

I tried it just today, I thought. But something told me to hold back on that information too.

"*Sonnen* . . . it is a two-edged sword," Lena said. "If you go out into the daylight, yes, you will die. Not because it is harmful—but because it is not enough. What is in regular sunlight, the healing within it . . . it comes too slowly, in too small amounts to be of any use. Too small a dose is damaging."

"It's too gradual," Donne said. "Some of the good stuff is in the sunlight, but . . . it's not enough. Not fast enough. So that there's no protection from the bad. The bad parts of the sun eat away at you much more rapidly than the good repairs you. In normal daylight."

"But during the *Sonneneruption,* it comes all at once, okay?" Anton said. "The healing. There's something more in the sun than just ordinary light."

"It is a substance all its own," Lena said. "But only during the *Sonneneruption* does it come quickly enough to perform the Cleansing. Cleansing the body of the . . . *Infektion* . . ."

"Infection?" I said. "So you mean . . . there's a cure for vampirism?" All three of them flinched when I said it.

"The *Sonneneruption* is the Cleansing," Lena said. "It drives the infection away."

I felt a pulse of pure cold electricity in my chest. *A cure. Sagan* . . . "So there's a chance we can be . . . human again?"

"That is how we believe," Lena said. "The *Verloren,* on the other hand . . ."

"But . . . the *Sonneneruption* . . . wouldn't it cure them too?" I said. "Wouldn't it cure vampires everywhere?"

"Yes," Anton said. "Do the math. Vampires, as you call us, would have long ago overrun the earth if not for periodic *Sonneneruptions.*"

"How often do they happen?" I said.

"The frequency is difficult to predict," Lena said. "They do not come at regular intervals. The last occurred when I was about your age, which was, as I said, in 1859. I was still human then. It came during the night in my part of the world. All were cured except for those who remained belowground for the duration. The *Verloren.* I was turned three years after the *Sonneneruption* by one of them."

I got up and stood away from the wall, facing them. "So you're saying the bad ones . . . the *Verloren* . . . they missed the boat, so they're bitter? And they take it out on the rest of us."

"Who knows what they think?" Donne said angrily. "They think about themselves and no one else."

"The only way they were ever able to confederate was briefly through their collective anger," Lena said.

"Was that the war?" I said.

Lena glanced at Anton, who looked as if he was about to speak. "The war," she said. She smiled a sad little smile. "If it could even be called that."

All of them were quiet for a little while. Then Donne spoke up.

"Why don't we just build a campfire and roast marshmallows?" she said. "Sitting here talking like this . . . is wasting time."

"Time is running out for you?" Lena said, smiling.

"Not running out for me, running out for the *Unschuldig*," Donne said, pointing at me. "She needs to feed."

"Well," Lena said. "I thought you were being impatient, Donne, and instead you were being wise. Please forgive me. And thank you." She turned to me. "Emma. Donne is exactly right. My manners . . . You should feed right away. You are not yet experienced enough to fast."

"Wait a minute," I said, slowly catching on to what they were saying. "You mean . . ."

Anton stood and clapped delightedly. "Good! We get to take you on your very first *Blutjagd*."

"What's that?" I said, feeling nervous.

"Blood Hunt."

Anton took me by the arm. Again I noticed how strangely smooth his skin was.

"It's so much better your first time if someone experienced goes with you," he said. He was genuinely excited at the idea.

Donne got up as well. "I'm not looking forward to it, taking along someone new," she said. She stared at me. "Nothing against you, Emma, only the risk factor goes way up when you're out with someone who doesn't know what they're doing. But I don't like thinking of you going alone. And besides, I need it myself."

"You're not . . . you're not saying what I think you're saying, are you?" I said.

"Of course!" Anton said. "The more the merrier. What about you, Lena, huh?"

"She's still fasting," Donne said.

"Oh, right," Anton said. He looked at me as if to explain. "Lena is amazing. I've never seen anyone who can go without it as long as she can."

"Don't be modest," Lena said. She nodded at Anton. "We all fast at one time or another, Emma. It is part of our . . . way. I suppose you could put it like that. Part of life as a *Sonnen*. We control the hunger, not the other way around. We use our faith and our will. It takes practice, but in time it is manageable." She glanced at Anton. "Don't stay down there too long. . . . Daybreak."

"Don't worry. We'll be quick. Come on," Anton said, taking my hand and pulling me along. "We'll show you exactly how it's done, okay? There are few things in life more thrilling than a *Blutjagd* with morning coming on."

I let myself be tugged away from the Stone House, thoughts flying. The first thing I realized was that we weren't heading in the direction of the road; we were starting down the mountainside through the woods. Within seconds I could no longer see Lena, only the stone blocks against the darker trees. In no time we were running.

This can't be happening, I thought. I was about to go down into Huntsville to drink some poor victim's blood?

"Wait," I said. "Stop, please. I don't think I'm ready for this."

Anton laughed. "Oh! You're ready, all right. You should have seen me my first time. I don't know what I would've done without Lena! I was terrified, if you want to know the truth."

"But . . . how can I . . . I can't," I said.

"You can," Donne said. Her eyes flashed at me. "If you won't, then . . . well, we'll know, won't we?"

"Know what?"

"That you aren't a friend. You might be afraid for us to watch how you feed. That could give you away. . . . You may even be a spy for the *Verloren*."

"Nonsense," Anton said with a laugh. "It's painfully obvious, is it not, she is no spy."

"Shut up, Anton," Donne said.

They both took my hands this time and we flew down the mountainside. As we ran, I concocted ridiculous plans in my head, ways of ditching them. Or maybe even preventing them from killing.

All too soon the trees were thinning and the ground began to even out. Then we were passing houses built into the rocky foothills. I could see streetlights ahead, an older neighborhood. They let go of my hands and we slowed to a gentle speed, still much faster than human walking, moving like quicksilver along the roads. Everything dead still because of the hour. Windows dark, porch lights out.

"There's a trick to maintaining a *Strecke*," Donne said quietly. "The hunting is tougher at this time of night. There just aren't that many people around. But that's why we choose it. The people who are out and about after midnight tend to be a different kind. Most of the time they're unattached. Young. Living by themselves."

"Or they're older, right?" Anton said. "Without many friends or no friends at all. Doing the lonely kind of night jobs people like that do. People who don't want to be around people."

"Or people who are so different—they don't want people to see how different they are," Donne said. "People like that are much less likely to give us away. And we spread it around. Different streets, different neighborhoods. Parts of town where unexplained things can happen but are rarely questioned."

I felt a little chill moving through me, listening to them talk about people . . . people we were about to attack. I thought about Sagan. . . . He was a late-night person, wasn't he? And there was nothing strange or lonely about him. That was just the hours available to do the job he loved doing. What about his family? What if the vampires took someone, one of his sisters, say. What then?

"That's why the *Verloren* always have to be on the move," Anton said. "They don't care how they do it."

"Oh, they care," Donne said. "They care about not getting caught. But Anton is right. The *Verloren* tend to be nomads, moving through the rural areas and from town to town, but in the city it's always the darkest, most violent places where they tend to feed. Places where awful things are expected. We—the *Sonnen*—might even outnumber them. But it always takes more good people to handle the evil ones. Because the evil ones don't live by any rules. Shhh!"

We saw movement up ahead. While they were talking, the older neighborhood had given way to small, funky businesses . . . used-book shops, health food stores, restaurants that served dishes made out of stuff like tofu and soy.

I could see the person Donne was watching now. An older guy filling a newspaper rack with the morning paper. Nobody else anywhere around, not a single light. He looked to be about as old as my principal, maybe late fifties. The man was wearing a blue jacket even though it wasn't close to cold. We were still several hundred feet away, but I could hear him cough into his hand.

I tried to think of something to say, anything that might stop them. I was horrified at the thought of fighting them while they tried to attack the poor guy.

"But . . . what if the person . . . is sick or something? What if they have some deadly virus?" I said. "Won't we catch it?"

This time both of the vampires laughed. "You truly are an *Unschuldig*," Anton said. "I haven't been on a hunt like this in a while. This is going to be fun!"

"They are the ones who have to worry about *Infektion*, don't you think?" Donne said. "You think you're the first person who has ever wondered about that? As if a human virus could do anything to us."

I had to ask it. "You said you don't know if we die of natural causes. Can we . . . be killed?"

"By the hundreds," Anton said. "During the war—"

"Of course we can die," Donne said, giving him a look. "We're living beings, not the undead. That's crap."

"Take out the heart or other vital organs, chop off the head, sever the body in half, there are plenty of ways," Anton said. "It's tough to do, but it's done all the time. But we should be concentrating. I'm hungry."

He drew back his lips at the thought, but I didn't see anything that looked like razor-sharp fangs.

I did what they were doing, studied the newspaper guy. He would open each rack, toss the leftover papers, stick in new ones, then let the whole thing bang shut. He was very focused, head down. An easy target. There didn't seem to be any possibility of him escaping; I saw a car, a little white Toyota, sitting up the street a ways, smoke coming out of its tailpipe. *Too far away for him to reach it in time,* I thought. I could feel both Anton and Donne tensing up the closer we came.

"Wait, come on," I said. "So we're just going to rush him and rip his throat out? This is insane. . . ."

They were concentrating so hard, they didn't seem to hear me.

A bunch of different thoughts crashed through my head . . . take them both on, they were smaller than me . . . yell something at the guy, tell him to get in his car . . . but I knew realistically he wouldn't make it three steps.

Or—my least favorite option—just run away, take off. Anton and Donne would never catch me. Starting on equal terms, I was ten times the athlete either of them was. Besides, they were hungry, needed to eat.

Yet what was I supposed to do, just let the man die? But . . . they had to do this probably every day, right? If I saved one life . . . what then? They would just go after somebody else. Thinking this way was driving me crazy. And all the while we were getting closer and closer. The man was banging each box down, moving on to the next, completely oblivious.

When we were only about fifty feet away, Donne stopped, crouching behind the corner of a little diner. "Are you ready?" she said to Anton.

Anton reached into his pocket and pulled something out. A little gold and white squeeze tube.

"I wouldn't forget. Not after last time," he said.

It was Donne's turn. She produced something I didn't recognize that was small and thin and metallic, like a silver pencil. Also a square of folded white cloth and a small brown bottle with a rubber stopper and no label. She splashed a little of the liquid from the bottle onto the cloth and clenched it in her small fist. It gave off a pungent—yet somehow sweet—aroma.

"Hey, what are you—"

I was never able to finish. Both of the vampires sprang at the newspaper man.

*   *   *

I say sprang, but they moved so gracefully, so soundlessly, it was more like watching swans skimming a lake than tigers pouncing. I could only call their movements beautiful, not deadly or monstrous or even threatening. It didn't feel like an attack; it felt like a dance.

Sagan, you would not believe this, I thought.

I followed along. Anton and Donne flung their bodies out in opposite directions, springing and bounding, sailing ten feet or more in the air. Then they touched lightly down on one foot and sprang again, as if closing the last corner of a triangle.

The old newspaper guy never knew what hit him. He didn't hear their approach and was leaning over jerking out a bunch of leftover papers when the vampires landed behind him. Anton took him first, pulling the man's arms down and pinning them to his sides. I rushed toward them, bracing myself mentally for Donne's attack, falling on the man's throat with her teeth, tearing him apart.

It didn't happen that way. Instead Donne reached around the man's shoulders while Anton continued to hold him and placed the wet folded cloth over his face, covering his nose and mouth.

I couldn't see the newspaper guy's face, but I could imagine his eyes going wide with terror for a moment. I don't believe he ever saw either of the vampires. His body jerked silently two or three times, and when Anton turned him around, the man's body went slack and his eyes were already closed. The vampires gently lowered him to the pavement.

Anton cradled the newspaper man's head in his lap as Donne pulled the guy's right arm out of his jacket sleeve, then stretched the collar of his T-shirt over to reveal a pale, smooth neck and shoulder. *Here it comes,* I thought, standing over them, dumbstruck.

Now Donne took the little pencil-like object she had been

holding in her left hand and drew a two-inch line across the top of the man's shoulder. Only it wasn't a pencil or a pen. It was some kind of knife—an X-acto.

The man didn't move or even groan as the warm blood welled up like red beads along the thin incision she had made. I actually saw Anton licking his lips. Donne let him go first. He lowered his head to the man's shoulder and began to drink in a way that looked like a passionate kiss.

I was surprised that he only drank for maybe twenty seconds. Then it was Donne's turn, and she drank in the same way, like a kiss. A way of feeding that was so delicate, so gentle, so completely the opposite of the brutal, violent way the monster Wirtz had torn at my leg. I was speechless. Donne saw me watching.

"This one is not for you, Fresh," she said.

She also spent less than a minute drinking. Her eyes rolled back in her head and then she shut them. It was over almost as soon as it was beginning. She lifted her head away from the cut, and there wasn't even a trace of blood on her mouth. She could have been giving the guy a hickey for all I could tell.

It was clear they were finished now. But instead of leaving the man and fleeing, Donne blotted the wound with a cloth and then Anton applied a little squirt of antiseptic from the white tube, which he rubbed in gently with his finger until the bleeding stopped. Anton replaced the man's jacket and they carefully carried him over to the sidewalk and set him down easily with his arm crooked beneath his head.

I felt as if I had landed on an alien world . . . that I was seeing something that went on all over the earth with all of us humans completely unaware.

"Now what?" I said.

"We wait," Donne said. "And watch."

She and Anton pulled me around beside a small building. We watched the man as he lay motionless on the concrete. "What did you use to knock him out?" I whispered.

"Ether," Donne said. "You can use chloroform too, but neither of them are easy to get unless you are close to a university."

"But how do you know how much to give him?" I said.

"You do it a few hundred times, you'll know," Donne said, again acting like I was a little dense.

"So . . . what are we waiting for now?"

"To make sure he's okay," Donne said.

"You're messing with me," I said. "You just drank the guy's blood . . . and now you're going to hang around and see if he's okay?"

187

"Yeah," Donne said. "Sometimes there can be . . . a reaction. Also, he is defenseless."

"What kind of creatures of darkness are you?" I said, almost wanting to smile.

"We're human beings," Donne said grimly. "Doing the best we can."

The newspaper guy groaned and sat up. We slipped away into the shadows.

"Okay . . . now what?"

"Now we do it all over again."

The next victim was a huge woman waddling out to the mostly empty parking lot at Walmart. We left her behind the wheel of her pickup and waited until she came to, coughing and looking dazed. "She must work in the bakery," Anton said, smacking his lips. "She tastes of flour." The third was a guy sitting alone playing on the Internet in a little guard shack out beside an industrial plant. They didn't even have to move him from his seat.

In each case Donne said the same thing: "This one is not for you." *Whew*, I thought. *I'm not complaining.*

I felt guilty even though Anton and Donne couldn't have been more kind . . . which I know is a weird word to use in conjunction with two vampires slicing someone open with an X-Acto. But I couldn't help feeling that they sincerely cared about their victims and did everything they could to minimize the damage, psychological or otherwise.

"But . . . don't they wonder who knocked them out? How they got cut?" I said.

"I'm sure they do," Anton said. "Unless they're drunk or otherwise incapacitated."

"But wouldn't they . . . report it to somebody the next day?"

"And what would you say to the police?" Donne said. "'I woke up with this paper cut on my shoulder.'" She laughed derisively.

I thought of the vampire bats feasting on the pig.

"What about . . . animals?"

"Doesn't work," Anton said. "Too far removed on the family tree, okay?"

"Okay . . . hospitals? Blood banks?" I said. "Couldn't you . . . couldn't we . . . eat there?"

"Believe me, we've heard all the jokes," Anton said. "Hello, sir! So this is a blood bank? I vant to make a withdrawal, please."

"The blood is no good," Donne said, frowning at Anton. "Oh, it's all right to use on humans. But it's not really . . . alive . . . anymore. We would quickly starve if we tried to live on it."

"So . . . a vampire can starve? To death?"

"Well, technically, we don't know what would happen if you carried it all the way to the end. And I sure don't want to find out."

"You said Lena was in the middle of a fast. . . ."

"That's right," Anton said. "She's incredible. Her willpower. Strength. I couldn't stand it, not that long. She can go for weeks."

"It's part of being *Sonnen,*" Donne said. "We didn't ask for this. Fasting is one way of keeping our dignity. Keeping our way of life separate from that of the blood-gorgers."

"The *Verloren,*" I said.

"Yeah."

The last guy we picked was a lot younger than the others and several miles away. His car was parked at a convenience store, and we waited until he had gotten his cheese curls and soda, then followed him as he drove back to his apartment complex.

It was thrilling keeping up with the car, running full tilt through yards, dodging around obstacles, hopping over fire hydrants and dogs, then flinging ourselves into the shadows whenever he turned or otherwise might see us. It more than satisfied my need for speed and the frenzied animal joy of the chase I had been missing since getting kicked off the soccer team. It was wrong that we were stalking the poor guy, but it didn't feel wrong. . . . It felt exhilarating. Like fulfilling every adventurous kid's nighttime dream of being able to chase a car through darkened streets.

Anton and Donne took the guy just as he turned the key in his apartment door. We caught him as he slumped into the doorway and hustled his inert body to the couch. They didn't seem worried, but I took a second to glance around just to make sure nobody else was home.

The sink was full of about a week's worth of dishes, and the table and parts of the floor were covered with wadded-up clothes. There were empty beer cans everywhere. Natty Light and Natty Ice. The apartment had a sour guy smell.

Anton and Donne were content to just leave the door open, but it felt weird, so I closed it behind us.

"Hurry up," I said.

It didn't take that long. They had the guy propped up on the couch, ready to go, when . . .

Donne lifted her head from the young guy's shoulder and, wiping her mouth with her forearm, looked at me.

"Your turn."

15. THEIR WORLD

I swore. "You're not serious."

"It's a little strange the first time," Anton said. "But you have to start somewhere, okay? We saved the best for last. The best for you. There's no reason to be nervous. As a Fresh you shouldn't be taking in so much on your first time. . . . It's best not to . . . gorge yourself early on. Look how easy we have made it for you. It's as private as you're ever going to get it. You will never make an easier . . . kill."

"What's wrong, Emma?" Donne said, eyeballing me suspiciously. "You have to be just about crazy hungry by now. Watching us feed."

Moment of truth time. I knew I wasn't ready to tell them about my scrambled status as a vampire. I needed to save that until I knew for sure it was okay. But if I refused to drink or just ran away, that would be even worse—that's all I needed, three more vampires for enemies. I wasn't comfortable with any of my options.

There was another. *I could drink.*

The mere thought of it horrified and disgusted me. Drink his blood? All warm and wet and oozy? My lips sucking at the skin of a strange guy's shoulder?

I had to decide something quickly or Donne would likely turn on me.

"Okay," I said. "Just give me a second." I knelt while Anton stretched the guy's shirt away from the pearling wound. *Think. You could just pretend. . . .*

"Just to let you know, I'm going to be watching you closely, *Unschuldig.*" Donne said the German word almost sarcastically, as if she didn't believe it. "If you are *Verloren,* I'll know it."

"If I'm *Verloren,* I would have already broken your skinny neck," I said, getting a little sick of her attitude.

"We'll see."

"Why the shoulder?" I said. "Some spiritual *Sonnen* reason?"

"Who wants a paper cut on their neck?" Donne said.

Anton was laughing.

"Oh, shut up," Donne said, kicking at him halfheartedly. She looked at me. *"Now."*

I leaned forward. . . . I could already smell the scent of the young guy's skin. . . . It wasn't entirely unpleasant. . . . In spite of the condition his apartment was in, he seemed clean.

"What about the . . . infection?" I said. "Won't he become a vampire? I thought you had to kill them to keep them from turning. . . ."

Donne looked like she wanted to spit. "That's for those animals. The *Verloren.* They have no control over their hunger. They drink so much, the greedy pigs . . . they leave themselves no choice but to kill. Or churn out more stupid Freshbloods like you. I told you, *Sonnen* are dignified. Civilized. We never take more than a little from each . . . person. Never nearly enough to turn them. Don't worry, if you start to gorge yourself, we won't let you go too far. Quit stalling."

My mouth was very close now. *Get it over with, Emma.*

I put my lips to the cut.

I knew what blood tasted like, of course. You can't play sports without having your lip shredded. I'd heard it described as "salty" or "coppery" or even "metallic." To me it was none of those. I didn't know what to call the taste. I just knew it tasted "foreign"—

definitely not something that was supposed to be running down my throat.

I kept my tongue curled deep in my mouth. Okay, so far I was keeping my supper down and managing not to show how awful this was. *Just pretend,* I thought, starting to count the seconds. *That's all.*

"I'm watching," Donne warned. "I'll be able to tell if you're swallowing or not. So you better get to it."

Oh my God. She means it.

Almost immediately the blood began to flow, as if the motion of my throat had created a vacuum. Warm, vile stickiness began to creep onto my tongue. Slowly my mouth started to fill with the stuff. Second moment of truth. Either I was going to have to spit it out all over Donne's feet, or . . .

I pinched up my face and swallowed. And kept swallowing. Now I suddenly tasted something familiar . . . but it wasn't a taste so much as a smell masquerading as one.

Beer! The guy has been drinking beer. I could taste it in his blood.

"Ulp!" I said, hiccuping sickeningly, feeling my whole insides convulse. I pulled my mouth away just in time. . . . Another few seconds and I would have vomited.

I hacked and sputtered while Anton laughed hysterically. I wanted to bust him in the face and came close to doing it until Donne grabbed my fist in her small hands, looking at me apologetically. And showing a rare smile.

"I'm sorry, Emma, but we had to know. I'm satisfied. You are so Fresh! There's no hiding it. I hope you got enough. He won't be under much longer. We should go."

I could still taste the greasy beer-smelling blood sliding down my throat into my stomach. *My stomach!* I immediately thought of my visit to Wirtz's mind, the dying woman's blood gushing down my gullet. *Ulp*. A wave of nausea hit me again, and I pushed myself away from the boy on the couch. I came to a standing position and took several long breaths through my nose until I felt a little better.

"Let's get out of here," I grumbled, and headed to the door while they bundled away my breakfast.

I felt better outside in the night, but the lingering effects of my "feeding" kept me wobbly. Anton got a kick out of watching my cheeks bulge every time I fought to keep from puking. They helped me make my way unsteadily back up the mountain.

I wondered what time it was. Then I remembered Sagan's gift and pulled out my pocket watch: 3:49 a.m. Not a lot of night left. Which got me to wondering where the *Sonnen* went during the day.

"That was so good," Anton said, and I wasn't sure if he was talking about feeding or the joy of setting me up.

"You knew that guy had been drinking, didn't you?" I said, trying to pass off my sickness as a distaste for beer.

"Oh! You should have seen what they did to me!" Anton said. "No beer, ha . . . whiskey! A drunk in an alley. Be thankful we looked around until we found someone . . . better."

He grinned so broadly and looked so silly and innocent with his black hair falling across his eyes that it kept me from beating him senseless.

"I thought you said Lena helped you through your first Blood Hunt?" I said, wiping my lips for the dozenth time.

"I'm sorry. I lied, okay?" Anton said. "The one who took me . . . He was a real *Arschloch*."

"*Arschloch*?"

"You don't want to know," Donne said.

"Think Chaucer," Anton said, laughing. "The 'nether eye.'"

"Whatever. So both of you were just jerking me around," I said. "All that 'this one is not for you' crap."

Donne didn't say anything, just frowned.

"Ho! Just wait till you get on her bad side," Anton said, winking. "Don't take it too hard, huh?"

The higher we climbed, the better I felt. Soon we were racing along again, bounding through the trees effortlessly. *I've got a guy's blood in my stomach,* I thought, over and over. *I drank his blood.* The strangeness of the thought was impossible to shake from my head.

"Were you . . . successful?" Lena said when we got back to the Stone House Hotel.

She had spread out the blanket they had used to capture me and was lying on her back with her eyes closed. For the first time I noticed her feet: they were small and so pale, if I hadn't had vampire eyes, it would have been difficult to tell she had toenails. Her shoes were leaning against the wall: small black lace-ups with rubber soles, like something you might wear on a boat.

"You should have seen her face!" Anton said. He smiled at me. "Green as grass, isn't she, Donne?"

Donne didn't reply, just stepped over and fell on the blanket next to Lena. "Why do I always get so sleepy after feeding?" she said, yawning.

Speaking of green, Lena opened her startling eyes and sat up. "Because it is nearly time for sleep. The sun will be rising soon."

"Where do you . . . live?" I said, very curious, but wondering if I was being impolite. "During the daylight, I mean."

Lena glanced at Donne. "What do you think?"

"I think . . . she's fine, Lena," Donne said. "You have never seen a more delicate drinker. She could teach us a thing or two about abstaining."

"It was the beer," I said, quick to remind them of my excuse. "I'll do better next time."

"The hunger is something we cannot control," Lena said. "But . . . no matter how many years you do it, the drinking is still an unnatural act. For we are still humans."

"So where do you sleep?"

They got to their feet, and I helped the three of them with the blanket. In some ways, it was the oddest experience of the night: three vampires and one half-vampire girl standing in the burned-out ruins of an old hotel and doing the most domesticated of acts: folding a blanket. It struck me as strangely comforting—how four people from completely different time periods each handled the blanket exactly the same way, folding it in halves and walking toward each other until we met. *Some things never change, I guess.*

We started into the woods behind the *Steinhaus,* skirting a small brook that tinkled over a long curved bluff face. I could hear the water striking on rocks below, and the path trended gradually downhill.

After all the excitement, it dawned on me. *I know someone born before the Civil War.* The tiny hairs on the back of my neck stood on end. . . . I could ask her questions and get firsthand accounts of things no non-vampire human being had ever seen. Well, that was alive to ask, anyhow. Where to start? I practically swooned at the possibilities.

We didn't walk far. The trail circled around to a place that brought us down in front of the little waterfall. A few feet away there was a long, overhanging ledge. Lena and the others ducked beneath the ledge. It went farther back under the lip of the mountain than I realized. It wasn't exactly a cave. . . .

"I would not live in a large cave," Lena said. "Not with the possibility of missing the next *Sonneneruption*."

A long shoulder of stone protruded from the wall. Lena lifted her dress above her knees as we crawled forward on hand and foot. We came to a place where a stone was wedged into an opening—moving it would be way beyond human strength. It looked like a dead end. Lena and the others dug their fingers into the dirt beneath the stone and hauled it out, revealing another low opening just wide enough to get our bodies through.

They replaced the boulder behind us. I thought about spiders and cave crickets, but the low ceiling quickly opened into a broad room with a ceiling tall enough to stand. At the far end of the room I could plainly see a long notch like a natural window opening onto the rest of the forest. To my super-eyes the light was nearly as bright as day, though I knew from checking my watch that sunrise was still at least an hour or so away.

"You can't see the notch in the wall from the outside," Anton said, walking over to it. "It's too high up, and it curves into the stone face of the mountain, right? It's our lookout place."

"Doesn't the sun ever shine through?" I said.

"No." He pulled a cord next to the opening and a thick rug unrolled down the wall, blocking out the night. The room filled with the lavender glow of the vampires' bodies. "We always leave it open after dark," Anton said, rolling the blanket back up. "We don't want to miss the next *Sonneneruption*."

"We live our lives outdoors as much as possible," Lena said. "It is another part of the *Sonnen* way of life. Besides, where else could we stay? The *Verloren*, always on the move, must constantly find new living quarters, most often in abandoned buildings lost in the wilderness—a blanket of fresh earth covering most of their bodies—or deep in the bowels of the city. Underground. Below concrete structures, whatever they can find. You will find shelter is one of the most difficult parts of our predicament, Emma."

"But in books and movies, vampires—I mean, people like us—they're always showing them in huge old houses or castles," I said. "Lots of times they're rich."

"Impossible," Lena said. "Think about it, Emma. We cannot own homes or land because we have no history."

"No social security numbers, no birth certificates, work records, fixed addresses, none of that, hey?" Anton said. "Even if we had those things, imagine trying to carry out all your business transactions after dark?"

"What they're trying to say is, Emma, that stuff you see in the movies, read in the books . . . the glamour, the romance, fabulous clothes . . ." Donne's voice trailed away. She stuck three fingers through a hole in her jeans and gave a nasty little laugh. "I had to steal these, and it's not getting any easier."

"No clotheslines anymore, huh?" Anton said, touching Donne's arm affectionately.

"I've got a social security number," I said.

"Sure you do," Donne said. "It's useless to you now."

I felt a tinge of sadness in her words and thought of all the things I had always taken for granted: cooked food, shelter, utensils, hot water for bathing. . . . The list went on and on.

"We do not mix with them often," Lena said. "The ones down . . . below." She lifted the hem of her tattered dress. "Anywhere we go, there is a constant danger of exposure. Here at least we have a warning because it is so easy to detect someone advancing on our home."

Home.

Lena lit an oil lamp. "I like it for the memory of the sun," she explained.

I looked more closely at the room. There were three mismatched chairs, all sitting at awkward angles because of the unevenness of the floor, and a small wooden table. Several battered cardboard boxes were grouped in a corner; the one on top was open and a threadbare sweatshirt and some white socks that had gone gray were spilling out. There was a smaller plastic bin that contained things like hand sanitizer, more gauze and antiseptics, baby shampoo, soap, and little metal tools that I couldn't identify. A large jug of water sat against one wall. Three sleeping pallets were arranged on raised frames of saplings with cushions for pillows. And against one wall flat planks served as shelves for . . . *books?*

I stooped to look, interested to know what a vampire would read.

"Anthony Adverse?"

"Don't look at me," Donne said, nodding at Lena. "She's the bookworm." She yawned again, pointedly. "I'd rather be . . . sleeping."

The books were thick and old, with white Dewey decimal stickers on their spines.

"So they give out library cards to vampires?" I said.

"Easiest to steal," Donne said, looking slightly offended.

"I deny this!" Anton said. "I'm no thief. They wanted to give me a library card. But only if I signed my name . . . in blood." He burst into peals of stupid laughter.

"Nobody else thinks you're a bit funny," Donne said. She crooked her arm around his neck. "But we love him anyway, don't we?" She kissed him briefly on the mouth.

I felt like an intruder watching them. Did they share a bed? I couldn't help thinking of Sagan.

"So how long have you been here?" I said to break the awkwardness.

Donne and Lena exchanged glances. "I honestly do not know," Lena said. "Perhaps three or four years? That is why I prefer the longer books. What else am I to do? When time is relatively . . . meaningless . . . you stop marking it."

"Except for sunup," Donne said. "Cutting it a little close, aren't you, Emma? Where are you staying? Don't you have somewhere to go?"

Lena looked at me. "You are welcome to share our home for the day, if you like. You are welcome to my bed. I was going to do some reading anyhow."

Donne frowned.

"Thanks, but I've got a place," I said, taking the hint. "It's . . . not real far away. It won't take me long to get there." I turned to Anton and Donne. "Thanks so much for taking me on my first . . . what did you call it?"

"*Blutjagd,*" Anton said. "You're welcome. It was fun. Thank you for not getting too angry at us, huh?" He kissed Donne again as if trying to shut her mouth before she said something snarky.

I knew I should go, but so many questions were broiling in my mind.

"Why do you use so many German words?" I said.

"It depends on the region," Lena said. "If you travel farther south, down into Florida, the words tend to be Spanish. In Louisiana and parts of Mississippi, French. It just so happens that

German tended to predominate here. I myself have a French background, but it all depends on what was being spoken in your area at the time of the last *Sonneneruption*. The last Cleansing. I would think that many of the old words would go away following the next one. Except among the *Verloren,* of course."

Lena settled into one of the chairs with a book, kicking her shoes off and folding her legs beneath her.

"Can I . . . can I come back? Can I see you again?" I said.

She lifted her emerald eyes from the book and smiled. "I will leave that up to you. But I am hoping so much that you will! It has been . . . a very long time for us."

"There are so many things I want to ask," I said. "The war. How you live. What you have been doing all this time." *Oh please, God. Especially that.*

"Good. Then I am hopeful you will join us," Lena said, and went back to her book.

Join us? Come live with them? I thought. And then I understood.

She wants me to become one of the *Sonnen.*

201

16. ERUPTION

On the way down the mountain, my thoughts were racing almost as fast as my legs. Mostly about how much I wanted Sagan to be able to meet my new friends. Which was completely insane. *Hi, this is Sagan, please don't eat him,* I thought, laughing to myself. He didn't even know about me yet. And I wondered, how would the *Sonnen* react? Was it even possible for vampires to be friends with someone who basically represented a midnight snack to them? Someone . . . normal?

Donne wouldn't like it if she heard me say that. I was hardly normal myself. I felt an overpowering sadness about how they were forced to live. Like animals. *No, insects.* Insects that came out at night to bite you and suck your blood. And how could anyone spend years in that grungy little room?

I was blazing around a hard, sloping curve, turning it all over in my mind, when a possible answer to both problems came to me: *Hey, that's the perfect idea,* I thought. Maybe Sagan could come up with a better place for the *Sonnen* to live? Somewhere out on the Space Center! We could help them, earn their trust, really get to know them. Then . . .

Oh God.

I didn't see that there was something in the road ahead because the long turn vanished into the trees. A police car was angled across one lane of traffic, its blue strobes flashing crazily. Another cop car was parked farther down. In between the two was a small green Honda that was missing a big chunk of its front end. A young guy in a T-shirt and shorts was sitting on the shoulder, head between his knees.

I say I didn't see it, but suddenly I did. I saw all of it in an instant of bright photographic detail, a microsecond before I hit the first car.

Spzzzt! Spzzzt!

Even before I opened my eyes, I knew I was in pain. A strange hissing noise was coming from somewhere close by. I was lying on something hard—I could tell that much too. Where?

I was under a scratchy blanket that had been pulled up to my shoulders. Something lumpy was beneath my head. I finally managed to turn slightly and felt my heart thump: I was stretched out on the pavement not too far away from the first cop car. The driver's door was heavily dented and skid marks showed where the car had bucked sideways several feet. But at least it was still resting on all four tires. My vampire reflexes must've kicked in at the last moment—as fast as I had been traveling, it's a wonder I hadn't rolled the vehicle over.

I could see the legs of people coming and going, could hear the wail of an ambulance in the distance. A police radio kept spraying out little bursts of crackly voices.

Spzzzt! "Monte Sano Boulevard." *Spzzzt!* "Two vehicles. EMTs en route." *Spzzzt! Spzzzt!*

The first cop, the one whose car I had rocked, was sitting in the front seat, hunched over something, arms moving. Probably writing on one of those steel clipboards. I could see his face clearly, head tilted in concentration. Above that I could see the blue strobes of the bubble gum lights cycling back and forth.

I ran my hands over myself under the blanket. I felt pretty much

203

okay, except for a sharp twinge in my right elbow. I must've thrown my forearm up at the last moment to shield myself from the crash. I tried sitting up, then lay right back down: the inside of my skull felt like an oily lump of pizza dough sliding around in a ceramic bowl.

Okay, rest a minute, let your head settle, I told myself.

My eyes focused on the flashing lights, the angry blue roaming back and forth like a neon finger on piano keys. I stared at the lights, feeling their intensity pounding the backs of my eyes. But instead of causing pain, they were making me feel . . . *Comfortable. So comfortable. Just rest,* I told myself. *Rest a minute. Then you can run. . . .*

Wirtz was standing next to me.

"*Sehr gut,*" the vampire said in his earthquake voice. "Very good."

At first I couldn't look at him, it was so hard to tear my eyes from the comfort of the blue lights. But then I did, and now I was looking up the length of his body at his awful smirking mouth. But he was staring at something else. One of the cop cars.

"Huntsville city police," Wirtz said. "So you ran away from home. I expected it." His shoulders rose as he heaved a heavy sigh. "You ran because you would rather save her, the little one, than save yourself."

Manda, he's talking about Manda, I thought.

"And now you are hiding somewhere in Huntsville, Ala-ba-ma. You have made quite a mistake, wouldn't you say, *Mädchen*?"

Can't you see him! I wanted to yell at the cops. *He's standing right there!*

I tried to move, but I couldn't. I was paralyzed again. The air around my body felt like foam rubber, encasing me within its grip. I wanted to cry out, to accuse him. "I know what you are! *Verloren.*"

"Oh, do not worry," Wirtz said. "No speeches tonight. I am not in the mood to implore. It is beyond that. It is plain you will not come to my Call. I have what I need. For now." He gestured at the police car. "Please go with them, if you like. It would make it so much easier for me to find you. But truly I don't care one way or the other. I'm coming, and I will so much enjoy the end of it, either way you choose."

At last I managed to get my arm out from under the blanket. Swung my fist at him. My hand passed through his leg. The vampire had dissolved.

I sloughed off the blanket and sat up. This time my head was feeling better. One of the cops noticed and came over. He had a thick porn 'stache and his eyes were blue. Square jaw. Almost no hair on his head.

"Whoa, you need to take it easy, darling," the cop said. He took hold of my hurt arm, making me wince, trying to get me to lie down again. "EMTs are on the way. Can you tell me the car you were riding in? Make and model? Who was driving?"

I pulled away from his grasp, grimacing at the pain. "I . . . I wasn't in a car. . . ."

He grinned like I was delirious or on drugs and nodded over his shoulder. "Well, sugar, something hit this officer's vehicle at a high rate of speed. I'm not trying to get your friends in trouble, but leaving the scene of an accident is a serious offense . . . so if you'll just tell me who was driving, maybe we can . . ."

I struggled to my feet. "I can't stay here. I need to go."

"Darling, you need to listen to me. You're going to be okay." The cop was trying to force me down, but I wasn't letting him. He had a surprised look on his face. "You've been in a car accident. The emergency folks need to check you out before you can go anywhere. . . ."

Other people were starting to come over, and I could hear the honking screech of a fire engine siren. The young guy I had seen sitting on the shoulder was now leaning against the smashed green car. An ambulance had pulled up next to him, and several guys were hustling out either door.

I couldn't go down the road now, too many people. I looked over the edge of the mountain at the lights of Huntsville twinkling below. The officer's grip on my arm went slack a moment. I tore loose from him, took a couple of long running strides and flung myself over the embankment.

I landed harder than I expected but was able to keep my balance. I barreled through thickets of vines and small, twisted trees and leapt over bush-choked gullies. Finally, after a lot of jouncy running, the ground started to even out again. I could still hear the cops' shocked voices calling from far above. The blue lights I could see for miles after that.

I was pretty scratched up by the time I found my way home. I got a drink at the faucet in the bunker and washed a little, then wearily climbed the rocket tower. The sun was starting to rise when I stretched out on the air mattress, cradling my injured arm. . . .

He knows I'm in Huntsville, I thought.

I wrapped myself in the tarp, shivering at the thought. *Okay, got to do something, Emma. Figure this out.* From what I remembered, there were a quarter-million people in this town. Besides, I wasn't technically in Huntsville at all, was I? The Space Center was its own little world, like the Vatican. With any luck, Wirtz wouldn't know to look for me here.

I had slipped up, let myself get distracted by all the crazy stuff that had happened with the *Sonnen.* I never would have run into that cop car otherwise. Couldn't let anything like that happen again.

If I was really careful, I could still make myself a very small needle in a pretty large haystack. And hey, if it came down to it, what was stopping me from just keeping on running? Moving from city to city, finding new places to hide each time? Then maybe, just maybe . . . I could—

No.

I swore and kicked the stupid tarp off. That's what the vampire was after, trying to get me out in the open. Wirtz had me going at this whole thing backward. *That's not me,* I thought. Not anymore. I had run away three times in my life, and I was sick of it. I never ran away from trouble on the soccer field, did I? What happened to that warrior chick who had stood on top of the chimney at the Stone House and shouted at the darkness? How had I forgotten so quickly?

I want the monster to come.

I needed him to come. I couldn't spend the rest of eternity jumping at shadows. A showdown with the vampire . . . it was the only way I could ever be free. The only way my family would finally be safe. I remembered something Coach Kline liked to say.

You're best when you're bold.

I lay back down and plunged into a dreamless sleep.

I don't know how long I had been out of it when something close to my ear screeched. I jumped up, my hand on the ax, but the sun was well up in the sky. I didn't know what was making the sound until I remembered the headset Sagan had given me. I fumbled for it in my bag.

It took me a second to remember how to work it. At last I flicked it on and thumbed the mike.

"Hey . . ."

The headset hissed in my ear. "You sound tired," Sagan said.

"Ow! Deaf is more like it. This thing is loud." I adjusted the volume, yawning.

"Are you getting enough sleep, Emma?"

If you only knew, I thought. "You sound like my mom."

"So, whatcha want to do? Are you hungry?"

I tested my elbow. It was sore, but not too bad. The whole strange night flooded into my head. I suddenly realized I was not only hungry, but—after last night—desperate for his company. "Starving," I said. "Bring me something."

"You're getting spoiled, you know that?" Sagan said.

"Yeah. Hurry before I get grouchy and kill a rabbit."

"Ha. Okay . . . just to conserve the wildlife." I could hear the grin in his voice. "I'll bring Schlotzsky's."

"Huh?"

"You'll love it."

I did. Schlotzsky's turned out to be big round sandwiches on black rye bread. "How'd you know I liked corned beef and mustard?" I said, taking a huge bite. It seemed like days since I had eaten. *Well, food that is.* My body squirmed involuntarily.

"Lucky guess," Sagan said.

We were sitting on the little picnic bench out behind the Solar Observatory. The day was turning hotter than yesterday, and the cicadas were starting to whine in the trees. Which of course made me think about summer and wonder what it would be like living out here during the other end of the spectrum. *Winter.* The thought of being homeless that long was depressing. Sagan was asking me a question.

"What?" I said.

He pushed a little strand of hair out of my face and waved his

208

hand in front of my eyes. "You were looking right at me," he said. "But even through your sunglasses I could tell you had that thousand-yard stare you get sometimes."

"Oh. Sorry. My mom used to complain about that too." *Used to.* Now I was talking about her in the past tense. I needed to call her. Papi too.

"It's like you're so completely gone, when you get like that," Sagan said. "I don't even know where you are. How to bring you back."

I took another bite, wanting to change the subject. "God, this is really good. Thank you."

I could still taste that college guy's beery blood in my mouth, if only in memory. I was dying to tell Sagan about my first Blood Hunt. But it was all so totally nuts. I wondered if I was changing in some important way, beyond the physical. When I first met the *Sonnen,* they had seemed strange to me, otherworldly. Now, just a few hours later, it was Sagan who was new and different with his white-blond locks and penetrating blue eyes. I almost felt as if we were a different species. I wondered if he could sense it.

"You're really quiet today," he said. "Anything happen last night?"

"No, not really." *Only the weirdest night of my life,* I thought. And there had been a lot of those lately. "Just kind of strange out here after dark."

"We need to talk about that," he said. "Changing your situation."

"Only that's not up to you."

"I know. But you can't keep living out here. Somebody's going to catch you sooner or later, Emma. Or you'll get hurt and won't even be able to call for help."

"Haven't we had this conversation before?" I said, looking away.

"Hey, don't zone out on me again."

"I'm not. I just get tired of having to explain myself."

Sagan put down his sandwich and got up from the table. "But that's the thing. You never explain. You just expect me to understand. What would you do if things were reversed? Say if I were living out here, homeless, sleeping in the woods, who knows where? How would you like it?"

I popped the last bite in my mouth and chewed. Made him wait while I drank some Mountain Dew. I thought about something Lena had said.

"Hey, the other day you told me about CMEs," I said.

"You keep trying to change the subject."

"I know. Please tell me again. About coronus massive—you know. There's something I've been wondering about."

"Coronal mass ejections. What about them?"

"What are they, exactly?"

"I told you. A violent ejection of material from the sun."

"So . . . you could almost call it . . . an eruption of the sun?"

"Sure. What are you driving at? I thought this solar stuff bores you."

"It does. Okay, so there is an eruption on the sun that violently throws material out. What kind of material?"

Sagan looked away, thinking. "It's a gigantic bubble of gas, mostly. Plasma, to be more specific. The plasma is made up of electrons and protons."

"Anything else?"

"Well." He tapped his fingers against his head. "Small amounts of other elements, like helium, oxygen, iron. Plus there's the coronal magnetic field to deal with. . . ."

"So when this solar flare—"

"CME," Sagan corrected. "There's a difference. A solar flare is an explosion too, but it's mostly associated with sunspots, emitting X-rays and UV radiation."

"And all of this stuff showers the earth?"

"If it's aimed in our direction. It affects the earth, yeah. Some is intercepted by the earth's magnetic field. The rest makes it all the way through."

"Radiation, protons, et cetera?"

"Sure."

"So how long does it take for the stuff to get here?" I said.

"With CMEs it can take as long as five days. But the effects of solar flares can reach us much faster. One erupted back in 2005 that hit the earth in fifteen minutes. That's one-half the speed of light."

"So what happened?"

"Not much. Disrupted satellite communications for a little while, that kind of thing."

"Oh."

He looked at me. "You sound disappointed."

"Well, I guess I was just thinking . . . that they were so much more powerful than that. That they really could affect things on earth."

"Oh, they can. But the real danger is for astronauts in space at the time of the eruption—"

"But I'm thinking about something really strong from the sun," I said. "Not just stuff that knocks out your Sunday NFL Ticket, but an explosion to end all explosions. Totally drenches us in particles or whatever . . ."

"The strongest are when they both happen at the same time," Sagan said. "A massive CME combined with a humongous solar flare."

"Does that happen often?"

"Maybe every few hundred years. We don't really know. People have been studying the sun for centuries, but real scientific data doesn't go back very far. So we don't have many long-range samples. Best we can do to figure out what might have happened back then is by analyzing stuff like particles found in ice core samples from places like Greenland—"

"So what's the biggest?"

"The biggest in recorded history?"

"I guess, yeah."

Sagan smiled. "That's easy. Carrington. It's called the Carrington Event because it was first seen by a guy over in England, an astronomer named Richard Carrington. It was a phenomenal solar flare that came out of a sunspot and pushed a monster CME straight at us. The CME got here in eighteen hours instead of the usual three or four days. So strong, you could call it a solar storm. When it hit, it set telegraphs on fire all over North America and Europe. Auroras were seen as far south as the Caribbean. In the Rocky Mountains the sky was so bright, miners woke up, thinking it was morning, and started cooking breakfast—"

"But when did it happen?"

"September 1859."

17. ESCAPE

A chill rushed through me. *1859*. The exact same year Lena had mentioned. The date of the last *Sonneneruption*. So it was true! That was the last time vampires all over the world were cured. And the vampire population had been building back up ever since. Ready to pop unless another *Sonneneruption* came along soon.

I got up from the table and walked around in a slow circle, thinking.

"Why are you so interested all of a sudden?" Sagan said.

"What?" I was still inside my head, trying to process it all.

"CMEs. Why did you want to know about them?"

"It's a secret," I said.

"Oh. Another one."

I didn't like being frowned at. "What's wrong with secrets?"

"I mean, when are you going to start trusting me, Emma? I thought after yesterday . . ."

He stood and tried to take my face in his hands.

"Stop." I pushed his hands away.

"What's wrong? It's almost like you've . . . been away somewhere or something."

"Nothing," I said. "Nothing's wrong. I just don't like you doing that when I'm trying to think."

"So what are you thinking about? Look at me. Stop a second. What are we doing here?"

"I don't understand. Me and you?"

He nodded.

"Me and you are fine." I looked into his eyes and softened my voice. "Look, I know I'm not making much sense. One thing you need to know about me . . . I've never been all that great at the whole . . . people thing. Mom always says I don't have enough patience for it. Either you trust me or you don't."

"I could say the same thing about you. Except I'm not holding anything back."

Now it was my turn to touch his face. He left my hand there.

"I don't want to fight," I said. "I trust you, Sagan. Surely you get that by now, don't you? The secrets are just . . . safety things."

"I want to keep you safe."

"You do. I mean . . . there are some things you can't do. Not right now. But I swear . . . I will tell you everything. When I'm ready. You have to believe me. I wouldn't have told you about— Wait, I know. Have you got a pen and a piece of paper?"

"Sure." He fumbled around in the glove box of his Jeep. "Here."

I took the pen and wrote something down. Folded the paper and stuffed it in the pocket of his jeans. Sagan started to pull it out. I stopped his hand.

"Don't look at it till you get home. Hide it somewhere safe and promise me you will guard it with your life."

"Wow. Okay, sure. What is it?"

"The address to my family's apartment."

Sagan kissed me.

"Um. I could do this forever," I said.

"Not me," he said.

"Huh?"

"I've got a secret too."

"Okay, what is it?"

He walked over and held open the passenger door to his Jeep. "Get in."

We went down to the main road and he turned left. When we got to the next big intersection, Sagan turned right. We had never been in that direction before.

"Another tour, huh?" I said, a little disappointed.

The road went a good ways with nothing on either side, just lowlands and soggy woods. Then up ahead I saw it. . . .

"Is that a guard shack?"

Sagan didn't say anything. Just pressed on the gas and the Jeep accelerated.

"You tricked me. You tricked me!" I said. "You're taking me off the base, aren't you?" I put my hand on the door handle. "Turn this Jeep around or I'll jump out."

Sagan nodded and spoke without looking at me. "You'll jump out doing . . ." He glanced at the speedometer. "Fifty-two miles an hour?"

"I will," I said. "If you don't turn around."

"Okay, go ahead."

He wasn't smiling. I unhooked my seat belt and leaned toward the door, ready to open it.

"You don't believe me, do you?" I said.

"Nope."

I opened the door. We were moving fast, but my eyes were so good I could see individual blades of grass whipping by on the shoulder. I leaned toward the opening.

"Hey!" Sagan yelled. The Jeep swerved a little as he grabbed at my arm. "What are you doing? Shut the door!"

I leaned a little more, tensing my leg muscles.

"Emma!"

I pulled the door shut and sank back into the seat, defeated.

"I can't," I said, as much to myself as to Sagan.

We passed through the gate and kept on going off the base.

"I can't believe you did that," Sagan said. "You were really thinking about jumping, weren't you? You're crazy, you know that?"

We drove a little ways not speaking, both of us hot. We were passing a big new subdivision on the left, stubbly cotton land on the right.

"So what's the big deal, anyhow?" Sagan said finally. "You left the Space Center to go mall hopping the other day."

"That was different."

"Different how?"

"That was just me, okay?" I said, shooting bullets at him with my eyes, though I was pretty sure he couldn't see them on account of my shades. "I wasn't in somebody's car. I could do what I want. I was in control of the situation."

"So it's that bad . . . what might happen to you . . . that you have to be on top of it every second?"

"Now you're starting to get it."

Sagan made a sour expression. "So you don't think I could protect you."

"No," I said. "Like I said, nobody could. Just tell me where we are going."

"I told you, it's a secret."

"Kidnapping me is a secret?" I said.

"I didn't kidnap you. I asked you to get in my car, and you did."

"But what if they had stopped us!"

"They never stop you going out, only coming in."

I sat back in my seat, pouting. "So what now?"

"Just wait."

"You're not taking me to the police, are you?" I said, again feeling the need to jump. "Please, swear you wouldn't do something that stupid."

"Of course not," Sagan said, looking offended. "I told you I wouldn't. Just hang on a little farther. We're almost there."

I anxiously watched the telephone poles we passed, wondering how I would feel if I saw my photo plastered there: MISSING GIRL. I also kept having crazy flashes of us pulling up alongside my mother's car. Even after I reminded myself that she was in another town thirty miles away, it still seemed all too possible.

I tried to distract myself by memorizing the turns we took, but there were too many. The last road we came to cut through the center of a quiet middle-class neighborhood. The houses were mostly two stories with medium-sized yards and flowers around the mailboxes. Sagan slowed to a stop in front of one of them. The house was a little bigger than some and had white frame siding with brick chimneys on either end. There were four cars in the driveway.

"This is where I live," he said.

"What?"

"I want you to come meet my family. I told them . . . last night I told them about you."

"You didn't!"

"Calm down, please. I didn't tell them you were . . . homeless. Just that we had met at school."

"I'm in high school, remember?"

"You could pass for a college freshman. We'll . . . make up a course we're taking together."

"Yeah, astrophysics."

"I'm serious. History. There you go. You're in my Western Civ class. We've been studying together. You've been helping me with that while I help you with . . . calculus. How about that?"

"Oh my God. I'm going to kill you, Sagan. Take me back. Take me back right now."

"But I already told them that you're coming. It's a cookout by the pool. That's an easy way to get to know new people, right?"

My jaw was hurting from clenching my teeth. "Oh sure. That's easy. Just me and about a million lies surrounded by strangers. Do you have any idea how stupid you are right now?"

"Yeah. I do. Really I do. But I knew if I just asked you, you wouldn't come. Please. Guaranteed pain free. They are really nice and easygoing. It would mean a lot to me. Please."

I couldn't look at his eyes.

"Please?"

This time I looked at his eyes, and then I was done. I blew air out of my cheeks.

"Anything else I need to know?"

"Yeah," he said. "Your name is Julia."

I swore as we walked around to the back. "*Julia*. Are you serious?" But inside I was thankful he had thought to protect my identity.

"Yeah, I've been reading *1984* lately," he said.

"Huh?"

"Julia? Winston? One of the all-time great love stories . . . well, until they put Winston's head in a cage full of rats—"

"Spare me," I said. We were already at the gate to the swimming pool and I wanted a chance to catch my breath.

I checked myself over. I was completely clean and wearing decent clothes, but my stomach was doing barrel rolls. Forget about the homeless vampire stuff. . . . It had been a long time . . . *years* . . .

since I had been over to anybody's house like this. Because of the curse.

I could hear screams and splashes coming from the back, the kind of sounds that always make you feel like an outsider.

What if his family watched a lot of TV, especially the local news? Would they have seen me? I tried to remember; did they put missing teenagers on TV? The only time I ever saw them was on those little Xeroxed posters at Walmart: HAVE YOU SEEN ME? The only missing people who ever seemed to make the nightly news all seemed to fall into one of two categories: (1) kids younger than ten or (2) hot, squeaky-clean moms. Forget about Channel 8 showing up at your house otherwise. I sure didn't fit either of those profiles. Plus my shades would help. . . .

"Did you tell them about my eyes?" I said.

"I think so. Yeah, I did," Sagan said. "Don't worry. I don't know who you're used to being around, but they're not like that."

"Not like what?"

"They're easy. They won't pounce or anything."

I wasn't so sure.

Sagan opened the gate. Nobody seemed to notice us at first; they were making too much noise and talking to one another. Then just when I thought we could safely make it to the sliding glass door and escape inside the house, a little kid screamed, "Hey, Sagan's new girlfriend is here!" and did a cannonball that threw water all over me.

They all stopped, looking. I was too nervous to count, but there were at least seven or eight heads bobbing in the pool and several adults arranged around the edges on lounge chairs. My first impression was of a lot of pale legs and blond hair.

"Hi, this is Julia, everybody!" Sagan said. "I promised you wouldn't scare her."

I glared at him. Good thing he couldn't see my murderous expression.

I was dripping but pretty much undamaged. "Hi," I managed to say weakly, giving a stupid little wave.

"Well, hello, Julia!" A tall, thin blond woman came over, taking my hand in both of her hands. Obviously Sagan's mom.

She steered me over to a man standing in front of a gigantic grill, a big oven mitt on one hand. He waved with a spatula. He was as tall as Sagan and had the darkest blond hair in the bunch, and rounder features than everybody else as well. Sagan's dad, I guessed.

"We've got you a place right over here," Sagan's mom said. "I hope you like tilapia. If not, we can put some pork on there. Honey! Did you bring out those chops like I told you?"

"No, fish is fine, really!" I said.

I had never felt more like an alien in my whole life. After spending the night prowling the city and drinking blood with vampires, the extreme normalness was making me dizzy.

"Glad to have you," Sagan's father said, taking the mitt off and shaking my hand. I found myself desperately focusing on the food: bunches of onions splitting open from the heat, green and red peppers, little ears of corn. . . .

Sagan introduced me around. My heart was in my larynx. There were siblings and an aunt and uncle and their two kids, an extra friend or three from the neighborhood. . . . It was impossible to keep all of them straight, so I just stopped trying.

After we sat down, I had to make up a few things about my dad, what he did for a living, the college football team we rooted for, that kind of thing, but I tried to keep it simple. I had trouble remembering names, except to notice that none of them were as unusual as "Sagan."

"The first kid is an experiment," Sagan's dad said. "You keep practicing until you get it right."

"So, Julia, Sagan tells us you are helping him with his history?" his mom was saying later. We were sitting at the world's longest picnic table, digging in. One of the little kids was absently kicking my shins beneath the tablecloth.

I gulped a little, having just shoved a giant wad of butter in my mouth along with a small forkful of baked potato. It's funny what you miss.

"Um. Yes, ma'am. That's the plan," I said, garbling the words. "And he's getting me squared away in math."

"So what are you planning for your major?"

"Well . . ."

"The counselors really don't push it so hard when you're a freshman, Mom," Sagan said. "They're just interested in getting you through the 101 courses."

"Yeah," I said, taking his lead. "Gotta be well-rounded."

"But . . . what are you interested in?" Sagan's mom persisted.

"I . . . don't know exactly," I said. "Papi—my grandfather—he always says I was born four or five hundred years too late."

Sagan's dad sat down, beads of sweat on his temples. "Whew, that looks good," he said about his own cooking. "So, Julia . . . if you could be any person in history . . . whom would you choose?"

"Oh, that's easy," I said. "An explorer. Like de Soto or Champlain or Ponce de León."

"That's an interesting answer."

"Not to do any of the bad stuff those guys might have done," I said quickly. "Just to see what it felt like to explore new places. You know? Before everything changed. See what the forests were like. The wildlife. The . . . Native Americans. Have some adventures.

Find out where maybe we got parts of history wrong. I've always wished I had come over with the settlers at Jamestown."

"But . . . didn't they end up eating one another?" Sagan's aunt said.

I bit into an ear of corn. "Sure, well. Papi—my grandfather and I read about it. Some archeologists say cannibalism is hard to prove. At least half the original colonists died, yeah. They called it the 'Starving Time.' Supposedly a man dug up his pregnant wife, salted her, cut her into pieces, and ate her. Captain John Smith even wrote about it. He said he didn't know 'whether she was better roasted, boiled, or barbecued.'"

I looked up from my corn and they were all staring at me, especially the little kids.

"This . . . is . . . um . . . good," I said.

We had homemade ice cream later. "This is the first time I've had this since . . ." I stopped myself.

"What?" Sagan said.

"Never mind. Just something from a long time ago."

He took me inside afterward. It felt extremely weird walking through his house. These people were so . . . involved. Artwork all over, photographs on every wall, and stuff that I couldn't even give a name to. Maybe you could call them . . . projects? Things with feathers and seashells and bits of colored stones.

"Come see my room," Sagan said.

We went upstairs and passed a bedroom full of beads and golden twirly thingies hanging from the ceiling that spun in beams of sunlight.

"That's Bree's and Jenna's," Sagan said.

Another room had books everywhere and what I think was a

cello . . . a violin on steroids, anyhow. A hat with pink-and-white-striped fur was propped on a lava lamp.

"Charlotte's."

We walked a little farther, then I made him stop, turning to look into his eyes.

"They're all really nice," I said. "Have I been okay?"

Sagan returned my gaze, brushing back my hair. "Perfect. Except for that part about John Smith barbecuing his wife . . ."

"That's not what I—!"

A couple of screeching wet kids brushed past, hurtling up the hall.

"You're beautiful," he said. "Thanks for coming. They all love you, you know."

"Sure they do."

"No, really."

"Is it like this all the time around here?"

"Only on weekends," he said. "The rest of the week's not so calm."

Sagan's room was not what I had expected. I had pictured posters of supernovas, planet models, astronomy textbooks. It was kind of spare. A laptop on a desk that was really only a wooden table. A bed with no headboard shoved up under the window. A dresser and an oak armoire with a dinky TV inside.

"Wow, this is really . . . neat," I said. "As in, where is all your stuff?"

"I get tired of all the crap all over the house," Sagan said. "This is my space. I like to keep things simple. Streamlined. So I don't have to spend a lot of time thinking about useless junk."

"I'm . . . impressed. No, really. Shut the door."

"Why?"

"Just . . . shut it."

Sagan shut the door, then turned around looking embarrassed. There was a life-sized poster on the back of his door: a cowboy with a bearded, scowling face, a broad-brimmed dingy white hat, and twin pistols crossed over his chest. The top of the poster said THE OUTLAW JOSEY WALES.

"Look out. Who's this?" I said, grinning.

"Um. You know. Come on, don't tease me."

"No, really, Sagan, who is it?"

"You're kidding, right? You know who it is; it's Clint Eastwood!"

"The old guy?"

"Yeah. Um, no . . . Well, it's a movie he made when he was a lot younger. You know, he used to be in all those Westerns."

"I seriously have never seen this."

His eyes got big. "But it's a classic! My dad's all-time favorite movie. He's the one who turned me on to *Josey Wales*. It has some of the most famous lines in the history of movies."

"Oh wow. So no wonder you hide this thing behind the door. So you can lie in bed all day and look at him . . ."

"Oh, shut up."

"Your secret's out!" I tickled his stomach and he knocked my hand away.

"Stop it. That's been up there since like . . . seventh grade."

"So why don't you take it down? You like it, don't you? Your hidden passion, to be a cowboy."

"Hey. That's not why I like it."

"So you get off on Westerns, huh."

"I mean it, quit teasing me."

"I'm not teasing," I said, still smiling. "But I can hardly resist. . . . The big astronomer who wants to rope little doggies."

"You mean *dogies*, don't you? Motherless calves?"

"See!"

"I don't want to be a freaking cowboy!"

I pinched him playfully. "So why do you like Westerns?"

"Not just any Westerns. His Westerns. Well, this Western."

"Okay. So tell me one of them." I crossed my arms. "I'm waiting."

"One what?"

"The famous quotes. You said this movie had the most famous quotes like . . . ever. So you must have them memorized, right?"

"You'd just laugh."

"No, I promise I won't laugh. It's important to you, so it's important to me, huh?" I was giggling under my breath as I said it. "Like, pick one. The most famous. The one I'm most likely to have heard."

Sagan was quiet, looking at me, probably trying to figure out just how deep he was in it.

"Okay. The one probably everybody remembers is this," he said.

He held up his arms like he was holding six-guns and put on a scowl that made him look kinda sorta like a Scandinavian Clint Eastwood. In a raspy voice, almost a whisper, he said, "'Are you gonna pull those pistols or whistle Dixie?'"

I stared at him, waiting for him to finish.

"Is that it?" I said.

He looked at me, disbelieving. "Well, of course that's it!"

"Never heard it."

"Not possible."

"No, truly, I've never heard it. I don't watch a whole lot of old movies, you know."

"It's not that old. Not like it was made in the Dark Ages or something."

I put my hand on the side of his face and pushed in a little closer. "Pistols, huh? So you got a thing for pistols. Ever fire one?"

"No." He grinned sheepishly. "Unless you count Halo 3."

"Okay, gimme another one. Another quote."

"No."

"Why?"

"I don't feel like it. You'll just make fun of me."

"Oh, come on. You get your feelings hurt too easy."

"I do not," Sagan said, puffing himself up a little. Now his arms were crossed too.

"Really. It doesn't take much," I said. "My mom would say you can dish it out, but you can't take it."

"I can take it."

"Okay, then tell me another one. Not something random, but— your favorite, pick your personal favorite. I swear, I won't make fun of you."

Sagan watched me.

I raised my hand, crossed my fingers.

He rolled his eyes. "I know I'll regret this," he said. "But . . . okay. There is the part near the end of the movie . . . Wait, I don't want to spoil it for you. . . ."

"Oh please . . . like I'm ever going to watch it."

"Okay . . . Josey, you know, Clint Eastwood, Josey Wales is a real loner because his whole family was murdered by some rene-gade soldiers. He's always pretending he doesn't care about any-thing or anybody else the whole movie, yet the entire time he keeps picking up these friends, you know? Misfits, loners like him, or just people who need help. Well, in the end he and his friends—women, children, old people—they're all about to be trapped in this cabin by the same bunch of murderers who killed Josey's family. And this . . . this is what he says. . . . Wait . . . no, I can't do it. . . ."

"Yes you can. Come on. Say it."

"Okay. Jeez, Emma. Okay. So they are heavily outnumbered. Basically going to die in that cabin. And Josey . . ." He swore.

I looked at him closely. . . . His eyes were shining.

Sagan dropped his head, raised it again. "So stupid."

"It's not stupid. Tell me what Josey said."

I watched him swallow. "Okay. He said this: 'When things look bad, and it looks like you're not gonna make it, then you gotta get mean. I mean plumb mad-dog mean. 'Cause if you lose your head and you give up, then you neither live nor win, that's just the way it is.'"

I suddenly felt my bottom lip quivering, my eyes bunching, blurring out. Sagan started to say something.

"I know, it's not what you—"

I leaned into him and touched my mouth to his. We kissed and it turned into a long kiss. His lips tasted of vanilla ice cream.

18. MONSTERS

Finally I just clung to him, feeling his breathing going in and out. I wondered what his folks would say if they came in.

"Wow," Sagan said. "Where did that come from?"

"I'm sorry about the way I was acting back at the base," I whispered. "I know it must have seemed pretty . . . strange."

"You're fine."

"I know, but . . ."

"What?"

"It's just . . . everything . . . it has all reminded me of what it was like. I had almost forgotten. Today has been a little bit like going back in time. Are your parents happy?"

"Sure, yeah. I guess so," Sagan said.

"So it really does work out for some people."

"Well, yeah. I mean . . . I guess it's just what you're used to. This is all I've ever known. So I guess you start thinking everybody is this . . . lucky."

"Will we be lucky?"

"Are you saying . . . ?"

"No, I'm just saying, us. Me and you. Not talking anything about white houses with a yard and two-point-three kids or any of that."

"You know, probably we never would have met," Sagan said. "If—whatever happened to you hadn't happened. So I feel . . . I feel lucky already." He tilted my head up to look into his eyes. "I don't see how somebody could be any more lucky."

"So . . . if something happened to me . . . would you—"

"Don't talk about stuff like that. I'm superstitious."

"You mean black cats and all that?" I said. I rubbed noses with him. "I'm surprised."

"No. I don't believe in ladders and salt over the shoulder and the number thirteen. I just mean in general. Like maybe it's possible to be so happy that . . . it almost doesn't feel . . . safe?"

"Oh yeah. I know that. I know it exactly."

"Why, do you think something is going to happen?"

"Something is always going to happen," I said. "Or it's boring. Who wants boring?"

"Safe. Right now I'll settle for safe."

"Not me," I said. "Well, my little sister, sure. If anything ever hurt her . . . it would kill me. Completely. But I've never cared about being safe my whole life."

"Please start," Sagan said.

The party didn't break up until well after dark. The finale to the evening was Sagan's sister Charlotte playing a concerto by somebody named Rostropovich on her cello. She was tall and slender and of course blond, and had pulled on jean shorts over her bathing suit. She was fourteen, and something about her intense concentration and the way everybody paid attention to her while she played broke my heart.

On the way back I made Sagan stop at a convenience store with a phone. "You have to stay in the Jeep," I told him.

Mom wasn't at home, so I left another rambling, teary message that basically said the same stuff I'd told her before: I'm fine, just checking in, don't worry, tell Manda I love her, I'll be home as soon as I can.

Papi was tougher, because he actually answered. He got right to it, no BS, just as I knew he would.

"*Enkelin,* where are you?" he said in his sternest voice.

"Papi . . . please, I can't tell you where I am. But I'm okay. I really am. Please . . . I know it's hard not to worry, but you have to . . ."

Papi swore. Something he never did. "Come home. *Sofort.* Immediately. No. Be quiet. There is no discussion, you hear me? Now. I demand you to come home now."

I started to cry. It felt as if I were tearing out both our hearts. "I can't, Papi. You know I would if I could. It's not me. It's something that has happened to me. I don't know what Mom has told—"

"You are killing your mother, *Enkelin.* Do you understand this? Every day you are gone. She is killed a little bit more."

"Manda, how is Manda?"

"Her too. She weeps every night. Weeps herself to sleep, do you hear? For missing you. Afraid for you. We are all so afraid. . . . If it is a boy, I will . . ." I could almost hear him spitting with anger as he grasped for the words. "If a boy has made you do this, given you drugs . . . I can't say. I can't say."

"It's not a boy, Papi. It's not drugs. You know I wouldn't lie to you! I have never lied to you. It's . . . something else. Something I can't say, because I have to keep everybody safe. If I tell you, if I tell Mom, anybody, nobody will be safe anymore. You have to believe me!"

"Then tell me where you are. Right now. I will be coming to pick you up. Just give me the address, the street, anything, I will be there. I am putting on my coat, *Enkelin.*"

"No, Papi. You can't. It would . . . everything would be too dangerous. I have to do this by myself. . . ." I trailed off into a whimper that I hoped he didn't hear. I rubbed my arm across my eyes, clearing my blurred vision. Tried to stand a little straighter.

"Papi . . . I swear to you . . . I will be okay. You know me. I wouldn't be doing this without a very good reason. You have always trusted me. All I am asking you . . . all I can ask you . . . is to keep trusting me. Don't think I can't do it. Don't believe that. I have to know you believe in me. It would help so much. . . ."

His voice softened and I heard him take a very deep breath. He let it out again. "I know you," he said, voice breaking. "I know you, *meine* . . . granddaughter. You must know it's not that I don't believe. You are my . . . strength. That is what I believe in you. But this . . . I only want . . . help you . . ." I heard him sniff. Was he trying not to cry?

"I love you, Papi," I said in a broken voice. "I'll be back. I promise. . . ."

After I got back in the Jeep, I wouldn't speak. Sagan drove me to the entrance of the Space Center. "What's wrong?" he said. I didn't answer and he tried to keep me in the car, almost fighting with me, grabbing at my arm.

"No," I said finally. "No!" And I broke away, running up the highway, loping so he wouldn't see how fast I really was. He tried to follow, but the traffic was going the other way. By the time he got the Jeep turned around, I was gone.

At least five minutes passed before I realized where I was going.

I had to wait for them outside their dirty little cave room for nearly two hours. I passed the time basically weeping and feeling sorry for myself. Papi's words blazed in my head: *You are my strength.* I was still cursed. Right now I was nobody's strength.

At last the vampires returned. They had been off on another *Blutjagd*, this time for Lena. They didn't seem surprised to see me. I still had my sunglasses on. I didn't want them seeing the condition of my eyes.

"Oh, it's you again," Donne said, scowling. "What are those for?" she said, pointing at my sunglasses.

"Sometimes my eyes are sensitive, even after dark," I said, pointing at Lena's oil lamp.

"That will go away after a while," Anton said.

"You smell of . . . cooking," Donne said.

"Thanks," I said. If I hadn't felt so rotten, I would have added, "And you smell of cave dirt." They all had on the same clothes as before. I was struck again by how slightly they were built. *Must be from all that fasting. . . .*

I waited for them to settle around me on the chairs. Lena stretched out on a pallet. "*Blutjagd* always makes me sleepy," she said. "You seem . . . sad, Emma."

"I'll get over it," I said, wondering if she were somehow tapping into my thoughts. I bit my lip. "Was it a . . . good hunt?"

"Three kills!" Anton said. "When Lena eats, she . . . eats."

We talked a good while about unimportant things. Then we talked about important things. Finally I started to feel a little better, hearing what their lives had been like. *Guess misery does love company.* Now they were telling me their stories.

"Many times people are taken from behind and never see who it was," Anton was saying. We were back outside at the *Steinhaus* sitting on the wall again. The night breeze felt good on my face after being in the stuffy room.

"But I did," Anton went on. "Mine was a woman who hid in the basement of an Episcopal church in Atlanta. We had moved down from New Jersey, and I came each week to deliver coal for my father's business. It was a November evening, dark very early. I can still remember wishing my jacket wasn't so thin. Hard times! Okay? The Great War was just coming to an end. If it hadn't ended soon, I was going to enlist. Fight the Hun. It seems like such an odd thing, hey? The history of someone else."

He smiled and went on. "I didn't know she was down there. I woke her dumping a load of coal down the chute. I don't think she was a bad person. Just starving and there I was. The coal bin had high walls and a low door. Sometimes the coal would pile up and block the door and I would have to go down and pull it free.

"She was squatting in the corner, her back against the bricks, asleep. She was much older than me. I was seventeen. She was so thin. Her hair was thin too. I didn't even know she was alive; her eyes flew open, staring at me. I tried to get away, but I slipped in the coal and slid down, eh? She was too fast. She was on top of me almost instantly. I can still feel the pain of her bite. Afterward she was still there when I awoke again. She told me over and over she was so sorry. She wept over me. She apologized for not killing me, for letting me live. Like this."

Lena and Donne were watching, not speaking, just taking it in. I wondered how many times they had heard this. It was weird listening to this guy who looked like a kid but talked like an adult from some other time period. Back whenever they used coal, anyhow.

Anton coaxed Donne to tell her story. "Come on. We each have to share. You know that."

"All right, all right," Donne said. "I was fifteen. It was a man. It was dark. He basically left me for dead. What more do you want?" She glared at me.

"I didn't ask you to tell it," I said.

"What's the difference, anyhow?" Donne said. "We're here, aren't we? Who wants to live in the past? I am the past."

"You are still young," Anton said. I realized that he was over a hundred himself. "Donne was taken during the Depression," Anton went on. "It has left her depressed." He laughed.

We sat there watching each other uneasily. Lena spoke up.

"I do not know if years truly count for us," she said. "As old as I am, I don't feel one bit older than the day I was taken. More experienced, certainly. But no older. I have watched the old many times over the years, and I have become convinced that they feel older because they are older. I mean, in their bodies. Otherwise, I think it would be as it is with us."

"How about you?" I said. "What's your story?"

"Great," Donne said, cutting her eyes at Lena. "Go ahead. It won't kill us to hear it again."

Lena smiled and nodded, then looked back at me.

"I was living in a small Utopian Christian community called Bixby in Tennessee. We were a closed society. Bixby had been founded by a man named Philip Orton who had once been an Anglican clergyman in Connecticut. Pastor Orton had a dispute with his church and renounced his formal faith, then came south with a handful of followers where landholdings were cheap. His dream was to found a Christian Eden.

"I say Christian, but half of us, the women, were totally without freedom and subject to the dictates of Pastor Orton at all times. This is the world I was born into. When I knew the pastor, he was past sixty. I remember he had flowing white hair and wore a tall, shiny beaver hat, even indoors. I cannot even recall a single picture in my imagination of him without it. Save one. And that one time was enough.

"The day it happened, I had been avoiding Pastor Orton for weeks. I could sense instinctively what he was after. I could feel it even as I sat in the pews of our small church. His ravenous eyes following me wherever I went."

"So he was a vampire?" I said.

"Patience," Anton said.

Lena went on. "I was coming back from the spring one afternoon with a load of washing when the pastor came to me behind the general store and assaulted me." She paused a moment, gathering herself. "I managed to fight him off, but I was terrified thereafter and was careful never to be alone with him.

"I had no one to tell about this. I wanted to tell my mother what had happened, but she was so enraptured with the pastor, it was impossible. My father . . . with him I did not even try. He was one of Pastor Orton's deacons.

"After that, I hid my face as much as possible and became something of a shut-in. I felt trapped. My life, at the ripe old age of twenty, seemed as if it were essentially over. And then he came."

Lena's eyes were glistening. She took in a shuddering breath.

"Who?" I said.

"I only ever knew him by one name," Lena said. "Valentin."

"You're kidding," I said.

"Wait, it gets even better," Anton said, smirking. Donne jabbed him in the ribs.

"That really was his name," Lena said. "The only one I ever knew him by. Valentin was a French Creole from Baton Rouge. He happened to be passing through our little community on the way to Boston.

"It was early spring. Valentin arrived in the middle of the night in a terrible storm. He happened to come to my door first. His knock woke me, and I opened the door to the schoolhouse where I was sleeping—I was the only teacher in Bixby—and there he was, sweeping his dripping hat low and bowing to me. It was as if the Lord Himself had stepped into that room. I had never known a man could be beautiful—the men of our community were so plain. I was awed by his powerful arms, huge chest, long black hair. His voice alone, that accent, simply melted me.

"You must understand . . . I was so innocent. Yet also so ready for change. I had thought of running away many times, but where to? And what would I live on? It all seemed so hopeless until Valentin came.

"He returned each night. I could not think to dare question this. It was too good. His visits were what I lived for. Even my parents remarked that my cheeks were glowing with a new vibrancy. We fell in love. Not in one night, no. We had to be secretive about it. Valentin would only appear long after dark, after the rest of Bixby was asleep. How I lived to be near him! I cannot tell you how intoxicating it was. We made plans. I was to run away with him. I had no reason to stay. He would be my protector.

"The night of my escape arrived. I had everything I owned tied in a small bundle. I left a farewell note in my mother's bread box and waited in the schoolroom. Valentin arrived. He had acquired a horse for me. You cannot imagine how thrilled I was. We were just about to leave when the schoolhouse door was flung open. There stood Pastor Orton. To this day, I do not know how he found us out. I only know what happened next."

Lena paused for another long moment. I'm not sure I was even breathing at that point. The night, everything around me, had disappeared. "Go on," I said. Lena collected herself and continued.

"One moment the pastor was bellowing in a fury, rushing toward us, and the next he was flung across the room so violently, his body was broken against the iron stove.

"Whatever Valentin had done, I had never seen it. It was almost as if avenging angels had been in the room with us.

"There was no turning back now. We plunged into the night, the forest. I don't know how long we rode, but we had to have traveled many miles from Bixby. We came to a natural glade in the middle of a vast forested wilderness, somewhere just over the border into Kentucky. Valentin set about putting together a makeshift camp there in all that wildness. I could not understand why he was hurrying so.

" 'I must leave you now,' he said when he was finished. 'I am sorry, but it cannot be helped. The sun will rise soon. You must rest. I will return at sundown.'

"I wept inconsolably. Valentin begged me to trust him and then he was gone.

"I tried to sleep, but every sound made me leap with fear. After the sun arose, it was the longest day of my life. I was so tired, unable to think clearly. All alone in that immense forest, terrified he would never return. I think I was slightly mad by the time the sun dipped below the horizon.

"And then he was there. The joy I felt was so overpowering, I collapsed. I must have slept several hours. When I awoke, Valentin was leaning over me in the light of a single candle. He was caressing me. He kissed me. I will never forget that kiss as long as I live. He removed my coat and shawl and began to unbutton my chemise. I trembled, but after all I had been through, all the terror and the joy, I felt I was ready for anything. Even that.

" 'Forgive me, my darling,' he said. '*Rien ne peut m'arrêter maintenant.*' "

"Which means?" I said.

"I was expecting a Creole phrase that meant he loved me

endlessly," Lena said, smiling sadly at the thought. "But it wasn't even Creole; it was Standard French, meaning, 'Nothing can stop me now.' That is what he said, and then he brought his face next to my ear and . . ."

"He took you," I said.

"He . . . drank from me. Drank from my throat."

Lena closed her eyes slowly and they stayed shut as if glued that way by the memory. She lifted her hand to her neck, touched a place just below her jaw. Her whole body seemed to sag.

"I was horrified by what he had done. Valentin was a monster. How could this man I loved have done this thing to me? I wanted to strike at him, kill him. I remember how feeble my struggles were compared to his strength. At last I simply left, and he let me go. I did not realize it at the time, but Valentin was tracking me through that forest. He waited until I was overcome with exhaustion, slumped over a stream trying to drink, before approaching me again. But he did not approach me physically; he did so through the Call."

"Wait. The Call . . . ," I said, immediately thinking of Wirtz. How he had used that word over and over, wanting me to come to him. Lena seemed to study me for a second before speaking.

"You have heard of this?"

"Please, go on. I'm sorry I interrupted."

"Very well. When Valentin approached me again, I was terror-stricken, yet he made no aggressive moves. He was himself. Perhaps you could say he wore me down. He was very gentle in his approach. At long last I could stand it no more. I was ready to fall into his arms, a kind of rapturous suicide. But he was not really there. Not in bodily form, only his . . . essence, what we call the *Wesentliche*. He explained through this disembodied messenger why he did what he did. Valentin had never intended to fall in love that night.

"'I had not known I was still capable of love,' he said, 'until that moment I came through your door and saw you. I was going to attack you, leave you for dead. I had been staggering blindly through my life. Which I did not think was even a life anymore. You brought me back. You were my salvation.'

"'Then why . . . ,' I said, touching my throat.

"'I am eternally sorry for that,' he said. 'It is my selfishness. I knew you would never assent to such a transformation. A union with someone like . . . me. What I had become. And so . . . I took you instead. Like stealing from heaven. I feel as if I may be struck down even now for speaking of such a place. Yet I am telling you the truth. All that I ask is that you somehow understand that this was the only way. Our only way. You could have never lived a normal life knowing this about me. And you would grow old as I remained forever . . . what I am. Please forgive me and consider what I have said. What I am now asking.'

"He thought it was his only chance. Our only chance," Lena said. Her eyes were bright with tears. "And so . . . he felt he must turn me. So that we would be frozen forever in that moment. Never again to age. To spend the rest of eternity with each other."

Donne rolled her eyes at this. Lena didn't seem to notice.

She didn't speak for a little while, as if she were caught up in a memory too painful to deal with. Finally she started again.

"Eternity . . . turned out to be scarcely more than a year. But in that time, Valentin taught me everything I needed to know about . . . what I was. When to hunt. Where. How to feed. In the beginning, I would not speak to him. I ran away several times. When he caught me, I would beat his chest, screaming and pleading. I was certain my soul was dying. Perhaps it was already dead."

Lena folded her hands across her lap.

"So . . . whatever happened to him?" I said. "Valentin? Why aren't you still together?"

"It is so . . . ridiculous," Lena said. "It was in 1862 . . . I forget the month. We were hiding in an abandoned farm beneath a puncheon floor . . . an old root cellar that smelled of decaying potatoes and onions.

"The cabin had been looted and burned. It was by pure chance that they did not come upon the cellar. When we came out, just after dark, we staggered into a nightmare world of flame, the sound of gunpowder discharging, the whistle of minié ball shot. We had stumbled onto a Civil War battlefield. Valentin took my hand and we fled. I could hear his heart pounding. . . .

"I saw the flash first, a huge outpouring of flame—it was a cannon. In my memory it made a sound like a mountain breaking open. We had passed directly in front of the Union lines. I do not even know the name of the battle. Probably a minor one. For me, however, it was everything. We were so close to the lines, even with Valentin's speed . . ."

Lena dropped her head, then raised it again.

"The cannonball . . . it took everything above his shoulders—he was taken from me just that suddenly. I was pitched into the mud by the blast and soaked in Valentin's warm blood.

"My life has never been the same since meeting him. Not a day goes by that I do not grieve for him in some way. Though it has a certain . . . crystalline . . . feeling to it now. An emotion captured in amber."

"Don't be fooled," Anton said to me. "Just listen to her sometime when she sleeps."

Donne seemed very far away. I wondered what she was thinking. As if hearing my thoughts, she spoke up.

"Tell her, Lena."

"Tell me what?" I said.

Lena stared at Donne as if deciding whether or not she should. "I suppose it would have come up sooner or later," she said, exhaling.

"What?"

"Valentin . . . wasn't just any old vampire," Donne said. "Was he, Lena?"

"No," she said, almost whispering. "He wasn't. He was French Creole, but he was more than that. He was . . . *Verloren*."

"Now wait a minute," I said. "You're telling me you fell in love with a *Verloren* guy? Wow. So I guess not all of them are so easy to pick out on sight. Not all of them are monstrous."

"Oh no," Lena said. "For you see, Emma . . . I was *Verloren* too."

19. CHANCES

I won't lie. The thought blazed through my mind that I might have been tricked. That I had wandered right into a nest of *Verloren* and Wirtz was waiting right around the corner. Or maybe there were no such creatures as *Verloren* or *Sonnen,* and the three vampires were just toying with me. They had all that time to kill. . . .

But looking at Lena's eyes instantly dispelled that thought. Vampire lore is full of tales about the suggestive powers of the vampire stare, but what I saw in her eyes reflected nothing but pain. Pain and loss and years of getting over it.

"But . . ." I didn't know what I was trying to say.

"Let me help you," Donne said to me. "You're wondering if this is all just crap, aren't you, Emma? The *Sonnen.* Explosions on the sun. Cures. Fasting. Admit it."

"But I saw what you did on the Blood Hunt," I said. "It was all so . . . different . . . from what I experienced. You care about the people you . . . drink from." I looked at Lena again.

"So . . . are you . . . both?"

"I was *Verloren* for a long time, Emma," Lena said, sounding tired. "It was the only way I knew. The only way I could survive."

"Did you . . . did you kill people?"

"Yes. Yes, I did. It is no excuse, truly, but I was . . . so broken. I felt I had been betrayed by the God I had grown up worshipping. First Pastor Orton, then the way He took Valentin away from me. The only happiness I had ever known. I was angry at the world.

Most of all, I was angry at the world of men. It was their fault entirely, the sufferings of humanity. I felt justified. No, I felt . . . righteous.

"I became almost like a . . . demon. There were stories told about me. There may be stories still, I don't know. I was called the Gray Lady. I was brutal, did not care whom I hurt or how. Then one night I barged through the doors of a church. . . . I do not even remember what kind of church it was. I was voracious, blood-driven. I only cared that there was someone inside, someone warm, whom I could . . . take.

"There was a man there. . . . He was . . . very young. He was kneeling in the front of the sanctuary, his hat placed beside his feet. His clothes were tattered and shabby. His back was to me. He had no chance. I flew to him the way a storm would fly across a continent. . . .

"Just as I was about to descend upon the man . . . I saw he was kneeling over a child in a small white casket. A little girl, perhaps about four years old. I had landed so lightly, I do not believe he ever knew I was there. I backed away from him and the dead child. Backed all the way out into the street. I flung myself down upon the steps and wept bitterly over what I had become.

"I wanted it all to be over. I waited for the sun, but when it came, I did not have the courage. I hid myself in the basement of a nearby home. An elderly woman lived there all alone. I could have taken her anytime I wanted. But I learned that I could fight against the hunger. One night the hunger was so strong, I fled into the darkness. I found shelter where I could, taking as little blood as possible from the people I encountered. Still, I felt I was an abomination.

"I could no longer tolerate what I had become; I was desperate to somehow make amends. By chance I traveled into Washington,

D.C., where there was a great need of nurses due to the war. I had no training, but they were short-staffed and required none. And so I became a night nurse in a war hospital.

"I was given the most repugnant tasks, owing to my lack of experience. My ward had eighty beds. The stench, in particular to my vampire senses, was unimaginable. I steeled myself each night by sprinkling my clothes liberally with lavender water. But do you know what frightened me the most, Emma? Attending those poor men, fresh from battle, with wounds so grievous, they spouted blood. My blasphemous hunger would become so intense at such moments, I thought I might be driven mad with shame at my ravenous desire. And yet, even as I fought to gain control over my cursed appetite, the struggle made me feel . . . better about myself. That I was not only becoming stronger in my willpower, but also somehow helping. I could feed them, bathe them, provide comfort, even attend amputations without being overcome.

"Then one night I was attending a dying man who had been grievously wounded at the Battle of Fredericksburg, and it came to me . . . I could become an engine of release for men who were suffering terribly. As he sank in and out of consciousness, I sang softly to him for a time, then fastened my lips to his throat and drank deeply to the last poundings of his heart.

"I am ashamed to admit the satisfaction this gave me, both physical and spiritual. I served in that hospital for the remainder of the war. I have no idea how many poor suffering men I helped spirit away while slaking my thirst. It was more than a way to survive. As odd as it sounds, it was a way to remain . . . human."

Lena put her arms behind her, leaning back against the wall.

"After the war, I stayed on as long as I could. But soon even the positions for night nurses became scarce, and I was forced to move on, because they wanted me to work daylight hours. I was so afraid the madness of my former time would return. . . . Then I heard the first inklings of the *Sonnen,* and I recalled the way I had been able to resist my hunger before coming to the hospital. I joined them and began fasting, and I have been with them to this day," she said.

My head was spinning with questions. Washington, D.C., during the Civil War? I had to ask.

"Did you ever see him?"

"Him?"

"You know . . . the president?"

"Oh." Lena smiled. "Yes, I saw him. Once, that was all. One night he made a tour of inspection of our hospital ward to cheer the troops, and I was there."

"You saw him. You saw Abraham Lincoln."

"Better than that . . . I spoke with him. The president touched my arm. . . ."

"Oh. My. God. What was he like?"

"Emma, he was a man. To me he was a man. Not the statues you see. He had the saddest, most serious face . . . but when one of the men made him laugh, telling him a joke about a Johnny Reb who was half mule, he was so different . . . so alive.

"He was wearing a black coat and a dark blue bow tie. His eyes were light gray. His face was creased, hair mostly dark, but peppery with gray; I remember wishing I could take a comb to it. His voice was slightly high-pitched for so tall a man. He was thin, but gave a sense of great physical power. His fingers were so long . . . when he touched me . . . I . . ."

She stopped and her gaze wandered over the Stone House Hotel, then out at the darkened horizon of the valley below.

"You know, I could have turned him, Emma. I do not like to

think about it, but I could have. It was a possibility. Just think of that . . . he could still be with us today. That haunts me, I must admit."

I was pretty much stunned into silence now. I just sat and looked at her and soaked it all in. I was thinking about the things she must have done, all those years . . . and what it all meant for me. That I could be sitting in this very same spot a hundred years from now . . . two hundred . . . and not be a day over seventeen. Ever.

It was too much to take in. Especially at night. Especially after talking to Papi. What would I remember about him a hundred years from now? Or Manda? Would I even remember her face? Mom's? I struggled not to cry. My mood must have been catching. I had never heard the three vampires so quiet.

"Can I ask you something?" I said finally. "All of you?"

"Of course," Anton said, leaning back.

"Living . . . so long . . . you must have learned a lot of things? Had a ton of experiences?"

Donne snorted. "That's what you would think, wouldn't you? Being the freshest Fresh I ever saw."

I bristled a little. "I don't know what I think. It just seems like . . ."

Lena waved her hand as if trying to get us to chill. "What Donne means to say is that so much of the knowledge we acquire ends up being useless, out of date, as time marches on," she said. "Imagine a college degree acquired in 1891 or even 1932; how useful would that be in the twenty-first century?"

"But the biggest thing is, you get sick of it," Donne said.

"Sick of what?" I said.

"People. Sick of being around people. Sick of working so hard to still be associated with them, still be a part of what they are. Human. Trying to hang on to the old life . . ."

"She is right; it's too much trouble," Anton agreed, lacing his arm around her waist. "All the hiding, lies, the close calls. And everything, everything has to be done in the dark. How many great experiences happen after dark? Truly?" He laughed again, and this time Donne punched his arm.

"But it is more than that," Lena said. "We do not have much contact with people. Hardly any, actually. It is . . . uncomfortable . . . if you have any kind of conscience at all. That is one of the great sacrifices forced upon us. We are quite limited in our experiences because we are limited in our relationships. Can you imagine spending a great deal of time with beings who are destined to become . . . your food?"

My scalp prickled. I felt so comfortable with them now, but every once in a while a shocking wall popped up between us. A wall that always reminded me that no matter how close we became as friends, they were trapped in a place where I could never go. I would never have to feed on anyone to live.

"And now . . . is there something you would like to share with us?" Lena said, breaking me out of my reverie. "We are so . . . curious."

I knew what she meant. I was holding back the story of my own transformation. Everything about Wirtz. My epilepsy. *The Call.*

"I . . . I want to tell you," I said. "You have all been so up-front with me. And I will. I promise. I just need . . . a little more time, okay?"

Donne started to say something, but Lena cut her off by lifting her hand.

"We understand," Lena said. "Speaking of such a horror when it is still so fresh and new is . . . trying. Take all the time you need."

I needed more than time. I needed a way to tell them what I was—a half-vampire human girl who was drawing a monster closer and closer to us all.

*   *   *

I woke up late the next morning feeling down. Today was Monday. Sagan had classes all week, but his schedule was especially full on Mondays, Wednesdays, and Fridays. It seemed like an eternity before I would see him again. Before the night would come.

Funny, I had never been a night person . . . now I couldn't wait for darkness to fall. Was I becoming something . . . different?

I took out the pocket watch he had given me. First block, English with Ms. Rose. That's where I should be right now. We were reading a book I couldn't stand, only now I might never know how it came out. Because I would never choose to read a book like that for myself.

After that, Chem II with its smells and sinks and test tubes. Then the project I was working on in history with my group. I didn't particularly like any of the kids, but we had been just that . . . a group. Algebra II. Whatever they learned this afternoon would be forever missing from my brain.

What if I never could go back? If I had to live like this basically . . . forever?

I would never find out my final averages in anything. Never attend another stupid pep rally. No more homecoming chatter, no brawny football guys beating some old junker to pieces with sledgehammers in front of a bonfire. No lunch line. People banging into you at the lockers. Guys saying crap about my boobs.

I had always felt so disconnected from school. So why was the loss of it bothering me now? There was nothing to stop me from learning on my own . . . but even more than I hated school, I hated the idea of not finishing. All that work. My hand cramping from taking notes. All the reading and projects and lugging sixty pounds of books through crowded halls. All of it cut off and done just like that.

I couldn't believe I was missing it. It's funny how when you get outside of something you hated, the hate isn't so strong anymore. There's a flip side, but it's not love, it's . . . the sense of being part of something, whether you wanted to or not.

I wondered if I had officially become the Lost Girl at school. Soon to be immortalized in a black-and-white photo—signifying death—hanging somewhere horrible like the cafeteria or the gym or the principal's office. Kids years from now would see my face and wonder who that sad, angry chick was. And somebody would say, oh, she's this weird girl that went missing years ago and they never found her. How's that for a memorial?

It made me sad in a way that I had never felt sad before.

I had to do something physical. I pulled on my trail shoes and ran into town. Cruised by the local high school just for the vibe. It turned out to be acres and acres of two-story, flat brown buildings made of blocks the size of washing machines. It looked like a fortress. Maybe that's what schools were expecting these days, an attack.

There were girls on the soccer field. They were okay, but looked as if they were only half trying. I wanted to be out there so bad, showing them how to really pound in a shot. Rush a defender.

Why not?

I jumped the short fence and raced onto the soccer field. I was wearing my jeans, but so what? Before I had even registered on their consciousness, I stole the next lazy pass setting up a shot, and then I was off, weaving my way around the girls, moving in and out as easily as if they were running in wet cement.

"Hey!" one of the girls yelled.

I knew girls like her. Tall and lanky, the kind that lulled you to sleep. Then, when you got too close, they would uncoil a leg like a bazooka, and your stomach or chest or—worst of all—your face would get whacked so hard, it took a little while for the pain to even start.

The tall girl took up the chase, screaming at the others to follow. "Come on, get her!"

Pretty soon I had half the team rushing at me from all sides. I moved with the ball in a way that was downright supernatural, dipping this way to duck one defender, swinging wide past three more, playing with them, really. Until I had the whole team and even the coaches—squatty ex-college soccer-type guys with legs like fire hydrants—all converging on me at midfield, screaming and cursing.

I barreled right through them, got my sights on the goal, swung my leg and bent the kick so hard, the keeper wound up horizontal in midair trying to stop it. *Too late*. It was in the net and I had jumped the fence again and was gone.

I wanted to die. I really did. Because it was over. Nothing was ever going to get that feeling back for me. Even if I killed Wirtz, went home, started going to school again—the thing I was best at, my greatest passion, something that meant everything to me personally—was done. *Forever.*

When I had first begun to understand my powers, I had thought I was a god. But now I knew the truth. I had lost everything, not because I was a god, but because I was a freak. And who wants to hang out with a freak except another freak? I was even more isolated than the *Sonnen* vampires. I was caught between two worlds, a foot in both, but all of me in neither.

I had never felt so lonely.

In the middle of the afternoon I ate pizza someone had left on a table in a mini-mall. I certainly was getting my quota of cheese these days. A girl came by wiping up, giving me a funny look, but she didn't say anything. I chewed a slice of lukewarm pepperoni and tried to imagine a life beyond hiding. Maybe I could convince Sagan to come with me. We'd go somewhere I'd always dreamed of going. Europe. South America. Some island. I would have to keep things secret as long as I could. If other vampires—if *Verloren*—ever found out about my special powers, would I be safe anywhere?

I daydreamed about a place where I could live with Sagan that was cool and wooded and kind of unpopulated . . . like Prince Edward Island. Wasn't that where Anne of Green Gables was from? But maybe it was overrun with tourists these days. Okay, my own island off the coast of Maine. We wouldn't need a big house, just a tiny cottage. I bet a vampire could sling together a cabin in no time. But then Sagan would have to know. But he'd have to know sooner or later anyhow. Surely he would start wondering why I never aged.

I tried to imagine a life like the *Sonnen* had been leading for centuries. Hiding, stealing, taking blood drop by drop from strangers. I wanted so much to help them. I wanted Sagan to help. But how could I ever tell him what I was?

Maybe the *Sonnen* could come and visit us up there? Sure, and we could all chop wood and skin rabbits and wait for the Cure. *Shut up.*

Late in the afternoon, my headset shrieked, shaking me out of my doldrums. It was still too early for Sagan, but I flicked it on delightedly.

"I'm skipping work tonight," he said. "Meet me at the observatory at six o'clock. I've got something planned."

I spent a good long while getting ready, then it seemed as if six would never get there. As much as I wanted to run, I forced myself

to stroll to the observatory so I would stay as neat and clean as possible. It was exciting, wondering what in the world he had in mind.

My heart was beating outside my chest when I saw his Jeep
swinging up the long drive.

"Get in," Sagan said, kissing my cheek and holding the door
open for me.

We got out on the main road and headed north. I wished the
seats were closer together.

"Isn't this the way to the gate?" I said.

"Yep."

"Sagan . . . I don't get it. Where are you taking me?"

"It's a surprise."

My heart thumped. "Wait a minute . . . not more family stuff?
Do I look okay?"

He laughed. "When do you ever *not* look okay? You look incredible. No, nothing like that. You're safe."

"Then what—"

"I told you, it's a surprise."

We left the interstate and then made several long slow turns.
After several minutes the Jeep rolled to a stop in a broad parking lot
and Sagan pulled up the hand brake.

The first thing I saw was a cobblestone canyon flanked by fancy
shops and restaurants. Banana Republic. A Mac store. P.F. Chang's,
the Chocolate Crocodile. And right in front of us, a huge Barnes &
Noble.

People were milling all over, some in shorts and casual stuff,
others with more formal wear. It felt strange after all my isolation,
almost claustrophobic, dodging in and out of the crowd.

"So where are we . . . ?" I started.

"It's a date," Sagan said. "It's called a date."

*   *   *

We headed down the cobblestone canyon. I was nearly dizzy by the time he pulled me through some big glass doors.

The noise instantly changed to a gentle indoor babble. The odor of cooking wafted deliciously beneath my nose.

"Food!" I said, mouth watering. Somewhere a steak was being grilled. I could hear the meat sizzling in a way that I had never heard it before. . . . The sound of a waterfall couldn't have been more beautiful.

"This is my family's favorite place," Sagan said, shaking out his cloth napkin after they seated us.

"O'Connor's!" I said, looking at the tasseled menu in front of me.

"You know it?"

I nodded excitedly. "I've passed the billboards plenty of times."

"You've never been?"

"Life in a single-parent family."

"With six we don't come here often, but we all love it."

The wood around us was dark and heavy and elegant, and a fire was burning in the big stone hearth. After being outdoors so much, I felt completely out of place, but I didn't care. I flipped through the menu, marveling at the choices.

"Why don't we start with an appetizer?" Sagan said. "You like lobster dip?"

Did I.

We had a baby spinach and strawberry salad. Then a crab bisque that was a kind of thick soup that nearly lifted the top of my skull off. An hour later I was popping the last little bit of blue-cheese-encrusted garlic prime rib into my mouth, practically moaning with pleasure. I didn't have words for the experience. Afterward I could only lean back in my chair and sigh contentedly.

"So you liked it?" Sagan said, grinning.

"*Like* is too small a word. Thank you." I squeezed his fingers.

"And for dessert . . ."

"Oh my God. I'm stuffed."

He checked the time on his cell. "Okay. I was thinking maybe an ice cream cone after the movie."

"Movie?"

Being in a theater was an even bigger shock to my system. All those heads, people laughing, gabbing. So normal. I felt like I needed six more eyes. We were about twenty minutes into the movie before I began to settle down. My alertness made me realize just how paranoid I had become.

It was a good show, something called *Karma Chameleon,* all about a girl who figured her karma was responsible for screwing up her love life. I thought it was cute and sweet that Sagan had picked a chick flick. So I never told him I would have rather seen the sci-fi epic where zombies overrun the very first city on the moon.

The theater was only about a third full—everybody else was catching lunar zombies—and most of the audience looked as old as my mom. I wondered what they thought when Sagan leaned over the popcorn tub and kissed me. Then he did it again.

After that I didn't think about anybody else at all. Not even vampires. We were just a boy and a girl in a dark room.

When we got out of the theater, most of the shops were closing, so there weren't as many people around. A shaggy-looking guy with a guitar and a small amp was playing ancient tunes in front of a synchronized fountain. We chose a spot just far enough away to hear without paying attention. Of course I could have listened from the parking lot.

"You probably think I'm crazy, don't you?" I said, taking a lick of ice cream.

Sagan smiled and kissed me on the temple. His lips were cold from the rocky road. I gently pushed him away to look deeply into his eyes. He blinked first.

"I don't think you're crazy," he said. "I think you're different. Different is good."

"But maybe I'm not different," I said. "Maybe I'm just like everybody else . . . only something happened. Something beyond my control, and it changed me. Changed me in a way that nobody would ever believe."

"Okay," Sagan said. "Can I guess what the change is?"

"If you want to. But you'll never guess right."

"Hmmm . . . you've got some strange new disease nobody ever heard of, cooked up in a government lab." He glanced at the balled-up napkin in my hand. "I'm . . . probably infected right now and don't even know it."

I laughed. "Next."

"Let's see. A genetic experiment in . . . human enhancement. They were trying to design this perfect new species. . . ."

"Perfect? Please."

"Girl DNA mixed with . . . I can't think of an animal that would be right. A cheetah? But where's your spots? Wait. That's a leopard, isn't it?"

I giggled. "Or a dalmatian. Nope, not even warm."

"You're killing me, you know that?"

"You've said that before. Okay," I said, laying my head on his shoulder. "How about this. As long as you don't bug me to death about it, I promise I will tell you. Soon."

"How soon?"

"I don't know. It depends . . . on a lot of things." *Like me staying alive.*

"Why did you frown just then?" he said.

I turned away. "I'm sorry."

He touched me on the chin, lifted my head up with his finger. "Hey, it's all right. It's going to be okay. Look . . . Emma. Tell me something . . . a secret about you nobody else knows. Not *the* secret. You know what I mean."

I looked off into the distance. I'd never really been the secret type until recently.

"Okay. As far back as I can remember, I have always been kind of desperate . . . desperate to believe life is more interesting than it really is. You know what I mean?"

Sagan nodded.

"That's why I'm always going on about history. I kind of use it as my evidence, you know? Of what life can really be. Does that sound totally stupid?"

"No."

The shaggy guitar guy—somebody was actually watching him now. A single man, short but powerfully built, wearing a little hat that barely covered the top of his massive head.

"When you think about it, we have more in common than you realize, Emma," Sagan said. He was holding my fingers. "Stars . . . some of them are already dead by the time we get to see them. We both want to be in places that are already gone."

"Except . . . my place has people."

"Don't screw up the moment." He pointed at the sky. "Maybe that star right there—maybe it once had life orbiting it? Maybe they were just like us. Only a trillion miles away and a million years ago."

"You think too much," I said. "But I like it."

"Both of us want to go to places where neither of us can go, because it's basically impossible," he said. "Why do you think that is? Why don't we want to be here?"

I snuggled against him. "I don't know. Right here, right now . . . is there anyplace else?"

20. FALLING

Back in the parking lot, I leaned against the Jeep. Sagan put his arm around my waist.

"You know, you keep giving me the best days of my life," I said. "I've never been on a date before."

"I kind of guessed that."

"How?"

"I don't know. You just kind of reminded me of myself a year or two ago. I didn't really date much in high school. Mostly a little bit of 'friend' stuff, you know? Hanging out with the editor in chief of our school newspaper because I was managing editor. Or a girl from the chess team. That kind of thing."

"You were on the chess team?"

"Yeah." He puffed up his chest. "Wanna make something of it?"

I swore. "Probably in the band too. Don't tell me. You played the tuba, didn't you? No! You dragged around one of those portable xylophones and—"

He kissed me.

"Mmmm. You don't kiss like a xylophone guy."

Sagan wrapped me in his arms from behind. I could feel his mouth in my hair. Every sensation was heightened to the point where I could barely stand it. Was this because I was a vampire? *Or something else.*

"You're a huge distraction, you know?" I said.

"That's my job."

I put my hand on his arm. "Just keep telling me that."

We sat in his Jeep a very long time, talking and making out. I didn't want to go. Finally the parking lot was empty except for us and a street sweeper that was zipping closer and closer to the Jeep, trying to give us a hint.

"Sagan," I said.

"What?"

"If you could live forever, would you want to?"

He put his hand on his chin and leaned away from me. "Well . . . geneticists say we're only about fifteen or twenty years away from basically beating all diseases, extending the life span indefinitely. Sure, who wouldn't want that? There are so many things I want to see, want to do."

"But really think about it," I said. "Forever. It never ends, okay? I know that sounds stupid, but think about what that means. Isn't it kind of scary? If you take it literally? To keep on going and going."

"You mean like, what will we finally come to? What will we become?"

"I guess, yeah."

"I don't know. I like what we are."

I was definitely becoming a night owl. After Sagan dropped me off, I wasn't remotely sleepy. Being with him was like taking a drug that left me burning and alive. After lying on the air mattress for over an hour, thinking about nothing but him, I cursed and dropped down into the grungy little room, looking for something to do to pass the time.

My mind screamed for a laptop—I couldn't remember ever feeling so disconnected from the world.

I sat at the moldy desk and took Manda's picture out, looking at it. After a while I put my hands on an imaginary keyboard. Started typing in keystroke combinations that were so familiar to me, they didn't even feel like a memory. This felt more like patterns I had been born with, patterns built into my fingers before birth.

Patterns.

The desktop felt spongy, almost wet, but my moving fingers barely noticed. I kept up my imaginary typing. And then I didn't notice anything at all.

When I looked up again, the vampire was standing in the doorway, framed by his lavender glow. My heart jumped out of rhythm. He was watching me, one corner of his jagged mouth turned up in a pleased little smile.

I had no weapons in here. Only things like batteries and bags of clothes.

I watched him, reflexes screaming. If I rushed him, hit him hard enough, maybe I could knock him off the tower—

I tried to stand, but I couldn't move.

My hands were still lying on top of the desk. *It's happening again,* I thought. Another seizure. I struggled inside the cushiony prison of my mind, curses rattling through my head. Wirtz came closer, filling the room. He studied the walls, the desk, the furniture. My eyes were the only thing alive in my body; I swiveled them left and right, doing my best to follow him, see what the vampire was looking at.

Wirtz reached for the filing cabinet drawers, fingers stopping just short of touching the handles. "You wouldn't want to open this for me, would you, *Mädchen*? So that I may see what is inside?" He laughed, an awful sound, like stones laughing. "I didn't think so."

The vampire suddenly leaned across the desk, the raw-looking wound on his scalp right in my face. My breathing stopped. I knew he was only an image, but my body didn't know.

"And what are you doing here?" He straightened up and my breathing started again. "A . . . room," the vampire said. "Industrial. Old. No *Verzierung* . . . ornamentation. I would say this is some-where in a . . . business? Am I guessing correctly? An abandoned business in Huntsville, Ala-ba-ma, where you have chosen to hide. With bags from . . . let me see, what is this . . . U-ni-ted Outfitters and *Nord* Creek. Interesting."

Now something else caught his attention. Manda's picture on the desk.

No, I thought. *Leave her alone. I'll kill you.*

The vampire looked at the picture a long time, smiling. At last he backed away from the desk and sat down in midair. . . . Wher-ever his physical body was, there was something to sit on.

"I want to tell you a story, *Mädchen*. A story about *Zubehöre*— attachments. One of the first of my children I ever . . . turned . . . was a young girl named Ava. Not very many years older than your-self. She answered my Call, even though at the time I did not know how to give it properly. I had stumbled upon this myself. My skill was simple, *rudimentär*. But Ava came, in spite of this.

"I took her on her first *Blutjagd*. We shared our private spaces during the long days underground. Time became meaningless to us. There was only the time I spent with her.

"One night I awoke and Ava was gone. I could not understand this. Had someone come and stolen her away? She would no longer answer my Call.

"I searched for years, but I was too . . . *unerfahren* . . . inexperienced . . . to find her. Decades passed. I fathered many more children until at last I became weary of the practice . . . only wishing to be alone. I came to find myself in the place you would call . . . *Nord* Carolina . . . in the mountains. I have always preferred mountains. More isolated; again, my preference."

The vampire's face changed. I couldn't read his expression.

"One spring, by the most extreme chance, I came across Ava again. She was standing beside the old colonial ferry landing on the Neuse River. Watching across the water as if waiting for someone. I watched too. Her golden hair, *jugendlich* appearance. I felt something I had not felt for . . . a very long time.

"Ava recognized me at once, called out my name in a kind of gasp when I approached. We came together in an embrace. I held her close. This way, you know?" The vampire crossed his arms over his large chest, hugging himself. "Close in such a way to never let her go again. Closer still, *Mädchen*."

The vampire drew his arms tighter and tighter around his broad chest. His pale face began to turn red and his jaw bulged with the effort.

"Harder still. Her eyes . . . were very large. Harder and harder I squeezed. Until . . . at last . . . her bones . . . began to crack. . . ."

The vampire let himself go and his long arms dropped to his sides. He took several breaths, dark eyes lowered to the floor.

"That is what I came to tell you tonight," he said. "This is the memory I have to share as a gift for you. All I care for . . . attachments."

Wirtz stood up from the invisible chair. The pale color slowly returned to his face.

"*Bis später.*"

He evaporated into the dark.

Bis später. I knew what that meant. Papi said it all the time.
See you later.

The room was still vibrating with the vampire's presence. I climbed up to the roof and collapsed on the air mattress, taking hold of the ax. Wirtz had come through so easily this time. Did that mean he was closer? At least he hadn't picked up any new clues.

Oh no. The bags. The vampire had seen my shopping bags from the mall. The mall that was only a couple of miles away. *He's tightening the noose.*

I lay there unable to sleep, alternating between terror that he might come back tonight and fury that he was only coming through in images, pictures. This was turning into psychological warfare.

I ached to take the vampire on in the flesh. I had passed the point of wanting only to survive. I was tired of his games. Wanted to ruin Wirtz, destroy him, crumble him into bits. I had to know more about where he was and what he was doing.

I found them sitting on the stone wall. From a distance, their lavender glow made them look like Japanese lanterns hanging in the forest.

"Well, Fresh," Donne said. "Just can't keep away from our range, can you?"

"Bite me," I said. I didn't have patience for her crap tonight.

"I might, but who knows how you will taste?" Donne said. Anton responded with his goofiest laugh.

"Good evening, Emma," Lena said.

"I've come to ask you something important," I said. "Your story about Valentin—you mentioned he once came to you when he wasn't in bodily form. It started with a *W.*"

"Wesentliche," Lena said. "That is the word you are searching for. What we call the essence."

"Yeah, that's it. I really need to know more about this. . . . Like how's it done?"

Donne snorted. "Oh, is that all?"

Lena smiled. "Knowledge of the *Wesentliche* is acquired over time, requiring great patience."

"Oh. But what if I needed to know right away? Couldn't you give me the Cliffs Notes version?"

Lena gave me a knowing look. "All right. The best way to start is with the *Feld*."

"*Feld*. That's another German word, right?" I came over and sat down next to her. "It means 'field,' doesn't it?"

"Yes," Lena said. "But not like a field of clover . . ." She looked at Anton. "You are better at explaining it."

Anton hopped down from the wall and drew a stick figure in the dirt with his index finger.

"Here, Emma. Let's say this is you, all right?"

"Okay."

He drew a circle around the stick figure. "This circle is your *Feld*. But it's not really a circle because . . . it's everywhere, you know?"

"All around me? Like a sphere?"

"More than that. Around you, inside you, throughout you . . ."

"So the *Feld* is some kind of . . . invisible force that is all around me, inside me, etc.?"

Anton snapped his fingers. "Exactly! Only a force acts upon something else. The *Feld* just . . . is. Understand? It doesn't do anything; it's just there. All the time. Wherever you go. Your *Feld*, mine, Donne's, Lena's, on and on."

"What about the *Verloren*?" I said.

"Sure," Anton said. "Everything has a *Feld,* even stones." He patted the Bear. "So there are trillions of individual *Felder*—or, as you might say in English, *Felds.* Even much more than that. Yet there is only one *Feld.* Stay with me, okay? Your *Feld* is also all *Felds* at once, all right? They are all connected, making up one giant *Feld* that goes all over and touches everything."

"So we each make up a part of this gigantic *Feld,*" I said.

"Yes and no," Anton said. "Each part also contains the whole, okay? In each of the small *Felds* there is a . . . picture . . . of the whole, you know?"

"Sounds like a hologram," I said, remembering something we had talked about recently in science.

"A what?"

"A hologram is a . . . picture, like you said. Only you can cut it up into smaller pieces, and the whole picture is always still there. No matter how small you slice it."

"Perfect!" Anton said. "That's really very good. Hologram. I will have to remember that. So—all *Felds* are connected, becoming one big *Feld.* So our actions ripple through everything. Once you learn how to tune into it . . . you can sense the approach of others by these . . . ripples. Their *Feld* announces them."

"Like Spider-Man's tingle," I said.

"Huh?" Anton said.

"Never mind."

"We use it to communicate. *Feld* is like a telephone wire. . . . You can speak through it when you know how." Anton's eyes brightened. "But *Feld* is also . . . health! You balance it and it takes care of you. The infection—when a *Verloren* attacks someone, they are really attacking that person's *Feld.* Understand?"

I nodded. "I guess so."

Anton jabbed his finger on the circle he had just drawn. "The

265

infection is not in the blood. A doctor couldn't find it. The infection is not an infection of the body; it's an infection of the body's *Feld.*"

"Wow. Okay, but how about the *Wesentliche?*"

"I'm getting there. When you're drinking from someone, your two *Felds* are temporarily joined," Anton said. "Mixed. Blended. If you drink long enough, they become permanently bonded, see?"

"Okay," I said. "But when we went on the Blood Hunt and . . . drank from those people . . . why weren't they turned into vampires?"

Anton held up a finger. "If you stop drinking soon enough, the *Felds* separate. Become two again. Unchanged."

I thought of Wirtz. How long had my *Feld* been hooked to his? *Long enough.* But why hadn't it changed me completely? *The seizure,* I thought. Something about my tonic-clonic must have screwed up the bonding process. Scrambled it. I shuddered.

"So . . . how do you know when to stop feeding?" I said.

Lena jumped in here. "It is instinctual. You know when you are approaching the boundary where the bond is forged. I hate to tell you this, Emma, but . . . once that boundary is reached, it creates a bond between your *Feld* and your attacker's *Feld.* This bond will extend through time without lessening."

My heart sank. *Not Wirtz. No.*

"You mean . . . I'll be glued to that creep for as long as I live? He can keep sending his *Wesentliche* through over and over again?"

Anton nodded. "The *Wesentliche* comes through and keeps coming through. With the *Feld,* there is always a sender and a receiver, okay? The sender has control. The receiver must submit." He held his finger up. "But wait! There is hope. Remember that this contact is a two-way street. It goes both ways, yes? The one who initiates the contact is usually the sender. But the sender also can be the one with the strongest will. With patience, years of practice, you can strengthen your will to fight against the bond, but until the infection is cleansed completely by the *Sonneneruption—*"

"Oh my God. Years?" I said.

"There is a shortcut," Donne said.

"Which is?"

"Kill him."

We were quiet awhile as I digested everything. "In the meantime, you must guard against *der Anruf,*" Lena said. "The Call. Resist it. He will try to use this against you over and over. This is the *Verloren*'s way of controlling others."

"Why? What do they want?"

Lena glanced at Donne, who was unusually quiet. "For some, the attachment can be . . . physical. In others, it is perhaps a twisted kind of loneliness. Power, a wish to dominate. Control for the sake of controlling. Now, however, they are being directed to go against their natural instinct for killing in order to strengthen their numbers. This is unthinkably difficult to accomplish. Imagine herding wild animals. It has taken an extraordinary *Verloren* leader."

"Who is it?" I said.

They looked at each other with worried eyes.

"Come on, don't tell me this is some kind of Harry Potter deal," I said. "You can say his name, can't you?"

Lena gathered her ragged skirts so that she could step down from the wall. "It is not a *he*, Emma. It is a she," she said.

Now we were sitting around the little table in the *Sonnen* hideout.

"It's not as dangerous talking in here," Anton said. "Surrounded by earth, stone, trees, things with big *Felds*. They help to mask our own."

"So who is she?" I said.

"I don't know that anyone among the *Sonnen* knows her original name," Lena said. "We call her *die Esserin*. In New Orleans, she is *la Mangeuse*. Further south, *La Comedora*."

"Which means?"

"The Eater," Lena said.

A wave of cold rolled through me. "Have you ever actually seen her?"

"Are you kidding?" Donne said, speaking for the first time in a while. "Do we look like the kind of people who would come within a hundred miles of someone called the Eater?"

"So where is she?"

"As far as we know, like other *Verloren,* she is always on the move," Lena said.

"I once heard she was in Tennessee," Anton said.

"Too close," Donne said.

"*Die Esserin* changed everything," Lena said. "She is the one who made the war."

"But how?" I said. "How did she get them to act together?"

"By using the *Feld* to offer them something," Lena said, "that even a *Verloren* would find difficult refusing."

"Which was?"

"The world."

"You mean . . . they want to wipe out all the human beings?" I said.

"Oh no, not at all," Anton said. "They would breed some . . . for food."

I tried to picture a world where human beings were enslaved to a vampire race, alive only for the . . . thirsty.

"But why can't anybody resist them? How can they control you the way they do?"

The three vampires glanced at one another.

"Through threat of torture," Lena said finally. "So unspeakable . . ." She hesitated as if she literally couldn't bear to say it. "The *Sonnen* call it *der Verlust.* The Loss."

"The *Verlust* cuts the victim off from her *Feld,*" Anton said.

"But . . . you said the *Feld* is everywhere, inside everything?"

"Oh, it's still there," Anton said. "Only the victim can't access it anymore, okay? To be cut off from the *Feld* . . . We've been told it's like . . . existing, but not existing. There is no escape. Soon, even thinking of escaping this . . . place without a *Feld* . . . is too hard."

"So the person . . . dies?" I said.

"The victim is still a living, breathing being. But with no sense of being connected to anything. Not the earth, not other people. Perfectly isolated and helpless, they care only to satisfy their basest needs."

"Are you saying they'll be like that for . . . eternity?"

"Now you're catching on," Donne cut in.

Lena gave her a frosty look. "We don't know that. You are frightening Emma."

"She needs to be frightened, little Fresh," Donne said. She spat on Anton's drawing.

"So what was the war like?" I said.

"It was really more of a battle than a war," Lena said. "The *Sonnen* did not want war. But as the *Verloren* grew in strength, it became a point of survival, if the *Sonneneruption* didn't come soon . . . and so the *Sonnen* united to locate the Eater . . . in order to kill her."

"Killing the head of the snake," I said.

"Yes," Lena said.

"So what happened?"

Lena didn't answer for a moment. She put a hand to her mouth, as if she didn't want to let the words out.

"The *Sonnen* who were sent against her . . . they underwent the *Verlust*. They lost their *Felds*."

All of this swirled in my head as I rushed home to my tower, the seed of a crazy plan beginning to form. Something Anton had said had given me an idea: *With the Feld, there is always a sender and a receiver. The sender has control.*

That's why I had been able to go to Wirtz when I had experimented with the playing cards. *I pushed first,* I thought. I had been the sender. Now it was time to go on offense again, and I intended to take the vampire right over the edge. But first I had a phone call to make.

I dug out the headset and dialed Sagan's number. It took him a while to answer.

"Hey . . . it's you." I could hear him yawning happily. "My . . . street sweeper."

"Sagan, listen—"

"Everything all right? What's wrong?"

"I'm fine. Please, I wouldn't ask you to do this if I didn't think it was important. But . . . it's in another town."

"Um, yeah, sure, what is it. . . ."

"Do you still have the address to my apartment?"

"Are you kidding? It's practically sewn to my skin." He was wide awake now.

"Tomorrow morning, would you please go to my place and check on them for me? Google the directions. I'd screw it all up."

"Really? Okay, yeah, sure."

"Don't knock on the door or anything. That would be a disaster. Just park and watch for them. They should be coming out about seven-thirty or a little after to get Manda to school. It would mean so much to me if you could just see them."

He yawned again, pointedly this time. "There's just one thing. . . ."

"What?"

"Don't you mean today instead of tomorrow? It's 3:22 a.m., Emma."

"Oh crap. You're right. Sorry, I'm losing track of time."

"I gave you a watch," he grumbled good-naturedly. "I love hearing your voice, though."

"It's really important." *So at least someone I trust will know where they are. In case—just in case* . . . I didn't want to finish the thought.

"Has something happened?" Sagan said.

"No! I'm okay. I just need you to go there. Don't worry about me. There's something I want to try."

"Wait—you're sounding all serious now. Like somebody leaving a last will and testament. What is it really?"

"I'm just scared for them, that's all. Okay, Mom drives a maroon Kia, so you'll be sure it's them. Just see if everything looks all right. I have to know."

"Are they in trouble? Come on, Emma, let me call the police!"

I swore. "No, God—Sagan—I'm sure they're fine. But if you call the police, the cops will force you to tell them where I am and I'll have to run again. I told you what would happen then. Do you understand me? If you think you know better than me and do it anyway—we're dead."

"Jeez, okay."

"And call me the second you get back."

"I'll call you from the complex; how about that?"

"Even better. Good deal. And don't get caught," I said.

"Caught by who?"

"My mom, who else?"

"So I don't need a gun or something."

"Sagan! This isn't a joke."

"Who's joking?"

I switched off the headset and shoved it back in the bag. Time to get ready.

I grabbed a length of nylon rope and dropped down into the feral room. I stepped off the distance to the back of the room, which turned out to be approximately fifteen feet, then cut a little over half that length in rope. I wrapped one end of the rope around my stomach and knotted it securely with three granny knots. Then I tied the other end to one of the legs of the prehistoric desk. Last, I plumped a few thick bath towels around any sharp edges, sat down, and made myself as comfortable as possible in the rickety old chair. Shook out the playing cards on the desk and went to work.

I was going to induce a grand mal seizure.

Actually, I wasn't really sure that I could. A big part of me hoped I would fail. But I wanted to know the vampire's location, and I figured this would give me my best chance. My simple, or "small," seizures generally lasted about thirty to sixty seconds, while a TC could go on for several minutes. I wanted that extra time inside the vampire's head.

I was scared to death of going there again—not to mention sickened—but I had to gain an edge somehow. Besides, who knew what else might happen? Maybe the "bond" between our two *Felds* was so deeply rooted, it would shake something loose in Wirtz's skull too. The way he had looked at Manda's picture—*so help me God*—I was ready to strike back any way that I could.

I checked the rope one last time. I had to work fast; daylight wasn't that far off. Wirtz would be going to ground soon. Then, as before, I started out by rapidly shuffling the cards before my eyes.

Then I laid the whole deck out in a checkerboard pattern, quickly flipping them over, one after another. Not a twinge. *Wish I had a strobe light.*

What was I doing wrong?

I tried just watching the cards, letting my eyes go in and out of focus. Finally I lapsed into a semi-doze, tipping back in the chair until a line of drool running down my chin woke me up.

I snapped forward, gasping. Remembering what I had done the last time I traveled to Wirtz. *My scar . . . I touched my scar.*

I looked at the pattern of the cards again, this time running my finger over the raised flesh on my leg. *Take me to Wirtz. Take me to Wirtz.* Then I added something new: I started rocking forcefully, getting into a vigorous rhythm that exactly matched each time I stroked my scar. *Take me to Wirtz. Take me to Wirtz. Take me to Wirtz.*

The chair squeaked violently as I picked up speed. *Faster, faster.* Finally I began to feel the sensation I had experienced before: the comfort of the rolled-up towel behind my eyes. The cards slowly melted, losing their shapes and colors, becoming a part of the desk. *Any second now . . .*

Wait.

That smell . . . Cinnamon and apples.

I opened one eye and I could see trees. The other eye was squashed against something pebbly and hard. I was lying on my side, somewhere outdoors. *How did I get here?*

For the longest time I couldn't move, then I tried to sit up, but the top half of my body felt as if it weighed twice as much as normal. I slumped back down on my side. My ribs hurt as if someone had taken a sledgehammer to them.

One of my hands was pinned beneath me. I raised the other

and tried to grab something that could help me sit up. There was nothing there. I could see my free hand moving against the sky, but I no longer had control over it. It didn't belong to me anymore.

"Mom?" I said, but I doubt the word ever left my throat.

Nobody came. Finally I managed to fall over onto my stomach. Got both hands under me and pushed. My body moved forward a few inches, then collapsed again.

I pushed as hard as I could and rolled over onto my back. I was looking up at the bluish black of the night sky: twinkling stars, little ragged bits of clouds. Everything hurt. Everything looked round. The world started to spin. I closed my eyes, but that made the spinning worse.

A warm liquid was spreading across my legs.

For the first time I noticed that a rope was knotted around my stomach. *Rope?* It was bunched up under my back, and that's where some of the pain was coming from. I angled my head to the left and opened my eyes again—there was some kind of tall metal structure there. I couldn't remember a thing. Not even my own name.

"Hello," a deep voice said.

My heart gave one big hammering lurch, then kept on beating rapidly.

With great effort, I struggled upright. A man was sitting on the ground across from me. He had a shirt that was gray and stained. Little corks for buttons. A long coat and dark pants, muddy boots. His legs were crossed, arms draped over his pointed knees, hands clasped in front of him. *Oh no. What is that?* There was a reddish-lavender glow all over his body.

Nothing made sense. Why would a man be glowing like that unless he was something—*something that was not a man.*

Oh God. The guy's head was seriously messed up, like he had been in some kind of horrible accident. A long pinkish flap of scalp hung over one eyebrow. It made me sick to look at him.

The man stood; he was really tall. He walked a little ways around the clearing, the lavender glow following. I turned and looked at what he was staring at: the huge iron and steel structure behind me. If only my memory would clear. Where was I? What was this place?

What was he going to do to me?

"So this is where you are," the man said. "I have been looking in the city, but you are outside the town limits, aren't you?" He put his hands in his pockets. "This tall structure is . . . industrial, I am sure. But not exactly . . . modern . . . is it, *Mädchen?*"

Why was he calling me that? The man smiled and licked his lips. His eyes were black as marbles.

"Who . . . are you?" I finally managed to slur. To my ears the words sounded syrupy and confused.

"She speaks," the man said, seemingly pleased. "*Sehr gut.* But there is something . . . damaged with you . . . *ja?*"

Was this strange guy German? I tried to stand and fell down on all fours again. A runaway gyroscope inside my skull made me sway in little circles. The stranger kept looking at the tower.

"There is something . . . familiar about it. . . . I would think this may be a *Försterstation* for observing fires . . . correct? But no, the structure is too elaborate."

The man came closer to me. I was still on all fours, so dizzy I could barely move. He knelt and looked straight at me, putting his arms out in front of him. He turned his hands up to where I could see the palms. Dipped his head until his stringy hair hung on either side of his face. But he kept staring into my eyes.

"Have you ever painted with watercolors?" the man said. "You cannot keep them from running together on the *Leinwand* . . . the canvas. They blend no matter what you do. We are like that, *Mäd-chen*. You are a part of me now. I am a part of you. Indivisible."

He kept his hands out in front of him. I felt something pulling.

The pulling sensation grew, but the man remained motionless. A giant magnet connected me to the steel of his fingers. I felt I would tip over.

I wanted to go to him. I didn't want to, but I wanted to. I began to walk on all fours to him. The rope trailed along behind me like a tail. The man waited, on his knees, head still down, arms still reaching.

Finally I knelt before him, our knees almost touching. The man was so much taller than me. I suddenly wanted to hold him. *Wanted to be held*. How? I was disgusted by him. I could see his face so clearly now, that horrible hooked nose and flap of scalp.

The man wanted me to kiss him. I wanted to kiss him. I started tilting my head to make it easier.

We were less than an inch apart. If I inhaled, I would be inhaling his breath. The man smiled. He was here to help me—

I blinked. I saw something there in his eyes. I saw images of . . . bodies . . . the walls of a room splashed with blood. Hair, clothing, furniture sticky with it. An empty sneaker . . .

A name fell into my head like a stone.

Wirtz.

I remembered where I was. Who I was.

Wirtz!

He still had some kind of hold on me. I couldn't move. So I stared at him from one inch away, willing the blood to come up into my eyes, heat them to the boiling point. I thought of the sun . . . Sagan's sun . . . the boiling bright merciless midday sun. Made it fill my brain. Made the sun float inside my head, filling every crack and crevice with light so intense, my skull couldn't hold it.

The vampire's image seemed to wobble a moment, then his smile turned into a grimace. He stood up and staggered backward, hands over his face.

For one brief moment I understood how the *Feld* worked. Understood that the one with the strongest will was the one with the power to wield it. For just a few seconds I was his master. *Turning his black little eyeballs to putrefied jelly.*

The vampire staggered once more. I broke free of his pull, his Call. Free enough to get to my feet. I took a jerking step toward him, driving him back. He kept backing up until he backed straight into the night.

21. DISCOVERY

I had trouble holding myself up. I sat down in the gravel and hung forward. I don't know how long I stayed that way. Maybe hours. The sun was coming up when at last I staggered to the faucet in the bunker and doused my head, splashed my face. I didn't know if I had ever been hurt this bad before.

I had barely enough strength to unknot the rope. How far had I fallen?

I took my clothes off and bathed cold water over my injured side again and again, taking as long as I needed. The pain started to ease a little, but it still felt as if I had been run over by a cement mixer. I risked a deep breath.

"Ohhhhhh."

At last I came out of the bunker and sat down on a cement wall. The top of the tower, which was the iron structure of the long arm, had to be close to a hundred feet high. I could see the open doorway of my little room, the next level down, say seventy-five or eighty feet above the forest floor. Enough to kill a human being about two or three times. The pain in my side, the feeling of compression, told me it was true.

Insane.

There was so much I didn't know about this *Feld* business. I had thought I had control. But somehow the grand mal seizure had screwed everything up: the vampire had pushed his way through instead. The temporary amnesia didn't help. And now he knew exactly what my hideout looked like. *Great.*

When I straightened up again, the pain was eye-blinking bad. But probing around, I didn't think anything was broken. I trudged up the tower, taking the stairs one step at a time. I almost laughed when I got to the little room at the top. . . . The desk had been jerked all the way across the floor, and a corner leg was sticking through the doorway and hanging out over space. The leg that the rope had been tied to.

I slept most of the day and woke in a rotten mood. Physically, I felt better. So much better, I could sit up without much trouble. I rubbed my side. Aching and incredibly sore, but not much worse than taking a nasty shot in soccer. A long curved bruise showed just under my ribs.

I hung over the edge of the tower and looked down. *Bad idea.* My head felt like it was going to snap off. It was impossible to imagine falling that far and not dying. Judging from the bruise, I must've hit one of the catwalk railings on the way down.

What was I made of now? And if Wirtz was made of the same stuff, what hope did I have of killing him?

I drank some bottled water and managed to hold it down. I was a little hungry, but I didn't feel up to doing anything. I lay down again, alternately dozing and dreaming of falling. When I woke a second time, the NASA traffic was leaving the base. I stretched and put my shoes on. I couldn't believe how much better I felt. The bruise was still there, but the pain was mostly gone.

*   *   *

I took it easy going down and even easier making my way through the woods. I felt dizzy a couple of times and had to bend over, holding my knees. My mood lifted when I saw Sagan's Jeep at the Solar Observatory.

"You're here!" I would have thrown myself into his arms but didn't want to risk it. Sagan stiffened.

"What's wrong?" I said.

"So you're . . . okay," he said.

"Well—"

"You call me in the middle of the night, acting all mysterious like it's Emma's Last Supper or something. You want me to check on your family, call you back from the complex. And then—"

"Wait! Stop! How are they, did you see them? Sagan, you have to tell me."

"They're fine, Emma. Just like you said they would be. Beautiful little girl, cute mom. I saw them walk down the steps, just like it was a regular, normal day, get in their car, and drive off."

"Oh my God, Sagan. You saw them, you saw them! That makes me feel so good!" I was holding back tears.

"And so I call you, over and over, just like you asked me to. And you never picked up."

"Oh no. I'm sorry. I had no idea. I must have turned it off! I was really busy with something and I wasn't thinking. Then after . . . well . . . I forgot to turn it back on."

"Meanwhile, I've been looking for you all day all over the center . . . sure something horrible has happened to you—that you're in trouble, hurt, who knows . . . and the whole time, you were fine and had just . . . turned . . . it . . . off. . . ." His voice was shaking. I'd seen him angry before, but I'd never seen him like this.

"You mean . . . you've been out here all this time? Oh no. I didn't realize! Oh wow. I'm so sorry. But I can explain."

Sagan walked over and sat down on the picnic bench. I followed.

"Hey," I said. "I didn't mean to scare you so bad. I had . . . a pretty rough night, see?" I pulled up my shirt to show him the bruise, but he wouldn't look at it. "But I'm fine now, okay?"

"You turned it off."

"Yeah."

"You want something to happen, don't you?" Sagan said, finally looking at me in the eyes again.

"Come on, you think I've got a death wish or something? You think I'm having fun here?"

"I don't know what you're doing. You won't tell me."

"Let's go get something to eat. We'll both feel better." I took his arm and he yanked it away.

"No."

"What?"

"I said no. You know how close I came to getting my father out here? Calling security?"

"You said you wouldn't do that. You promised."

"I know I promised and it was stupid to promise. If you're too . . . stubborn . . . to take care of yourself, then somebody's got to do it for you."

I looked at him hard. He was looking away from me again. "You almost said 'stupid,' didn't you? You almost called me stupid."

"No."

"I can't believe this. You think I'm stupid."

"Emma, if you want to twist my words around, then . . ."

"Then what?"

"I don't know."

He got up from the bench and walked to the door that led to the cafeteria.

"You coming?"

I stood watching, purposely making him wait.

"I said, are you coming?" Sagan repeated.

"What do I want to go in there for?" I said.

"Okay, so leave."

"I can't believe it," I said. "Now's the time you choose to dump on me? After what I've been through? You have no idea. . . ."

He sagged a little. "I've been up since three in the morning, Emma. I'm tired and a little bit freaked out and pissed."

"And that's *my* fault?" I swore. "How is that my fault?"

"Now you *are* being stupid."

He brushed past me and headed the opposite direction, down the sidewalk toward the Solar Observatory.

That did it. I caught up with him.

"Hey, guess what," I said as he put his hand on the observatory door. "You know that moon-landing thing? The one that supposedly happened in 1969? I don't believe it. I think they filmed it in Arizona. Just like they said on that British documentary. The whole thing was fake. Are you hearing me? Completely fake."

Sagan stopped but didn't turn around. He stood there, arms dropping dejectedly, head lowered.

"Awww, did I hurt the poor widdle astronomer's feelings?" I said, regretting it the moment I said it.

"Emma," Sagan said, still not turning around. "You talk a lot about your grandfather. Did . . . did I ever tell you about my grandfather?"

I didn't answer. I knew I had gone too far, and his quiet tone scared me.

"My grandfather was an astronaut in the Apollo program back in the sixties. One day they were doing a routine test on the test stand down at Cape Kennedy. He and the other astronauts were in their space suits. Kind of a dress rehearsal. Something was wrong with the wiring in the capsule. It sparked, and because the capsule was full of nearly one hundred percent oxygen, the spark caused a fire. An inferno. It happened so fast, was so intense, they couldn't get the astronauts out. He died, Emma. He died in that fire on the test stand. Never got to finish his dream. Never got to see Neil Armstrong walk on the moon. Never got to walk there himself. They named a school after him. Right here in this town. My grandfather."

I was still looking at Sagan's back. He didn't move. I could see the blood running out of his fingers, leaving them white, he was clenching his fists so hard.

I waited before saying anything. I wanted to touch him, but I didn't dare. Finally I opened my mouth, but not much came out.

"I'm sorry," I whispered, then realized he hadn't heard me. I said it louder. "I'm so sorry, Sagan. I didn't mean . . . what I said. I didn't know, really I didn't. I wouldn't have said it if . . . I'm sorry. I didn't mean to stick you like that. It was . . . cruel."

I watched him spread his fingers, clench, spread them again. He finally turned around.

"What is wrong with you?" he said.

"You'd understand if . . ."

"If I knew? You know, Emma, I'm starting to think there is no reason for you being here. You just are. That's all. You didn't want to be at home. You got bored, so you had to pull somebody else into it, your little adventure, didn't you?"

"I can't believe you just said that."

I turned and headed back down the sidewalk. Sagan chased

after me, grabbing my arm. I pulled it away and he fell against the wall, surprised at my strength.

He caught up with me again. I put my hand against the middle of his chest and shoved. Sagan shot backward hard and banged against the wall.

I was moving up the walk again, not looking back. I had done it. Ruined the best thing ever. Destroyed it. Maybe that was all that I was good for. Destroying things. Maybe Lena was wrong. Maybe I was *Verloren* after all.

My brain was in a fog. *Maybe I should leave the Space Center completely. Go somewhere else.* There were other places I could hide. Maybe Wirtz would never find me. I could even . . .

Someone was coming up the walk toward me.

It was a NASA security guard. A heavyset older guy with a jacket and a cap and an official-looking blue uniform. A big black handgun was strapped to his hip.

I would have seen him from a mile away, heard him even, if I hadn't been so distracted by the fight with Sagan. The guard was not a hundred feet away. I was dead. I was dead.

Only a split second and I would be out of the shadows and the guard would see me. I panicked and did the first thing I thought to do . . . didn't stop to think about my hurt ribs, but took two steps and leapt, flying up the side of the building. I grabbed the rolled metal edge at the top and flung myself over onto the roof.

I looked down for the guard. He was still coming; nothing had changed. *Thank God.* He hadn't seen me. He was just staring straight ahead. Then I saw Sagan.

He wasn't moving. He was standing on the concrete walkway looking up. Looking at me. He had seen.

* * *

I ran back to the tower, but I didn't climb up. I saw the bunker and dashed inside. Tore my clothes off and threw them down on the cold, dirty floor. Kicked my shoes into a corner. Cranked the faucet on full blast and started slapping my naked body with water. The water was frigid, but I didn't care. I scooped it up in handfuls, beating my skin with it, slamming it into my face.

I wanted to clean it away. Clean it all away. As if being a vampire were something that was on my skin. I knew I couldn't, but I couldn't stop trying. I scrubbed and scrubbed, kept pounding handfuls of the cold water in my face, on my arms, stomach, everywhere.

I was talking to myself as I did it, barely conscious of what I was saying. *I'm a monster. I'm a freak. A monster. A freak. A monster. A freak. Monster freak monster freak . . .*

Finally I slipped slowly down the cinder block wall until I was slumped in the water. The faucet was still on full blast, beating against my legs. I wrapped myself in my arms, hung my head, all my hair in front of me, seeing nothing, hearing nothing but the roaring of the water as it drowned out my sobs.

I fell over on my side. The water was getting deeper and deeper until my ear went under and my hair floated around my face.

I didn't care what happened anymore, I didn't. I was used to fighting, but I didn't know how to fight something like this. It wasn't possible.

The water was still roaring. I didn't move for a long time. I didn't want to move ever again. What was the point?

I closed my eyes and tried to pretend I was the water. All of me would just wash away into the darkness and disappear into the ground.

*   *   *

I had gotten so used to the sound of the water, the silence made me suddenly feel deaf. I didn't move, just lay on my side with one ear in the water, legs drawn up against my stomach.

He knelt beside me and put his arms under my back. I felt myself go limp as he lifted me up and pressed his body against mine. We didn't speak. He held me a long time. I had never felt that before—someone holding me while I had no clothes on. I was surprised it felt the way it did. I would have thought I would be ashamed, embarrassed. But I didn't feel any of that. I just felt like I was sinking into him, the way I had wanted to sink into the water.

"Does this mean you're not going to leave me?" I said.

A long time later, after I had gotten dressed and most of the water had dribbled away, we were sitting just outside the bunker, our backs against the concrete. I reached over and touched his hand.

"How did you find me?" I said.

"You're not invisible, you know. Just walked into the woods and kept walking. You went in the same direction where I'd seen you come out before. Like I said, not many people know about the old test stand anymore. It made sense."

"I'm sorry . . . I'm sorry about what I said. I didn't mean it. I don't know why I did it. I think . . . maybe I was using it as an excuse to push you away. Because I was afraid, Sagan. Afraid for so many reasons. If you knew everything . . ."

He squeezed my fingers. "I'm going to know everything, because you are going to tell me everything. Starting at the very beginning. So much of what I thought I knew . . . it went out the window when I saw you scale that wall."

"You're wondering . . . what I am."

Sagan smiled. "So . . . you're not on the run from some government lab? Like in the movies?"

"Not even close. But if they ever found out . . ."

"I'd never see you again, right?"

"Pretty much."

"Were you . . . born this way?"

I hung my head, looking at the ground. "Sagan, there's something . . . I have to tell you. And you're going to have to believe it. You won't believe it, but you have to. Because if you don't . . . well, that's it. I wouldn't know what to do. But even saying that . . . you won't believe it."

"Really? It's that bad?"

"It's that . . . impossible. I can't even believe I'm going to tell you. I don't know what you might do."

He frowned. "Hey, give me some credit."

"But . . . this is more than that. It's not just what I can do. That's not the strangest part. The strangest thing is what I am."

"God, Emma, what is it already? Are you radioactive? From another planet? Or . . . let's see . . . you got bombarded with gamma rays and—"

"Shut up. Just shut up. This is hard." I sat there, mind going blank. "All right. I'm just going to say it."

"Okay. I'm right here. I'm not going anywhere. I promise. You can tell me you are from the center of the earth, the vanguard of a race of superchicks hell-bent on world domination. One mall at a time . . ."

"Be serious or I won't say a word."

"Okay. Serious. I can do serious. You just got a sample over at the observatory."

"No, I mean it. I'm going to kill you if you don't take this seriously. This is my life here. I wouldn't make this up."

"All right already. Put me out of my misery!"

I took a very long breath . . . held it awhile . . . then finally let it slowly out. I had to do it again. I closed my eyes. *Just say it.*

"Sagan . . . I'm a vampire."

22. THE GLADE

It was interesting watching his face. I wondered if he was basically the very first person—human being, I mean—who had ever been told something like that. I caught him with his mouth open. It stayed open. He didn't speak. Didn't even look close to speaking.

"See why I didn't want to say anything?" I said finally.

"You mean . . . you're one of those people who has read a ton of Anne Rice books and now you want to be a vampire, so—"

"No. I'm serious. I am a vampire. Not the pretend, wannabe kind. The real thing."

"You're saying . . . vampires are real."

"Yes."

"Not the goth offshoots . . . but the real deal. You drink blood from people . . . turn into a bat . . . fly . . . sleep in a coffin full of dirt."

"You promised you wouldn't do this," I said. "You said you would be serious."

"I . . . am serious, Emma," Sagan said. "What do you expect me to say?"

"I expect you to think I'm crazy. But I'm asking you . . . I'm pleading with you . . . to believe me."

"Okay, you want me to be honest?"

"Please."

"I wouldn't have believed you if I hadn't seen you go up that wall. But . . . being honest, remember? I don't know how to believe in something like vampires."

"Well, you better learn."

"I . . . I don't have any."

"All right. I've seen you out in the daylight lots of times. Just another myth, huh?"

"No. That's real. Only . . . there are some vampire things that don't apply to me."

Sagan stood up. I almost couldn't bear looking at his face. He didn't look like he disbelieved me. . . . He looked . . . sad. Like he had lost someone very important to him.

"I know what you're thinking," I said. "I told you you would think I was crazy. I told you that over and over."

Sagan had his hands on his hips. He was walking back and forth, as if refusing to make eye contact. Then I realized it wasn't that. . . . This kind of news wasn't something you could take just sitting there. It came out in your body.

Finally he looked at me again. "I don't think you're crazy." He said it very quietly, as if someone might overhear. "Maybe I'm crazy. Because nothing you have done has seemed crazy to me. Well, except living out here."

"Breathe," I said. "Please."

"I'm breathing. I'm here. I haven't left."

"It . . . rearranges everything, doesn't it?" I said. "When I figured it out, I got sick. I mean, physically ill. For days. All this amazing stuff had been happening to me, and somehow I was still getting up each morning, not questioning it so much, just amazed over and over. I think it made me numb. Then when I realized what it was, I got so sick, I felt like I was dying. And I think I was. I mean, the Emma I used to be . . . she is dead. . . ."

"You're not saying like undead, are you?"

"No, of course not. I'm alive. But the person I was before

that . . . she's gone. Well, I'm still here. I'm still me. But once I understood . . . it just wiped me out. It was too much to take."

Sagan was looking kind of ill himself.

"You're not going to throw up or something, are you?" I said.

"No. Please don't take this the wrong way, Emma, but I just don't see how it could be real. What makes you think you're a vampire? I mean, obviously, beside your wall-climbing skills. Were you bitten by a radioactive spider?" He grinned, but it was a sickly kind of grin.

"I was attacked," I said, instantly erasing his grin. "I didn't remember it at first because I had a grand mal seizure, a tonic-clonic, right in the middle of it. You sometimes come out of a seizure with a kind of amnesia about what happened. Well, that time my amnesia lasted for days, weeks."

"Wait a minute. You're telling me you have epilepsy?"

"A seizure condition, yeah."

Sagan swore. "And all this time you have been living out here by yourself with a seizure condition. And you didn't tell me."

"I figured if I told you that, you'd turn me in. You know, for my own safety."

"Okay." He sat back down next to me as if his legs would no longer hold him. "Tell me all of it. Everything."

So I told him everything: all about that day at the soccer tournament, breaking Gretchen's nose, taking the car, and winding up in the hospital. The changes.

"So . . . you saw him?" Sagan said. "The guy . . . er, the vampire . . . who attacked you?"

"That's the worst part," I said. And I told him all about Wirtz, how he had fed from my leg and then later on appeared to me the night that I ran away.

"And he keeps coming back," I said.

Sagan was looking down at his hands when I finished. I think it was something he had to do. . . . Maybe looking at the most familiar things in the world, his own hands, was his way of keeping his feet attached to the ground.

"You gonna flake out on me or what?" I said.

Sagan raised his head slightly. "Or what."

"Which means?"

"I don't know what it means, Emma. You're right. I've been begging you to tell me the truth and . . . now I don't know what to think."

I stood up. "You want me to show you something, don't you?"

"I want to trust you. That isn't trust, making you prove it."

"But it would help, wouldn't it?"

Sagan got up too and looked at me, almost as if he had never seen me before.

"Maybe I don't want proof," he said. "Maybe I'm afraid of proof. You're the best thing that has ever happened to me, you know? Maybe I don't want it to be true."

"You think I'm lying."

"No. And that scares me."

"So why are you into astronomy?" I said. "What do you hope to find out there? You know, I've seen footage from those moon missions. We watched some of it in school. And I've seen the pictures from the Martian rovers. You know what? Boring. It's rocks, Sagan, just rocks. That's pretty much all they've found, isn't it?"

"They're trying to determine if there was liquid water and—"

"Big deal. What are you really looking for out there? Water? No way. Aren't you looking for something huge? Really different?

Strange beyond your wildest dreams strange? What about all those books you read as a kid. . . . Would you have read them if the whole secret, the whole danger, the mystery—if all it ever turned out to be was barren places full of useless rocks?"

"What are you saying?"

"I'm saying . . . maybe you *are* ready for this. More ready than you think. Papi always says there's a reason for everything. A reason things happen. Maybe that's why I found you, right? Out of all the other people on this base. What would anybody else have done . . . I mean anybody . . . if they had caught me here, breaking into a building, searching for food?"

Sagan breathed out. "Turned you in."

I took hold of his arms and looked straight into his crazy blue eyes. "You have to understand something. I have been living with this. Living it. Just pretend it's real for one minute and put yourself in my shoes. Wouldn't you be practically desperate for someone else to know? Someone important to you? Someone to believe in you?"

"Yeah."

"But you would be so scared of telling them, because it's too crazy, it's impossible. . . . It's for the kind of people who believe in bigfoots and UFOs. . . ."

"I believe in UFOs. . . ."

"There you go," I said, letting go of his arms and smiling. "So you're telling me you can believe in little green men . . ."

"Gray, they're usually gray. . . ."

"Okay, little gray men with heads shaped like gigantic lightbulbs and big black footballs for eyes . . . how they come and abduct people, etc. . . ."

"I didn't say I believed in that," he said.

"Okay, they are real, anyhow. You can believe in that, but you can't believe that there might be another kind of human being out there? Human beings just like us, for the most part, who just happened to be in the wrong place at the wrong time and got infected . . ."

"Infected? So now you know what causes vampirism?"

Whoops. I wasn't sure he was ready to hear about the *Sonnen.* "Just throwing some possibilities out there," I said. "But imagine those people. . . . They didn't ask to be made into vampires, but they were. And so now they have to live and somehow keep away from the rest of the world. . . . Think of what that would be like."

"And feed off regular people."

"Exactly."

"It doesn't sound like a disease; it sounds like a curse," Sagan said. "A nightmare."

"Not a real glamorous way to live, huh?" I said. "Hiding in dark dank places by day, stalking other human beings just to stay alive."

"And you're telling me you're one of those . . . people."

"Yeah. Except for the drinking blood thing and the sunlight thing. Everything else about me is full vampire."

"But that would mean . . . you have . . ."

"Superpowers, basically. Like the way I've been getting in and out of the Space Center. It's not all that tough, really. I just jump over the fence."

"Ten feet high with razor wire, and you jump over it?"

"Pretty regularly."

"So that's what you never wanted me to see, huh?"

"Well . . . of course."

Sagan shook his head and then ran his fingers through his hair. "But that's the thing; you've got it all worked out, haven't you? You can explain anything by these powers, can't you?"

"I'm just telling you the truth. Like the mall. You want to know how I got those clothes? I ripped a few doors off their hinges. And when the cops came . . ."

"Cops?"

"They would have caught me if not for my . . . skills. They even shot me with a Taser and it didn't stop me."

"This is nuts, Emma, nuts!"

"I can show you the holes where it stuck in my shoe. See?"

Sagan rubbed his eyes and walked in a little circle that came right back to me.

"So basically, you have a choice," I said. "You can believe me and . . . maybe have the biggest adventure of your life. Or . . . you can think I'm just some chick who got off her meds, ran away from high school . . . and lose me for good."

"Meds. You must be taking something for your . . . condition," Sagan said.

"I was," I said. "It's a prescription drug called Dilantin. I haven't taken it for a while, and I had a seizure and fell off the tower last night. And I saw him here."

"Him?"

"Wirtz. The vampire who turned me."

"Turned you. God, Emma. Do you know how that sounds?"

"Yeah."

"And you saw him here?"

"Well . . . a projection of him." I explained about Wirtz and the *Feld* without giving specifics about the other vampires.

"So . . . you think . . . this vampire, Wirtz . . . you think he is using the *Feld* to get inside your mind?" Sagan said.

"Yeah. But only when I'm experiencing some kind of seizure, apparently. That's the only time I ever see him."

"And he can see the things around him when he's here?"

"He seems just as solid as you sitting there. But I've been experimenting some. If I can tap into his *Feld* first, then I have control. Well, as long as I don't have a tonic-clonic. But time is running out."

"What do you mean?"

"Wirtz is getting close, that's what I mean. He's seen my tower now. It's going to get really dangerous around here very soon. I need to be ready."

"So . . . you're really going to fight this . . . Wirtz guy. . . ."

"Yeah. And I came here to do it." I pointed up at the test stand. "This is basically . . . my siege castle. And there's something else. . . . He won't stop. I know that. He won't stop until . . . one of us is dead."

"So you're saying you've got to . . . you've got to kill him. And you actually think you can."

I took his hand. "Look. Let's make this easy. Let's not even call it proof. How about a demonstration?"

I led him to the most private place I could find—the secret glade in the woods.

"But you're hurt," he said. "That's the most gruesome bruise I ever—"

I tugged my shirt up where Sagan could see. The bruise was already going away.

"Did I tell you I also heal incredibly fast?"

Sagan shook his head. "Okay, so what next? You're not going to bite me, are you?"

I laughed. "Maybe later. But I had something a little different in mind."

We stopped in front of the sign I had found before.

DANGER!
BURIED MUNITIONS
NO TRESPASSING
DO NOT DIG WITHOUT GPR PERMIT

"Not cool," he said. "We really shouldn't be here, Emma."

"I know we shouldn't, you goofball. I shouldn't even be on the base. Would you believe I ran through this meadow the first day I was here and came through without a scratch?"

Sagan swore. "So you really are Superman, huh. Nothing can hurt you?"

"Oh, I can be hurt. You should have seen me last night. I was just lucky. Extremely lucky. So what's a GPR?"

"Ground-penetrating radar. They use it to locate buried objects. Chemicals. Bombs. Canisters of mustard gas."

"Mustard gas!"

"Before NASA, this place was an army base," Sagan said. "Still is. Going back to World War II. So why are we here? You mentioned something about a demonstration."

"Okay. But not here. I'm never setting foot in that field again. Take me someplace safe—preferably a forest."

It was only a short distance away, so we walked. Sagan was still holding my hand, and that made me feel better. *He still wants to touch me.*

"How's this?" he said.

"No mustard gas?"

"Just trees."

"Okay." Now that I was going to do it, I was suddenly nervous. How would he react? "Look, this is hard. . . ."

"I thought it was going to be easy?"

"I don't mean physically hard. Just . . . please don't freak. It's going to be kind of crazy."

Sagan smiled. "I won't. Why would I? It's going to be interesting."

"You promise?"

"Sure."

I let go of his hand and picked him up. Tucked him against my side like a six-foot-long football.

"Hey, wait a minute!" Sagan yelled, struggling to get free.

I was off, bounding through the trees like before. I was hardly aware that I was even holding him, except that my balance was off.

"Oh shiiiiiiiiiiiiiii . . . !" Sagan yelled, his words whipped away by the wind.

I was using my left hand to grab tree branches, flinging myself from one tree to the next like a monkey, then dropping to the ground and bounding upward again. It felt the way it always did: exhilarating. I shifted Sagan around to my shoulders, carrying him fireman style. It didn't slow me down a bit.

At last I came to a stop and put him down. He fell over and lay on his back.

"God. God." He said it over and over as he struggled to catch his breath.

"What are you breathing hard for?" I said, grinning. "I'm the one doing all the work."

I squatted next to him, not winded at all, and waited for his head to catch up to his body. At last he blinked and rubbed his eyes.

"I can't believe . . . you just did that," he said.

"Okay. How about this?"

I found a dead tree and shoved hard. It fell with a huge jolt I could feel all through my legs, the tree looking rubbery as it bounced like a pencil you twiddle between your fingers. I glanced at Sagan, pleased to see that his eyes were bugging out.

I tried to pick the tree up, but it was like trying to palm a basketball. . . . My hand was too small. I had to get both arms around the trunk to hoist it into the air.

"Where do you want it?" I said.

"What else would you like to know?" I said when we were back at the tower.

I had to admit, after the shock of finally being caught, I was enjoying this. I had always been a show-off.

"I don't even know what to ask," he said. "Well, technically that's not true. I have about three million questions. But I'm not sure where to start. All I know is stuff from TV shows and movies. Can you be seen in a mirror?"

"Yep. I'm solid. Physical. That would be defying the laws of physics." *Thanks, Anton.*

"Okay, you said you don't drink blood. . . . How?"

"I haven't figured that one out yet. When I was attacked, I had a seizure while he was still . . . feeding . . . and somehow I figure it scrambled my transformation. So I only got part of the total package. Same thing for sunlight. Except that I have to wear these." I tapped my sunglasses. "I'm pretty much blind in regular daylight."

"So . . ."

"As far as I can tell, all of the good, none of the bad. If you don't count the fact that I'm homeless and a crazy vampire is out to kill me."

"But why?"

"Who knows. It hurt his ego that I got away the first time? Or maybe he's just bitter. . . . He definitely wants to know my 'secret.'

So all I have to do is tell him, no problem, just be born with epilepsy and you're halfway there."

Sagan turned and looked up at the tower in the distance. "You really think this is the best place to fight him?"

"It's pretty much the only place," I said. "Think about it. . . . Would you want to fight somebody like Wirtz out in the open?"

"I wouldn't want to fight him at all."

"You assume I have a choice."

"Well, at least I can see why you didn't want to go back home. You would draw him right to your family. But what if . . . what if I got us a little place somewhere, an apartment! Wouldn't you be safer there?"

"I would feel cornered. Here at least I can see. I can move around, maybe get some advance warning, slow him down."

"But what's to stop him from just climbing up there and killing you?"

"You want to see?" I said.

So I took him up the tower and showed him my defenses. The trip wires, deadly garden tools, chemicals, all of it.

"A hoe," Sagan said. "You're going to kill this . . . monster . . . with a hoe."

"That's basically for good luck," I said. "A hoe is my all-time favorite tool from working in Papi's garden. Besides, in a pinch . . ." I slipped the hoe out of its hiding spot, spun 180 degrees, screaming, "Yahhhhh!" The corner of the hoe was embedded in the tower's metal hide. Sagan's face went pale and he softly swore.

"I didn't even see that, Emma. No joke. How did you move that fast?"

I pulled the hoe out and set it back into position. "I don't know. Just part of the deal, I guess. I figure it's like this. . . . If you're a slug and you're turned into a vampire, you're going to be a sluglike vampire. But if you're a top-notch athlete . . . well, it's multiplied."

"Don't get cocky."

"Sagan, I have to be cocky. Haven't you ever played sports? You can't go into something like this without being cocky. You'd be dead before you got your hands on your first weapon."

He shook his head. "I feel like any minute some guy with a camera is going to step out from hiding and tell me I've been punked. If I hadn't seen what you did in the woods . . ."

"Now do you see why the cops could do nothing to protect me? My family? Nobody but another vampire can stop this guy. He's too fast. Too strong."

"A bazooka."

"You'd die trying to load the thing. How do you think they've kept hidden for thousands of years?"

"They? So there's more than just the two of you?"

"Oh no. You make us sound like a couple. Yeah, there's lots more."

"How do you know?"

I stood there gazing at him, realizing my mistake and trying to decide whether to lie my way out of it or tell him everything. *Everything. Tell him all.*

23. HOSTILE

"I've . . . I've met some of them," I said, waiting for Sagan to react. This time his face didn't change.

"Real vampires. You've met them. Here, like locally?"

"Yeah."

"Blood-sucking, coffin-dragging—"

"They aren't like that. They're . . . good people."

"Good people who run around in the streets at night, killing—"

"But they don't kill anybody," I said.

I told him about Lena, Donne, and Anton, along with the warring vampire factions. Sagan caught on quickly—it's not that I was afraid he wouldn't, but more concerned that he might blow a circuit somewhere in his head because of the all-out strangeness of everything he had to absorb. So I fed it to him in manageable chunks.

Sagan took a long inhale and let it out slowly. "Any more stuff like this, and I'm liable to lift off," he said.

"Hey, I've got an idea," I said. "Let's take a break. There's still a little light left."

The sun was almost down; the state park would be closing soon. But it was great to see the Stone House Hotel in the daylight for a change. It looked like the familiar place I had loved so much growing up. The playground was covered with screaming kids. People were jogging, walking their dogs, throwing Frisbees. Talking about vampires here felt ridiculous.

"I've been here plenty of times," Sagan said, climbing up on one of the low walls. He walked along like a tightrope performer, arms out for balance, swaying dramatically with each step. He walked all the way to the end of the wall and hopped down in front of me. "And I've never been sucked on once," he said with a grin.

"Be serious," I said.

"So you're saying you could lead me right to them, this very moment."

"I could, yeah."

"But they would be asleep."

"I don't know if Lena sleeps all that much, but probably."

"So just anybody could stumble into this little place and find them there?"

I looked at the trail that ran along the edge of the mountain. "It's a little tough to see it, especially with your eyes. Human eyes, I mean. I almost didn't see it and I was right there with them."

"A caver could find it," Sagan said.

"Probably. They cover the opening with a big stone. But what would you find? Three homeless people who might not be in all that good of a mood. Call it home delivery."

"Huh?"

"Vampire pizza."

He laughed.

"They must have some kind of alternate plan," I said. "The oldest has been a vampire since 1862. That's a lot of years of dodging people. I bet they have that kind of stuff figured out."

Sagan looked in the direction I was looking. "It's right down there?"

"Yeah."

"So you really want me to meet them?"

"Not right now, but soon. And only if you feel up to it and they agree. Are you scared?"

"Well . . . interested, sure. Scared? Next question."

"Really I'd rather do it at the Space Center. You'd be on your own turf, so that would be better for you. And maybe they wouldn't feel as uncomfortable as they would if a human were inside their . . . home."

"Me surrounded by three vampires and you wouldn't want them to feel uncomfortable."

"Four vampires."

"Three-point-five," Sagan said.

"Okay. But you'll like them. I hope they'll like you."

"Hope?"

"They will! Only, Donne seems to have a little trouble with guys. She's with Anton, but I get the impression she kind of bosses him around."

"Is that unusual?"

I hit him on the arm. Night was falling as we walked back to the Jeep.

"So this Wirtz guy, he's *Verloren,* and you don't know where his hideout is," Sagan said as we drove back down the mountain.

"I don't think he has one," I said. "Lena says the *Verloren* are mostly loners and nomads. They're the violent ones, remember? They can't hang around any one place too long or they'll be discovered."

"And they—the *Verloren*—they answer to some kind of queen or something—"

"*Die Esserin,*" I said. "Only, I don't think she's a queen. Just the first *Verloren* who was able to get some of them to cooperate, at least to a certain degree, from what Lena says. I get the feeling she is really different . . . that anybody who can do the kind of thinking she has done would usually move over to the *Sonnen*. But for some reason she didn't."

"Power hungry," Sagan said. "She wants to take over the world. Turn us . . . human types . . . into cattle."

I looked at him. "You're grinning again."

"I'm sorry, but I have to. Or I'd go crazy. It's too much. Human beings infiltrated by vampires who want to breed us for food and others who worship the sun?"

"I don't know if they actually worship it."

"Okay, they're cured by it. The very thing that is supposed to burn them alive or turn them to dust, whatever."

"I told you, it's because they need a huge dose of it, quickly . . . something that comes from the sun. That's why I was asking you about CMEs the other day. I know it all sounds crazy. That's why I tried so hard to keep you out of it. The *Feld* . . ."

"Now that part I can believe," he said.

"But that's the craziest part!"

"Only if you don't know anything about quantum physics. My turn to show you something."

Sagan let me out on a little side road that ran alongside the Space Center. He parked the Jeep and waited, leaning back, his arms folded.

"I hate to sound like a cliché, but this I gotta see."

I was a little self-conscious. "It feels weird doing it with somebody watching. I feel like a circus performer or something."

"True. Okay."

I looked back at him one last time, took two steps, bounded into the air, and sailed over. Landed so lightly on the other side, I barely rustled the thick layer of old leaves underfoot.

"God," Sagan said.

"What?"

"Just . . . God. It's going to take a while getting used to this, Emma."

I walked over to the fence. "Stop looking at me like that."

"I can't help it. It's just so . . ."

"I know, I know . . . it's weird." I put my fingers through the wire. "But don't ever forget, I'm still me."

"Come here," Sagan said.

He put his face against the wire. Our lips met at a space in the fence.

Soon we were sitting in the control room of the Solar Observatory. Sagan ran some of his comet-hunting routines while we talked so no one would think he had disappeared. Then he clicked a mouse and leaned back in his chair.

"There you go."

I looked at the screen. It was a Wikipedia page on something called the "zero-point field."

The electromagnetic zero-point field is loosely considered as a sea of background electromagnetic energy that fills the vacuum of space.

"Sound familiar?" Sagan said.

"So you think this is the *Feld*?" I said.

"Sounds like it, the way you describe what it can do. Actually, it's what you do in it. With it. Within it. See how slippery a concept it is?"

"Oh, believe me, I'm slipping away already."

"Don't be funny."

"If I didn't know this stuff was possible, I would say it sounds about as fake as ESP."

"Lots of quantum physicists believe in ESP. More and more of them are starting to believe there really is a connection between all of us. And we're all individually connected to the universe."

I thought of what Lena and Anton had been telling me.

"Some think we're evolving in ways beyond the Darwinian," Sagan said. "We started out with the geosphere, which was inanimate matter. Right now we're in the biosphere, which is animate matter. But soon, maybe real soon, we'll be moving on to the noosphere."

"Don't tell me. . . . That's where we all turn into soap bubbles and fly off into space—"

He kicked my foot. "It's where human thought begins to transform the biosphere with pure mind power. Using the zero-point field to predict future events or rearrange molecules to turn substances from one state to another. It'll be like alchemy. Magic. Anything you can imagine."

"So . . . you're thinking maybe vampires . . ."

"Maybe their special abilities let them tap into stuff we haven't been able to yet, at least on a big scale."

"That makes it sound like . . . vampires are some kind of leap ahead."

"Sure, it's possible," Sagan said.

"But that means . . ."

"Yeah."

"You're on your way out," I said, giving him a pinch.

I was miserable waiting for him to get out of his classes the next day. Sagan called around lunchtime and told me he had come up with all sorts of plans for upgrading my defenses.

"I know of some stuff we can borrow from a couple of places on the center," he said. "We'll have to wait till everybody leaves, but if we hurry, we could get them set up tonight."

A few hours later we were standing outside a big industrial building with peeling white paint. We walked around to the back to an area that was crowded with steel canisters, forty-gallon drums, and black hoses leading to portable compressors.

"My dad has an old friend who runs this shop," Sagan said. "This is where they keep the stuff they don't use anymore, equipment that is no longer needed."

"Junk, huh."

"Except there's nothing wrong with it. They have new stuff coming in, so they put the old stuff out back. Eventually they have a government sale where people bid on it for pennies on the dollar."

"So they won't mind us borrowing it for a while?"

"No way. They won't even know it's gone for months. We can bring it back . . . after . . ."

"I don't like the sound in your voice when you say that," I said.

"Try not to worry." He patted the side of a tank that was a kind of yellow cube on wheels with a wicked-looking spray nozzle. "These babies have the potential for being downright hostile. NASA uses them to blast rust off the old rockets for repainting. Come on, let's get loading. This is our best chance with nobody out here."

It took three trips with the Jeep to get everything back to the test stand. I told Sagan I could have hauled the stuff on my back and gotten it there even faster, but he talked me out of it.

"What would security think if they saw some chick running down the road with a compressor on her back?"

It took a lot longer than we thought to get the new stuff in place.

"Looks like the only source of water is down in the bunker,"

Sagan said as we walked back down from the tower. "We'll need about a million miles of hoses." He sighed. "Some heavy-duty extension cords, a decent socket set, what else?"

"I can get all that tomorrow," I said, a Home Depot twinkle in my eye.

"No way, no more stealing," Sagan said. "We can find it around here; I can bring the sockets from home."

We decided to knock off for the night and get something to eat. Later we were sitting outside the Solar Observatory, gobbling up Mexican. The sky was beautiful with a partly full moon.

Sagan sat back against a tree. "So you think I'm going to let you do this by yourself?"

"You have to," I said.

"No way. You have to swear you'll let me be here, or I'm blowing up the whole deal."

"We've been over and over that. You'd get yourself killed. I'd have to . . . watch you die. That's exactly what somebody like Wirtz would want. Somebody here who was helpless—"

"Whoa, I'm not helpless. There are other ways to fight this . . . thing . . . without giving him the advantage."

"Like how?"

"Like with brainpower. You say somebody with a bazooka couldn't stop him. Which only means you can't fight him in conventional ways. It's gonna take something very different."

"Chain saw works for me."

"I'm serious, Emma."

"You think I'm not?"

"It's you who is going to get yourself killed if you try to fight him straight up," Sagan said.

"Thanks for the vote of confidence."

"No, I'm not meaning to insult you. I'm just saying . . . you are giving him way too big a slice of the percentages if you do it that way. Even with your vampire powers, he's bigger, more experienced. One slip, he could have you."

"So what are you saying?"

"Out-think him. Tip the odds in your favor as heavily as possible. Don't rely just on raw fury."

I smiled at him.

"Don't smile at me," he said.

"I'm not making fun of you."

"Then why are you smiling?"

I tried to think of how to put it into words. "It's . . . hard to explain. And . . . to tell you the truth, it kind of makes me feel like crying. I'm tired of crying."

"Why crying?"

"Because . . . you care, you know? You care so much. I don't know how to say it. . . . It's like . . . I belong to you, you know? Not in this controlling way, but . . . I'm messing this up, Sagan." I touched at the corners of my eyes with the back of my hand, careful not to get any salsa on my face. "It's like I'm . . . yours. I'm important to you. . . ."

"Well, of course, you . . . crazy person." He said it so softly, it didn't sting, but made my heart feel as if it were expanding instead. He reached across and touched my arm. I could have melted just then. I coughed and blinked.

"Okay. You were saying you want to fight this guy," I said. "And not get murdered in the process. How do you do that? I'm telling you, you wouldn't stand a chance. . . ."

"Tell that to my WoW friends," Sagan said, clenching his jaw.

"WoW?"

"World of Warcraft. I don't care who you are. I don't care what powers you have. If you're coming at me, you better bring it. Because I will eat your frigging lunch."

I would have laughed at the sheer ridiculousness of it if it wasn't for the look on his face. He meant it.

"But this isn't a game," I said.

"Everything's a game," Sagan said. "When you get down to it. Everything in life is ultimately some kind of strategy. If you have a better strategy than the other guy, he's going down. Like I said, it's all in the percentages."

I was feeling my heart growing again. "So . . . what makes you think you can even out-think him?" I said quietly.

"Trust me, Emma. He doesn't want any part of me."

I couldn't talk for a good while. I just couldn't. Because my heart was about to burst and I wanted it to burst.

I packed him off into the Jeep with a long kiss and felt lighter and freer than I had felt in ages. I wanted that lightness to continue. *Time for a little confession.*

"His name is Wirtz," I said to the three *Sonnen.*

We were walking through a grove of tall hardwoods up at the state park not far from the rim of the mountain. At the mention of the name, they all stopped walking at once.

"What?" I said.

"Emma, you are certain this is the person who turned you?" Lena said.

"Yeah. I'm not sure how to spell it. But that's what it sounds like. Why?"

"This . . . *Verloren* . . . he's a bad one. Really bad," Anton said. "The *Verloren* don't really have a structure, but if they did, Wirtz would be high up there."

Donne made a face like somebody had just sprinkled dirt on her tongue. "You are so lucky to be alive, Fresh."

Lena put her hand on my shoulder.

"You love history; let me tell you another story."

"There once was a family that lived in the Temperance Community of Telfair County in the state of Georgia in 1818," Lena said. "The father operated a large plantation there, with a boatyard, gristmill, and a brick factory. He was said to be a hard, driven man. Ruthless and lacking in mercy. Other than his business interests, he had but one love in this life, his only son, a boy named Karel.

"One night in March, the father and his son were camping on the banks of the Ocmulgee River, where the brick-making clay was extracted. A small band of Creek Indians saw their campfire and crept up on the two.

"Karel was instantly killed and his father badly wounded. The Creeks then proceeded to scalp them both. The father was forced to watch the scalping of his beloved son. Then it was his turn. The Creeks peeled back the flesh while the man was still alive. The father did not scream, but lay as still as death, withstanding unimaginable pain in order to escape with his life.

"Then, as it happened, someone else arrived on the scene of the torture, almost unnoticed at first. She was tall and slender and appeared to be very, very young. Certainly no older than twelve or fourteen. The Creeks paid her no mind at first, supposing they could kill this frail child at their leisure.

"Instead of immediately fleeing, the girl came forward as if to watch what they were doing, curious. Then she reached down, took the first Creek by the hair, pulled his head back . . . and opened his throat with her mouth. She did the same with the next. The third, the one who was scalping the father, threw down his scalping knife and fled. The girl pursued him and took him on the run.

"You see, Emma, there was more than one predator abroad in the woods that night. But this kind of predator hunted alone.

"The girl returned to the scalped man where he lay on the riverbank. Again, curious. She knelt and drank from the body of the child first, while his blood was still warm and alive. Then she turned to the father . . . and took him too."

Lena looked at me with an expression that chilled me to the soles of my shoes.

"That young girl walking alone in the forest—seemingly no more than a child—was *die Esserin*. And the man who had been scalped was Wirtz. He answers only to her Call."

We walked a ways farther without speaking, then I finally told them everything about that terrible night in the Georgia mountains. Even how my epilepsy had enabled me to escape. Everything but my scrambled condition as a vampire.

"Wait," Donne said, making us stop. "He drank from your leg?"

"Yeah," I said. "He started to go for my throat, but after I hit him, he acted all offended, as if he expected me to be honored to be 'chosen' to feed him. I wish I could have broken his nose. Driven it into his brain, actually."

"You . . . hit . . . him," Donne said. "Whoops."

Anton's mouth opened in apparent wonder. "It's considered a great insult to strike a *Verloren*, Emma."

"The throat is sacred to *Sonnen* and *Verloren* alike," Lena explained. "*Heilig*. In his mind, Wirtz would have been honoring you had he taken you there. You dishonored him by striking his face."

"It's the worst thing you could have done," Anton said. "It's no wonder he's after you so fiercely, eh?"

I couldn't believe what I was hearing. "Are you serious? I was supposed to just lie there and let it happen? Be honored to have my throat torn open?"

"Bingo," Donne said. "In the eyes of a high-ranking *Verloren,* you didn't play the game fair. A human girl actually striking a being so superior to her? It basically never happens."

I stopped walking. "You almost sound like . . . this is all okay with you."

They stopped beside me. "I am sorry, Emma," Lena said. "We didn't mean to hurt your feelings. It is only that . . . it has been so long."

"So long what?" I said, turning to face her.

"Since we have known anyone who dared to fight back."

We were sitting at our usual place on the stone wall at the *Steinhaus.*

"The throat," Lena said, "is an instrument. Much more than an instrument of the voice or of sound. It is a kind of . . . transmitter, using the *Feld,* of course. It transmits thoughts, communications, even feelings. The *Verloren* are most attuned to . . . aggression, base lust, anything discordant. They use a very narrow spectrum of the *Feld*'s true possibilities. But they are effective in the way that they use it."

"You could say aggression is their frequency," Anton said. He was lying back with his hands behind his head and his eyes closed.

"What about the *Sonnen*?" I said. "What is your . . . frequency?"

Lena seemed to think about it a moment. "Perhaps you are ready to begin."

"Begin what?"

"Learning about the *Kehle.*"

Now Lena and I were seated side by side atop the chimney at the Stone House Hotel, looking at the lights glimmering across the valley. The same chimney I had shouted from the night we met. There was just enough room for the two of us.

Lena had sent the other two vampires back to the hideout. I got the feeling she was afraid of embarrassing me if they were watching.

"It is good to be up here," she said. "Somewhere high that is not so . . . encroached upon by the larger *Felds* of things like trees, even the ground. Let us begin. . . .

"The *Feld* is not something that can be fully explained in words," she continued. "It must be experienced."

"So how do we do it?" I said.

"You are so new," Lena said. "I wonder if you will like the answer."

"Try me."

"All right."

Lena reached over with her hand and placed all five fingers on my neck as if she were about to choke me. . . . I flinched a little, surprised, but her fingers rested so lightly there, I didn't feel threatened. But there was another feeling—one I didn't have a name for—that stirred the instant her skin met my skin.

"As I said before, the first and most important thing you must know is that the *Kehle,* or the throat, is *heilig.* Sacred. The most sacred part of the body. Many say it is the heart, but that is not true. There are several reasons for this. First, the throat is the seat of the voice. . . . Say something."

"What do you want me to say?"

"All right, Emma . . . that was out loud. Now . . . say it, not out loud, but keep your mouth closed and speak deeply within the *Kehle.* Your throat."

I wasn't sure what she meant, but I thought I would try it anyway. *What do you want me to say?* It felt kind of stupid; the noise that came out through my neck was like some creature's in a cheap horror movie.

"Do not worry about the sound," Lena said. "You will get better at controlling it. It is the vibration that is important. If you want to control the *Feld,* you must learn to control it through the vibration of the *Kehle.* Try again." She kept her hand on my neck.

I repeated the words, mouth closed, speaking deep within my throat. I didn't feel so self-conscious this time.

"Did you see?" Lena said. "I could feel your words, your voice, with my fingers as much as I could hear them with my ears. Second, even more than the lips or the mouth, the throat is also the seat of love, passion. There are those who say that the kiss was invented because the throat was too tempting, too dangerous. There is such a natural instinct to taste your lover's skin just here. . . ."

She trailed her thin fingers over my neck, making my skin pulse and tingle deliciously. I couldn't help feeling a little strange. No girl had ever touched me this way. I'm not even sure Sagan had.

"You are uncomfortable," Lena said. "And for this you must be at your most comfortable, or the lesson will be a failure. Close your eyes and think of something . . . pleasurable . . . and that may help."

I closed my eyes as her fingers continued to trail over my skin and thought of Sagan. *His lips there. His mouth.*

"Um . . . I'm not sure how relaxing this is," I said, giggling a little nervously.

"It will be easier as we go along," Lena said. "You haven't been touched many times, have you, Emma?"

"It shows?"

"Please, keep your eyes closed. Continue to focus on your pleasurable image."

Sagan popped into my head again . . . the way he looked this afternoon as we wrestled the compressor into the Jeep. Shirt off, the wetness of his skin, the strong line of his jaw punctuated by tiny beads of shining sweat.

"Don't let me fall," I said, smiling and breathing deeply.

"The throat, the *Kehle,* is the center of a person's *Feld* . . . ," Lena went on. "You can make adjustments within your *Feld* by what you say in your throat. You can even communicate over long distances with other . . . vampires." She squeezed my neck gently. "Especially those who have tasted you here."

"Oh great, like Wirtz," I said.

"Shhh," Lena said. "He would be the easiest, yes. But focus on the good. The words do not even have to be audible. Only that they must be spoken words within the throat."

What do you want me to say? I said again in my throat. It didn't seem silly at all now.

Again Lena's hands moved lightly over my flesh, almost stroking.

"Are you ready?" she said.

"I think I . . ."

She sank her teeth into my neck.

24. THE FEEDING

I know I jumped a little, because both of us nearly fell off the chimney. But Lena wouldn't let go. I could only turn my head so far, but—acting on an instinct deeper than I could explain—I kept my eyes cut hard to the side, staring in horror, desperate to see what she was doing.

After a little while the muscles that controlled my eyes began to ache. Lena was still attached to me, drinking. I reached for her, but she clasped me with both arms. . . . I knew I was stronger, I knew I could break away . . . but for some reason, I wouldn't let myself do it.

Almost immediately I was flooded with the most intense sensation of . . . comfort . . . I had ever experienced. But this wasn't the comfort of a seizure—part of me was terrified and furious, afraid that I had been tricked, that all this was just an elaborate scheme to turn me over to Lena's side. But the other part . . . the other part of me was in orbit.

The less I resisted, the better the sensation. I knew she was draining away my heart's blood and I didn't care. My whole life I had been asleep—the nervous twitch of daily living, the sense of always being on my guard, ready to fight, to attack . . . it all began to evaporate with each drop of blood I lost.

I couldn't struggle against this feeling. It wasn't a lack of strength; it was a lack of will. I wanted her to drain me. I wanted her to carry me as far inside her world as she could . . . even farther. There was nothing wrong with what we were doing. There was nothing wrong with me loving this feeling. This overall feeling of being needed, adored, wanted.

At that moment in time, I had never felt more important to anyone. Not my mom, not Manda, not Sagan. I was important to her, to Lena. That was all that mattered. The thought of leaving this feeling was painful. It was like seeing the real world for the first time. *Seeing the inside of the universe*. Knowing the way it all worked even if I couldn't say it in words. What I was experiencing was beyond thought. Thought was no longer necessary. Everything was already there that was needed.

I felt Lena's lips gently suckling at my neck, could almost hear the ticking of the blood rhythmically slipping into her throat. We were no longer two people, but one person. But that didn't begin to describe it. We weren't just one person . . . we were all people. Huge masses of people and souls and thoughts and non-thoughts, which was all there was and all there ever would be. I was separate but not really separate. I was small, but I was unimaginably large. I couldn't think, but I did something that was more than thinking. It wasn't a thing that took effort like thinking did; it was a thing that took non-effort. Letting go. Opening. And in that opening I saw . . .

Oh.

If this was death, then it poured out slow and sticky sweet and wasn't really a leaving at all, but a kind of arriving at this new place where I had always been, but just didn't know it before. *Take me. Take me all the way there.* But she already had. There wasn't any "taking"; this was more like "releasing." Letting the prisoners go. Nothing to worry about ever again.

Wham.

Lena had pulled her mouth away. I slumped forward, nearly toppling over the edge of the chimney. She caught me and held me there in her arms.

"I almost . . . I almost . . . could not . . . stop," she said. Her lips and teeth were red. She licked them with a red tongue. "I have never . . . Emma . . . please . . ."

"Oh wow." I wiped my eyes.

I didn't want her to ever let me go. Lena ran her shirtsleeve over my neck; it came back smeared with blood. *My blood.*

"Your . . . blood . . . is so . . . sweet. I . . . I can still taste it," she said, whispering. "I can taste the sun in your blood. My God, Emma. It was like . . . feeding. It *was* feeding. I didn't intend to really feed— I had eaten so recently! I only wanted you to fully experience the joining of your personal *Feld* with that of another. Your neck was so pristine! But once I began!—it was all I could do to pull away. I wanted you so much. I cannot understand it . . . why there is still so much . . . of the sun in you."

I didn't know what to say. I was still slumped against her. It felt strange to be held that way by someone smaller than me.

"That is enough for now," she said finally. "We need . . . to come down. I need . . . to let go of you. I might start again. It would be . . . too dangerous."

When we joined Anton and Donne, they looked at us with strange eyes.

"Something happened, didn't it?" Anton said. "I knew it. I knew there was something different about her."

I didn't know what to say. I was still a little bit in shock. The wounds in my neck throbbed, but it felt more like a pulse than a pain. As if what Lena had done had somehow made my body, my spirit, still move in rhythm to the beat of her heart. It was frightening.

Lena didn't answer Anton's question. She was sitting across the room from the rest of us. She had cleansed her face, though I noticed she held the rag she had used close to her nostrils as if sniffing the last traces of my blood.

I held a cloth to my neck. The cloth was damp with alcohol. Lena had warned me to keep it there while we were inside the little cave room, even if the bleeding had stopped, to blunt the scent.

Donne watched me curiously without saying a word.

Later, after things had settled down, I had something important to ask and was looking for the right moment. Finally I just blurted it out.

"I need your advice," I said. "The thing is, is there any way you can help me? Against Wirtz?"

Lena thought a long while before speaking.

"I'm sorry, Emma. I wish so much that we could, but we don't dare provoke the *Verloren*. Another war would be . . . utterly devastating. Any act of aggression . . . would be a terrible provocation."

"They've already been provoked, as far as I'm concerned," Donne said. "We'll be lucky if some of them don't come snooping around here now. She'll draw them to us."

"And how is that my fault?" I said.

"It is not, of course," Lena said. "But the *Verloren* have a kind of primitive code of honor they call the *Fütterung*. The Feeding. This does not mean literal feeding. It means there is no greater death, no greater sacrifice to be made in their world than to give oneself willingly in service to the warrior. Who in your instance would be Wirtz."

"You haven't answered his Call," Anton said. "So you've never submitted to the *Fütterung*, okay? In his mind, you haven't lived up to your end of things."

I thought of the girl, Ava. What had happened to her when she had resisted the vampire.

"That's why he's coming for you," Anton said. "It's the only way to satisfy his wounded honor."

"Oh boy," I said.

"So thank you for messing everything up," Donne said. "We were doing all right until you came along, Fresh. They'll come again, I know they will. . . . It will happen all over." She turned her face away.

"I don't get it," I said. "No wonder you *Sonnen* lost the war! If all of them are like you, Donne—"

"Emma!" Lena said. She spoke so sharply, I knew immediately I was supposed to drop it.

She motioned to me silently, and we left the cave and stood beneath a tall hickory tree that had moonlight fanning through its leaves. The sound of the little waterfall muffled our voices.

"That is why she never speaks of it . . . the night she was turned," Lena said. "*Verloren* . . . So often when one is in the throes of blood frenzy, the *Blutraserei*, a different sort of lust comes over them as well."

"You mean she was—"

"Assaulted," Lena whispered. "Can you imagine the horror? To already be suffering the greatest . . . theft . . . that can be suffered in a life. To have every choice from that moment on colored by the actions of another. She didn't fight back. She knew she couldn't, that her only hope of living was in choosing to do . . . nothing."

"Oh wow. I'm so sorry. I didn't know."

"Donne was a damaged spirit for years. You cannot believe

what it took to gain her trust. If not for Anton . . . He can be so much like a very bright . . . child. Locked inside a kind of perpetual . . . immaturity. Yet that is why she trusts him. He reminds her of her lost brother. Perhaps it is her only way of trusting a man."

"I didn't know," I said. "No wonder she didn't want to tell her story. I was thinking. . . . Oh, forget it. It's not important."

"What? Tell me."

"I guess I just thought she didn't like me for some reason."

"Give her time."

"Probably I should go," I said.

"It might help if you were to come back inside a moment. I have something to ask you, and the others need to hear this as well."

We went back inside and sat down again. Donne seemed to be okay, but she was almost leaning against Anton.

"I wanted you two to hear this," Lena said. She turned to me. "All right, Emma. What is it? Have you decided yet? Which side you will choose?"

"Well, sure," I said. "I thought it was pretty obvious that I'm on your side. Why would I go with the *Verloren* after what Wirtz did to me?"

"So you are ready to join us?"

The way she asked it felt almost formal . . . as if we were about to partake in some kind of weird vampire ceremony. I didn't know how to respond.

"I . . . I want to," I said. "I really do. There are just some things. . . . Well, it's all so different for me. I don't know if I'm ready to . . . wait like you guys do. I don't know if I have the patience for it. What if the *Sonneneruption* doesn't come for another hundred years? Two hundred? Sagan said the last one, the flare from 1859, was the strongest in five hundred years. . . ."

"Sagan. Who is Sagan?" Anton said.

"I knew it," Donne said after I had spent the past hour explaining about Sagan, how our friendship had developed. "I knew there was something you were hiding from us."

"You're right," I said. "I should have told you. But . . . I didn't know how you would take it. I figured you just might throw me out."

"Well, your instincts were right on," Donne said, fuming. "You've betrayed our trust. Told someone about us—someone we are forced to hunt to live. A person who is going to betray us sooner or later."

"Sagan would never do anything like that!" I said, struggling to hold in my temper. "Don't you believe there are good people out there?"

"Of course we do, Emma," Lena said.

"Only we've never known any of them," Donne said.

"That's because you've never tried," I said. "And I know why. Because . . . you think you can't. They are what we . . . consume. I understand that. But please—you have to make an exception in Sagan's case for your own good. He can help! I know he can."

"How?" Anton said.

"I don't know all the technical stuff," I said. "But he has . . . instruments he can use, ways to forecast what the sun is going to do at any given time. Predict the changes. He would know about the next *Sonneneruption* the moment it leaves the sun! Before anyone else in the whole world."

"This is true?" Anton said. He seemed ready to jump at the chance. I explained as much as I could remember about STEREO and the Solar Observatory. I was laying it on kind of thick, but . . .

"Lena?" I said.

"I see no harm in it, I suppose."

"Outvoted again," Donne said, scowling. "But why would this *Vollmensch* help?"

"What's that?" I said.

"Human, a human who has never been turned," Anton said.

"Because he told me he would," I said. "I believe him."

"Why?" Donne said.

"Because . . ." *Because he loves me,* I wanted to say.

I loved watching Sagan work the next day. I couldn't help sneaking glances every so often, especially when he got hot and pulled his shirt off and hung it on the railing. Something about the way his muscles moved . . . it made me feel this weird tingly sensation in my mouth. I wondered if I had this power before becoming a vampire. As if my senses were opening up in ways that I never could have imagined.

"So they're really coming tonight?" he said, taking a drink of water.

"Huh?" I was checking out his Adam's apple sliding up and down his throat. "Oh yeah. They said they would."

"And you really think it's okay?"

I tried not to look worried. I could still hear Donne's voice ringing in my ears.

"Okay, okay, I'll go! I'll go. And if we don't like him, we can just take him."

"Donne!" Lena had said.

"You know it's true," Donne had said. "What else can we do? He will know."

"She's right," Anton had said.

"It's fine," I said to Sagan, trying to sound perky and positive. "You have to look at it from their perspective. They've been so isolated. Their whole world has been about hiding, staying unseen, unknown. But when I explained all about the observatory, the things you can do . . ."

Sagan grunted, almost laughing.

"No, really. You could help them so much. Maybe even find a new place for them to live on the base."

"Just what I need," Sagan said. "Four of you running around loose out here."

"Be serious."

"I am. I'm sorry. I just can't really believe it. No matter what I've seen, what you've shown me . . . vampires are real? And I'll be meeting three of them tonight?"

"Yep. It's a big step for them. I practically had to make you out to be a sun god to get them to come."

Sagan stretched magnificently, the little golden hairs on his arms glistening, a vein in his neck throbbing out a measured beat. *Hmmm, maybe I was right.*

"Can you see that?" he said as we positioned a tank behind a steel pillar and strapped it in place with bungee cords.

I leaned back, shading my eyes to look. "Nope. Not unless you're coming up from the other side, and then you would probably just think it was part of the test stand. Thank goodness for rust."

"Best camouflage there is," Sagan said. "Okay, how's that?"

I checked out his handiwork. "Good stuff. I'm impressed. I never would have guessed what a nasty mind you have lurking inside that angelic head of yours."

Sagan was concentrating so hard, I'm not sure he heard that last part. "Some of this probably seems like overkill, but . . ."

"Papi always says he would rather be loaded for bear and face a *Rotluchs* than the other way around."

"What's a *Rotluchs*?"

"Bobcat," I said.

"They have bobcats in Germany?"

"Guess so if they have a word for it."

"I like the way your papi thinks."

"Me too. I hope you can meet him someday."

"Plan on it," Sagan said.

We sat on the edge of the structure, mopping our faces with stolen high-end towels. The sun was going down. The sky to the west was turning scarlet as if the clouds were filling with blood.

"Hey," I said. "All this stuff we're setting up . . . be honest . . . will it work?"

"You're supposed to be the cocky one, Emma."

"I know. But . . . if this were an experiment . . . what would you say the percentages are?"

Sagan was quiet a little while. "You prepare the best you can. You try to increase your odds, but once you've done everything you can do—"

"I know; it's out of your hands. But will it work?"

"Well . . . it's got to, to a certain extent, right? Wirtz is a physical creature. So he's got to have physical limitations. These things we have set up—they will have some effect. The only questions are these: how big an effect, and—maybe more important—can we hit the target?"

"There you go with that 'we' stuff again."

"You're stuck with me for the duration, Emma."

"Until I decide to stash you somewhere safe."

"We'll see."

"Sagan . . . do you worry at all about . . . killing someone?"

He stood up and turned away from me, leaning against the railing and looking somewhere over the fields. "We're talking about a monster," he said. "That's what you called him."

"I know. But he used to be a man."

"Well, the problem is, it's not real to me the way it's real to you," Sagan said. "You've seen vampires. Experienced what they can do. Being out here with you today, setting things up in the bright sunshine . . . it feels more like we're getting ready for Halloween. It doesn't feel real. So it doesn't hit me that way."

He spat and watched the small white blob fall all the way to the ground, wafting on the air currents as it fell.

"So . . . is it going to bother you? What we're doing, I mean?" I said.

"Do we have a choice?" Sagan said. "We've got to come hard and with deadly force. If we try to be humane . . ."

"We'll die. I get your point. It's starting to feel a little too real," I said. "You think this is what soldiers go through right before they go to war?"

"I don't know. I don't think it has completely sunk in for me. I wish I could see what you have seen."

I shuddered. "No, you don't."

Night had fallen at last. We were standing outside the Solar Observatory, excitedly waiting for Lena, Donne, and Anton to arrive.

"You ready for this?" I said.

Sagan flashed a shaky smile. "Sure. I hope I am. Is there spinach in my teeth?"

"You'll be fine. Just don't think of them as . . . you know . . ."

"Vampires? Oh sure. That'll be easy. Especially if they lick their lips a lot."

"They're people, remember? Human beings caught in a . . . bad situation. They want to be cured, be normal again. What they are doing, the sacrifices they are making and all—it's pretty amazing. Lena is the leader, but Donne is the most suspicious. Win her over, and you'll have all three of them. Or not."

"Thanks for the vote of confidence. So if I don't win her over . . . ?"

"You'll be on the menu."

"Oh boy."

"It'll be fine." *Please let it be,* I thought. *Please.* "They're really nice, I swear. Besides, I told them you have a plan."

"I do?"

"Yeah. Ways of helping them out. Even if it's just to find them a new home that's not so . . . dirty. Just remember this is every bit as weird for them as it is for you. Maybe more."

"Oh, I'm sure."

He kept looking up.

"They're not going to fly in," I said, almost giggling.

"What do I know?"

At last we saw them. Three small dark figures moving slowly up the drive. I had asked them to take it easy on the speed once they got close to the observatory for Sagan's sake.

"Showtime," I said.

Sagan was holding my hand, but now he pulled free. I'm not sure why. I think maybe he just didn't want to look weak. *Afraid. He's afraid of looking afraid.*

"Hi," I said to the vampires, trying to sound cheerful and pleased. "Well, here he is, just like I promised." I took Sagan's hand again. He looked at me and looked at my hand as if comparing it to theirs. I gestured to the three of them in turn. "Sagan, this is Lena, Donne, and Anton. Guys, this is Sagan Bishop. My . . . my friend."

I had known this would be a little awkward, but this was off the scale. I could see Donne's nostrils flaring as if her vampire senses couldn't help but sniff the wind for the scent of Sagan's warm human blood. Anton was breathing through his mouth instead of his nose. I couldn't tell anything from Lena's expression.

"Hi," Sagan said, giving a little wave. "Nice to meet you."

I noticed he swallowed as he said it, but I gave him points for the steadiness of his voice.

Lena started to say something, stopped, then started again. "Um . . . hello . . . Sagan," she said. "I want to . . . thank you for inviting us. For demonstrating so much . . . courage."

"No problem," Sagan said, which sounded instead like there were actually a lot of problems he had with being here, only he was willing to look past them.

"This place is very . . . large," Anton said, staring this way and that. "I can't believe it. . . . NASA."

"Yeah," Sagan said. "Would you like to go inside?"

They were still about ten feet away from us. I thought about vampires shaking hands with a human and almost started to laugh. Would it be like a human being shaking hands with a shark?

25. THE EYE

Sagan let us in with his badge and we walked down the long hall to the observatory.

"I need to turn on the lights," he said, sounding apologetic.

He turned the round dial on the wall, slowly bringing up the illumination. Each of the *Sonnen* lifted a hand to their faces to blunt the brightness until their eyes could adjust.

The vampires were keeping their distance. *They're afraid of him,* I realized with a shock. What could Sagan possibly do to them? But it was true; they were scared. I could see it in the way they stood, legs apart, hands ready, prepared to flee. It had taken a good bit of courage for them too.

I tried to think of some way to loosen everyone up. "Um . . . maybe it would be better if we all just sat around a table?" I almost said, *Just like . . . people.*

"All right," Lena said. "But first . . ."

She crossed the room carefully but also gracefully to where Sagan was standing. He must have weighed twice what she did. I sometimes forgot how slightly built the *Sonnen* were without anyone else around for comparison purposes.

She held out her hand.

"I am so happy to make your acquaintance," she said. "Emma has told us so much about you. Thank you for having us."

Sagan hesitated just slightly, looking at her hand, then her eyes.

He reached out and touched her fingers, then shook her hand warmly. He had a surprised look on his face.

"You thought my skin would feel . . . cold, didn't you?" Lena said, smiling.

"I . . . I didn't really know," Sagan said, blushing.

All of the vampires tensed a little; I could almost read their minds, the way they became unnaturally observant, noticing the blood rising to his face.

Anton stepped forward. He and Sagan shook without any trouble.

"You are very . . . tall, eh?" Anton said, grinning shyly.

I looked at Donne. She came over reluctantly, but then just stood there, nostrils wide.

Say something, I mentally beamed at her. I wondered for a crazy moment if she looked prettier than I did to Sagan.

"Nice . . . to meet you," Sagan said, taking her small hand.

Donne ran her tongue over her bottom lip, making me wonder if human blood gave off a kind of overpowering fragrance to a vampire's nose.

Shut up.

They let go of each other's hands and stood there watching. It almost felt as if I were intruding, witnessing something that was meant to be private.

The room wasn't hot, but beads of sweat had formed on Sagan's brow. I could tell without even touching him that his pulse rate was way up and his skin temperature was rising.

As if to break the tension, Anton waved his arm at all the computers, marveling at the technology. "This is a very interesting place." I noticed his accent seemed self-consciously heavier. "So many machines. I enjoy so much thinking about . . . scientific things."

Lena was still standing in front of Sagan with Donne and Anton at either side. He was a head taller than all three of them, but he suddenly seemed . . . surrounded.

"Please forgive me for staring," Lena said. "You see . . . it has been a great many years since I have . . . spoken . . . with someone like you."

"Wow," Sagan said, exhaling nervously as he said it. "This is . . . kind of surreal."

"All right, you may stop circling the prey," Lena said, and we all laughed a little bit. She tugged at Donne's arm and the three of them sat at the huge conference table. Sagan and I took seats on the opposite side.

"Now that we're all here . . . ," I said.

"What do we have to talk about?" Donne said.

I was surprised she had spoken, and it took me a moment to collect myself.

"Um . . . about . . . friendship," I said. "You know, new possibilities. Why can't . . . people like you . . . be friends with humans, that kind of thing."

"Well . . . how about because they're our source of food, or have you forgotten?" Donne said. She didn't even glance at Sagan.

"Donne!" Lena said.

"No problem," Sagan said, blushing again.

"Would you please stop doing that," Donne said.

"What?" Sagan said.

"You're blushing," I said, then turned toward Donne a little angrily. "He can't help it. You just called him food."

"I told you, it's no big deal; I'm cool," Sagan said, taking my hand and then looking at Donne. "Sorry about the . . . autonomic reflex."

"Donne?" Lena said.

Donne put her lips together, looking down at the table. "I . . .

I shouldn't have said that. It's just . . . I don't see how we can ever make this work; I'm sorry."

"Nobody said it would be easy," I said. "But . . . what if . . . we could maybe form some kind of pact? We could call it . . . mutual assured . . ."

"Destruction?" Donne said. She wasn't smiling.

"Like . . . an agreement. You know. Working together. This is a really small start, but . . . who knows . . . it could take off and really grow. Maybe someday both types of . . . humans . . . could join forces and work together against their common enemy."

"And you believe . . . under a scenario like that . . . humans would . . . just provide us with what we need?" Donne said.

"I think so . . . yeah . . . I think as long as—"

"It would never work," Donne said. "Somebody would foul it up. Surely you can't be that thick."

I glared at her. "I didn't say it would be perfect. That's why I said start small, work our way up from there."

Sagan raised his hand. "Hey, as the resident snack, I'd like to say something."

Everybody turned to stare at him.

"I hate to say it, but I agree with Donne. It would never work," he said. "Just imagine how . . . other humans . . . would react. There would be protests. All kinds of cults—for and against—would spring up. There would be a whole bunch of new government regulations . . . assuming the government ever got done trading blood for experiments. Religious leaders would go completely nuts. One thing we . . . humans . . . generally don't do well is large-scale stuff. Every once in a while we pull off a miracle, like landing on the moon." He winked at me. "But so much of that was an engineering problem. We are great at engineering problems. But something like this? We can't even get people in neighboring countries to like each other."

"You are correct, I am afraid," Lena said. "It would not be practical, Emma. I am sorry to spoil your grand plans."

"But . . . what if we started right here?" I said. "Just see where it goes? We could help, couldn't we, Sagan? With the *Sonneneruption*?"

"Help like how?" Donne said.

"We could . . . act as a kind of advance-warning system, you know?" I said. "I know you spend as much time as possible outdoors, but what if the *Sonneneruption* came during the day? You'd be dug in somewhere, completely oblivious to what was going on. You could miss it entirely . . . then be stuck for another few hundred years."

"Most of the eruptions last more than a day," Lena said.

"I'd have to agree, Emma," Sagan said. "The really powerful ones can wash over the earth for hours."

"Still . . ."

"Forgive me for saying," Anton said, "you're young, Mr. Sagan, but you're not going to live two or three hundred more years, are you? So it's likely you may be . . . gone . . . before the next *Sonneneruption*. It's not possible for you to live that long, is it? So how could this help us?"

Sagan grinned. "My great-grandfather is almost a hundred."

"Isn't it better than what you have now?" I said. "Maybe . . . when the time comes . . . Sagan could turn it over to someone else, someone younger?"

"Got me in the retirement village already, huh?" he said.

"Anton is correct," Lena said. "And besides, it is not fair to expect a lifetime commitment from anyone, no matter how well intentioned."

"But we could do it while we can," I said, feeling the meeting slipping away, not going at all how I had imagined it would. "So you could live a better life in the meantime. And we could band to-gether to fight the *Verloren*."

"So that's why you got us out here," Donne said. "You're still looking for us to help, huh? Help spark a new war, worse than the last."

I bristled at her tone. "So you'd rather hide like rats in a hole?"

"I'd rather live, thanks," Donne said.

"Hey, time-out," Sagan said, raising his hand. "Why don't we just do what we can do? And let the other stuff sort itself out? No-body has to save the world tonight. But we could make things bet-ter for you, right? Emma has told me about your situation. I'm sure I could find something a lot better for you out here—there are plenty of empty spaces where you could—"

Donne pounded her small fist on the table. "How do we know we can trust you?"

"I don't know," Sagan said. "You've trusted me this far. Well, Emma, actually. I can only give you my word."

"That you won't give us up?" Donne said.

"Even if I wanted to, what would I say?" Sagan said. "Um, ex-cuse me, Officer, but there are three vampires living up at the state park and—ouch!" I pinched his leg under the table.

Donne got up from her chair, staring at me hotly. "You told him that too?"

"Okay . . . yeah . . . Well, actually, I took him there and—"

"Now what are we supposed to do? Move again?"

"No, really! You don't have to move. Sagan would never tell anybody." I looked at Lena. "I'm sorry. I guess I screwed up. I should have asked first. It's nothing sinister, it's just—I have a tendency to jump the gun. And I didn't show him exactly where you live. No-body is going to storm your place or anything. Please trust me."

"Try living like this, dealing with the *Verloren,* for a hundred years . . . we'll see how trusting you are," Donne said. But at least she sat down again.

"That's the whole problem," I said. "The *Verloren* are wrecking things for everybody. Somebody needs to get their attention."

I noticed Anton had been holding his hand up.

"What?" I said.

"Emma, I appreciate your feelings, okay?" he said. "But there's nothing that can be done about the *Verloren*. They're just too strong."

"I am afraid I must agree with Anton on this point," Lena said. "There truly is no means of standing up to them at this time, not before the next *Sonneneruption*. The risk of provocation is too great." She turned to Sagan. "And I understand if you do not want to help us in light of this decision."

"Okay, okay," I said, desperate to swing the mood in a different direction. "Sagan, maybe this is a good time to show off the observatory?"

"Um . . . sure," Sagan said.

Everything felt a little somber as Sagan got set up, but things warmed a bit as he went into his routine. He gave the *Sonnen* the same basic tour he had given me. It was interesting to watch their faces and hear their gasps of astonishment. Some of their ideas about science and astronomy were pretty antiquated, and they seemed in awe of the technology, almost to the point of disbelief.

"You are saying it is possible to know . . . how soon?" Lena said when Sagan was explaining about solar flares and coronal mass ejections.

"From here we could have advance warning of as much as eighteen to twenty hours in most cases."

He pulled up the same information he had shown me about the Carrington Event. Even Donne seemed fascinated. Sagan and

Anton got into a technical discussion of the *Feld* that—even as important as it was to my situation—ultimately bored me catatonic. I sat there yawning and not trying to hide it one bit.

"Okay, I can take a hint," Sagan said.

Afterward we all sat down at the picnic tables outside. It felt so much better to be under the stars, where the darkness masked our differences.

"I am Sicilian," Anton was saying. "But by birth I am a good old USA boy. My grandpapa, he came to this country from Sicily. A barrel maker, okay? Can you imagine they used to have jobs like that?"

Sagan was full of questions, most of them the same ones I had already asked. But he came up with a few new ones of his own.

"Did you ever get to see them again? Your family, I mean?"

"Once, yes. It was very sad," Anton said. "My mama; she cried so much that I was missing, you know? I couldn't take it. I had to leave."

"Do you ever . . . wonder what happened to them?"

"Sure I do. I still do sometimes if I think about them too much."

"We could find out, go to something like Ancestry.com," Sagan said. "I could show you how."

Anton grinned broadly. "Is this true? This is something we could really do?"

"Sure. With a computer it's pretty easy."

Anton's eyes practically sparkled. "I have a sister—Rosa—I would really like to know what happened to her."

"Sure, we'll do it."

Sagan then got really quiet. "Talking about . . . the *Verloren*. You say their numbers are increasing?"

"Yes," Lena said.

"So is it dangerous? To be out alone at night? I mean, more than it used to be, say, like twenty years ago?"

"Are you saying . . . what are the chances?" Anton said. "Of encountering *Verloren*?"

Sagan nodded.

"No worse than the odds for encountering a serial killer, I would say."

"Thanks, Anton," I said.

"No, you misunderstand, Emma. I just meant that the chances are really very small. It's a big world out there, okay? But who can say when something is going to happen?" He pointed at one of the oak trees at the edge of the forest. "Who is to say this tree, it suddenly falls down on your head, Mr. Sagan, as you're making your way up the sidewalk? Something terrible could happen, but most likely it wouldn't."

"It's just that . . . knowing you are . . . real, you know what I mean? It changes everything," Sagan said. "I will never be able to be out at night, after dark, and not think about it after this."

"But you're careful already, am I right?" Anton said. "Don't go into bad places."

"What . . . what if one of my sisters . . . what if she were in your *Strecke* one night, completely by accident. And you . . . you took her."

"We wouldn't take all of her," Anton said, laughing, thinking he had just made a fabulous joke.

Sagan remained serious. "What I'm saying is . . . I would feel funny if I saw her with some . . . unexplained cuts on her shoulder."

"Would it make you feel differently about us?" Lena said. "About helping us?"

He took a couple of breaths. "I hope it wouldn't. It would just seem . . . weird. A little scary."

"I wouldn't blame you for feeling that way," Lena said. "Do you think any one of us would not have felt the same?"

"I know . . . it's not your fault," Sagan said. "You are what you are."

Donne smiled for the first time all evening. "I have an idea."

"What?" Sagan said.

"Where do you live?"

"I'm not sure it's fair to my family," Sagan said. "Not that I don't trust you. I wouldn't be here otherwise. But I signed up for this gig. They didn't."

"But it's only right, isn't it?" Donne said. "You know where we live. If we're going to trust you, then . . ."

"Okay. Okay. One condition," Sagan said. "I drive."

It took even more time coaxing to get Lena into the Jeep.

"I have never been in . . . one like this before," she said, eyeing us fearfully. "Couldn't we just run alongside?"

"I'll keep it down to fifty or less; how about that?" Sagan said.

Donne said she had been in cars plenty of times, and Anton was more excited than scared. The three of them finally piled into the small backseat, while me and Sagan got in front, and we zipped out the main gate headed west toward Sagan's neighborhood.

"Why, this is . . . exhilarating!" Lena said. "I can feel the wind . . . !"

Sagan grinned. "I told you my baby would move. Got her up to forty-five."

I was proud of him. If he was nervous about where we were going, he wasn't showing it. I was the nervous one.

I glanced in the backseat. They were sandwiched in there, all right, their combined lavender glow in the low light filling up the small space.

We turned off the main road and zigzagged through neighborhoods before finally coming to Sagan's street. His house looked smaller in the dark. I was surprised to see so many lights on, and some of the upstairs windows didn't even have curtains. Instead of pulling into the driveway, we stopped alongside the curb in front.

Nobody got out or spoke. I didn't know what Donne was after. Then I realized she was watching the tall second-floor windows. Pretty soon a blond head came bobbing down the hall; it was Sagan's sister Bree. I licked my lips nervously, wondering what Bree would think about three vampires checking her out in her pajamas. She was followed by Jenna, bouncing along behind her, cute as a doll.

"Let's get out," Donne said.

She was sitting in the middle, but practically climbed over Lena. Soon all five of us were standing on Sagan's front lawn in the moon shadow cast by a Bradford pear tree.

"Aren't you worried they might see us out here?" I said to Sagan.

"Not this time of night," Sagan said. "Everybody hits it pretty early."

"Hits it?" Lena said.

"Goes to bed."

"Okay, so you've seen his place," I said to Donne. "Satisfied?"

"Not quite," she said.

Suddenly she was standing next to the front wall of the house, moving so fast that even with my eyes she was little more than a blur.

"Oh no." Sagan saw her now. Donne was climbing the side of his house. He swore and started to run across the grass.

"What's she doing!" I hissed at Lena, and we took off after him.

Donne had already reached the first window. I had no idea what she was holding on to. Her limbs were splayed out around her like a four-legged spider.

"Hey!" Sagan said, as loudly as he dared.

I was already past him, moving up the wall in a single leap to land beside Donne. I grabbed one of the shutters and held on, hoping it was fastened securely.

"What are you doing!" I said.

"Watching," Donne said. "How many are there?"

"How many what?"

"How many brothers and sisters does he have?"

"Three sisters," I said. "Now are you gonna get off of his house, or do I have to drag you down by your hair?"

Donne didn't say anything, just flowed back down the side of the house like mercury.

I stopped her in the yard. "What were you doing up there? What's this all about!"

"Come on, let's go," she said. "Before one of them sees us."

She ran back to the Jeep with the rest of us following, and the three *Sonnen* all climbed back in.

"Wait just a minute," Sagan said, furious. "You better give me some kind of an explanation for what you just did or . . ."

"Or you'll . . . what?" Donne said. "Turn us in? And what's to stop us from killing you first?"

"Donne!" Lena said. She turned to Sagan. "I am so sorry; she does not mean what she says."

"Of course I don't," Donne said. "I just wanted to see."

"See what?" Sagan demanded, eyes blazing. Anton was holding him back.

"I wanted to memorize their faces," Donne said. "The faces of those we promise to never hurt."

The trip back was quiet. Sagan could tell I was pouting.

"Don't worry, I'm okay now," he said, speaking softly.

"I know."

"Then what is it?"

"Well . . . what happened just now, with Donne. It made me remember . . . something I saw. Something I didn't want to tell you about. Because I didn't want to scare you."

"What did you see?" Sagan said.

"I was experimenting with the playing cards, putting myself into an absence seizure to test my powers on the *Feld*. I saw . . . I saw Wirtz kill someone. A woman in her kitchen. He's out there somewhere right now. He's hunting for me, but he's killing people. It was horrible, Sagan. So horrible . . ."

There was a tap on the back of my seat. "You realize we can hear every word you're saying?" Donne said.

"Yeah."

"So you visited Wirtz?"

"Yeah."

"As a *Wesentliche*?"

"Well, no," I said. "That's why it was weird. It was so different from what I had expected."

"How so?" Lena said.

"I didn't just visit him—I was inside him, you know? I had to go wherever he went, do whatever he did. But I was seeing through his eyes. . . . I followed this poor woman into her kitchen, carried her back to the bedroom, snapped her neck. . . . It felt like it was me who killed her. Not Wirtz. That's why it was so—"

"Stop the vehicle," Anton said.

"What?" Sagan said.

"Stop the car. Now!"

We were sitting on a bench in a Wendy's parking lot. The *Sonnen* had asked Sagan to go inside. I could see him through the glass eating a Frosty. He gave me a worried little wave with his spoon.

"She has to be," Anton said. "It makes sense, doesn't it?"

"But there have been so few . . . ," Lena said.

"I'll believe it when I see it," Donne said. "No pun intended."

"What?" I kept saying.

"Anton thinks you're an *Auge*," Donne said, rolling her eyes.

"What's an *Auge*?"

"See, Lena, she doesn't even know herself!" Anton said.

"An *Auge*, Emma, is an Eye," Lena said. "Meaning, one who can see through the eyes of another."

"Is that good?" I said. "I figured all vampires—I mean, all of us—could do it. It's just something I stumbled onto by accident. Another way of using the *Feld*, right?"

"It's the *Feld*, oh yeah," Anton said. "The *Feld* is the medium for the sight. But not all of us have it. In fact, none of us do. I have never known an Eye personally, only what Lena has told us."

"It is an extraordinarily rare gift, Emma," Lena said. "Putting your *Wesentliche*, your essence, out onto the *Feld* is one thing . . . but to go inside another . . . that is most rare of all. But the strongest power of an Eye is not the physical—it is the ability to see deeper than that. You are privy to the mind of the person you enter . . . his innermost motivations, judgments, secrets. A true *Auge* can look inside and see whether one is *Verloren* or *Sonnen* at heart."

"But I wasn't just clued in to Wirtz's thoughts," I said. "It was more like I *became* his thoughts. His hunger, lust, cruelty. I wanted that woman he killed. I wanted her so much." *Her blood, her body. Her death.*

"Are you sure this is what you experienced?" Lena said. "That it was not simply a dream or your imagination?"

"Yeah, well, I've only been able to do it once, but it was no dream. It was completely real. Too real." I had a terrible thought. "Wow. So . . . you're telling me that Wirtz, the whole time he has been looking through my eyes—"

"Oh no. He is not an *Auge,*" Lena said. "I would stake my life on it. He can communicate through his *Wesentliche,* but seeing through another's eyes—that is beyond his ability. It is especially rare in *Verloren.* I do not know that I have ever heard of one. . . ."

"Die Esserin," Anton said. "Aren't you forgetting about her?"

"Yes, well, of course," Lena said. "She is one. It is how she became their leader."

"It's that rare, huh?" I said.

"One comes along maybe only once every hundred years or so," Anton said. "We sure could have used you during the war! They were always ahead of us, knew everything we were doing."

I looked at Lena. "So . . . does this mean I'm safer than I thought I was?"

She shook her head. "I am afraid not, Emma. It is more dangerous for you than we imagined."

"Why?" I said.

"The Eye is a two-edged sword," Lena said. "Think of it this way. Which glows more brightly, is easier to find, a lighthouse on a hill or a lantern in the woods?"

"So I'm the lighthouse in this scenario?" I said.

"You are when viewed from the perspective of the *Feld,*" Lena said.

"Which makes it easier for Wirtz to find you," Anton said. "You stand out."

"Wait—so what am I supposed to do?" I said.

"You're the Eye," Donne said. "What do you see?" There was an undeniable smirk in her voice.

"There is a way," Lena said quietly, "to know."

26. DYING PLACE

"You are sure you wish to do this?" Lena said.

The three *Sonnen* were arranged in a small circle around me back at the Stone House Hotel. I was feeling a little claustrophobic. Sagan was sitting nearby, looking nervous.

I felt for Lena's bite marks on my neck. They were still there, but thanks to my vampiric healing abilities, the wounds were already shrinking.

"Yeah," I said, gulping a little.

Lena nodded and looked at the others. "Her blood is . . . a powerful draw. It is so full of sunlight, even now. I cannot warn you enough about this. I hadn't intended on feeding when I was teaching her about the *Kehle,* and yet . . ."

"We'll be fine," Donne said, looking exasperated. "Let's just get on with it."

You'll be fine, I thought. *What about* me?

The moon was high now, but Sagan was holding a flashlight. He came over. The sudden brightness made the other four of us blink.

"Wait a minute," he said. "You're not going to . . . bite her, right?"

"No," Lena said. "That is not necessary. Only that we are close to her throat."

"Slow down. Let's think this through," Sagan said. "What if . . . what if you can't control yourselves? There will be nothing I can do to stop you, right?"

"Afraid not," Anton said, winking. "But I promise—not a drop!"

"Emma, you don't have to do this," Sagan said. "Surely there must be some other way. . . ."

"There is no other way," Lena said wearily, sounding like what she was . . . a woman who had been alive more than 150 years before Sagan was even born. "If she is truly an Eye, we will be able to see what she sees. Please trust us. Only the *Sonnen* can accomplish this—*Verloren* don't have the willpower."

"I'll be okay," I said, taking his hand and giving it a quick squeeze.

"All right already," Donne said. "We'll be here all night at this rate."

"Very well," Lena said. "Emma, please hold as still as you can."

I swallowed a sour lump of fear and held my head as motionless as I could. Forced my breathing to be more regular, deeper. "I'm ready," I said.

Lena moved closer and raised her hand. She was holding Donne's X-Acto knife. She placed the razor tip against the bite mark on my neck, made a little flicking motion—I winced—and the wound was open. My blood, warm and wet, began to ooze down my neck.

Lena put the knife away and re-formed the circle. The three vampires closed their eyes. Their faces were less than a foot away.

"The center of your *Feld* is released with the opening of the *Kehle* and the releasing of your blood," Lena said softly. "As your blood flows, so flows the *Feld* within. Our hunger is drawn to your blood. As your blood draws our hunger, with it, it will draw our *Felds*. Our four *Felds* will unite as one, and we shall see what you shall see."

She still had her eyes closed. The whole thing felt a little embarrassing, like I was taking part in some weird cult ritual. *Especially with Sagan watching.*

I tried to ignore him. "Okay, so what do I do?"

"You must do what you have been doing to join with him," Lena said. "The *Verloren,* Wirtz."

Okay, so now this was really feeling dorky. I had no idea if I could pull it off with anybody else around. "I don't know," I said. "But I'll try."

I could still feel the blood on my neck, kept wanting to swipe it away before it reached my shirt collar. Instead I put my hands down and began to stroke the scar on my leg through my pants, saying the words.

"Take me to Wirtz—"

"No." Lena's eyes popped open. "In the *Kehle.* The throat."

"Oh. Right." I closed my mouth and started speaking the words within my throat, feeling the familiar rumble. Only it didn't seem so ridiculous now.

Take me to Wirtz. Take me to Wirtz. Take me to Wirtz.

I stroked the scar faster and faster, but nothing seemed to be happening.

"Maybe I'm too self-conscious for this," I said.

"You can do it," Lena said. "Please keep trying."

"What if I sit down?"

"Standing is better," Lena said. "Sitting would impede the flow."

"Okay."

Take me to Wirtz. Take me to Wirtz. Take me to Wirtz.

Instead of closing my eyes, I glanced at Sagan. He looked concerned. I concentrated on his eyes, nothing else.

Take me to Wirtz. Take me to—

Everything went away, like fingers snapping—the forest,

Sagan, the *Sonnen,* the stone walls around me . . . all of it disappeared in an instant, as if a door had opened beneath me and I had fallen through into darkness.

My arms shot out from my sides uncontrollably, flailing around. I knew the *Sonnen* had to be right there, but I couldn't feel a thing in any direction. I was sinking into the blackness like a swimmer losing strength in the middle of the ocean.

Dying, I'm dying.

What happened next was hard to explain. Inside my panic there was something else. A change coming over me . . . *It feels good,* I thought. Like nothing I had ever felt before. *Letting go. I'm letting go.*

I was angry with myself, even in the joy of letting go, or because of it. Because I no longer had control. That was it . . . it made me angry, letting go of control, giving it to someone else—angry that it could feel so good.

A liquid bliss began spilling over me. *Is this what it feels like in the womb?*

The darkness slowly peeled away and my vision gradually cleared—I could see the outlines of objects around me, some of the colors they were giving off. But instead of the *Steinhaus,* I could see darkened buildings around me. Some of them had signs. MONSANTO, SAIC, RAYTHEON. The grounds around the buildings were dotted with pools of light and shadowy shrubs. I could see striped parking lots, roads lined with jogging trails, and decorative lampposts encircling a huge artificial pond shimmering with reflected light.

I know this place.

Sagan had driven me through here on our date. It was called Research Park, a sprawling high-tech industrial park only a mile or two from the Space Center.

I became aware of a presence.

. . . Someone is here with me. . . .

This is what it felt like: once at Papi's house I had found a pair of long white gloves that had belonged to my grandmother. This was like pulling on those gloves . . . except it was the vampire's body I was slipping on, every inch of it.

My feet touched the ground and I felt myself running. We moved together, darting from bush to bush, dipping around corners. And then there was no more "we"—there was only "I."

Fight it. Fight his mind. Remember who you are, Emma.

I saw something up ahead: a jogger moving down the sidewalk. A guy out by himself late at night because he worked some crazy shift. He had his shirt off and was wearing those tiny jogging shorts with a split up the hip, showing off his muscular thighs. He had a great body and he knew it. Only no one was there to see. *Well, no one except me.*

My eyes were glued to the man—the beauty of him. But then I started to realize that the beauty was really coming from inside my hunger. I wanted him.

Please. Somebody come.

The jogger might as well have been running in cookie dough the way I closed the gap. I slowed when I was about twenty yards behind. Could feel my breathing and the rhythmic tap-tapping of the jogger's shoes.

Please, anybody. Help him.

I willed the trail to flood with people, drive me back into hiding. No one came. The jogger took a long looping curve toward a darkened belt of woods. I could see apartment lights on the other side.

I loped soundlessly behind, feeling the pull of a sickening, bottomless hunger. I wondered why I hadn't taken him already. It would have been so simple.

I could hear the rush of water as we approached a bridge that crossed a shallow creek. I let the jogger get all the way over the bridge, and now he was bathed in the bright orange lights of a parking lot.

The jogger picked out one of the apartment buildings and ran up the stairs. There was a narrow landing at the top. I tried to see the apartment number, but the young guy's body was blocking it. *Yes. Inside. Yes.* I waited for the jogger to put his key in the lock and swing the door open, then I leapt up to the landing and pushed my way in behind him. I swung the door shut with a backward fling of my hand.

The jogger turned around, saw me, and swore. At first it looked as if he would come after me, but then he got a good look and backed away, throwing one hand up to his mouth. I felt horrified for him. The jogger tried to rush into a bedroom in the back, but I had him by his neck before he was halfway across the living room. I threw him down on the couch.

"What . . . what do you want, man?" the jogger said, voice trembling with fear.

"We will get to that in a moment," I said, mouthing the words that were not mine. "But first . . . I need your key."

"My key, man? Why do you need my key? Oh God, come on, don't hurt me. I'll give you whatever you want, but oh God."

"Your key," I said.

I extended my arm. It was hard to look at the guy on the couch, who was now basically scrabbling against the wall. He was staring right at me; I was the person who was going to hurt him.

"I . . . I threw them on the table, man. Over there on the table." The jogger unclasped his hands and was shakily pointing.

I walked over and picked the keys up, then made the poor guy show me which one was the right one to the front door. I pushed him, hurrying him.

"On the floor."

The jogger tried to stand beside the couch. I shoved him down on the worn brown carpet. He looked pathetic lying there, short shorts, shiny-chested, one arm up, pleading. I gave him a kick that sent him skidding across the rug into the kitchen.

I want him in the kitchen because . . .

I fell on the jogger, gashed open his throat. The young guy screamed, then his voice was nothing but a tortured gurgle.

I began drinking.

I want him in the kitchen because . . . because . . . it will be easier to lap up the spills.

353

I fell into darkness again. This time there was no comfort in the void, only pain. I was slipping into my own death. I was the man lying in his kitchen spurting dark blood all over the linoleum. I wanted to be him. Because I didn't want to be Wirtz. Not ever again. I was trading my death for the relief.

But there was no relief. Only pain and more pain and falling. Everything felt attached to me in my falling. . . . I had torn through the universe and was pulling it into the hole after me.

But even as I was falling, I was still inside the vampire. I got up from the jogger, his hot blood still running down my chin. Walked down the hallway to a bedroom and started blocking the windows with blankets.

"Catch her! Catch her!"

Someone close by was shouting. I could feel myself sliding out of Wirtz's body and back into my own.

My eyes popped open. The *Sonnen* were still arranged around me, but they were rigid, as if in a trance.

I pitched forward.

Sagan forced his way into the circle just in time for me to topple against his chest. He put his arms around me.

"Hey, are you all right?"

I couldn't speak. I clung to him for a long time, feeling dizzy. The *Sonnen* were still in their circle. Finally words started coming back to me. I started shouting.

"I know where he is! I know where Wirtz is! We've been there! Sagan, do you know what this means? As soon as it's daylight, we can go. He'll never be more vulnerable. We could go there and kill him, Sagan. Kill him in his sleep . . ."

The three *Sonnen* vampires were staring at me.

"What?" I said.

"Daylight, Emma," Anton said. "You said daylight."

"I knew there was something," Donne said, jaw tightening. "I knew it."

"I need to sit down," I said, going over to the wall and finding a spot.

Donne followed. "So when were you going to tell us? Don't you think this was a pretty important thing to let us know about? What other secrets are you hiding?"

"Nothing. That's it," I said.

"How are we supposed to believe you?"

"Okay . . ." I sighed. "I apologize for not telling you up front. You want to know the truth? I was afraid you wouldn't accept me for what I am." I looked around at the three of them. "I needed you guys. I figured you would kick me out . . . or worse. Vote me off the island."

"And what makes you think we won't now?" Donne said.

"So what does this mean?" Anton said. "What are you?"

"I have a theory, " I said. "I guess you could call me half vampire, half human." I explained about a seizure scrambling my transformation.

"So you can go out in the daylight," Donne said.

"Yeah."

"And you don't drink blood."

"No. Well, just the once." Nobody smiled.

"And we're supposed to believe you, Fresh?"

I took Sagan by the arm. "I brought him to meet you, didn't I? How's that for trust?"

He smiled sheepishly.

I was hoping for Lena to weigh in. So far she had been silent. Now she was walking over.

"I cannot speak for Donne and Anton," she said. "But nothing has changed for me. I can understand why you did what you did, Emma. And I can understand Donne's suspicion. But here we are. And in spite of being only half vampire, as you say, you are most certainly all *Auge*. Perhaps the most powerful one I have ever known."

"Just imagine it," Anton said. "Being able to go out in daylight. The advantages would be incredible, huh?"

"You're right: she doesn't face the same dangers we face," Donne said. "But it's more than that, Anton. If Wirtz wasn't on her tail, she could go back and live with *them*." She gestured accusingly at Sagan.

"Hey, what did I do?" he said.

Donne turned on him aggressively. "What *haven't* you done, don't you mean? When have you or your kind ever had to hide? When were you ever not in control of the entire planet? When—"

"I thought you said they were human," Sagan said to me.

Donne lunged at him and I lunged at her. We collided with Sagan wedged between us.

"Enough!"

Lena was there, pulling us apart.

"We are forgetting something," Lena said when things had calmed down.

"What?" I said.

"What you intend to do in the . . . daylight."

"Oh. Going to find Wirtz while he's sleeping, you mean?"

Lena looked dismayed. "I cannot tell you how dangerous that would be. Perhaps not to you personally—"

I swore. "Me personally? He's coming to kill me personally. I would say that's pretty dangerous, wouldn't you?"

"You misunderstand," Lena said. "I am speaking of the *Sonnen* . . . as a whole. You know my feelings about provoking the *Verloren*."

"They're monsters, Lena. If you keep running from them, if you never fight back, you know what will happen—"

"We have no choice," Lena said.

"Neither do I."

Driving back to the Space Center, I took a cloth Sagan offered and held it against the knife cut in my throat.

"This has been a very, very weird night," he said, patting my leg.

"You can say that again," I said.

"This has been a very, very weird—"

"Jerk." I punched his arm. "What was that 'I thought you said they were human' crap?"

He let go of the wheel briefly and stretched. "Just trying to keep it light. Are you okay?"

"Watch the road. I feel okay. Well . . . I'm scared."

"Me too," Sagan said. "You think she's right? Lena?"

"I don't like thinking about stuff like this in the middle of the night," I said. "It's too strange."

"No joke, you really want to do this in the morning?" he said. "Break into a dead man's apartment to kill a vampire?"

"Don't you?"

He was silent while I watched stripes passing under the Jeep. "Do you like them?" I said. "The *Sonnen*?"

Sagan ran a hand through his hair. "Vampires. What's not to like?"

357

27. THE APARTMENT

Nine-thirty in the morning. I had slept, but only fitfully. Everything had a foggy air of unreality.

The apartment complex was a good bit nicer than the one I was used to: tennis courts, a little waterfall that splashed down into the pool, brick instead of vinyl siding. The parking lot was mostly empty; everybody had already gone to work. I could see the building right in front of us, the one from my *Auge* vision where Wirtz was hiding.

I was holding a mini-sledgehammer from Home Depot, feeling ridiculous and terrified at the same time. We had gotten the stake from a big real estate sign I had uprooted and shaved to a sharper point with a hatchet.

Sagan had a wicked-looking Japanese sword lying across his lap—something his great-grandfather had brought back from World War II.

"This is insane," he said.

"You're right," I said.

"I still say we should call the police."

"And tell them what? That I saw a guy murdered in a vampiric vision last night? And then they find the guy, and where does that leave us?"

Had last night even really happened? I put my hand on my neck. The fresh cut Lena had made was already mostly healed. The light of day and the green garbage cans in the hall where the buildings joined together made all that stuff seem imaginary, impossible.

But I recognized those wooden stairs, worn smooth in the middle by years of feet. I could see the jogger's door, though I couldn't read the number from this angle. The white plastic shades on his windows were pulled. That's the way all of the windows in the complex looked. Like they all were hiding something.

"Here are our options," I said. "I go up there and check and nobody's home, and it was all just a weird, whacked-out vision—"

"Or . . . the kitchen is covered with dried blood and there is a vampire sleeping it off," Sagan said.

"Wirtz would have lapped that up."

"Good God, Emma."

I turned to face him. "Look, the first thing I'll do when I get inside is get some light coming through those windows. Then what can he do?"

"Kill you?"

"Not funny."

"I wasn't meaning to be funny. What if he's waiting for you and gets to you before you can get the curtains open?"

"Then I should break in through a window. Establish a beachhead of sunlight. What could be safer?"

"Leaving."

"He's so close, Sagan. Do you realize this spot is only a little over a mile from the Space Center? He knows what he's doing. This might be my only chance to catch him before he catches me. What would you rather do, face him when he's trapped and helpless or wait for the big showdown with a vampire at full strength?"

"Neither." Sagan looked at me a long time. He held up the Japanese sword. "And this is for . . . ?"

"The head. That's what Anton said. The stake is just to hold him down. Then you chop off the—"

"You're serious?"

"I have to be," I said.

We parked as close as we could. Got out and went up the stairs. The door at the top was smudged around the knob from use. The number was 218.

I was wearing rubber dish gloves. I looked around before seeing if the door was locked. Nobody in sight. The far end of the outdoor hall was a balcony that hung over a grassy slope. It would be a simple jump, even for Sagan. But I knew that was ridiculous. No way Wirtz could follow us out here: there was far too much light.

"I don't like this," Sagan said.

"Hush."

I put my hand on the knob . . . cold, even through the glove.

I turned it slowly . . . very slowly. It clicked and held firm in my hand.

"Locked," I said.

"We could knock."

I raised my fist and Sagan caught my arm, swearing.

"I was kidding!" He let go. "Wait."

"What?"

"A pretty nasty image just popped into my head." Sagan pointed at the peephole. "Wirtz could be looking at us right now. Ready to jerk it open and yank us in."

I shaded my eyes against the light. "He'd get toasted if he did that. . . . Look at the angle of the sun."

I walked to the opposite balcony. *Shoot.* There was another door there. Another apartment.

"What?" Sagan said.

"I was hoping there were windows on the back side, but there's another apartment there."

"So?"

"So somebody might see me scaling the wall on the front of the building. You'll have to keep a lookout."

I walked back down the stairs with Sagan behind me. I edged along the front, looking at the wall. I needed something to hang on to. No spider hairs in the palms of my hands, thank you.

I was pretty sure I could bound my way up there, get my fingers in a crack near the top. Even if I missed the crack, what was the worst that would happen? If an eighty-foot fall couldn't kill me, a twenty-foot one would be like stubbing a toe.

I stuck the handle of the mini-sledge in my belt. For once I was thankful I had hips, or my pants would be down around my waist. "Give me the stake." Sagan handed me the stake and I tried sticking it in the other side of my belt. "It's too tight! It won't fit."

"Whew. Let's go," Sagan said, acting like he was turning around.

I undid my belt, then redid it just tight enough to keep the stake from slipping out. "That's better. Okay, if you hear a lot of noise after I go in, yell for help," I said. "Wirtz would be surrounded with nowhere to go."

"Surrounded by who? And you'd be just as dead. I've got a ridiculously bad feeling about this."

I was running toward the building.

I made the jump easy enough and clung to the side of the wall like a fly. It wasn't hard at all to lower myself hand over hand in the brick mortar cracks down to the jogger's front window. Except the stupid stake kept digging into my back. I adjusted it and peered through the cracks in the plastic blinds.

Nothing.

But my eyes should have been able to see inside. Something was blocking the light.

I felt a long swallow rising in my throat. "Here we go," I whispered.

"Be careful!" Sagan said. "When you get in, unlock the front door!"

"I will." *Just as soon as I know it's safe.* "Is everything clear?"

"If I lie, will you come down?"

"No."

The screen had to go first. I didn't want to just rip it out if I didn't have to, but all the little white tabs you were supposed to pull were on the inside. Finally I managed to wedge my thumbnail through the glove between the edge of the screen and the window jamb. I pulled and the screen resisted, then finally came loose in my hand.

"I had to bend it a little," I said to Sagan, dropping it to the ground. "See if you can fix it."

"Don't worry about that! Just hurry."

The window was locked; I could see the latch was still in place. *Going to have to break it,* I thought. Holding on with the toes of my shoes and one hand, I used my other hand, lifting gently on the frame, then harder until the wood splintered and the latch tore loose and dropped inside the apartment.

So quiet. My heart was trip-hammering. I wondered if a vampire's super-hearing worked as well when he was asleep.

Calm down. If he reaches out here to pull you in, he's fried.

A dark blue blanket was hanging over the opening. I touched the blanket and drew back my hand with a little shock. There was something solid and heavy behind it, holding the blanket in place.

Great. It was set up like an alarm system. . . . If I pushed the solid thing over, Wirtz would hear the crash and come running.

I put my hand against the solid thing—*whew*—it wasn't a body, but instead something that felt hard with an edge to it, like an overturned table.

I leaned in and put my ear to the blanket, listening. Still nothing. Okay . . .

I got my hand against whatever it was and started slowly moving it back, as soundlessly as possible. It took very little effort. The whole time I was pushing, I watched the edge of the blanket moving farther and farther away from the window opening. Expecting any second for Wirtz's leering face to thrust itself into view, stopping my heart.

There.

At last the blockage was far enough away for me to slip inside. I pulled my hand back and the blanket came with it, until it covered the window again. I thought about jerking the blanket down, but the table would still be blocking most of the light and the vampire might hear the blanket coming loose.

I also hated the idea of sliding around the edge of the blanket—leading with my head, of all things. *He's waiting right over there, Emma.*

I compromised and pulled the blanket down slowly. Very slowly.

Something was holding it at the top. . . . There was a lot of resistance—it had been threaded through a curtain rod.

I was right: I was looking at the top of a table—a wooden kitchen table with thick white tiles in the center.

"Hurry!" Sagan hissed below. "A truck is turning in!"

I put my fingers on the edge of the table and with paralyzing slowness slid it sideways. The room looked empty. I got my foot over the sill and slipped through.

Just a living room. A white leather chair and white leather sofa, both cheap and slightly cracked. No pictures on the walls—guys can be so spare—but at least there was a single drooping rubber plant in the corner. A little shelf held a Walmart stereo; skinny arms of wires ran out to black speaker boxes perched in the corners of the ceiling.

I could see everything in here so easily, it made me wonder how dark it really was. Somebody strong had pushed the table over here from its nook in the kitchen.

I took a couple of steps across the carpet, the very same carpet where I had seen the vampire push the jogger down. The kitchen was empty. The floor looked like it had been mopped. . . .

Licked.

The apartment had an odd smell . . . not a closed-in, musty smell . . . but of something different. Alive, but nothing that smelled human. Again I felt that lump rising in my throat.

I shoved the table over all the way and sunlight came through. *Good.*

The layout of the apartment was simple. The front door opened onto the living room, with the kitchen off to one side with a single hall going into the back. Apparently there was more than one room back there. Let's see, one had to be the bathroom, so the others were probably two bedrooms. . . .

I took a step into the kitchen, taking infinite care not to make a sound. But to a vampire's ears? Might as well be an elephant tiptoeing around in here.

I really didn't want to look in the sink, but I did. . . . Nothing but dirty dishes. But that wasn't the source of the strange smell.

Kitchen to my right, living room to my left. I took a step into the hall. Four doors ahead of me. No, five. The one at the end of the hall was probably a linen closet.

I took another step, blood pressure rising. I looked behind me: the living room, now bathed in glorious, delicious morning sunlight, made me feel stronger. I raised the mini-sledge and pulled the stake out from my belt. Took another step forward in a low defensive crouch. *I've got you cornered. What are you going to do? Drag me into the back bedroom and . . .*

I decided to open the first door. *Whew.* Empty except for a few coats, a red hoodie, and some folding chairs. A little red Dust Devil was mounted on the inside wall.

The next door was already open—I could see the edge of the tub and shower stall. Thankfully, the shower curtain was drawn back. The window was stuffed with the shower mat and a bunch of blue towels. A thrill of horror ran through my whole body.

I didn't want to go into that little space, the bathroom. If I couldn't get to the window in time, Wirtz could come in right behind me and trap me there. Would Sagan hear me?

I sprang to the window and jerked everything down: floor mat, towels, shades. More light blasted in. He had to know I was here now. *Unless vampires sleep like the dead. Shut up.* The bathroom closet was nothing but shelves. I raised the mini-sledge over my head, sunlight washing over my shoulders from behind. Stepped warily back into the hall, standing for a moment in the block of light I had just let in. Three more doors.

The narrow one at the end—I took another couple of steps and pulled it open. Like I thought, a linen closet stuffed with shelves, a vacuum, and a metal air-conditioning thingy. Not enough room for a vampire. I closed it again.

The weird smell was stronger now . . . definitely coming from back here. I tried to slow my breathing. The last two doors were on the left and right, both closed.

Which first? Left, because it would have a window.

I slowly opened the door with the hand holding the stake, ready to run, kill, pass out.

The window across the room from me was blocked up like the others, but I could immediately see the space was empty except for a desk, chair, computer, and some boxes. I tore the blankets from the window, letting the light in. Slid the closet doors back and let light fill in there as well. Nothing but a folded-up stair climber.

One left.

It would have to be the other one. The bedroom with no window. If I were allergic to sunlight, that's the one I would have chosen.

I hated more than anything leaving the room with the light. I left the door open to the hall, but the angle of the sun wasn't good here. None of it would shine directly into the room I was about to enter.

The last door was slightly ajar. Nothing but a strip of blackness on the other side. I could see into the blackness, sure; if I watched through the crack and moved my head from side to side fast enough, I could even make out a shape, the edges of something. . . . It definitely wasn't furniture . . . too irregular. *The jogger's body. Oh no.*

I pushed the door open with a finger.

A bed had been turned on edge and was leaning against the far wall. A dresser, chest of drawers, nightstand had all been pushed into a corner next to it. To make room for . . .

Oh my God.

There were sleeping bags on the floor. Empty sleeping bags.

Here was the source of the smell hovering throughout the apartment that I couldn't identify. The bags weren't just filthy; they were coated in soil. Each one had a layer of dirt probably half an inch thick. Not Alabama red clay, but dark, loamy-looking earth. Almost black. Almost wet. The kind of soil you never saw in this state.

As if . . . *As if it was brought in from somewhere else.*

The closet was the last place. No window to uncover. Whoever was in there, they had a pretty good chance of getting between me and the door. After that . . .

I stepped closer to the closet and listened, one foot angled toward the hall. If they were in there, they were holding their breath. I thought about a way I could slow them down. I lifted my leg, aimed a kick squarely at the place where the two closet doors came together.

Slam.

By the time the closet doors had swung in their tracks, crashing against the inside wall, I was standing in the sunlit living room, breathing hard. I waited. Heard nothing. I waited some more. Finally I couldn't stand it—I walked back up the hall and peeked in. One of the closet doors had come off its tracks. I could see nothing inside but the jogger's clothes.

I looked back at the sleeping bags and for the first time noticed it—the imprint of bodies in the alien black soil.

I let Sagan in. We were standing in the jogger's bedroom.

"Six." Sagan swore. "Emma, how are we going to fight six vampires?"

"I don't know. The same way you fight one, I guess. Over and over again."

"Suppose they all come at once?"

"You were so confident you could out-think anybody. So? What do we do now, Mr. Warcraft?"

A hurt look passed over his face.

"I'm sorry," I said. I squatted and lifted the corner of one of the sleeping bags. It felt heavy and sodden. "Any ideas?"

"Move to Saskatchewan. Change your name. I've seen how quick they . . . you . . . people can move. With the defenses we have set up . . . we could handle . . . two . . . maybe three. But this . . . this is suicide."

"So I just throw up my hands and let them take me?"

"No. Of course not. But I don't know, Emma. This is way more than . . . I don't know. . . ."

I dropped the edge of the sleeping bag. "I know what's creeping you out," I said. "It's not how many there are, is it? It's seeing this stuff. It's made it too real, hasn't it? It was fun when it was all pretend, wasn't it?"

"Now you're pissing me off."

"Good. I need you pissed off. I need you to help me, Sagan."

"Great. You need my help. I thought I was the chump you keep saying would be dead the instant they got here."

"I'm sorry. I deserved that. Okay, so here are the facts. They're stronger and faster than you are. I'm asking you to back out now, Sagan. It's too much to ask."

"You want me to go when you need me the most."

"Good. I was only saying it to be saying it. All right. Six vampires. That doesn't mean we can't come up with a strategy, does it? That's where we even things out. I need you to think. They are coming for me, Sagan. Six *Verloren*. What are we gonna do about it?"

"You have to . . . give me a little while. Let's look around some more."

"There's nothing else here."

"Humor me."

We went back over the apartment top to bottom looking for any kind of clue we might have missed. All we found was stuff that made us both heartsick: the jogger's clothes hamper. The music he liked to listen to. (Alternative.) A picture of a little girl with bouncy brown pigtails, holding a toy horse. *Sister?* I thought about Manda and nearly started to cry. I brushed the tears away angrily.

Sagan found the jogger's wallet lying kicked under a chair.

"Paul Freeman," he read, pulling out the guy's driver's license.

Paul was a good-looking guy who had turned twenty-six years old three days ago. And now? Was he in pieces somewhere?

"So . . . not much to go on, but here's what we know," Sagan said. "They were here, but for some reason they left. Assuming what you saw last night was in real time . . . it means they only stayed part of the night. So why bring this stuff in here?" He waved his arm at the filthy sleeping bags. "Doesn't that kinda indicate they were planning on staying awhile?"

"Maybe . . . maybe they got set up, then something spooked them. . . ."

"What could spook six vampires?" Sagan said.

"Maybe they somehow knew we were watching?"

"But all you ever saw was Wirtz and the jogger, right?"

"Yeah, that's true," I said.

Sagan walked back and forth along the row of sleeping bags, touching the handle of his grandfather's sword to his bottom lip.

"I think . . . here's what's more likely. They're closing in, tightening the circle. But the closer they get, the more often they have to change their base. Because they have to hide each day. Wirtz knows how close he is to finding you, so this is kind of a staging area. . . . He followed Freeman home mainly just to grab this place.

A place that is only a mile or so from the Space Center, a couple of miles to the tower. He's called some of his nastiest followers. . . ."

"*Nasty*'s the word," I said.

"So now that he's set up, he brings them into his new HQ. Where they can start getting ready for the final assault."

"I don't know if Lena would say that *Verloren* do that much planning."

"Well, this isn't exactly long-range stuff here," Sagan said. "Surely somebody will notice Freeman is missing sooner or later. He must have had a job, relatives. So this is a very temporary deal."

"Okay . . . but why go to the trouble of fixing up a . . . haven . . . something like this, and then not even use it?"

Sagan rubbed his chin. "Uh-oh. You know what it could mean?"

"What?"

"They found something even closer."

We moved faster after he said that. Rolled up the sleeping bags, dirt and all, and slung them in the Dumpsters. With any luck, today was garbage day and they would be part of a landfill somewhere before Wirtz and his killers came back. *If they come back.*

"You think . . . they really need the dirt?" I said as we sped away in the Jeep. "I mean, you know, dirt from their native land to sleep in? Like . . . Dracula?"

Sagan downshifted and waited for the noise to subside before answering. "Well . . . so far just about everything we've found out about vampires at least feels scientific. The whole thing about the zero-point field, electromagnetic particles from the sun. Maybe it's just a comfort thing, you know? If the *Verloren* tend to be nomads, maybe that's what they do to feel at home . . . bring a little home with them."

I frowned disgustedly. "One thing's for sure, they'll know we're on to them now. I don't know if that's a good thing or a bad thing."

"Maybe it's good," Sagan said. "If it makes them uncomfortable, knowing, hey, we can hit them too if they aren't more careful . . ."

I looked away at a long stretch of green no-man's-land between the middles lanes of the interstate. I was thinking about the jogger. Other innocent people who would be in danger. *Six vampires.*

"There has to be something more we can do," I said. "The longer this goes on, the more people they will—"

"Maybe there is," Sagan said.

28. NIGHT VISION

Sagan put down a sleeping bag—a clean one he'd brought from home—next to the tower stairs and walked back to the Jeep. He returned several times with his arms loaded with a Coleman lantern, a gym bag full of clothes, and other things I didn't recognize in sacks and boxes.

"Night vision Webcams," he said, taking one out to show me. "I don't know why I didn't think of this sooner."

I was surprised by how small they were. Five of them, one for each side of the tower and a fifth for the top. They weren't much larger than a handheld digital camera. Each came with a four-foot "stalk" that we plunged into the ground around the base of the tower and tested for the best viewing angles. The last one we strapped to the little airplane beacon on the roof.

"Wireless," Sagan said. "My dad knows some people who are into tech like you wouldn't believe. This will give us more eyes to even the odds. All I have to do is watch from my laptop, and—"

"I've been thinking about this," I said. "It's different now that we know there are more. It's crazy what I'm asking you to do. It's . . . it's stupidly dangerous."

"Stupidly, huh? You saw what we're up against. You need help now more than ever. Around-the-clock help. That's me. They're too close, Emma."

"But . . . Sagan . . ."

"What did you think? That you could call me up and I would come running? They might have you dismembered before I even put my foot on the gas."

"You want to know the truth?"

"Sure."

"You've done so much already. Now that I've seen how close they are . . . I don't want you anywhere near this place when they come."

"Pulling a Clint Eastwood, huh?" Sagan said. "The lone gunman fighting off the band of murderous cutthroats—no pun intended. But in the end he wasn't alone, remember?" He put down the box he was carrying and took my face in his hands. "A little faith?"

"I'm just trying to be realistic. You think I want to watch something horrible happen to you?"

"Who says it will? Look, it's stupid arguing about this. They're close, Emma. I may not be an *Auge*. But I have a little intuition of my own. He's coming soon."

"What if I kick you out?"

"I'll just keep coming back."

"This is crazy," I said.

He picked up the box again and headed up the stairs. "Maybe so. But from now on, it's our crazy, not just yours."

"An iPod docking station?" I said, fishing through his stuff. "What are you going to do, recharge the *Verloren* to death?"

Sagan looked thoughtful. "Electrocution . . . hmmm . . . now there's an idea."

"Sorry, fresh out of transformers," I said.

I held up his white iPod shuffle. "So, whatcha got on here we can listen to?"

"My playlist is off the proverbial chain," Sagan said. "Stephen Hawking. Brian Greene, *The Elegant Universe*. *Membranes and Other Extendons*."

"Yuck. I take it back. That's assault with a deadly weapon. Hope you remembered your earbuds, Bud."

"Don't leave home without 'em."

"So . . . what're your parents going to think?"

Sagan leaned back again, putting his hands behind his head. "What they don't know won't kill 'em."

"Won't they wonder where you are?"

"In that house? Half the time I don't even know if they are there. I'll check in from time to time. It'll be fine."

After we had finished unpacking, we climbed up to the roof of the tower to watch the surrounding forest turn golden in the fading sun. I could see the runway lights of the nearby jetport.

"No lavender lights," I said. "That's always a relief."

"I wonder if we need to set up a wider perimeter," Sagan said. "To give us a little more notice. Something like motion detectors. I bet we could score some at Radio Shack."

"Let's talk about something else."

We stretched out on the air mattress and watched the sky turn different colors, holding hands.

"Man, what a view," Sagan said. "I should have brought my rich field telescope for later. . . ."

I sat up.

"What?" Sagan said.

"I need to show you something before it gets dark."

Sagan made a face. "In there?"

We were standing deep in the bunker where I bathed, all the

way back in the shadows where the steel net hung over the opening.

"That's the deal. Besides, I thought you liked caves."

"I do. But why can't I be up there with you when they come? Helping to hold down the fort."

"Because you can't fly."

"Neither can you." He grabbed the steel mesh and shook it. "So you think this would slow them down?"

"I don't know, you tell me."

"It's pretty stout. And stuff like this that's a little flexible is often tougher to defeat than a solid wall. But I think I'd rather die out in the open."

"Sorry, nope."

"But what if . . ."

"Sorry, Sagan. Those are my terms. We can't mess this up. You don't get a do-over."

"I wasn't . . . trying to make fun about it," he said. "That's just me. I can't think doom and gloom all the time. It's not the way I'm wired."

"Who's thinking doom and gloom? If we do this right, we'll—"

"Kick some serious bloodsucker butt?" he said.

"That's the plan."

"Did I really just say that?"

We spent the rest of the evening stashing supplies behind the net. Afterward Sagan brought in some dinner from a local pizza place called Terry's. I had practically forgotten how good hot, greasy, bubbly pizza was. I was in ecstasy hauling each delicious bite to my mouth and lifting the strands of cheese from my chin.

"Heaven, complete heaven," I said, picking up another slice.

"Huntsville's claim to fame."

"Not the space program, huh?"

"Well, that too."

When we had finished eating, we lay back on the air mattress counting the stars as they came out. A slight breeze was flowing across the top of the test stand. Sagan pulled off his shirt and I played my fingers across his bare chest.

"My biggest fear is that we won't get enough warning," I said. "That you'll be up here with me, on top of this tower, when Wirtz and his buds drop in."

Sagan turned over onto his stomach to look at me.

"Okay, you're the strategist," I said. "We've got plenty of stuff to fight them with. But what else can we do?"

"Well . . . in the classic battle sense, you try to divide and conquer. You know, somehow get them separated so they aren't all coming at you at once."

"What's the best way to do that?"

"If we hit them hard enough as a group . . . that might force them to separate, try to surround you coming from different angles. If that doesn't work, we could use me."

"You?"

"Yeah. If I'm down there in the bunker, I could be a kind of bait, draw some of them away. That would split up the group."

"You're kidding, I hope."

"I wish I was," Sagan said. "Do you still have that toothbrush?"

When we finally settled down to sleep, Sagan touched me on the nose, then took me in his arms. Started kissing my eyelids. I adjusted my body to be closer to his. I loved the warmth coming off his skin. I kissed him.

"It's still not . . . completely registering," I said. "We have to—"

"Quiet."

I shut up and for a long time that's all we did. Talked with hands and mouths without words.

Now he was on his back again, arm crooked under his head. I wondered how I could possibly sleep with him lying next to me.

"You know what we need?" I said.

"More pillows?"

"Nope. A rope to tie you off. I bounce, you splat. Remember?"

I was dreaming.

Sagan was with me and we were walking beside some railroad tracks. The tracks ran up a little hill, then back down again. At the top of the hill we came to a group of smooth boulders that surrounded a place shaped like a funnel. I wondered where the funnel went. A strange orange light came up from below. Sagan went over the edge first to look and . . .

He was gone. Just like that.

He had slipped into the stone funnel, which was really an endless chasm shaped like a tube that dropped straight down. I could still see him because the entire chasm was lit with orange light. I saw Sagan falling the whole way, his body twisting, getting smaller and smaller.

The worst thing was knowing that he was changing on the way down. The fear caused by the endless falling was changing him. He was strange and different to me before he was even dead.

I woke up sometime in the night when I heard my grandfather speak.

"Emma."

That's all he said, but I heard it so loud and clear, just as if he were sitting right beside me, that I sat straight up looking wildly over the forest. The only thing moving was a truck whining up a grade in the distance.

"A phone," I said, shaking Sagan's arm.

"What's up?" he mumbled, sitting up and rubbing his hair.

"I've got to get to a phone. Now!"

We flew up the driveway to the Solar Observatory and ran inside.

"Just pick any of them," Sagan said, hustling me into one of the offices. "You have to dial nine to get out. All it will say on his redial is 'Government'—"

"God, Sagan." My hands were shaking so bad, it was hard for me to dial.

He stayed in the doorway watching for security. Papi's phone rang and rang. I hung up and dialed his number again. No answer.

"He's not there," I said. "I can't get him! I'm calling my mom. . . ."

"Hello?" Manda's voice ripped into me.

"Manda! Oh my God, Manda. It's so good to hear your voice!"

"Emma! Emma!" She was squealing and screaming so much, for a while that was all I could hear.

"Manda, where is Mom? What's going on!"

"Oh, Emma," Manda wailed into the phone. Several seconds passed before I could get her to calm down enough for me to understand. My heart pounded. *Papi's hurt. He's sick. He's dead.*

"Mom . . . Mom is at work," she finally managed to get out. "She made me stay here and Ms. Peterson checks on me. It's . . . Papi, Emma! It's Papi! Where are you, Emma! Why don't you come home? Please . . . I don't know what to do."

I felt as if a bucket of ice water had been tipped over my head. *Oh God.* "Manda, Manda, what's wrong with Papi?"

"I don't know! Emma, I don't know! He's in the hospital, they said."

"Who? Who said?"

"The man! The man who called. Papi . . . he's in . . . he's in the hospital!"

"Is he okay? Where? Which?"

"Huntsville," she said. "I don't know. I don't know! He's in Huntsville. But, Emma, I . . ."

"Manda, calm down, sweetie." Tears were running down my face. "Calm down and tell me, does Momma know? Have you talked to her?"

"I don't know! I don't know! I'm supposed to keep the door locked and call Ms. Peterson if I can't get Momma, but they're not there! Emma!"

"Look, Manda, it's going to be okay! Everything is going to be okay. I'll take care of it. All right? I'll go see about Papi. You go back to sleep. Everything is all right. I'll talk to you tomorrow, okay?"

"But, Emma!"

"I'm sorry, sweetheart, but I've got to go."

I hung up and we ran back outside.

"Hey, wait up, I'll drive you," Sagan said.

"There's not time for that."

"You're telling me you can run faster than a car?"

"Yours, yeah. Besides, I can run in a straight line."

"Okay, so I'll follow you."

"Stay here." I said it with so harsh a tone, with so much weight on the words, he stopped and stared at me.

"Are you okay, Emma?"

"No."

"I can't just hang around here, worrying about you."

I took him by the shoulders. "Look, Sagan . . . I can't worry about both of you at the same time—"

"Since when do you have to worry about me?"

"Since we trashed their HQ. They're out there somewhere. I can't deal with this if I have to deal with worrying about you too."

"So do it in the morning."

I glared at him. "He could be dying, Sagan! And you want me to wait? I have to see him. It's my fault, you know that, don't you?"

"I *don't* know that, and neither do you. It could be anything. Besides, you only did what you had to do."

"He doesn't know that!" I said. "He's lying up there thinking something awful has happened to me, and it's killing him. I have to go show him, don't you understand? I have to do this for him. I'll be okay. I promise."

Sagan sagged with resignation. "I don't like it. Do you have your headset?"

"I'll get it. I'll get it right now. But I've got to go."

"What am I supposed to do in the meantime?"

I nodded at the observatory. "Go work for a while. Find a new comet and name it after me. It'll take your mind off things and I'll feel better with you in there."

"Be careful."

I crossed my finger over my chest. "You got it. I swear. Now let me go!"

"Emma . . ."

"What!"

"You know."

"Yeah. I do."

A light rain had started to fall. It just seemed to make me run faster. I cut through neighborhoods, stomped over the tops of cars, buzzed between trees. The hospital was somewhere downtown, that's all I knew. When I ran out of directions to try, a guy at a gas station set me straight.

I took mostly back roads, moving through neighborhoods and industrial sites as the crow flies.

When I found the hospital, the first entrance I saw said EMER-GENCY. I ran up the walk and through the sliding doors. Thank goodness it looked to be a slow night. A handful of people were in the waiting room, most of them older. One young guy with a crew cut had an arm wrapped in bloody bandages and was leaning against a Coke machine. I ran up to a counter where three women waited behind computer monitors.

"He's in room 332 in the cardiac unit," one of the women said. "But visiting hours were over at eight. There's really nothing you can do tonight, hon. You can come back tomorrow morning, sit with him at breakfast."

"Thanks."

I knew better than to just blaze through the doors and get se-curity hunting for me. I asked my way to the parking garage, and halfway there I found a service elevator—one of those big ones they used to bring people up and down in gurneys. I hit the button for the third floor.

The elevator opened onto a long hall and just outside an empty waiting room full of drink machines, plastic chairs, and a TV no one was watching. The room numbering didn't make sense. I had to double back twice. At last, there it was: 332.

The door was open and a soft light was glowing in the corner. My heart went up into my mouth . . . Papi looked so small. The thin sheets were drawn up under his armpits, his chest barely rising and falling. He had one of those thin transparent tubes with the two nostril plugs hooked into his nose. His eyes were closed.

Off to one side was a gently beeping monitor that looked like it was registering vital signs. Whatever he was doing, it was rhyth-mic, which almost scared me more than if it had been spiking and dropping all over the place. *Brain dead.* I hated it when thoughts like that popped into my head. But Papi's lines were steadily blipping, if weakly. A little bag like a cylindrical accordion was hanging from a metal post, periodically expanding and contracting. The room smelled of old people and some kind of antiseptic.

I went to the side of his bed. Papi's mouth was slightly open and I could see his crooked teeth and the tip of his whitish tongue. His arms were outside the sheets, running exactly alongside his body as if . . . *As if he's ready for his coffin.*

One of the reasons I was freaking was because I had watched too many bad hospital dramas on TV. I knew just enough to scare myself.

I took his hand in my hand; his fingers were cold.

I didn't know if I should wake him. I didn't know if he was even asleep. Wires ran from some machine up under his hospital gown through the curly gray hair of his chest. Had he lost weight? I was used to thinking of him as barrel-chested, but he looked almost emaciated.

"Papi?" I said softly, wondering if he was awake enough to hear me. . . .

I touched his arm and shook it very gently. "Papi, can you hear me?"

I sat on the edge of the bed and waited that way a long time. The sounds in the room were creepy, the little periodic soft beep from the monitoring equipment, the patter of rain on the glass, the "breathing" sound the little accordion bag was making. I had always hated hospitals as long as I could remember.

I suddenly felt his body start, rise up against the tug of all the things he was attached to.

"*Enkelin . . .*"

"Papi! Oh, Papi!" I leaned over and threw myself into his arms.

He hugged me as gently as a baby. His hands were shaking as he lowered them to the bed.

"You crying?" he said, a little croak in his voice.

I sniffed and brushed my hand across my eyes. "No, I'm not."

"Ho, you can't fool this old wolf," he said, smiling. He looked around, lifting one arm and weakly gesturing. "It's this place. It makes you think I am going. And *ja*, I am going . . . going right out of here. Got my tomato plants in. Corn coming along. You should see it. A lot of rain this spring."

I looked at the window. "It's raining now, Papi."

He didn't look. He wouldn't take his eyes away from me. "It's so good. It's so good to see you." His voice got suddenly stern. "You . . . you tell me . . . where have you been? Why were you gone?"

"Please . . . please don't make me tell you that. I'm all right. . . . You just think . . . about getting better, okay? What happened? What did they say? You're going to be okay, aren't you?"

Papi tried to snort, ended up coughing for a long time instead. "I was leaning over in the backyard," he said when he got control of himself again. "Turning on that faucet, you know . . . the one next to the clothesline? *Mein Gott,* it feels like an elephant sat down on my chest."

"But . . . the doctors, what did they say?"

"Doctors." Papi made a soft little disgusted sound. "What can they tell you?" He reached a hand to touch his chest, then had to put it down and reach with the other one, because the first hand was dragging too many tubes. "Here. What do they know about what is in here? Nah. Not important."

"Yes, it is," I said. "Don't say that. Don't. You'd better not . . ."

I couldn't finish it. I couldn't say, "You'd better not die."

"Some boy . . . he hurt you, huh? Make you a little bit crazy?"

"No, Papi. No. It's not that. It's not drugs. It's not any of those things. It's not anything for you to feel bad about. I just had to go away for a while."

"Your mother . . . you know you are hurting your momma so bad."

The tears started flowing again, so hard my shoulders were shaking.

"Hey . . . hey . . . here now, my darling girl. It's going to be okay, you know. Whatever this thing is . . . whatever it is has hold of my *Enkelin* . . . you are going to beat it, you know that?"

I tried to speak, but I was still shaking. I raised my head finally. "I'm so sorry, Papi. I'm so sorry. It wasn't my fault. Running . . . it was the only thing I could do."

He patted my hand. "There is always something you can do. You left your *Familie* out of things. Your mother . . ."

"I know, I know. . . ."

"You talk to her, *ja*? You go to her, you have a little talk." He coughed again. "Back to . . . back to school, *Enkelin*."

"I know, Papi, I know. Soon. I hope it can be soon. I'm doing the best I can."

He closed his eyes, started looking sleepy again.

"Papi. Papi? Do you need something? Are you okay?"

"I'm . . . okay. Just sleepy. These fools, they give me what they give me."

I bent and kissed him on the cheek. He waved his hand at me and made a face.

"Oosh, I need a shave." He was drifting off, eyelids rising and lowering. He said something that I couldn't hear. I leaned closer.

"What? What, Papi, what did you say?"

He whispered, "You know you are always . . . my . . . my *Kämpferin*."

His fighter.

*   *   *

I found a courtesy phone in the waiting room, called the Blue Onion, and left a message for Mom. Then cried like a stupid baby the whole way out of the hospital.

He had always been so strong. . . . It killed me to see him lying there like that, wasted, damaged at his core. *That's what happens when you hurt someone you love,* I thought. *You damage their center.*

It was raining harder when I reached the street. The pavement was slick, reflecting the reddish glow of the streetlamps. I took off at a run that sent streamers of water flying up from my feet.

Sagan's Jeep was still parked in front of the Solar Observatory when I got back to the Space Center, and some of the lights were burning in the cafeteria. My shoes scraped wetly on the cement as I walked up the path to the observatory entrance.

I reached into my pocket for the headset gadget and pressed the button that made a little shrieking noise that was supposed to pass for a ring.

"Emma—" There was a big burst of static as Sagan answered, cutting him off.

I thumbed the talk switch. "Hey, I'm back. Come let me in."

Another burst of static. The fancy electrical stuff inside the dome must be messing with the frequency. I pressed the button again.

"Hey, did you hear me? I'm outside. Let me in. I've been running my legs off. I want to sit down."

I waited a little while, then saw Sagan hurrying toward the air lock. He pushed open the inner door and started reaching for the outer one. He was saying something through the glass as he put his hand on the handle. I have never been good at reading lips.

"What?"

385

Sagan cracked the door slightly. Not like he was going to open it for me, but to tell me something.

"Run," Sagan said through the crack in the door.

"Huh?"

"Run, Emma. Run."

29. WHISTLE

I stood there paralyzed a moment, looking at his eyes.

"Run! Run!"

I reached for the door and jerked it out of Sagan's hands, almost tumbling him out onto the sidewalk. I yanked him up and within less than a second I was at a dead run down the driveway, Sagan slung over my shoulder in a fireman's carry.

Something solid and heavy slammed into my legs, making them buckle sideways. Sagan was thrown off, rolling over and over in the grass and leaves next to the path.

I got up feeling as if my face were on fire from scraping the pavement; a squatty, muscular guy was standing over me. I lowered my shoulder and sprang at him with all my might, driving my fists into his big gut.

The squatty man's eyes popped wide and he let out a tremendous "Oomph!" and sprawled back against the observatory building. His meaty elbow knocked out a section of glass with a tinkling shriek as he crashed against the metal window frame.

"Let's go!" I yelled.

Sagan had gotten to his feet and was staggering toward me. We had just started to run again when three more *Verloren* collapsed on top of us, pinning us to the ground. My mouth was driven into someone's side and I could barely breathe. I kicked and screamed, wildly lashing out with my arms.

The vampires each had an arm or a leg. They lifted me up,

tugging so hard, I was scared for a minute they might rip me into four parts. One of them got a huge arm crooked around my throat, crushing my windpipe. There was nothing I could do.

Sagan was jeered at and prodded as the vampires forced us inside the observatory. Two muscular *Verloren* had me by either arm while a third huge vampire—the one with his arm around my throat—kept shoving me from behind.

Once inside the conference room, the three vampires held me against a wall of louvered doors that housed the blue cables leading to the satellite feeds. The other two vampires threw Sagan down on his back on the conference table.

"*Stinkender Mensch,*" the stocky *Verloren* snarled.

Whatever that was, you didn't want to be it.

Sagan writhed and struggled until finally I could see him weakening. He knew what I knew. Without our weapons, we were dead.

A tall figure was standing in the back of the large room. He came slowly over. For the first time since encountering him on that lonely Georgia mountain, I saw Wirtz in the flesh again.

His eyes were as black as I remembered, features pointed, and the flap of skin above his right eye looked almost moist, as if his scalp had been peeled away yesterday, not hundreds of years ago. I could see thin little fingerlets of pinkish veins running through the exposed tissue.

He came closer until he was too close, leaning over me so that I was aware of every filthy inch of his body. His coat was dirty and ragged and his shirt sweat-stained, though the skin of his face was taut and unnaturally dry, like yellowing paper.

He licked me.

Wirtz's hot fleshy tongue moved over my cheek like a slug that had traveled through centuries of filth. I tried to twist away, but the others held me still. I tried to bite him, but he snatched his head away.

I spat in his face.

I had expected to make him furious, but instead the vampire touched his finger to my spittle and then touched the finger to his tongue. I could see his Adam's apple bob as he swallowed. His broad shoulders immediately hunched forward and he almost seemed to retch a little. Then he closed his eyes and drew in a long breath through his narrow nose.

"So it's true, then," the vampire said in his deep voice. "You have eaten . . . *Nahrung.*"

"I don't know what that is," I said.

"Food," one of the monsters holding me said. "You have eaten human food—"

Wirtz raised his arm for silence.

"And the *Blut*? Do you . . . drink it?"

"How did you find us?" I said.

Wirtz grabbed my whole face in one hand and squeezed. His fingers smelled of old soil and wood bark. He kept squeezing, harder and harder.

"I asked you a question."

I swore and gritted my teeth. "Never developed . . . a taste for the stuff."

Wirtz let me go and turned away, thinking.

I looked at the other vampires. They were younger than Wirtz in appearance. The two holding me had to be brothers; both dark-skinned with short cropped hair, of average height, but well muscled. Wearing dirty jeans and T-shirts. If I hadn't known they were vampires, I would have sworn they were in their late teens to early twenties.

The third guy holding me looked older, maybe late twenties,

and he was a kind of giant, taller and much heavier than Wirtz, with curly blondish hair and a baby face. Big-boned, heavy legs, a barrel chest. He looked monstrously strong. He was wearing a ragged mechanic's outfit that had once been blue but now was stained a mahogany color.

The stocky *Verloren* holding Sagan looked to be in his mid-thirties and had on an old dark suit that was torn at the knees and discolored in several places. Underneath was a filthy cream shirt that was ripped here and there, exposing his olive skin. He had a shiny scar running across his crooked nose.

The last *Verloren* looked slim and graceful, with small features and short trimmed hair. She was wearing a dark, stretchy jumpsuit and would have been beautiful if not for the chilling fact that her face was frozen in the most lifeless expression I had ever seen.

"You're . . . the friend of this . . . *Vollmensch*?" Wirtz said, nodding. I looked at Sagan lying on the table and hurt all over for him. Not only was he being held down by vampires, he was also the only one of us who couldn't see in the dark.

I didn't say anything.

"Human. He is . . . a human." Wirtz spoke the word as if he were talking about a disgusting little piece of slime that had crawled out of a sewer. Something that wasn't even a man.

Again Sagan struggled and bucked, but the *Verloren* girl pushed him back down with a single hand. *She's missing one of her thumbs,* I realized.

"They'll be here soon," Sagan said, his voice distorted.

"Who?" the woman said softly, leaning mockingly close to his ear. *Kill her. I want to kill her.*

"The . . . police . . . ," Sagan said. "We called . . . we called the police."

"Good," Wirtz said. "I'm thirsty."

Sagan started to say something else. Wirtz gestured, and the girl clapped her hand over Sagan's mouth. Wirtz came over to me again. I closed my mouth to keep from tasting his smell.

"You asked how we found you," the vampire said. "The big symbol—NASA—I saw this while you and I were . . . joined. . . . After that it was only a matter of time."

The tower, I thought. *He saw the logo on the tower.*

"It's truly too bad, all of this," Wirtz went on, looking at the stocky guy. "Is it not, Bastien? She could have been a *Kriegerin.*" He turned to face me again. "Do you know this word? A . . . warrior. If only you had honored my Call. But now . . ."

We stared into each other's eyes for a moment, and I wondered if there was something to it . . . the idea that a vampire could control you with his gaze. I had a sense of falling into something black and bottomless. I blinked and shook my head and the spell was broken. Wirtz sat down in one of the conference chairs and crossed his legs.

"So, you think this is the *Ende,* girl?" he said. "Don't you? That's what you are waiting on. No, this is the beginning. We are here to unlock your secrets."

"I don't have any secrets."

The vampire looked at his hand as if admiring his nasty fingers.

"How do you do it? Go out into the daylight? And how do you live without blood?"

I stared at him, waiting.

Wirtz gestured at the girl. *"Lilli."*

The female *Verloren* twisted Sagan's face so it was smashed against the table. She looked as if she was about to break his neck.

"Stop!" I said. "You should know! You did it! You . . ." I swore again. "When you attacked me. You. Did. It. Somehow things got scrambled. It's nothing I did. It just happened."

"Should I believe you?" Wirtz said.

"I don't care if you do or not. It's the truth."

"But you do care. You care very much." He glanced at Sagan. "As I am going to show you. But first . . . no more lies. Tell me the truth. There is some *Würde* in that. Dignity."

"I'm telling you the truth. It was an accident."

He stood again and touched the side of my head with the tip of his finger, drawing the finger down the line of my hair to my ear. I jerked away.

"We know that you have . . . family . . . somewhere nearby," Wirtz said. "A sister. Whom I would very much like to . . . kiss."

I cursed him a third time.

"It's all right," the vampire said. "I understand these things so well, *Mädchen*. You have a few moments where you still have thoughts, awareness. Right now your mind has never been more . . . open. That is all there is now, inside you, this openness. I think when someone . . . dies . . . there is so much to be learned in the last moments. When there is no reason anymore to think wasteful thoughts, everything is so clear."

I glanced at Sagan.

"So. Are you going to tell me?" Wirtz said.

I don't have any secrets, I thought. *I only have hate. That's all you're leaving me with, so I want to be dead. I have to be dead. Go on and finish it.*

"Let him go," I said, nodding at Sagan. "Let him go and I'll tell you anything you want."

Sagan struggled fiercely, trying to say something.

Wirtz smiled. "You are worried about your pet *Vollmensch*?

Why do I want to give up something I already have? Every part of his life has always been mine. You know a little about the *Feld*, I think? His whole life has been spent in bringing himself here. Making of himself a gift . . . to me."

I wrenched at the arms holding me. "Do what you want with me! But let him go. Leave him alone!"

Wirtz looked up. "The *Vollmensch*—he is more important . . . than your own life?"

"Yes," I said, choking. "Yes, he is."

"Then tell me what I want to know. How is it you can go out in the daylight and eat the humans' *Nahrung*?"

"I told you. I don't know. I don't! But I think maybe it was because of my . . . epilepsy."

Sagan tried to say something. The stocky *Verloren*, Bastien, tightened his hold on him, making him wince.

Wirtz looked at Lilli. "Epilepsy?"

"*Ergreifungen*," she said.

"Ah!" Wirtz said. "And so that's what it was. When I was . . . drinking . . . the bright lights, nothingness? *Ja?* You suffered a . . . seiz-ure . . . and because our *Felds* were . . . *verbunden* . . . joined— the seizure came to me as well. Is this right?"

"I guess so. I don't . . . I don't remember things during a seizure. I think it scrambled us somehow. Scrambled my transformation. It's not something I can just do. It was an accident. It can't . . . it can't help you."

"Oh. You believe I want to be helped?"

"Don't you?"

Wirtz walked up to me again. "You are still . . . *unerfahren*. Young . . . inexperienced. There are things you come to realize in time, *Mädchen*. There is no help coming. There is nothing . . .

good . . . out there that hears you when you pray. Once you realize that . . . what is one to do with this *Leben* . . . this life? I tell you this. The years go by. Until nothing is left but . . . curiosity."

"You're crazy."

Wirtz sighed deeply. "Oh. You have just now come to that conclusion? Let me tell you something. Who is sane? When we are born here . . ." He extended his arms and walked in a slow circle. "We are crazy. This . . . *Leben* . . . is the nightmare. All of us are sleeping and we can never wake up. Nothing matters. There is only each night and the night after it. You follow them or you die. But this is not something you can do for yourself. There is no dignity in a death like that. Someone else finds the courage for you. I have found it for you."

The vampire turned and sprang across the conference table, where the woman Lilli and the stocky man Bastien were holding Sagan. Wirtz pushed Lilli aside, grasped Sagan by his hair, and twisted his head back, exposing his pale neck.

"Let him go!" I yelled. "I told you what you wanted to hear! There's nothing else you need him for!"

"Oh, you are so wrong to say that," Wirtz said.

"What do you want!"

"It is something you owe me, not him. And so I will take this thing that you owe me. And this is how I will take it. I want you to watch while I do . . . this."

He sank his teeth deep into Sagan's neck.

Sagan grunted in pain and arched his back sharply; a look came over his face that I had never seen before. The realization that this was it, everything was finished. It felt as if my insides were collapsing.

Wirtz remained attached to his neck, drinking deeply.

Lilli licked her lips as she watched, probably waiting her turn along with the others. They were going to drain him. They were going to drain him right down into death. And there was nothing I could do to stop it.

I fought with all my strength against the three vampires holding me.

Wirtz pulled back from Sagan's throat and looked at me, smiling broadly. His face was slick with Sagan's blood. There was even a little bit on the tip of his long nose.

"Sie werden wie ein Schwein sterben," he said. And sank his teeth in again.

Then I saw it: Sagan gave up. Stopped fighting. Went so completely limp that I think the vampire could have finished the job without anyone even holding him.

"Sagan!" I screamed.

I managed to break free for just a moment, digging my fingers into the face of one of the dark-skinned brothers and smashing the other in the jaw with my forearm. But the huge third *Verloren* clung to me stubbornly, wrapping his giant arms around my chest before I could even touch the conference table.

Sagan's hand started to twitch. It was the only part of him that was still moving. As if his hand had a separate little mind that realized it was dying too.

I couldn't believe how quickly it was all happening. . . . Sagan was so alive, so fresh in my memory—and now he was becoming a thing in a dream that I didn't even know anymore. His flailing arm stretched out farther and farther, as if it were losing its muscular ability to even hold itself taut.

I closed my eyes.

What was it Lena had said? About the Call?

That it wasn't something you did out loud, it was something you did down deep in your throat.

Help us, I said, feeling the vibration as I spoke the words on the inside. The giant vampire smiled at me stupidly. The noise I was making must have sounded like a groan.

Please, Lena. Please come to me and help us. We need you. Lena. Donne. Anton. Please come help us or we will die!

I opened my eyes.

It was still true. Sagan was on the table, dying.

Please please please!

Something Sagan had once said when I was barely listening now flared in my mind:

Stars . . . some of them are already dead when we get to see them.

My eyes clouded up again. I blinked furiously to clear them. . . . *Stars. See them.*

"Sagan!" I yelled. "Sagan, can you hear me? Please, Sagan!"

His hand stopped flopping for a moment, then the fingers straightened, went still. Wirtz lifted his head from the wound in Sagan's neck and smiled sweetly at me. Enjoying this so much.

"Josey Wales!" I screamed the name as loudly as I could. "Remember . . . remember Josey Wales, Sagan! What did he say? Remember! What did he say! Josey Wales! You gonna pull those pistols or whistle Dixie?"

Sagan snarled deep in his throat and lunged. Wirtz had temporarily been thrown off guard by all my shouting. Sagan got his hand on it, the computer mouse. Clicked the button. I closed my eyes.

The room exploded with light.

I could see it, hideously intense, even behind my closed

eyelids: the huge, enormous, gigantic, blazing 3-D ball of the sun. *Sonnen.*

The same image Sagan had shown me that very first time, only this time it was blaring full force in real color. A smothering, double-barreled volcanic assault of blinding illumination.

The vampires in the room screamed, a sound so monstrously anguished, it was almost alien to my ears. I felt the hands grasping me fall away as the young *Verloren* sank to the floor, crying out in pain as digitized sunlight blasted over them. The light was so intense, I was afraid to open my own eyes but had to stumble sightlessly forward to the conference table, where I threw myself on my stomach and slid across, hoping I was aiming in the right direction.

I slammed into something that felt almost inert and I realized at once it was the slumped body of the stocky vampire with the scar across his nose. The one Wirtz had called Bastien. I heaved him out of the way and dared open my eyes a slit; sunlight lanced my brain, forcing me to clamp my eyelids shut again. But I had seen enough: Wirtz was crawling away from the table, in obvious pain. Only the female seemed to be groping with some sense of purpose, reaching where she thought Sagan would be.

But I got to him first. I tugged hard and his long body slid away from her clutching fingers. Lilli shrieked with rage. I started to sling Sagan over my shoulder but he said, "No, I can see. Let me lead."

I peeked again and, bracing my hands against the table, lifted off the ground and gave the female vampire a brutal kick in the neck that sent her sprawling against some computer monitors. Sagan caught my hand and guided me past the chaos of writhing *Verloren* bodies and out into the hall, where I could open my eyes again.

He staggered on the long run up the hall and I caught him.

Blood was running down his neck, leeching into the top of his shirt, a little red starburst blossoming on his collar.

"Let me carry you!" I threw an arm around his waist, lifted him up. We were moving much faster now.

"How long do you think it will last?" I said as we rushed through the air lock.

"Not long," Sagan said. "Not . . . the same stuff at all. Not natural light."

I shoved him in the passenger seat of his Jeep.

"No, let me, you don't even—" he started.

I ignored him and jumped in the driver's seat.

"Keys!"

My heart plunged into my stomach as I watched the front door of the observatory while Sagan fumbled in his jeans. *Come on, come on!* Nothing yet. I grabbed the keys and slammed the Jeep into gear, turning off the driveway and smashing into the woods.

"What?" Sagan said.

"Lights! Where's the lights?"

I ran my hand frantically over the dashboard. I didn't need the lights to see, but to be seen. I wanted the *Verloren* to see.

"Here." Sagan took my hand and guided me.

The lights flamed on, but now the forest was too bright; I had to throw my arm partly across my eyes to cut the glare. We bounced and rocked on the uneven ground, the cones of the lights bouncing too, little saplings disappearing under the beams.

As we raced toward the secret meadow and the tower, Sagan coughed and his cough sounded liquid. I wondered with fresh horror if he was bleeding deep inside. . . . Had his jugular been severed? *Oh God.*

I pulled at his shirt, trying to see, but it didn't look like the bloody flower at the top of his collar had spread much farther.

"Hey, get your hand on that," I said, trying not to panic. "Compress it."

I pushed his hand to his neck and drove on. I came to the edge of the forbidden meadow with the buried munitions and skirted around it, driving as fast as I dared, branches whisking by on either side.

"Hang on."

We jounced crazily on the long downslope to the bunker and I jammed the brakes, fishtailing on the gravel at the bottom. I leapt out and hauled Sagan inside.

"I'm okay, I'm okay," he kept saying. "They'll figure out where we went. . . . They'll be coming soon."

"I know, I know."

Sagan undid the hidden padlock at the back of the bunker and I hurried to haul open the steel mesh. He got to his feet and lurched toward me but not fast enough to satisfy my vampire reflexes. I took hold of him and shot through the small opening, dragging him behind me. Then I started scrabbling in the boxes we had stowed there, swearing.

"I can't believe we didn't put the first aid kit on top!"

I tore his shirt open. The bleeding had mostly stopped, but a clear fluid was leaking from the wound. I swiped it away with cotton balls and splashed the cuts with hydrogen peroxide.

"Ouch! Hey!"

"Sit still."

Sagan grimaced as the bite marks foamed. Then I swathed his throat with gauze, going round and round his neck.

"You were so brave," I said, tying the gauze and trying not to cry. "I couldn't believe how brave you were. Were you thinking about that the whole time? The STEREO image?"

"Not at first. I remembered it when I saw the red light glowing on the bottom of the mouse. . . . That's the only way I could find it. But I knew if I tried to grab it, he would be too fast for me. I thought if I let my body go limp, played dead, I could bluff him into letting me go. Then you gave me the perfect chance when you started yelling." He swore and touched his neck.

I kissed him on the forehead. "Are you okay? Please tell me you are okay."

He took a deep breath. "Yeah. I was mostly faking it, I told you. But they're coming," he said weakly.

"We're ready for this, remember?" I said. "They're not. It ends right now. You got your radio thingy?" I pulled my own headset out and put it on.

Sagan patted his pocket. "Yeah. Emma, I don't know. . . ."

"I don't know either. I trust your plan. I trust you."

He looked a little better now, not so pale. I got him some water, but he pushed it away after only a couple of swigs and scrounged through a box, pulling out long red highway flares and a set of night-vision goggles.

"No flashlight?" I said.

"Too risky." Sagan pulled on the goggles. "These have infrared illumination. Even if I have to go where there is no ambient light, like deeper into the cave, I'll still be able to see."

He fired up his laptop.

"What kind of battery life do you have?" I said.

"Max of about four hours with heavy video use." As soon as the computer booted up, the five Webcams appeared on the screen as individual greenish squares. "Okay, we're good to go." He looked at me, squeezing my hand. "Be careful."

I kissed him again.

"You too."

I closed and locked the steel mesh behind me as we had

planned and ran out of the bunker. Rushed to the top of the tower and took a 360-degree walk around the roof. What Sagan called position one. The only point higher was the steel spike with the blinking red airplane beacon that rose about thirty feet above my head.

I waved into the Webcam.

"Can you see me?"

"Yeah." Sagan's voice came through sounding scratchy. "Anything out there?"

"Nothing yet."

I looked for the bunker but couldn't see him. . . . He was too far inside.

"I'm looking at the cams," Sagan said. "So far just a lot of greenish-looking metal and trees."

"How are you feeling?"

"Just took an Advil. I'll live. Remember, don't let them catch you in a place where all of them can get at you at once. Do what we talked about to keep them separated. Don't forget if they come from the—"

"I remember, I remember."

I reached down and yanked the pull cord and the generator roared to life. The *pockata pockata* rhythm was kind of comforting. I didn't really need it anymore—everything had a full charge—but I wanted to do two things—confuse the vampires' sensitive ears, but mostly send a message:

Here I am. Come and get me.

30. UNDER SIEGE

I strapped on a carpenter's belt full of tool caddies and Velcro pouches. We had figured it was best to travel light, so the biggest weapon I carried in it was the handheld angle grinder with the diamond cutting wheel.

I ran to the edge of the roof and threw my body out into space. I landed on the long iron arm that once held rocket engines over the blast shield far below. Sagan called the arm a gantry. This was position two.

I ran to the middle of the gantry and grabbed the chain saw and cranked it—it took several pulls, then finally caught. I gave the trigger a bunch of angry squeezes, filling the forest with a hostile ripping sound.

I lowered the idling chain saw over the railing on its nylon rope, leaving it dangling in midair. I touched the rope to stop the chain saw swinging, then ran back to the tower.

"Okay," I said into the headset mike. "Everything's ready."

Sagan swore.

"What! What is it?"

"Thought I saw something. But now I don't see it."

I started breathing again. "Hey . . . Sagan . . . if we get through this . . ."

"When we get through this."

"I want to . . ."

I paused. Squinted into the gloom. My heart fluttered. *Yes.* Six balls of lavender light were moving through the woods, coming fast, one a little ways out in front of the others.

"Emma!" Sagan said. "You there?"

"I can see them!" I said. "I can see them coming! They've taken the bait. They're moving in a straight line from the observatory."

"Be ready to move. What are they doing now?"

"Heading right for the meadow."

Now the vampires were beginning to spread out. I wondered if Wirtz was the one out in front, but something told me it could be the girl, Lilli. She had been the least affected by the solar image.

The first lavender ball paused at the edge of the meadow as if expecting something nasty.

"Where are they?" Sagan said.

"They're . . . they're at the edge of the minefield . . . but now they're stopping," I said. "Almost like they know it's dangerous. Come on. Come on! What's holding you up!"

Two of the lavender figures came up behind the first, while the others spread wide, as if looking for a way around.

No! Come on, do it. Do it. Please.

Suddenly they were moving forward again, really flying, running straight across the secret meadow.

"They're running through it!" I said into the mike. "But nothing . . . nothing's happening! It's not even slowing them down!"

The headset crackled over Sagan's swearing.

"Get out of there, Emma! Get out of there now!"

The *Verloren* were taking shape as they left the clearing and came down the long slope toward the bunker. I could see them as distinct figures now. I was pretty sure it was the female up front; she was moving more gracefully than the others. Seemed to have more purpose.

I felt my teeth come together with a click, my face tightening. This was it. It was real.

I thought of Papi lying in his hospital bed. One of the few things he ever said about war.

In war there is only the fear and what it does to you, Enkelin. *If you cannot do this brutal thing, then it will be done to you. It's not fair. There is no fair. It is only who is still standing at the end. Time for fair . . . that is later.*

I crouched behind a stanchion, trying to block as much of my own feeble glow as possible.

You can do this, I told myself.

The glowing figures broke through the last of the trees and approached the bunker. They paused near the entrance and stood as a group as if debating something. *Wanting to look inside.*

"What is it?" Sagan said.

I touched the headset. "Shhh! They'll hear you!"

I could see the figures gesturing, pointing. *Something there.* They crowded around the entrance to the bunker, looking. My heart pinged in my ears.

I lowered myself to a little platform at the edge of the feral room with the desk, ready to drop to the next catwalk, thirty feet below. . . .

The vampires moved away from the bunker, swarming toward the base of the test stand. I pulled myself back up to the gantry, breathing rapidly.

"It's okay, it's okay," I said into the mike. "They were at the entrance to the bunker. Now they're coming toward the tower."

I could hear voices: the *Verloren* calling out to one another; I couldn't understand the words. It was German, some kind of signal.

"I can see them!" Sagan said. "Clustered around the eastern side of the tower, but still on the ground. Pointing up."

I heard Wirtz's deep voice: *"Links. Rechts. Ausschwaermen."* Three of the figures peeled away to my left, two of the others to my right.

"Whisper if you have to," I said. "It looks like they're splitting up, each taking a section of the tower."

"Maybe," Sagan said. "One of them . . . yeah, he's starting to climb the east face!"

"Is it the stocky guy? Bastien?"

"Can't tell."

I heard the climber curse. He had just gotten tangled in some of the noisemakers I had strung at odd angles all around the tower. I could hear him angrily tearing at them, then the noise stopped.

I ran back to the main body of the tower and launched myself over the edge, dropping to one of the smaller catwalks, landing as lightly as I could.

I touched the mike on the headset. "Position three. Where is he?"

"Climbing again," Sagan said. "About a quarter of the way up but coming at an angle . . ."

"I see him."

It was Bastien, all right. Rather than leaping, the burly vampire was climbing hand over hand, grabbing anything he could hold on to and throwing himself higher. A chill shot through my chest. If he managed to get those big mitts on me . . . I shook away the thought and reminded myself that I knew the tower a lot better than he did.

"This way!" Bastien shouted.

I swung over the edge of the catwalk and clung beneath it as the vampire scrambled up the side of the tower like an enormous crab. He got closer and closer while I felt my heart pound, waiting for the best moment to let go. The *Verloren* passed not thirty feet away, scuttling toward the top of the tower. I waited a few more seconds to be sure he was gone, then climbed back up onto the catwalk.

Sagan buzzed in my ear. "Two more."

I looked down. The two other vampires below were on the move now: it was the guys who looked like brothers. They called back and forth to one another, almost appearing to run in midair as they jumped from the ground and started bounding up the tower in the same general direction the stocky *Verloren* had taken.

"I see them," I said.

"And there are two others coming up the opposite side," Sagan said. "Except they're using the stairs."

"Where is Wirtz?" I said.

"None of them are him. I've lost him."

No time to think about that right now. The brothers were climbing the tower diagonally, circling it the way stone stairs wrap around a ziggurat, higher and higher.

Closer and closer.

The earpiece coughed.

"Hey, you there?" Sagan said.

"Here!" one of the brothers called. "I see! Look! Her *Glühe*!"

My glow. He's seen my glow.

"Gotta go!" I said, and ran back to the place where the catwalk joined the tower and scrunched behind a thick support column. Gooseflesh raced over my arms. *Now. It's happening now.*

The *Verloren* who had seen me dropped to the catwalk not twenty feet away, smiling.

"This is not a very good hiding place, *Mädchen*," he said, taking a step toward me. Pointing at my tool belt. "So, are you planning on building something?"

I just looked at him.

"It's okay if you don't want to tell me. After I am finished with you, you will want to talk. Assuming you can still speak."

The *Verloren* dropped his shoulder and sprang.

I flipped a switch on the squat yellow cube I was standing on and raised the sandblaster's spray nozzle. The vampire's eyes went wide with shock.

"*Scheisse—!*"

I squeezed the trigger. A scouring mix of sand and water hit the *Verloren* dead in the face from point-blank range.

He screamed and was knocked back, throwing his hands up to cover his blistered eyes. I charged after him, dragging the sandblaster bouncing and clanging, raking his face and arms mercilessly. The vampire staggered backward. I kept coming, afraid to let up for a second, hammering him with the skin-peeling spray until he was driven to the end of the catwalk.

Now he had nowhere to go unless it was over the side. The vampire gathered himself and charged again, bellowing in blind rage. I sidestepped him and squeezed the trigger. This time he got a full blast of the lethal sand right in the ear. The *Verloren* collapsed against the railing, holding his head and moaning, legs starting to buckle.

Something moved behind me. I swung the sprayer around—not fast enough; the second brother crashed into me, throwing me against the railing. I let out a yelp of fear and pain as my back bent over the side. The *Verloren* swore and drove his hands into my stomach; only my grip on the hose and the weight of the sandblaster kept me from plunging over.

I twined my legs through the catwalk and hung on, fighting to aim the sprayer, but the vampire was too close—the nozzle was pointing straight up between us, jetting harmlessly in the air.

We fought over the sandblaster nozzle, spitting and cursing.

The vampire was taller than me and stronger. He leaned in hard, pushing me backward even as he pulled against the sprayer. The tools in my tool belt were cutting into my stomach, but I was afraid to let go of the sprayer to try to get to them.

Now the top half of my body was almost horizontal, hanging over nothing but fifty feet of dead space. The fall wouldn't kill me, but the *Verloren* would as I lay there stunned and helpless.

I started to slip, one foot coming free. . . .

The vampire leered triumphantly, his face so close, I could see up his nose.

"Goodbye, *Schlampe*."

Up his nose.

I stopped trying to pull back on the sprayer and instead shoved it against the vampire's muscular chest—jammed the sandblaster's nozzle right beneath his flaring nostrils.

Squeezed the trigger.

The *Verloren*'s eyes widened in horrified surprise as sand exploded up his sinuses at 6,500 pounds per square inch. For a moment it seemed as if every square inch of his face bulged; his eyes almost came out of their sockets and his skin flooded with purple.

The vampire let go of the sprayer and staggered backward, groaning. He put his hands to his face and blood gushed violently from between his fingers. I couldn't move, just stood there against the railing watching in shock. The vampire looked at me, but I could tell he wasn't seeing me. He trembled all over, stumbled forward a couple of steps, and fell at my feet, lying still.

I still had my hand on the trigger of the sprayer, scouring nothing but the air. I let off the trigger and heard my ragged breathing. The vampire wasn't moving.

I swung around wildly, looking for his brother *Verloren*.

Nothing. He was gone.

*   *   *

I looked up. Above me was a small metal door with a platform about ten feet over my head. The door was closed, but I had already battered the lock. I threw down the sprayer nozzle and leapt up to the platform and hauled myself inside, slamming the door behind me. I jammed an iron bar we had placed there across the door and sank to my knees, still breathing hard and trying not to cry.

"No. No. No."

I waited for the shaking to stop, terrified something was going to crash against the door. I was in a hallway that stretched from one side of the tower to the other. The hallway was choked with fallen ductwork, wires, assorted hoses, old electrical panels.

I could stay here. This was a place we had thought of to use as a last resort for emergencies. I sat there staring straight ahead. Some amount of time had passed. I didn't know how much. Seconds? Minutes? Sagan had said . . .

I suddenly realized he had been talking in my ear the whole time.

"Emma! What happened! Are you okay!"

"Yeah, yeah, I'm . . . I'm okay!" I fought to keep from crying.

"Where are you!" Sagan said. "I saw someone fall! I've been calling and calling! Are you okay? Are you hurt!"

Hearing his voice was like taking a long drink of cool, clear water. I was sobbing hard now. "I said I'm okay, all right? I'm at position eight with the doors barred."

"Are you safe there? What happened!"

"I got . . . I got two of them with the sandblaster. The young guys who looked like brothers."

"Are they . . . are they dead?" I could hear the quiver in Sagan's throat.

"I don't know. I don't know! I blinded one and . . . I think he jumped over the side. The other . . . he . . . I . . . I think maybe he's . . . Oh my God, Sagan . . ."

"Emma . . . are you really okay? Are you hurt?"

I touched my side and stretched painfully. "I'm all right. Where are the others?"

"Two are on top of the tower, just looking around. The stocky guy, Bastien. And the big guy . . . the giant."

"Any sign of Wirtz? Or Lilli?" I wanted to keep asking questions to stop thinking about what I had just done.

"Nothing," Sagan said. "I saw the girl on the north face a little while ago, but she's disappeared. Then I heard something nearby. I don't know what it was. . . ."

I swore. "And you're talking to me? They'll hear you!"

"It's okay. There's nobody here that I can see. I'm so stupid. I should have . . ." His voice trailed away.

"What?"

"I don't know. I should have come up with something better. Some other way to keep you safe. I should be up there helping. . . ."

"You are helping. Just keep watching, keep me ahead of them. . . ."

"Emma . . . this is too much. Sneak down and let me out. We'll make a run for it to my Jeep."

"Where? Where can we go?"

"I don't know! Anywhere away from here."

"Sagan . . . they'll find us. Worse. They'll find our families sooner or later even if they don't find us. We have to stop them. We don't have any choice. I'm going to move again."

I brushed at my eyes and made my way toward the other end of the hall, dodging around the debris. I put my ear to the metal door. *Nothing*. I lifted the bar as quietly as I could and held it like a weapon while I slowly pulled the door open.

No one there. I was looking out onto another small platform with stairs leading down to the right and left. I waited, listening, then stuck my head out farther to where I could see the entire west wall of the tower. Nothing in any direction. And then—

"Emma! Look out!"

Sagan didn't have to tell me. The baby-faced vampire had dropped out of the sky right in front of me. At first I thought he was floating. Then I saw it—he was holding on to a sagging loop of old black hosing that was stretched practically to the breaking point under his weight. He smiled.

I threw my body back into the hall and barred the door shut, scrambling away from it. There was a massive crash and the door buckled and the bar bent. I ran toward the other end of the hall. There was a crash against that door and it buckled too.

Bastien?

I didn't wait to see. I stood in the center of the hall and kicked off the floor, flinging my body straight up through the tile ceiling. Flakes of asbestos and rust rained down around me. I was immediately tangled in a jumble of wires and piping. I swam through it, pushing and pulling things out of my way. I was moving horizontally, doing my best not to step on the fragile ceiling tiles just beneath me.

Something smashed through one of the tiles and an iron fist locked itself around my right calf. I caught a glimpse of the giant vampire's face. I aimed a brutal kick at his massive jaw and planted my shoe in his fat cheek instead. The force of the kick would have separated a normal human being's skull from his shoulders, but the tall vampire only lost his grip momentarily; I threw my body forward and kept moving.

Another set of fingers blasted through one of the tiles and caught my ankle. I kicked again, this time stomping the *Verloren*'s wrist with all my might. The giant vampire wouldn't let go. He started to haul me back down as I clung furiously to the thickest pipe I could reach.

Please please please!

I kicked crazily, only one hand on the pipe now. Then I remembered—I had a utility knife in my tool belt. I didn't have time to think about what I was doing. I drew the knife out by the handle and brought the curved blade slashing down. The knife struck the giant vampire's thick fingers, lopping off the tips of two of them and gashing a third to the bone.

The big *Verloren* shrieked, wrenching my leg hard as his enormous hand jerked away. I almost fell and the utility blade skittered out of my fist, clattering on the hallway below.

I kept moving. More hands burst through the tiles, punching holes of light on either side of me as I desperately twisted and turned my body to keep away. I came to a white bucket and could go no farther. A whole tile exploded behind me and four massive arms grabbed the metal frame holding up the ceiling and started to rip it down.

A long section of ceiling collapsed into the hallway. I clung to the piping, feeling horribly exposed. I could see them now, Bastien and the giant *Verloren*, looking up at me angrily, crouching to spring. They flung themselves at me, tearing through the last of the ceiling.

I got my fingers on the rim of the white bucket and tipped it.

Five gallons of industrial-strength swimming pool chlorine fell in a snowdrift of chemical pain directly on the *Verloren*'s faces, making a big *flumph* sound. A cloud of the stuff curled up, searing my nostrils and stinging my eyes. I shut my mouth and sprang blindly toward the long opening in the ceiling the vampires had made.

I slammed against the metal floor and the wind rushed out of me in one huge grunt. I opened my watering eyes and staggered to my feet and ran, lungs screaming for air, not daring to breathe until I got outside. At the last moment I turned to see both *Verloren* on their knees, clawing miserably at their faces and making gagging and choking sounds.

I burst through the partly open door onto the platform and took in huge gobbling inhales of the night air. I could hear furious shouts behind me.

Climb, I thought. *Climb.*

I kicked off, propelling my body to the side of the test stand structure. I landed as lightly as a cat, then nearly fell, the way a cat sometimes does when something is more difficult to cling to than expected.

The rusty hide of the tower was studded with huge hexagonal bolts the size of dinner plates, and that's what I was hanging on to. Only the bolts didn't protrude as far as I thought, so there wasn't a lot to grab.

The hallway door slammed open below me and Bastien roared out onto the little platform, face dusted white with chlorine, puckered eyes blazing red.

"Töten Sie Sie, töten Sie Sie, töten Sie Sie!"

I frantically scaled the sheer cliff face of the tower, lunging from handhold to handhold on the bolts, Bastien right behind, snorting like an enraged animal.

Sagan was yelling something into my earpiece, but all I could think about was getting away from the monster on my heels. At any moment he was going to grab me by the ankle and fling me off the side of the tower.

I slipped on one of the bolts and Bastien's huge hand clutched at my leg, but he didn't get a firm hold and I pulled free. I got my

413

balance again and shoved off with the tips of my toes, praying it would give me enough momentum to make the next catwalk.

I soared upward, hands banging the bottom of the metal walkway, fingers grasping to hold on as I twisted up over the railing and landed, feet already moving.

I ran down the catwalk, searching for a particular beam. . . . When I was moving this fast, one beam looked pretty much like another. The catwalk ran out into a flat wall of raw steel.

Bastien thumped onto the catwalk behind me.

"Komm, sie ist hier!" he yelled over the side. No translation needed: "She is here!"

The *Verloren* barreled toward me. I reached over the edge of the beam above me, fumbled, then grabbed it—the nail gun hidden there.

I gripped the gun with both hands and fired a burst of sixteen-penny nails straight into the vampire's chest. Bastien grunted as the nails slammed deep into his body, but he kept coming. Now I aimed dead at his face and unloaded sixteens as fast as the gun would let me. *Pop pop pop.*

Bastien grimaced. I could see black dots appearing on his face—the heads of the nails—but still he came on. Now there wasn't time to throw myself from the catwalk. I could only brace for the collision.

"Töten Sie Sie, töten Sie Sie, töten Sie Sie!"

Bastien hit me with the force of an out-of-control car, smashing my body against the metal wall at the end of the catwalk. A screw gouged a hole in my back.

The stocky vampire pressed into me, the stink of the chlorine flooding my nose. The barrel of the nail gun drove into the *Verloren*'s big stomach, twisting sharply in my hands until it was pointing straight down. The gun went off and a sixteen-penny nail shot through the top of my foot.

I screamed more in surprise than pain. I couldn't feel the nail at all. All I could feel was terror now that Bastien had me in his grasp.

The nail gun fell to the deck between us and Bastien got his beefy hands around my throat. The scar on his nose turned bright red and his eyes were shiny with hate. Blood was trickling down all over his face from where the nails were embedded.

I fought to get my hands up, but the vampire's heavy gut pressed me back, keeping my arms pinned. I couldn't breathe. He was crushing the life out of me. Then my fingers touched something hard and metallic at my waist. *The angle grinder.*

I wrenched the angle grinder out of the belt but couldn't raise it. Bastien still had his hands on my throat. My windpipe was collapsing, stripes of blackness starting to swim before my eyes. If I lost consciousness . . .

I flipped the switch on the angle grinder with my thumb, feeling the wheel catch and the tool start to vibrate with a screechy whine. I jammed it against the *Verloren*'s body with all the vampire strength I had and brought it up in a terrible arc. . . .

Bastien's eyes bulged. The tool's diamond blade dug in with a meaty gulping noise and something warm spurted over my hands. *Blood.* I kept driving the grinder into his body. Bastien let go of my throat and started furiously grabbing at the grinder, but the wheel was cutting his fingers to pieces.

The *Verloren* tried to push away, clutching desperately at my shoulders, arms, my face, coating me with his blood. I could feel his big arms losing their strength.

He took a couple of steps backward, turned, and staggered

toward the far end of the catwalk. Bastien only made about three more steps before slumping to the metal grate beneath our feet. He whimpered and rolled over onto his back, body shuddering, eyes open. Then he stopped. Everything stopped. I could still see the nails in his face.

416

31. GROUND

I doubled over coughing, still feeling the awful crushing pressure of Bastien's thick fingers on my neck. I dropped the angle grinder and held my hands in front of me, painted with the *Verloren*'s blood.

"Emma! Emma, please!"

I realized that Sagan had been yelling into my ear for who knows how long, but for just a moment I couldn't answer. I didn't know how to form the words.

Pain broke me out of my shock. My back hurt from where the screw had gouged me, and my punctured foot was throbbing. I lifted my shoe dumbly and saw blood ticking from the bottom. I slipped my shoe off; the nail had torn a hole in the top of my foot just above the fleshy V between two toes and passed all the way through.

I put my shoe back on. My heart felt as if it were beating outside my chest. I couldn't stay here. There were at least three *Verloren* left. Four, if the brother who had fallen had recovered. I scanned above and below frantically. . . . Not a single ball of lavender. Probably they were keeping out of sight and regrouping now that they knew I had weapons.

"Sagan." My voice was so raspy, I doubted he could hear me over his own shouting. "Sagan! Shut up. Listen . . ."

"Emma! Thank God, thank God you're all right! I could hear, but then . . . nothing! You wouldn't say anything! I was afraid you— God, Emma, what happened!"

"He's . . . dead. . . . Bastien is dead."

"How?"

"Forget it. What about . . . what about the rest?"

"Are you all right?"

"I'm okay! Come on, help me!"

"One of them—I can't tell who it is—he's climbing up the side the gantry is on."

"And the other . . ."

"The big guy? He still hasn't come out from the hall," Sagan said. "Position . . . um . . . eight. You sound . . . Are you hurt?"

"I'm . . . Just a minute."

The nail gun was too clunky to hang on to, but I couldn't just leave it for the vampires to use against me. I picked it up and hurled it over the side. Far below I could hear its firing mechanism burp twice as it hit the ground, then everything was still. I stepped over Bastien's body and staggered toward the tower.

"What about on top?" I said into the mike.

"They're not there anymore, but—"

"Hang on. Don't say anything for a little while. I want to go up and look."

I avoided the catwalks but instead took the stairways, favoring my sore foot, until I came to a little platform near the top that was a kind of balcony leading to nowhere.

I listened intently. Nothing. I wiped my blood-sticky fingers on my jeans and spat, trying to shake off the feeling of sickness that was washing over me. I doused my face and rinsed my mouth from a little water bottle Sagan had insisted I keep in my tool belt.

I swore.

"What?" Sagan said.

"I forgot to pick up the angle grinder!"

"Can you go back and get it?"

"No. I left it next to Bastien. . . . Stupid. Where are they now?"

"There's nobody. . . . Wait. The door to position eight—the hallway—it just opened and closed, but nobody came out!"

"You're sure? Maybe you didn't see them."

"I don't know. They're so freaking fast."

"Which side?"

"The side under the gantry."

I checked my tool belt. No weapons left on me except a small steel vial of hydrofluoric acid, a solvent so powerful, NASA used it to etch glass. Sagan said HF would eat through your skin and instantly go to work chelating the calcium in your bones until you were dead. I was pretty much terrified of using it.

I ran out onto the nearest catwalk and felt beneath it for the double-bladed ax we had attached there with bungee cords. It would be kind of clumsy to carry around, but I felt safer holding it as I jumped up to the roof.

There was no one there. The generator and my other things looked as if they hadn't been touched. I slipped the ax's long handle through my belt.

"I'm at position one again," I said into the headpiece.

"Yeah, I see you."

"Where are they? What are they doing?"

The headset made a clipped little chirping noise like a cornered bird. I gasped a little, feeling the sound in my heart.

"Sagan? Sagan, are you there?"

I waited for him to speak again, every nerve strained to the snapping point.

"Sagan!"

I ran across the top of the tower and leapt onto the big gantry. Ran toward the end of the long iron arm so that I could get a better look at the entrance to the bunker. I stopped and leaned over and could see pretty much everything: the low block walls protruding from the hill, the concrete face of the bunker, the blank doors and observation windows, and even a little ways inside. All was still. I touched the mike.

"Sagan! Where are you? Sagan!"

Something caught my attention out of the corner of my eye.

I looked toward the end of the gantry. At the far end was a ladder-like web of steel that ran straight down all the way to the rocket engine exhaust pit below. It was the fastest way down, other than falling. I started toward it.

Someone was there, standing at the other end in a cloud of lavender light.

It was the giant baby-faced vampire. He was crouched and holding a length of pipe in his left hand. Like Bastien, his face was still white from the chlorine I had doused him with. When he noticed me looking, he swung the pipe, catching it with a loud smack in his right hand. Blood from his injured fingers was dripping on his shoe.

I looked to my right, over the railing at the nylon rope that was knotted there.

The *Verloren* started toward me. I grabbed the rope and pulled hard. The end of the rope flew up in the air and I caught it with my fingers. What?

The rope had been cut.

"Are you looking for something, *Wespe*?" a voice said from behind me.

I whirled around. Standing on the opposite end of the gantry was the vampire I had sandblasted who had flung himself off the tower. His face was pitted and raw and his eyes looked as if they were full of blood. He was holding the smoking chain saw. I was trapped between them.

*　　*　　*

I slid the ax out of my belt, trying not to look afraid. I watched the *Verloren* with the chain saw. He nodded at the giant vampire.

"Be ready to catch her, George," he said. "I have taken her sting. She's coming your way."

The giant called George didn't say anything, just stood there cradling his pipe. The other vampire looked at me again and licked his shredded lips. He took a couple of steps toward me, giving the chain saw trigger a growling burst. Choking clouds of bluish oil smoke filled the gantry.

"I hear there is sunlight in your veins," the *Verloren* said. "I think I will split you open and find out."

I felt as if I were inside an insane dream. I looked up. Nothing but cage all around, laced with big steel crossbeams. If they decided to rush me, I would be overwhelmed. I could try wriggling through the gap over the railing to climb on top of the gantry, but I was terrified that the vampire with the chain saw would get there before I could pull my legs all the way through. *And then . . .* The thought was too awful.

I felt dizzy. *No, not now, no! My head . . .* I was terror-stricken by the possibility of a seizure. I took a deep breath. Both vampires advanced a couple of steps closer, taking their time, obviously wary.

Wary. I had a flashback. This was a feeling I was used to. *Where?*

Yes. Yes.

Verloren were so big on respect, an honorable death. I stooped and laid the ax at my feet, as if it were a kind of offering.

The vampires looked at each other, wondering where this was going. I fought my dizziness and battled to keep my voice steady.

"What's wrong?" I said. "I thought *Verloren* were supposed to be big-time warriors. Fighters. Afraid of nothing. And now you're

421

afraid of me? A *Mädchen*? A girl? Why don't you go back down and find someone who isn't so afraid."

Instead of waiting for them to run, I cried out myself and ran. Straight toward the big vampire called George. I heard the snarling roar of the chain saw flying at me from behind. I kept charging the huge *Verloren*. Now the giant ran at me, raising the steel pipe to crush my skull.

At the very last moment, just as we were going to collide, I dropped down and threw my body into the nastiest slide tackle in the history of soccer, my butt scraping the steel floor of the gantry, leading with my feet.

My trail boots caught George square in the ankles just as he was swinging the pipe, all his momentum carrying his huge body forward. The big vampire had his legs taken out from under him, was knocked headlong off his feet, and sailed over me as I slid beneath him.

I twisted out of my slide just in time to see the *Verloren* with the chain saw, the one who had been chasing me. . . .

He couldn't stop. . . .

George screamed. The whirling chain saw struck him on the side of the head, then skittered down his arm to the elbow. I felt the sound of the chain saw as much as heard it—the shrieking it made as the chain sank in deeply, through muscle and flesh and tendons. It jerked for a second against the bone, then the giant vampire's forearm flopped on the gantry floor. The pipe he had been holding dropped from his dying fingers. The hand lay there, spasmodically curling and uncurling.

Blood spouted from the stump of George's arm, throwing a ragged red stripe across the other vampire's face.

Some of the blood splashed into the other *Verloren*'s mouth. A look instantly spread over his features that made me cold all the way to my shoes. The vampire yelled something unintelligible. Dropped the chain saw, lunging . . .

I jumped to my feet . . . but the *Verloren* wasn't lunging at me. He fell on George. Took the stump of the giant vampire's arm . . . put it to his mouth . . . and began to suck in each pulse of the hot blood.

For a moment I stood there watching, paralyzed by something deeper than fear. George mewled like a wounded animal, kicking and writhing, head bleeding, trying to pull his arm away from the other *Verloren*'s mouth, and pleading in garbled German.

Du bringst mich um. Du bringst mich um.

I didn't want to know what the words meant. The vampire who was drinking clung on like a shark with meat in its jaws.

The ax was still lying where I had put it, not ten feet from where the two vampires were struggling together. I broke out of my trance and raced to pick it up.

Do it. This is your chance. Kill them. Kill them both.

I raised the ax. Clenched the handle so hard, it felt as if it might snap under my fingers. My hands shook. The vampire who was drinking didn't even look up. He was gorging himself in a way that was so monstrous, so uncaring, I . . .

I couldn't do it. I couldn't. I lowered the ax and started to slip it through my tool belt, turning to go to the ladder. . . .

Something slammed into me from behind. I fell to my stomach on the steel floor of the gantry and the ax flew out of my hands. The vampire was on top of me, the one who had been feeding on George. His face was a blood-soaked animal's face. He pinned my wrists and twisted his head back and forth violently, trying to get at my throat. I pushed back as hard as I could, but it was all I could do to keep his teeth from tearing into me.

The vampire strained his neck, manically trying to lower his mouth. He was making a high-pitched shrieking noise, desperate not to kill me, but to consume. The blood on his teeth dripped on my face. Slowly he bent my arms back in his fury until I could feel his breath on me, could see the red scratches in his eyes. I turned my head sideways, but his mouth descended closer and closer. . . .

I heard a shuddering *thunk,* then another one. A blow so terrible, I felt it as a vibration through my whole body. The *Verloren*'s eyes changed, lost focus; slick blood pooled on my chest and started down my shirt.

The vampire slumped against me. Someone was standing over him, clutching the long-handled garden hoe.

It was Donne.

"You came, thank God," I said. "Thank God."

I shoved the dead vampire off of me and staggered to my feet. Donne dropped the hoe, looking with horror at her hands.

"What have I done . . . what have I done . . . ," she said, running back to the tower and collapsing into Lena and Anton's arms.

They stared at me without speaking. I realized what I must look like to them. Crouched over. Sweating, furious, chest heaving. My face, neck, and arms splattered, clothes soaked in blackening blood, fingers sticky with it.

"What was I supposed to do?" I said, pleading with my bloody hands. "Stand there and let them kill me?"

Anton started to speak, but Lena held up her hand.

"You were supposed to run, Emma. Hide. That was what you were supposed to do. All of us have made sacrifices. We cannot change our lives. This is out of our hands. The *Sonneneruption* . . ."

I growled deep in my throat. "I'm not waiting for some mystical solar flare while they butcher my family! I don't have time for this. Sagan is down there—they might be after him right now!"

"You are an *Auge*," Lena said. "We answered your Call. We came to protect you."

"Then fight them with me!"

"No, but we can take you away from here."

I wanted to grab her and shake her. "What's happened to you? Don't you care who they kill? If we don't do something, people I love will be dead tonight! If you won't help me . . . you're just like them. No. You're worse. You're cowards—if that's what it is to be a *Sonnen* . . . screw you."

I turned to run back to the gantry.

Lena grabbed my arm, spinning me around. "Emma, stop!"

I almost hit her. . . . Something in her eyes made me lower my hands.

"It was me," she said, starting to weep. "I was the one. The leader of the group that attacked *die Esserin*. I sent them . . . I sent them to their deaths. It was me. It was me."

I looked at her a moment, then hurled myself onto the gantry, running for the ladder.

I jumped the last few feet into the iron exhaust chute at the bottom, gulping in pain because of my injured foot. Clambered out and slipped to the ground. Nothing moved. I threw myself behind a corner of the tower and listened. The only sounds I could hear were the chain saw idling far above and George's mutilated cries.

My impulse was to rush straight to the bunker, but I touched the headset; the mike was still on.

"Sagan, can you hear me?"

I repeated the words several times and waited, but the earpiece only buzzed and hissed.

I ran in a wide arc toward the bunker, avoiding the entrance, and positioned myself behind the slope of the hill. Through one of the observation holes I could see where Sagan had been sitting on the other side of the metal screen. The boxes were still there, but nothing else. He had moved.

I felt as if ants were crawling over my heart. My only choice was to go inside the screen and try to find him. I raised my head, looking at the trees, the top of the bunker, anywhere Wirtz could be lurking. Nobody.

I threw myself flat on the grass and crawled where the little hill rolled down to the concrete blocks. I edged over the wall and crouched, listening. I could hear water dripping far away. I ran in to see if the padlock was still fastened. . . .

I went blind.

Whatever hit me, it felt as if a concrete wall had collapsed on my head. I don't know how long I was unconscious. I only knew I was awake before my eyes were open.

A vampire can see through her eyelids. Not clearly, but enough to make out shapes, lights and darks. That's what I was seeing now. As if my head were crammed with wads of cotton soaked in gray and black paint.

I opened my eyes; the world was blurry and slow. But this wasn't the aftermath of a seizure. I could immediately tell where I was. Above me I could see the iron skeleton of the test tower on one side and the low cement walls of the bunker on the other.

I was lying on my back and could feel a trickle of blood running down my temple. I raised my head unsteadily; it ached terribly. I tried to sit up and discovered my arms and feet were bound with heavy chains. The chains were anchored in the gravelly soil with four long iron spikes as big around as baseball bats.

Someone stepped into my field of view.

The vampire's lavender glow shifted and flowed over his body like fog moving around a living statue. His expression was almost sad.

"I must admit I am . . . disappointed," Wirtz said. "You will never be a *Kriegerin*. You have no honor." He gestured at the tower. "I gave them to you, those four . . . *Verloren*. They were yours to release . . . but you could not finish them in an honorable way, could you?"

I started to twitch and jerk uncontrollably, pulling against the spikes, but my arms were spread out as far as they could reach like da Vinci's famous drawing of the man inside a circle. I couldn't get enough leverage to use my strength to pull them out.

I had failed. Failed. Was dead, gone, finished. And Sagan with me.

I wished I had enough liquid in my mouth to spit out the dryness. I didn't know if I could speak. I felt as if I was about to start hyperventilating. My eyes flitted around the clearing frantically. It was over. Everything was over.

No. Think, Emma.

I forced myself to focus on the vampire's long face, concentrating as hard as I could. Took several long, deep breaths. Willing everything to slow down.

"Where is he?" I said, speaking softly so maybe he wouldn't hear the terror there. "Tell me what you did with him. What did you—"

Wirtz dropped something hard and metallic on my stomach.

Sagan's laptop.

It was still warm. I closed my eyes, feeling tears on my cheeks. Wirtz took the laptop away. I heard him take in a long, resigned breath. In some weird way I felt almost comforted. Ready for it all to be over. The dumbest little pictures came into my head. Walking through our apartment, nobody at home. Dishes in the sink.

Manda's little shoes with the flowers on them sitting on the kitchen counter . . .

"It is truly too bad, all of this," the vampire said. "If only—"

I opened my eyes and cursed. "Shut up. I don't have to listen to this. Just do it. If you're not going to tell me where he is, what you did with him . . . just get it over with."

Wirtz didn't seem to be listening. His eyes were focused on something else. *My tool belt.* He bent and touched the little metal vial containing the acid.

"And what is this?"

I couldn't believe he thought he had the right to keep asking me questions. I was about to curse him again when an idea came to me.

"It's the drug I use to induce a seizure," I said. "You asked about my secret; that's the way I do it. I make myself have a seizure."

The vampire fumbled with my belt and slipped the vial out of its pouch. "Drug. Are you saying this is some kind of . . . *Pharmazeutik?*"

"Yeah, it's from a pharmacy. It's a seizure medicine. But I discovered by accident, if I take too much, it induces a seizure instead. That's what gives me my powers."

Wirtz's eyes narrowed as he held it out in front of him. "A *Vollmensch Droge?*"

"A human drug, yeah."

He unscrewed the cap, letting it fall at his feet. Put the vial beneath his nose and sniffed the acrid aroma, making a face.

Take it. Take it.

"Oh, you want me to take some?" Wirtz said. "Test it out on myself? Drink this acid? Perhaps I should just pour it on your face."

Oh no.

The vampire held the open vial over my face, tipping it slightly. He tipped it farther and farther. I held my breath.

"No, I think not," Wirtz said.

He put the vial to his lips and drank it down in one long gulp. I could see his Adam's apple bobbing.

The vampire grimaced horribly and made a sound like something was caught in his throat. He turned away from me, staggered a few steps toward the bunker, and doubled over and vomited. At last he straightened up, wiping his mouth, and flung the vial away.

He got down on his knees, close to my face, eyes flaring. I could smell the searing stink of the acid on his breath. His lips were bleeding.

"You think I care about life in this world?" Wirtz said, breathing into my face. His voice had a terrible ragged edge as if his insides had been ground into hamburger. "You need to understand this, *Mädchen*. I care about nothing. I told you, after this many years, the only thing I have is . . . curiosity."

I turned my head away so I wouldn't have to look at him and struggled to find my voice. "I know . . . I know about . . . your son," I said.

The vampire pushed away from me and stood. He took a grungy handkerchief from his pocket and wiped his sweating face. Returned it to his pocket and swallowed several more times, coughing. He took a step toward me.

"That person no longer exists," he rasped. "He never existed."

Wirtz lifted his arms, spreading them out wide. "You know, *Mädchen,* there is a dream that there is a life beyond this one. But you know what the truth is? This life . . . it is the dream. It is the thing that is not real. Lilli."

My heartbeat quickened. The female vampire appeared at his

side just as if she had been standing there all along. She looked down at me with that same expression. *Dead. Used up.*

"The time has come," Wirtz said in his shredded voice. "We are going to do what should have been done before. *Der Verlust.*"

"What . . ."

Then I remembered. *Der Verlust.* The Loss.

He was going to cut me off from my *Feld.*

32. THE LOSS

Lilli knelt beside me. She turned her face away and draped her body over mine, lying on her back at an angle across my chest, so that the skin of our bare throats was touching. She was heavier than I had expected. Her flesh was warm. I twisted my head, trying to look into her face.

"You don't have to do this," I whispered into her ear. "You don't have to do what he says."

Lilli turned her blank eyes to me, our lips so close, we could have kissed.

"You are right," she said in a quiet, controlled voice. "I don't have to do what he says." She paused a long time. "I *am* what he says."

I suddenly realized what it was—this thing she was doing. What had the *Sonnen* called it? *Fütterung*. The Feeding. *She's sacrificing herself.*

Wirtz knelt beside us and looked at Lilli almost tenderly, then tore her shirt open at the collar. He lowered his teeth gently to her soft skin. I watched, heart pounding, as the vampire lingered there almost playfully; then his teeth fastened hold.

The bite made me flinch in surprise. It was nothing like what the vampire had done to Sagan in the observatory. Instead of ripping her open, Wirtz's teeth pulled and tugged slowly at the soft skin of Lilli's neck, stretching the flesh agonizingly back and forth, tighter and tighter. The skin didn't tear right away. I couldn't stand it, but there was nothing I could do to stop it.

Torturing her. Wirtz was torturing her.

The sound of the vampire's teeth pulling slowly at her skin made me think of the way a cat would pull apart a mouse. It seemed to take forever for Lilli's skin to finally break. I wanted to scream. At last I could hear the flesh of her throat pulling free with a sound like thick wet cloth ripping; a terrible little cry escaped from Lilli's mouth straight into my ear. The blood instantly spurted and spilled over her neck, pooling down my own neck and shoulders. It was very warm.

Lilli gasped sharply as Wirtz made the opening larger and began to feed. I could feel her heart speeding up all the way through her back, could feel the twittery lurching rhythm through my own chest, joining with the beating of my heart as our *Felds* slowly came together as one.

Wirtz drank a long time. My mind felt like a room that had no door or windows and all the air had been sucked out. He drank so long, I thought, *Surely she is gone now. Lilli can't still be alive.* But she was. I felt the dull thump of her heart getting weaker and weaker, the beats further and further apart. He was killing her. That's all it could be. He wanted Lilli dead for some insane reason.

"And now," Wirtz said, lifting his bloody mouth from the steamy wound at Lilli's throat and looking at me again, "I am giving you another chance."

"You . . ."

"Oh no. I'm not letting you go. I am giving you one last chance to regain your honor."

My throat . . . he meant he was going to take me at the throat this time, assuming I behaved myself. I jerked against my restraints.

"You must remain still," Wirtz said, bending forward. "In

order for the *Verlust* to come, I must be able to drink from both at once."

I tried to use my head as a weapon, striking at him. The vampire took my head in one hand and pinned it to the side. He lowered his mouth and tore at my neck with his hot, wet teeth.

The pain was so intense. . . . Even with the chains holding me down, I lifted up in the air, arching my back. It was so awful, I couldn't make a sound, had to use every ounce of my energy to focus on surviving his tearing bite.

Wirtz made the tear in my neck right next to the tear he had made in Lilli's throat. He fastened his wide mouth between us, still pulling at the dying Lilli's blood while beginning to take in some of mine. And I knew . . . somehow I knew what he intended to do. What the *Verlust* was.

My Feld. *He's going to join my* Feld *to hers*. Then he was going to suck Lilli to death while I was still alive. And my *Feld* . . . It would die with Lilli.

"No!" I screamed.

Already I could feel Lilli's dying seeping into me, even while I was so alive. A frosty, spongy numbness pushed its way under my skin, filling my veins. . . . My fingers straightened as the cool tide of her leaving poured down my arms all the way to my fingertips.

That's exactly what it was. *A leaving*. Everything was leaving me. Even anger, hate, bitterness. *My soul*.

The noise Wirtz made as he drank was almost a cooing sound, the obscene flip side of the noise you made to lull babies to sleep. I tried to think of Manda. I tried to think of Sagan. . . . They were receding further and further into the gloom of some other night. Until I didn't care. Not anymore.

Everything was slowing down. It was so quiet now, I could hear individual leaves fluttering in the forest. Water rippling on the river.

The air above my head filled with billowing lavender light. I could feel Lilli leaving her body even as her deadweight was settling on top of my chest. I was going too. She was taking me with her.

A seizure. If I could only have a seizure, I thought. But why? Who cared? Who would remember me? I was just this angry, mistrustful girl who felt cursed and hated everybody and everything. It was good that I was going. The world would be better off. Whatever was inside me, whatever spark of uniqueness I contained, it deserved to be snuffed out. I only wanted everything to stop so I could dream myself into a wall of lavender oblivion. . . .

The very last thing was a sound.

I had always thought there would be something surprising about death. Something so unexpected, it would make the bad parts not quite so bad because I would be filled with wonder. But I never knew the surprising thing would be a sound. But then, this wasn't death, was it? The *Verlust?* And the sound wasn't so much surprising as it was incredibly annoying, invasive. A shrill, screaming blast of noise that made tears come to my eyes because I couldn't clap my hands to my vampire ears to shut it out.

Then something incredible happened. Wirtz pulled away. I could feel the unbelievable relief of his mouth leaving my neck, the pressure of his hand leaving the side of my head.

I wasn't gone. I felt really weak, but I was still here. I tried lifting my head, but Lilli's body was still there too. But even though I could barely move, when I opened my eyes, I could see Wirtz kneeling, then standing, looking somewhere past me, his features showing a murderous irritation.

It had to be the sound. So infuriating and painfully shrill, it was destroying his concentration. Wirtz stepped over us and walked into the big open space between the bunker and the tower.

There was a fire there that had not been there before. . . . No, it was too bright for a fire—more like an exploding shower of sparks. Then I realized what it was, some kind of fireworks going off. One of those cone-shaped gadgets you light on the ground on the Fourth of July.

Only the cone was lying on its side. It was throwing out a huge shower of horizontal sparks, and every once in a while a big ball of colored light shot straight across toward the woods like an over-turned Roman candle. The whole effect lit the gravel clearing as bright as day to my sensitive eyes. I had to squint to look at it directly.

Next to the fallen cone was a small black cube. Even with my mind gone bleary, I somehow knew that's where the sound was coming from.

Now Wirtz was moving toward the cube, shielding his eyes with his upturned hand. The sight was so bright, I could only see the vampire in a long black silhouette. The silhouette moved toward the cube at an angle that kept Wirtz from being pelted with the gushing sparks.

He was only a few feet away when he stooped and started to crab-walk closer, still shielding his eyes, the cube shrieking so loud, it had to be pure torture on his ears. I tried lifting myself as he bent to examine the black box. . . . I had barely enough strength to arch my back. Lilli's inert body made me feel as if I were trying to climb up through the dirt in a grave.

Her head lolled against my cheek and saliva from her open mouth ran along my jaw. I glanced at Wirtz—he was still looking at the cube. Reaching his hand out to touch it, then pulling his fingers back. I would never have another chance.

I flexed my arms and instead of trying to lift the iron spikes up out of the ground, I started pulling them toward me. I could feel them move just slightly; I was weak. I couldn't tell if the movement was from the iron bending or the spikes leaning sideways through the dirt. I tried again. The spikes barely budged. I slumped under Lilli's weight, my back flattening against the ground again. I tried flexing my legs. I couldn't do it. *I'm sorry,* I wanted to say. I didn't know who I was saying it to. *I'm so sorry.*

Wirtz was right. The only thing left was curiosity. I watched his silhouette from my sideways position. He was reaching for the black cube again.

I felt the Jeep before I saw it . . . felt it underneath my back as the vibrations radiated through the ground and up into my bones. It wasn't making a sound—it couldn't, the shrieking of the black cube was demolishing every other sound—but I could still feel the motion of the Jeep's tires as it crunched across the clearing.

What was this? I turned my head slightly . . . could see the Jeep angling across the big open circle, headlights off, one figure in the driver's seat, three other figures behind it, pushing. Pushing the Jeep forward . . . gathering speed.

Oh my God.

Sagan was driving the Jeep and the three *Sonnen,* Lena, Anton, and Donne, were pushing on the back bumper, running hard into the clearing, the Jeep gaining soundless, stealthy speed, moving so fast it looked as if it just might take off.

Wirtz touched the cube and the shrieking sound cut out; in the same instant the huge bulk of the Jeep crossed into the shower of sparks, hurtling straight at the vampire, the hood bursting through the sparks like the prow of a square ship lifting up in the air over a cresting wave. . . .

The grille of the Jeep smashed into the vampire head-on, ramming him viciously backward. Wirtz sprawled grotesquely across the clearing, arms and legs flying in jerky bent angles to his body. He landed again twenty or thirty feet away, but the Jeep didn't even slow down as it trucked him a second time, smashing his face to the ground with a heavy, crunching thud that bounced through my skin.

Sagan slammed on the brakes and the Jeep skidded to a stop on top of Wirtz. Sagan had already jumped from the door, leaving it hanging open, and was running toward me.

The mist in my head cleared. I bucked in the air again, and this time Lilli's body slipped off me and fell away. I retracted every limb like a dying spider pulling its legs in, feeling the resistance of the iron spikes starting to give. I jerked the chains taut at least three more times before Sagan had even reached me. Each time gaining a little bit of slack, but it was still so hard. I was still feeling the effects of the *Verlust*.

Sagan bent over me, the night goggles pushed up on his forehead. A trickle of blood was running down his neck from where I had tied off the gauze on his wound, what seemed like a century ago. I was yelling things at him and he was making shushing noises back to me, working at the chains without getting any closer to getting me loose. I watched helplessly as the Jeep lurched slightly, Wirtz pinned beneath it but moving. Still moving.

"Come on!" I screamed at Sagan.

The *Sonnen* were there now, pulling and tugging at the iron spikes as I jerked and strained. Donne got her spike loose first, then went to help Sagan with his. Slowly the four of them drew out the spikes one by one until there was enough slack to unknot the chains wrapped around my ankles and wrists.

The light from the fireworks was dying as the last of the sparks frittered out from the cone. The front end of the Jeep began to lift, higher and higher, the vampire beneath it getting his back into it now.

I tried to stand but fell. Sagan and Lena caught me. I twined

437

my arms around their necks and we started to run, Anton and Donne leading the way.

The Jeep was rocking and trembling now and suddenly the whole mass came off the ground, the hood rising almost vertically.

"Go! Come on!" Sagan said.

"This is all we can do!" Lena said to him. "You must hurry! We will take care of the others. You have to go now!"

The three *Sonnen* ran toward the base of the tower. Sagan helped me stumble toward the bunker. We were out of weapons, and both of us knew there was no way we could make it through the forest before Wirtz caught us. The Jeep suddenly lifted off and was now doing a slow barrel roll in midair. It landed on its side with a huge crash, then fell over upside down.

We stumbled through the bunker entrance clinging to one another. When we reached the steel net at the back, Sagan fumbled to get the padlock open.

"Hurry, hurry!" I said.

We fell through on the other side, Sagan landing on top of me, jamming the lock closed behind us. He helped me stagger across the concrete pad to the oil drums lining the far wall.

"Quick!" he said.

He let go of me and grabbed the top of one of the drums, swinging it around in a little circle. "Help me!"

I was dizzy and didn't know what he wanted at first. Sagan started rolling the drum on its edge toward the metal curtain. "Wait!" I said, understanding.

I was still wobbly, but my strength was returning. I grabbed the first drum and heaved it off the ground; it came down hard on the concrete next to the steel curtain and split open, spilling the gas. Grabbed another and threw it. Another. Another.

Wirtz was limping toward the mesh curtain. His clothes were

bloody and torn and his face was one big scuff mark. He fell to his knees in front of the curtain and got his fingers under the mesh and began to lift.

At first nothing happened, then the steel curtain started to bend and buckle. I kept hurling oil drums—gasoline splashed all around the vampire and the fumes started to choke me. Wirtz was only inches away from getting the curtain high enough to slip under.

"Stop!" Sagan yelled, pulling back on my arm.

He was holding one of the red highway flares we had stashed in his box. He yanked the cap off, turned it over, and feverishly scratched the flare against the striking surface until it burst into flame. Sagan threw the flare at the gasoline drums and we ran deeper into the cave, stumbling and falling and running again.

It took longer for something to happen than I expected, then a feeling of air pressure came rushing over us, making my ears pop, followed by an enormous flash of light. A big, concussive *whoosh* of air beat against our backs with the sound coming right after it, a roaring explosion of fire that filled every space behind us. We both fell to our knees. I looked back, and the entrance to the cavern had been filled by a gigantic fireball that was rushing toward us.

We helped each other up and ran. I could feel my legs coming back and we started to pick up speed. I tugged at Sagan's hand and plunged straight into the main channel.

"Do you think he's . . . ?" Sagan yelled.

"I don't know. I don't know! Just keep running."

The passage was wide, but the ceiling was low. Even with my vampire eyes and Sagan's night vision, we had to be careful not to hit one of the stalactites hanging overhead. Every part of me had become sensory, all focused on one thing: finding a place where we could survive.

"What about a side tunnel; shouldn't we—"

"No, too easy, he'd find us," Sagan said. "The King's Chamber! We've got to make it to the King's Chamber. The opening is just about impossible to spot if you don't know where to look."

I didn't know what he was talking about, then I remembered— the hidden crack in the wall we had slithered through where he had shown me the collapsing ceiling and the blind crayfish.

I kept running, letting him be my guide. Nothing seemed familiar. The crazy flowstone walls and columns had morphed into shapes not recognizable as landmarks. I thought about carrying Sagan but was too afraid of stumbling and dropping him on the rocks. The hole in my foot felt as if the nail were still there.

We stopped once and listened. . . . Nothing but the distant roar of the flames. We kept going.

At the end of the first long hall, the ceiling shot up a good thirty feet or more, but the floor was no longer smooth. It was covered with huge pieces of breakdown.

The brokenness of the landscape slowed us down. I clambered and leapt over one rubble pile after another, hoisting Sagan over the worst places. It felt as if at any moment Wirtz would be right there, flying at us from a side passage, dropping from a crevice in the ceiling, reaching up from a pit to grab our legs.

We moved deeper and deeper into the earth until I was near sobbing from fear and disorientation. I heard rocks tumble somewhere. There for a mini-second, then gone. The acoustics of the cave made it practically impossible to judge the direction. We dashed down a long slope, tripping over football-sized chunks of stone, then the ground became more rippling and smooth.

"Almost there," Sagan said, panting a little. "You just have to get to the lake and then follow the shore to the north until the ceiling cramps down."

I could smell the water and then just over a rise I could see it.

The lake was even bigger than I remembered but just as alien. The floor was rounded and smooth. I could see the dusky mounds leading down to water. The whole grotto was throbbing with dim, greenish light. It was almost impossible to believe this was the same place where I had first kissed Sagan.

"This way," he said, taking my hand and pulling me along. "You're going to have to help me. . . . Even with these goggles, it's gonna be close to impossible for me to see it. The shore turns back north, and there's this wall that sticks out a little ways, and you circle around it where the ceiling suddenly gets really low, and—"

"And . . . what?"

The voice came from behind me. A growling rasp of a voice.

I turned and he was there, Wirtz. Not thirty feet away.

The vampire seemed to have brought his own light with him. Beyond the usual lavender, there was a faint halo around his body, and I realized the glow was coming from the embers of his own burning. His hair was gone; smoke was rising from the scorched bump of his head. His clothes were in smoldering tatters, hanging from his body like burned flags in some places, stitched to his blackened skin in others. He stank of char.

"Well," the *Verloren* said. "Look at . . . what you have managed to do to me, *Mädchen*." He touched his arms, then dropped them by his sides. There was a painful catch in his voice. "It has been interesting, which is a better day than so many thousands and thousands of others. But even an interesting day comes to an end."

Sagan moved closer to me, taking my hand and squeezing it speechlessly. I didn't have to look at his face to know what he was telling me. *I'm sorry.*

"It's not your fault," I whispered to him.

"I agree," Wirtz went on. *That stupid hearing of his.* "You know, you both gave it a good try. But now you will never leave this cave alive. Oh, there might be a way for you, *Mädchen*. You are fast. Perhaps fast enough to outrun me? But you'll never do it carrying him. So. There is something interesting left for us. It is *Ihre Wahl*. Your choice. Are you of the *Sonnen* or the *Verloren*? Do you make the sacrifice or try to save yourself?"

He waited. I didn't speak. I knew nothing I could say would help anything now. Sagan knew. He knew I would never leave him here to face Wirtz alone. There was no reason to even say it.

"Ah." The vampire took a step toward us.

Sagan got in front of me, putting himself between Wirtz and me. I swore because I started to cry. Because I wasn't crying for the obvious reason . . . I was crying because of what Sagan did. Because of how stupidly brave he was.

I thought Wirtz was going to laugh, but he didn't. "So. You are going to let the *Vollmensch* make the choice for you? But I have to tell you. This is not really a choice. If he stays where he is and you stay where you are, I will have *euch beiden*. Both. Which is fine with me, if that is what you want."

Sagan still hadn't said a word. He stayed in front of me and fished in the pocket of his jeans. Pulled out his cell phone and opened it up.

"Oh." Now Wirtz did laugh. A laugh full of razor blades and rust. "So you want to make a call? Do you think you will get any bars down here, *Vollmensch*? Maybe to your friends. Get them to come help you. No? Then call 911; I insist."

Sagan didn't dial. He closed the phone and put it back in his pocket. Then he slowly turned to look at me.

"I wish I could see you better," he said. "But you're mostly just outlines and shapes." He pulled off the night vision headgear and dropped it at our feet. Then he took me in his arms and pressed me close to him, his lips next to my ear.

"You know, Emma . . . this is where I'm supposed to say, 'Save yourself.'"

He let go of me and straightened.

"Save me," Sagan said. "Save me."

He took two running steps and jumped and landed in the lake.

33. BREATHE

Sagan disappeared beneath the silky black water. Gone.

My knees were weak. My heart . . . It was under the water with him. *No. No!*

I stared at Wirtz and he stared back. Then he lunged.

And I knew, even as I saw Wirtz coming, moving almost like a night cloud, my mind was so clear in that moment . . . I knew what Sagan meant. I turned and dove in the black water after him.

The water was cold, jerking my breath up in my chest. I plunged in deep. Immediately I felt a surging current take my body, pulling me under, deeper, farther away. *Toward the river.*

I could see in browns and blacks: long, fluted humps of stone, washed smooth as marbles by the movement of the water over eons. I pinwheeled my arms trying to keep from striking the sides. Too many thoughts pouring in. *Sagan. Drowning. Wirtz.*

Then I saw him, up ahead in the tube we were thundering through: Sagan, looking like a tangled shape that couldn't possibly be human, but was. He was jerking and kicking, miserably probing with his arms to find anything, but at the same time not finding anything, because that anything could kill him.

We were totally submerged. How long could he hold his breath?

I stroked hard after him, rushing with the current, and swimming was better because at least I had some control. But I didn't know what to do once I reached him. I did my best to grab him gently, but even that contact was more like a collision.

Bubbles flew out of Sagan's mouth. I could see his eyes. I wanted to put my mouth on his, give him some of my air. But it was impossible. We were moving too fast; it was too dark, the current too strong. I could only grab onto him and stroke for the river, hoping it wasn't much farther. . . .

Something changed. We were still underwater, but the smooth rock walls of the tunnel fell away. The current was rushing hard as ever, but it had joined a bigger, more sluggish one. *The river.* We had made it outside.

I had my hand on Sagan's belt loops, tugging him backward against the slower current. The water was warmer. I could make out little details on the bottom: plants, submerged objects, the wooden legs of—

A dock. I could see a long wooden dock that protruded out into the deeper water. The bottom was rising now. Soon we'd be able to stand. I kicked hard for the surface and used one arm to blast Sagan up and out of the water.

Breathe. Breathe.

He was coughing. I had thrown him so far, when I came to the surface, he was on his knees in the muddy silt not far from the slope of the riverbank. I broke the surface and stroked toward him, watching him try to stand, then fall over, catching himself with both hands. But we were out. We were out and safe and . . .

The water behind me exploded.

He must've followed me the instant I jumped. *Wirtz.* I was still half turned toward Sagan, watching him crawling up on the bank to lie in the grass, then the vampire was there, crashing into me.

I was driven down in the silt, floundering with my back on the muddy bottom. Nothing around me but the thrashing of the sea-green water and millions of bubbles and the shocking sight of the vampire's face, half scraped away by Sagan's Jeep.

I fought the vampire's hands, working to keep them off me, trying to come up again and again, getting pushed back down. And then . . .

I felt Wirtz pulling away, and my head came up out of the water. Sagan was screaming something at me, running into the water and screaming.

"Stop him! Stop him, Emma! We have to . . ." He plunged past me, heading straight for Wirtz. "Help! Help me, come on!"

The sun had risen. During that time in the cave. It was just a low orange ball peering through a finger of cloud and trees on the horizon. But the sun had come up.

I could barely see—my sunglasses were in my tool belt—had to nearly close my eyes as I pushed off and flew past Sagan, tackling Wirtz around his stomach and locking my arms. He went under, but the water was too shallow. He was so buoyant, I lifted him up into the light again.

The vampire fought against my grip, tearing desperately at my fingers and kicking. We both went under again. It was harder to bring him up this time as he fought to get to deeper water. My heels were skidding on the silty bottom. My face was plastered against his back, my eyes closed against the dimly burning sun.

Sagan must've gotten to us then, because I felt him grab Wirtz's legs. Wirtz kicked hard and Sagan was thrown out of the water. But the kick caused the vampire to lose momentum. I lifted him into the sunlight again and worked to keep from losing ground, hauling his body toward the shore.

I could feel the vampire's strength waning as mine grew. Now he began to shake all over, vibrating in my arms. I raised him higher. I was afraid to try to throw him on the shore, afraid he would get away with one last effort. He took me under one last time, but the water was so shallow here, parts of his body were still exposed.

Sagan took hold again.

The vampire gave up trying to kick us loose and started stroking for deeper water. Trying to find his way back to the cave, his only hope. We hauled back against him. Wirtz's body was jerking manically and he was moving, but not making much headway.

Then he gave that up and fought his last fight. I clung tightly as he rained blows on my head and shoulders and back and then tried his teeth. Then his fingernails. Sagan kept losing his hold and grabbing back on. We pulled Wirtz back to the surface. The sun was getting higher and higher. Wirtz's body began to shake, and it was nothing that he was doing. The sun was shaking him.

His body began to vibrate in our arms like a washing machine that had been thrown off balance. He vibrated faster and faster, arching his back. His hands lost their grip on me and fell back over his head. We had him in the shallows, both of us on our knees pulling him farther and farther into the light until we had the *Verloren* on the weedy grass at the edge of the river.

He never stopped shaking, only vibrated faster and faster, every muscle tensing, the toes of his half-burnt boots pointing and lifting, fingers spreading and flexing.

I squinted my eyes open just enough to see his eyes wide, his mouth wide, tongue protruding. He was trying to say something. Wanted us to hear it. His voice was so far gone, I would have had to put my head closer to understand the words, but I didn't dare, figured it was one last trick. One last chance to taste my throat. And then I knew it wasn't a trick because in his eyes I could tell that he

447

was seeing something that wasn't me. So I bent to listen, and the vampire spoke.

"So . . . after all . . . it is, isn't it? Would you . . . look . . . at that. I knew you could. I knew. Thank you. Thank you. Thank you . . ."

His eyes closed. His body began to shake itself to pieces. Burnt clothing fell away, long ragged fissures opened up in his skin, his teeth came loose, one after another, and passed into the blackness of his throat. Then his tongue. Then the muscles and tissues under the skin, and it was too much, we had to let go, and the powerful *Verloren* turned to smaller and smaller bits before our eyes. Finally just cells and particles of cells. And he was gone just as if he had never been.

I let myself fall back and blindly crawled backward up the bank with Sagan. I don't know how long we lay there. I was touching his hand, not holding it. That's all the energy I had left. Our heads were turned toward one another and we didn't speak. My eyes were mostly closed, just feeling the river water trickle down the side of my face.

"Over," Sagan said finally. "Over."

I think maybe we slept a little. I don't know.

"So why did you come out of the bunker?" I said.

I had my sunglasses on. Sagan was looking at the sky. The sun was all the way up now.

"I lost the signal for the Webcams and couldn't hear you anymore on the headset," he said. "Maybe it was damaged when you . . ."

"I know. Maybe so."

"So I came out. I wanted to help. I couldn't find you. I put my laptop on the wall and climbed up the stairs. I ran into the *Sonnen* coming down. I thought it was all over. I thought they were

Verloren. They had been looking for you. Then we saw what Wirtz was doing. The . . ." ·

"The *Verlust*."

"Yeah. So I thought of the Jeep. I know, stupid, right? But it was right there. I just needed a couple of distractions. Something to cover up the sound. And something to temporarily blind him. I had the sound cube back on my desk and the firework was in the Jeep. I let Anton do it. He threw them out there. I was scared to death the cube would get damaged and not work. Thank God for Bose."

I actually laughed a little. "And you got them to push it so you wouldn't have to crank the engine."

"Yeah."

"Did you know it was close to sunrise?"

"I didn't think about it," Sagan said. "I guess that's why the *Sonnen* cut out when they did. I realized it when we were in the cave. Something Wirtz said about the end of the day."

"So you took your cell out—"

"To check the time. Yeah. So I knew the sun was coming up. You remember what I said about being down in a cave? How it messes with your sense of time? I finally felt like I had Wirtz at a disadvantage. He was on my turf. I was one step ahead of him. I didn't know if he would follow us but figured either way he was dead or we were safe. . . ."

I wriggled my hand into my wet jeans and found my pocket watch. I couldn't get it to open. Somewhere along the line it had been crushed.

"Oh God, I'm sorry. It's destroyed," I said, holding it up for Sagan to see.

He frowned, and then we laughed. Laughed so hard, I started crying and then I couldn't stop crying until Sagan held me a very long time.

*   *   *

Sometime later, when I could finally speak again, and he could let me go without me feeling like I was falling off the earth, I said, "You know, when we jumped in—that channel—it could have gone anywhere. It could have squeezed down into some kind of pipe that was too tight for our bodies to fit through. We would've been stuck there. Drowning."

Sagan smiled, but it was a shaky smile. "Yeah. But I figured there was too much flow. It had to be something wide going to the river. The thing that scared me the most was hitting a rock."

Now I smiled. "I saw your eyes."

"Not funny."

"So why didn't you tell me?"

"Tell you what?"

"What you were going to do?"

Sagan rolled over. "Oh. I knew Wirtz would hear it. He would know. But I thought you could figure it out."

I touched his fingers. "What if I hadn't?"

"But you did."

I thought about it a little while. "There are so many other things. . . . What do you think he was talking about? Wirtz? The last thing he said."

"I'm tired," Sagan said. "I can't think anymore. If I don't get up now, I just might lie here forever."

"Would that be so bad?"

"Come on. We've got a Jeep to flip over."

I wasn't ready to go home yet. We drove into town and spent the day in a hotel room that was so cheap, it had no phone. We lay on the bed and talked a long time about what I should tell my mother. What lies would she believe. But the more we talked, the more we understood that nothing I could say was going to be good enough. I would have to be good enough. Just me.

I lay on top of the covers and wondered if I would ever see the *Sonnen* again. I had to. Had to thank them. I wanted to learn more. Most of all, I wanted to know them because I wanted to know people who were going through a curse that forces you to be alone and had found a way to not be alone anyhow.

Would it ever really come, the *Sonneneruption*? Sagan said we had entered a period of historic solar activity. If the sun did explode, would they still be on their mountain, my Lena, Anton, and Donne? Did I want to be there too? Would I let the cure sink into my skin, carry me all the way back to where I used to be?

Some of this stuff I said out loud, some just to myself. Sagan lay beside me, listening and not listening. He tried holding me, but I couldn't stand it. It was too much. So we lay there not touching and the shades were drawn, but I couldn't sleep. Then I slept for ten hours. All my dreams were of the outdoors. Nothing was in color.

That night, after a shower and some fresh clothes, I was ready. Almost.

451

I remembered the number of his room, 332, so we didn't even have to stop at the desk. Sagan waited outside watching the TV that never noticed when no one was there.

"Enkelin!"

My heart swelled. Papi was sitting up, and for a little while I fell apart completely; he looked so much better. It was easier to hug him, and for a long time that's all I did. I told him some things and didn't tell him others. I had Sagan smuggle in a jamocha milk shake for him. Other than my grandmother's strudel, jamocha shakes were Papi's favorite sweet thing in the world.

I sat the milk shake on the little rollaway table in his room. Water condensed on the side of the cup. The water began to form little beads. When the beads got heavy enough, they ran down and collected around the base. By the time I left, the water was spilling onto the floor in a tiny trickle and the shake was past drinking. Neither of us cared.

The parking lot hadn't changed a bit. Our building was just as seedy. All except for one window that looked brand new. We sat in Sagan's Jeep staring at the steps that led up to my door.

"Just tell them . . . that you will tell them . . . someday," Sagan said.

I blew out a heavy sigh. "You don't know my mom. She will kill me, then raise me from the dead again for an explanation. She might not even let me through the door."

"She'll let you in."

"She'll never let me see you." I started to cry, and he dried my tears with his shirt.

"I'll see you. I'll never stop seeing you."

We kissed, and I realized it was the first time since Wirtz . . . well.

"You want to go in with me?" I said. That felt safer.

"No. That's too much," Sagan said. "Hi, Mom, I'm a vampire! Some other vampires tried to kill me! And oh, hey, here's my new boyfriend."

"I see what you mean."

He kissed my hand. "It'll be okay, Emma. I know how my mom would be if I disappeared and then came back."

"Okay. Now?"

"Yeah. But come here."

I leaned across the seat and fell into his arms. I pulled away and looked at the stairs. The door. The kitchen window.

"Just think, tonight you'll get to read to Manda."

I took a long breath. He always said the right thing.

I couldn't stop crying, even after I shut the door to the Jeep. My sleeves were soaked. I walked toward the steps. Turned and looked at the blurry image of Sagan, his yellow hair blowing. He had lost part of an eyebrow when the gasoline had exploded. There was a long slashing cut across his cheek that was probably going to leave a scar. I told him it made him look like Josey Wales.

I swallowed and slowly climbed the steps. Stopped in front of the door. My door. I stood there facing it, hands at my sides. Wondering just exactly how a girl who was half vampire was supposed to get by in this world. Wondering if I should knock.

Then it came to me. A family is like a hologram. It doesn't matter if there is only one other person. Or two. Or six, like Sagan's. No matter how you divide it up, when they love you, you're never half anything. Each part is always a whole. Your family is your *Feld*.

I raised the little knocker and rapped several times. Listened. I didn't hear anything. Then I heard running.

ACKNOWLEDGMENTS

A book like *Throat* would not be a reality without the encouragement, faith, and support of special people. I would like to thank my editor, Joan Slattery, along with Nancy Siscoe and Nancy Hinkel, Allison Wortche, Meg O'Brien, Kate Gartner, Artie Bennett, and all the other folks at Alfred A. Knopf; Cecile Goyette; my agent, Rosemary Stimola, and her colleagues in the agenting world, Stephen Moore and Bastian Schleuck; Ann Marie Martin of the *Huntsville Times;* my German translator, Katarina Ganslandt; my sister, Rikki Lynn Halavonich; and Kathleen O'Dell. Special thanks to my family for bearing with me all the times I had to disappear into my study, and to my wife, Deborah, who has read this book nearly as many times as I have and always sees the forest as well as the trees.

R. A. NELSON is the acclaimed author of *Days of Little Texas,* winner of a *Parents' Choice* Recommended Award; *Breathe My Name* ("Incandescent"—*Kirkus Reviews*); and *Teach Me* ("Hypnotic"—*The Horn Book Magazine*).

He lives in north Alabama with his wife and four sons and works at NASA's Marshall Space Flight Center. Visit him on the Web at ranelsonbooks.com.